THEODORE TERHUNE STORIES

Ten Trails to Tyburn

A THEODORE TERHUNE MYSTERY

BRUCE GRAEME

With an introduction by J. F. Norris

Moonstone Press

This edition published in 2021 by Moonstone Press
www.moonstonepress.co.uk

Introduction © 2021 J.F. Norris

Originally published in 1944 by Hutchinson & Co Ltd

Ten Trails to Tyburn © the Estate of Graham Montague Jeffries,
writing as Bruce Graeme

ISBN 978-1-899000-34-0
eISBN 978-1-899000-35-7

A CIP catalogue record for this book is available from the British Library
Text designed and typeset by Tetragon, London
Cover illustration by Jason Anscomb
Printed and bound by CPI Group (UK) Ltd, Croydon, CRO 4YY

Contents

INTRODUCTION

The Mystique of Books, the Power of Fiction

We enter the realm of pure fancy in *Ten Trails to Tyburn* (1944), another bibliomystery in which books and manuscripts help lead to the solution of a mysterious death. As in the third Theodore Terhune mystery, *A Case for Solomon*, the ownership of a book—or rather a set of books—is the key to solving the overarching mystery of who killed Peter the Hermit and why. Even more important is the world of fiction itself. *Ten Trails to Tyburn* is not only the title of the novel but also that given to a series of short stories that are sent anonymously to Terhune and Detective-Sergeant Murphy. Someone knows more than they are willing to share about the death of Peter the Hermit. Rather than phoning the police and reporting simply what they know, this shadowy messenger has concocted a series of stories that will incriminate the culprit and ultimately lead the police and Terhune to the person responsible for Peter's death. A fanciful and baroque way to divulge clues and a motif that not only belongs to the fantastic realm of the "Golden Age of Detection", when murderers would often intentionally lay out a plethora of false clues, but also represents a plot gimmick that could only spring from the mind of Bruce Graeme, a mystery writer in love with the idea of mystery writing and mystery plots.

Why the elaborate ruse? Well, without it there would be no novel, would there? We learn the reason for these odd stories, something of a coded puzzle sent piecemeal and requiring expert literary interpretation as well as a bit of library research, in the last chapter. It's a fitting coda to the many other mysteries presented in yet another complex plot. And you will, of course, be left to discover that all on your own. This odd narrative device, a bit of metafiction that seems decades ahead of its time, allows Graeme yet another way to explore the power of words on minds susceptible to imagination, exploit the love of books as almost a power unto itself, and posit the unconventional theory that literature can serve as an eccentric inspiration for justice.

Graeme has found myriad ways to use books and manuscripts as unusual clues in his varied and imaginative crime novels. Writers, especially, fascinate him. In *Ten Trails to Tyburn* he is given an opportunity to show how revered authors of classic works have the power to influence the imagination of would-be writers. As Swinburne proved to be the talisman in *A Case for Solomon*, so we have the work of French short-story author Guy de Maupassant in this, the fifth novel in the Theodore Terhune series. And just as identifying the owner of the Swinburne volume was tantamount to tracking down the murderer of the man found in the woods in *A Case for Solomon*, so will the ownership of a set of Maupassant books lead Terhune to Peter the Hermit's devious killer. To be more specific, it is the inquiry into some missing volumes from an almost complete set of Maupassant short stories that triggers a search as tiring as a fox hunt through a heavily wooded and hazard-filled forest.

Book ownership, fiction writing and the art of creation itself are recurring motifs in Graeme's crime fiction. A pattern begins to reveal itself as the reader travels through the pages of the mystery novels in the Theodore Terhune series. Without books and Terhune's vast bibliophilic knowledge, it seems no murder case in Bray-in-the-Marsh can be brought to a satisfactory conclusion. Even outside the Terhune novels readers will have a chance to explore further variations on Graeme's theme. In *The Coming of Carew* (1945), published one year after this fifth Terhune mystery, a fictional character seems to come to life and commit crimes duplicating those that previously occurred only on paper. In *No Clues for Dexter* (1948) it is playscripts, rather than a novel or book manuscript, and the re-enactment of some stage business that provide Inspector Dexter with one of his most eye-opening bits of "evidence". And in *The Undetective* (1962; also available from Moonstone Press) we have a writer's alter ego, one that exists solely as a wholly fictitious pseudonym, being investigated by police as a primary murder suspect.

Terhune is not only obsessed with finding the owner of the Maupassant book but comes too late to a realization that his own profession could have brought about an early end to the case. Angry with himself for forgetting his chief talent in being the best bookseller in the surrounding villages, Terhune tells Murphy that had he only remembered the buying habits and tastes of his regular customers he would have remembered that there is only one person who enjoys purchasing books in foreign languages. The puzzle of the manuscripts has led him to spend too much time on "decoding" those stories inspired by Maupassant, and this involved task has distracted him from what is easily the biggest clue, the one that could have led him and Murphy to uncover the true identity of the elusive Alec Foulis.

Most interesting in *Ten Trails to Tyburn* is the rare instance of a crossover character in a Graeme mystery novel. Jeremy Cardyce, a sixty-year-old barrister and fellow bibliophile, turns up in a cameo appearance to help Terhune and Murphy clear up some truths hinted at in one of the stories sent by the anonymous messenger. Ultimately, Cardyce helps confirm the true identity of Peter's brother, whom Terhune has learned used multiple names over many years. I say "cameo appearance" because Cardyce was previously the protagonist in his own adventure, several years prior to the publication of *Ten Trails to Tyburn*. The elderly lawyer was introduced in *Cardyce for the Defence* (1936), a case that involved his goddaughter's impending divorce. On page one of *Cardyce for the Defence* we learn that our protagonist is not only a lawyer but an avid book collector. The opening scene has Felicity, his niece, interrupting Jeremy in his study while he is reading one of his dusty tomes. In order for Felicity to sit down he must clear piles of books from the furniture and set them teetering on other piles that litter his book-crowded room.

When Cardyce first meets Terhune in *Ten Trails to Tyburn* he overhears a comment about the familiar smell of old books and how Terhune feels immediately at ease in the lawyer's house. The two are kindred spirits: being bibliophiles allows for an instant friendship. Never mind that Cardyce mistakes Terhune for a policeman—an error Murphy quickly rectifies—their mutual love of books makes the job of asking for Cardyce's assistance all that easier for the two crime solvers.

Graham Montague Jeffries (1900–1982), better known as Bruce Graeme, was married and had two children: Roderic and Guillaine. Both his son and daughter went on to write books and interestingly also used their father's alter ego surname for their own pen names. Guillaine Jeffries, as "Linda Graeme", wrote a brief series of books published between 1955 and 1964 about a girl named Helen who was a ballet dancer in theatre and on TV. Roderic Jeffries followed in his father's footsteps and turned to writing crime fiction, using his own name and the pseudonyms Roderic Graeme (continuing his father's series about the thief turned crime novelist Blackshirt), Peter Alding, Jeffrey Ashford and Graham Hastings. In addition to more than sixty crime, detective and espionage novels, Roderic wrote a number of non-fiction works on criminal investigation and Grand Prix racing.

Late in life Graeme gave his Elizabethan farmhouse in Kent to Roderic and his wife. Graeme moved up the road to a bungalow and would have lunch with his son and daughter-in-law once a week. According to Xanthe Jeffries, Bruce Graeme's granddaughter, he remained in Kent while his son's family moved to Majorca in 1972. They remained close even while apart, and Graeme would visit in May every year, on his birthday.

When I asked for any family stories she might share with Moonstone Press readers, Xanthe very politely complied with an anecdote-filled email. I learned that her grandfather kept a couple of marmosets as pets and had inherited a Land Rover from his son when Roderic moved away. She also wrote of his annual visits to Majorca: "If the weather was not to his liking," she reported, "we never heard the end of it. On his last trip to us he became very worried about having to travel back to the U.K. via Barcelona." Apparently he was concerned about Spanish customs law. "When asked why he told my parents that his walking stick was in fact a swordstick!" Clearly, Graeme was something of an adventurer himself.

In future volumes of Theodore Terhune's adventures, soon to come from Moonstone Press, Graeme will continue to elaborate on his recurrent motifs of the intermingling fictional crime and real crime, the mighty influence of literature on imaginative minds, and the ability of a love of and respect for books to bring people together. *Ten Trails to Tyburn* may be the most experimental and fanciful of the Terhune books, the one least resembling anything remotely realistic when it comes to what actual murder investigations are like, but one must admit that Graeme has done something daring here. Using fiction as the primary tool to guide the police to the solution of a devilishly committed murder must be admired as an ideal of how literature has the power to triumph in the end.

J. F. Norris
Chicago, IL
July–August 2021

Chapter One

"**M**r. Terhune!"

Terhune glanced absently at his assistant. "Yes, Anne?"

"Could I leave early, please? It's already half past four, and only two people have come in since three o'clock."

He stared through the plate-glass door at the empty Market Square. There should be no difficulty, he thought, in disposing of a copy of the 1822, the first, edition of David Carey's *Life in Paris*. It was in good condition; all the coloured plates, twenty-one in number, were intact; all the pages were clean with the exception of page 27, on which there was a smudgy imprint of an inky finger; the title pages were clean...

He chuckled, and, for the fourth time, glanced at the opened title page with its quaint sub-title—*The Rambles, Sprees and Amours of Dick Wildfire, of Corinthian Celebrity, and his Bang-up Companions, Squire Jenkins and Captain O'Shuffleton; with the Whimsical Adventures of the Halibut Family*. Phew! The sub-title alone was worth a few pounds. £5 was the price he was being asked to pay, but it was worth quite that; less than three weeks ago more than double that price had been given for a copy of the same edition with two of the illustrations torn out...

"Please, Mr. Terhune—" Anne Quilter appealed.

Terhune realized that Anne had been speaking, but as to what she had been saying... He smiled apologetically. "I'm sorry, Anne. What were you saying?"

"Could I leave early this afternoon? Mother isn't very well—"

He packed her off quickly, after grumbling at her for not having asked sooner. Tuesday afternoons, like Friday afternoons, were invariably slack periods, more especially when a bitter north-east wind was blowing. It wasn't likely that anyone would be dropping in before five o'clock, he told her in all sincerity.

But no sooner had Anne Quilter disappeared round the corner of Windmill Wood Road than somebody entered the bookshop.

"Hullo, Terhune. Am I in time?" Brian Howland spoke somewhat breathlessly, as though he had been hurrying.

"In time?"

"Aren't you closing? I saw Anne Quilter crossing the Square a moment ago."

"She left early this afternoon; her mother isn't well." Terhune glanced at his watch. "I shall not be closing for another thirty minutes."

"Good! Then I'll change this book. Has that Inspector French title come in yet?"

"It came back this morning. I think Anne put it on one side for you." Terhune moved over to a shelf reserved for requested books. "Ah! Here it is."

Before he could complete the exchange of books the shop was again invaded. Alicia MacMunn fluttered in.

"Ah! There you are, my dear boy. I have a message for you." Then she paused abruptly as she recognized Brian Howland.

"Good afternoon, Mr. Howland. What a stranger you are! And how is that dear little boy of yours? He was *so* ill, wasn't he? Scarlet fever, wasn't it? Or was it jaundice? I have such a bad memory for colours."

Howland shook his head. "Neither of my boys has been ill for the best part of a year—touch wood! I think you must be thinking of Boothby's boy, Mrs. MacMunn." Boothby was a rival dentist, who lived and practised in Willingham Road, a short walk from Market Square. "He had German measles about three weeks ago."

Alicia laughed shrilly. "How stupid of me! Of course! I was think-ing of Teddy Boothby—"

"Rex Boothby," Terhune corrected.

She was not one whit abashed. With a gesture of her elegant hand she dismissed the entire affair. "And Mrs. Howland," she went on. "I do hope she is well. It is *so* long since I have seen her."

Howland knew that his wife and Mrs. MacMunn had sat together on a hospital sub-committee four days previously. He also knew his Alicia MacMunn.

"She is fine, thank you," he replied gravely. "But not liking this cold snap very much." He picked up the novel which Terhune had pushed across to him. "Thanks, Terhune. I must hurry back—Elsie promised to have tea all ready by the time I returned."

"I shall come with you, Mr. Howland," Alicia announced deter-minedly. "I have just remembered that I want to speak with your dear wife about our Christmas Bazaar—"

"But you have a message for Terhune—" Howland glanced uncer-tainly at the door, unable to decide which was the lesser evil—to wait for Mrs. MacMunn, at the risk of appearing anxious to overhear the message, or to seem, perhaps, even more rude by hurrying away in face of Alicia's self-issued invitation to his home.

"A message—" Alicia gazed blankly at Terhune.

"From Julia?" he prompted.

"Why, of course! How *perfectly* stupid of me!" She laughed good-humouredly at herself—one could forgive Alicia MacMunn almost anything because she had the saving grace of being able to laugh at herself. "Julia asked me to let you know that she will be calling here just after five—she wants to talk to you about the tennis club. She is across the Square—at Miss Amelia's—" The message given, Alicia lost interest in Terhune. She faced Howland again. "Are we ready, my dear man? I really must tell Mrs. Howland what happened at the hospital sub-committee last week…"

As the two people passed out of the shop Terhune began to tidy up, preparatory to closing for the night—it was most unlikely that anyone else would be calling, he reflected for the second time. He tidied his desk first, by collecting all the spread-out letters, papers, loose sheets of catalogue proofs and so on, and then pushing them higgledy-piggledy into the top drawer. Then he made one pile of some loose volumes which were lying around, waiting to be priced. Others, disturbed by borrowers, he replaced on their respective shelves.

He looked at his watch again. 4.47. Only thirteen more minutes to go, so why wait for the hour before lowering the blinds, he thought. If Julia intended calling he could well do with the thirteen minutes in order to have the tea-table laid before her arrival. With that intention in mind he moved across to the right-hand window.

With his hand on the blind-cord he paused. Through the plate-glass window he saw two people wheeling bicycles across the Square, and there was something about their purposeful walk, and the course they were taking, which warned him they were making directly for the bookshop.

One of the two people—the man—was known to Terhune. What was his name? Somers—Sneli—no—Snaith. That was the name! Snaith. Andrew Snaith. Or Arthur Snaith. Terhune couldn't remember which for the moment, but he was sure it was either one or the other.

Snaith, he recollected, lived at Great Hinton, and was in the habit of dropping into the bookshop, about once in every five or six weeks, to buy books. For the most part he rummaged among the books which stood on shelves marked: 'Any volume, *6d*.' Or, occasionally, he looked at those priced at *9d*. each, but he never paid more than 1/-. His choice of books had always been catholic, but, of course, it had to be at these prices. On one occasion he had purchased a shabby copy of *The Plays of John Galsworthy*, and one of John Creasey's thrillers. Another time he had taken away a collection of O. Henry's short stories, Bret Harte's *Waif of the Plains*, and the second volume of *Swann's Way*, by Marcel

Proust—he had subsequently asked Terhune to look out for a copy of the first volume. Apparently he had some aptitude for reading foreign books in the original, for once he had bought the paper-covered *La Rana Viajera*, by Camba (from the *6d.* shelf), and once a rather nice copy of de Maupassant's *Une Vie*— at 1/-.

Snaith and his female companion entered the shop. Snaith moved automatically towards the *6d.* shelves: the woman remained close to the door—shyly, timidly, disagreeably? Terhune could not decide. As Snaith passed Terhune he said: "Good afternoon, Mr. Terhune. Getting a bit nippy out of doors. There'll be a heavy frost tonight, I shouldn't wonder. Anything fresh on the sixpenny shelves today?"

"I think there are some you haven't seen," Terhune answered shortly. He wasn't feeling pleased at this last-minute call: Snaith had a habit of taking his time over choosing his shilling's worth of books.

Perhaps Terhune's attitude—he was still holding the blind-cord—warned Snaith that his visit had been ill-timed.

"We're not too late, are we, Mr. Terhune? Are you shutting up for the night?"

"Just getting ready, but we don't actually close before five."

Snaith was relieved. "Time enough for me to find a book for tonight." He took a pair of steel-rimmed spectacles from his pocket, fitted them, and peered at the books. "*A Housemaster's Letters*," he mumbled. "Sounds like punk. *Captain Dieppe*, by Anthony Hope. I remember reading that when I was a kid. Didn't think much of it at the time. I was looking for another *Prisoner of Zenda*. What's this? *Trial of Mussolini*. I read that years ago, during the war. *Poverty Lane*, by H. H. Tiltman—that sounds about my mark!" he commented bitterly. He took the book down from the shelf and was about to examine it, when he looked up at Terhune. "By the way, have you ever met the missus, Mr. Terhune?" He indicated his companion with a nod of his head.

Terhune hadn't met Mrs. Snaith before. He smiled and nodded, and inspected her as she nodded in return. She was, he saw, a woman of considerably less than medium height, and aged about the middle forties. She was dressed—well, not smartly—for how could anyone look smart in the cheap clothes she wore?—but with a degree of *chic* not usually to be found in the quiet surroundings of rural Kent, Her hair was blue-black—even blacker than Julia's. Her complexion was olive, and in that respect, too, she resembled Julia. But there all resemblance finished. Julia's eyes were always expressive, whatever her mood, but the eyes of Mm. Snaith were ice-blue, with the dullness of indifference. Her lips were thin and colourless.

Snaith closed the book with a snap. "I'll take this one, and another, if I can find one I like." He paused, glanced at his wife. "Would you like one, my dear? You haven't anything to read?"

"I have too much mending on hand to have time for reading," she replied shortly.

Terhune believed there must be an inference behind her words, but her voice was as flat as the expression of her eyes, and as colourless as her lips, so he could not be sure.

Snaith was not disconcerted by her reception of his offer. "All right, my dear. Next time, perhaps..." he said cheerfully, as he turned back to the bookshelves.

For nearly half a minute there was silence in the bookshop. Then Snaith went on: "A. G. Street! I've liked most of his books. What's this one about? *Hitler's Whistle*," A pause, and then: "*Dammit!* I've read it. Don't you remember the story of the cowman, my dear, who was asked by a magistrate about the speed of a car which had injured one of the man's cows? 'It were giwaine a sight too fast to slow up quick,' the cowman said." Snaith laughed heartily—a fruity, boisterous laugh he had—but not a flicker of interest passed over his wife's face, and she remained silent.

Snaith went on imperturbably: "I'll take this one, Mr. Terhune. *Rome for Sale*, by Jack Lindsay. I like stories of old Roman times. They were the times right enough, when a man could have a dozen slaves about the place to do all the work of the house." He tucked the two books under his arm and passed over a shilling to Terhune. "Good night, Mr. Terhune. I'll be in for some more books one of these fine days." With a heavy tread—for he was a biggish man—he crossed the shop to the door, opened it, and passed out. Mrs. Snaith followed. They wheeled their bicycles to the road, mounted them, and rode off in the direction of Great Hinton.

Terhune grimaced at the backs of the departing pair. They—or, at any rate, Snaith—had caused his precious thirteen minutes to vanish. Julia might appear at any moment—and the kettle even wasn't on! He hurried back to the blinds, let them down, locked and bolted the street door, and made a joyful rush for the staircase which led up to the rooms he occupied above the shop. He was about half-way up when two bells rang simultaneously—the telephone and the private door. Between Scylla and Charybdis, as it were, he was at a momentary loss to know which bell he should answer first. Should he be too long answering the 'phone the unknown caller might impatiently disconnect. On the other hand, Julia was not one to remain outside a closed door without losing both her good humour and her temper.

He hurried to the door, opened it, and saw Julia.

"Come in, Julie—won't be a moment—" He began to move away.

"Theo—"

"Telephone—listen..." There was no time to argue the matter out. He left Julia to look after herself and made a rush for the 'phone. "Hullo!" he spluttered, just a trifle breathlessly. Good lord, he thought: was he out of condition?

"Hullo, Mr. Terhune."

Terhune recognized the voice as belonging to Detective-Sergeant Murphy, attached to the police at Ashford.

"Are you free for the next thirty minutes or so?"

"Well—er—" Terhune glanced sideways at Julia. Murphy, no doubt, was ringing up to suggest a drink and a chin-wag: quite often in the past, time and circumstances permitting, he had 'phoned and suggested a meeting. On this occasion Julia presented a complication. If she were in one of her 'possessive' moods—mostly occasioned through being bored by the company of people she disliked—she wouldn't hesitate to show her annoyance at any interference with her plan for a restful hour alone with him. On the other hand, Julia disliked Murphy far less than she did the average person; she respected his practical intelligence and willingness to work hard.

Terhune decided to take a chance—Julia appeared to be in an amiable mood.

"Yes, Sergeant, I think so. Are you somewhere near?"

"At Hilltop Farm. Do you know it?"

"Is it the farm on the right, past the *Dusty Miller*, with three stacks to the west of the house?"

"That's the place. Well, there's a body here—"

"Not another crime, Sergeant? I don't believe it!"

Murphy laughed. "You don't have to, Mr. Terhune, because there's no crime this time—only a plain, everyday death from natural causes."

Much to his own annoyance, Terhune felt disappointed. "Who is it—Giffen?"

"Giffen! Good lord, no! You mark my words! That old rascal will outlive the lot of us in spite of his fifty-odd years. No, it's Peter the Hermit. The doc here says he died from heart failure, senile decay, malnutrition, exposure—"

"The whole jolly lot?"

"More or less, but you can talk to him yourself if you wish."

"You want me to join you, Murphy?"

"If you have the time. We've found something—well, interesting: something to start your imagination working."

"It's already doing that, Sergeant. By the way, may I bring Miss MacMunn with me?"

"Of course. Then I'll expect you in ten minutes or so from now?"

"Sooner than that if Miss MacMunn has her car with her."

Terhune rang off, and found Julia just behind him. She looked unusually excited.

"What has happened, Theo? Has somebody been murdered—a Mr. Giffen?"

The eyes behind his tortoiseshell glasses twinkled mischievously. Julia excited about the prospect of his becoming involved in yet another crime! Well, at least it proved that her taste was not static. He could still recollect the occasions, not so long ago, when she had caustically referred to his activities as a notoriety-seeking, amateur detective. An unfounded charge, as it happened, for his was a shy, retiring nature, and he detested notoriety. For that matter, he had never deliberately sought out the few cases of sleuthing in which circumstances had involved him—though it was true that he had found them to possess a fascination—a morbid fascination, his conscience accused—which, it now seemed, was spreading to Julia.

"My dear Julie, Mr. Giffen is alive and well."

"But I heard you ask if a Mr. Giffen had been murdered!"

"That's what comes of eavesdropping."

"Are you trying to be rude to me, Theodore Terhune?"

A year ago the same question would have made him look anxiously into her eyes for danger-signals, but during the intervening twelve months their friendship had ripened, and she had stopped being on the defensive.

"I shouldn't dare, Julie: you are my master at that game."

"You are a beast, Theo," she said without malice. "Who has been killed? Is it anyone I know?"

"Nobody has been *killed*. Somebody has died from natural causes."

"Oh!" He was ready to swear that her inflection was one of disappointment. But she went on more casually: "Why does Sergeant Murphy want you to join him?"

"He says he's found something I might like to look at."

Julia's interest was rekindled. "What is it?"

"I don't know; Murphy didn't say. But the sooner we get there the sooner we shall know—"

"That's not a very subtle hint that you would like to borrow the car and make haste," she pointed out, leading the way towards the private door by which she had entered. "Who has died?" she continued, as he opened the door for her.

"Peter the Hermit."

She stopped and faced him. This time she really was angry.

"If that is how you are feeling—"

He stepped quickly out of the door and joined her on the pavement. "The old chap with the dirty white beard who used to sing outside the *Almond Tree* every Sunday morning."

"That poor old man!" Her eyes smiled at him. "I'm sorry, Theo dear. I thought you were trying to improve upon the old joke about Queen Anne's death."

They stepped into the car; she turned on the ignition and pressed the self-starter. As she put the car into gear, and turned the corner into Market Square proper, she continued:

"Why did you call him Peter the Hermit?"

"That is what everybody calls him. I'm surprised that you had never heard of him by that name. Didn't you know that he lived the life of a hermit?"

She nodded. "Vaguely. But it is so long since I've seen him I have almost forgotten about him. Besides, I've always taken it for granted that the story of his being a real hermit was an exaggeration."

"So did I until the day when I took a couple of dozen books to Mrs. Fawcett at the time she had that hunting accident."

"I remember. She broke both her legs and did something to her back."

"As soon as she was well enough to read she asked me whether I would take her a selection of books. I did so, but you know what Mrs. Fawcett is when she starts talking—"

"Too well. She won't talk to *me*, however, if she can avoid doing so. I once told her a homely truth about her chattering tongue. Go on, my pet."

"Her property, Strangeways, adjoins Giffen's farm. In a rash moment I happened to mention the woods which divide the two properties. I should have known better. Those woods are a sore point with Mrs. Fawcett."

"Why?"

"For two reasons. The first because her father and Giffen's father once went to law to settle who really owned them—and her father lost! She's never forgiven the Giffen family in consequence. The second reason is due to Giffen's allowing Peter the Hermit to live in the woods. Mrs. Fawcett didn't like the look of the old chap and was quite convinced that he was in the habit of stealing her eggs. She wrote a letter of complaint to Giffen and, as far as I could make out, practically ordered him to turn the old chap out of the woods."

"So, of course, her letter had precisely the opposite effect?"

Terhune chuckled. "You know what men of Kent are like when one tries to dispute their rights. Giffen told Mrs. Fawcett that he had offered to let Peter the Hermit live in the woods for the rest of his life—and Giffen lived up to his word."

"What do you mean when you say that the old man lived in the woods?"

"The story, as I know it, is that Giffen's son—the one killed in Sicily during the war—at the age of fourteen or so built himself a kind of wooden shack in the middle of the woods so that he and his friends could play Red Indians and cowboys. Some years later Giffen was having a day's rough shooting in the woods when he saw some smoke coming out of a hole in the top of the shack. When he investigated he found Peter the Hermit there; in fact, he had been there already more than three months. Anyway, for some reason or other Giffen let the old chap stay on, and there he has been ever since—but there's Murphy waiting for us."

Julia brought the car to a stop beside the man from Ashford.

Chapter Two

M urphy raised his hat to Julia, and smiled his greetings to them both. The detective-sergeant had a very commonplace type of face: round, healthy, somewhat heavy-jowled, stolid and without much character except in his alert eyes. It was, however, an honest face, and rather attractive when it smiled.

"Glad to see you, Miss MacMunn. I hope you and your mother are keeping well."

"Quite well, thank you, Mr. Murphy. And you?"

"Blooming, thank you, miss. This cold weather suits me." He glanced at Terhune. "I hope you're not expecting too much, Mr. Terhune. There's no mystery about old Peter's death, poor old chap, but, as I told you over the telephone, I've found something which might interest you, you being a writer."

"What have you found, Mr. Murphy?"

The detective chuckled. "I don't want to spoil the surprise, miss. You shall see for yourself if you will come with me." An expression of concern abruptly banished what remained of his smile. "Drat it! Why didn't I think to warn you to put on some old shoes—especially you, Miss MacMunn—?"

"Don't worry about my shoes, Mr. Murphy. I happen to have on an old pair of brogues because they are my warmest."

Terhune wore an ordinary pair of light shoes, but he was not going to be discouraged from following Murphy. "Never mind a little mud, Sergeant. It won't be the first time these shoes have been smothered."

The statement was quite untrue, but it eased Murphy's concern. He indicated a cart-track which joined the road where he stood: the track was a short one and, at a point where the fringe of a substantial area of woodland would have prevented farther progress, it turned left into a large-sized farmyard. They walked as far as the limit of the track; there they found, on their left, a closed five-barred gate, moss-green with age; on their right, an unbroken hawthorn hedge which marked the boundary of Mrs. Fawcett's land; in front of them a barbed-wire fence, and a stile which gave access to a footpath leading into the woods.

They climbed the stile, and walked along the footpath in Indian file, Murphy leading. Very soon the clustering trees and undergrowth closed in upon them. They found the air charged with the pungent but not unpleasant odour of rotting vegetation; a brooding silence—disturbed only by the occasional scuffling of rabbits and game birds—and the premature twilight emphasized by the interlaced boughs from which the cold winds of the last few days had stripped the last leaves.

Terhune, in the rear, was at ease, even happy, to find himself segregated from the world beyond by a thick belt of trees; a townsman by birth but a real countryman at heart, he loved Nature in all her moods, in any surroundings. Julia, country born—in the district in which she lived—was indifferent to the eerie charms of their cloistered isolation; she was self-confessedly intolerant of natural beauties, and a worshipper at the shrine of more worldly culture. But Murphy, Dublin born and London bred, had still not conquered an inherent aversion to Nature solitary or Nature cold and dormant. His walk lacked his usual confident assurance, and when he spoke, as he did presently, his voice was muffled.

"These woods aren't the place I'd choose to live in," he said.

The words, hushed though they were, seemed to penetrate the immediate border of trees and undergrowth, first to become flat and lifeless, then to be lost as if sucked into infinite nothingness.

"Listen to my voice," he continued resentfully. "It gives me the willies just to hear it. I'd choose a workhouse, or even jail, in preference to—to this blinking morgue."

Terhune laughed—the echo travelled so far that distance distorted the sound of it, and mockingly tossed it back at them.

"See what I mean?" Murphy added before Terhune could speak. "That didn't sound a bit like your voice, Mr. Terhune. Not to me, it didn't. Woods may be fine places to picnic in, on a hot day in mid-summer. But at this time of the evening, and with a wind blowing to freeze one's bones—well, give me a comfy seat before a blazing coal fire any day of the week."

"I agree," Julia said. "But I am sure you don't, Theo."

"I don't. I won't say that I don't like these woods—all woods or forests, come to that—better in spring, summer and autumn, but even in winter there is beauty to be found by all who care to look for it." He waxed eloquent. "The shapes of the trees, for instance. Winter is the only time when one can properly see their intricate structure. Look at that oak ahead of us on the left, Julie. I'll bet it's a couple of hundred years old if it's a day, but it's a darned sight more handsome now than it was when it was ten years old. Don't you agree that it has majesty? Its very attitude breathes defiance at anything Nature can hurl against it—"

"Lightning, for instance," Julia interposed drily.

"You're a Philistine, Julie. But even a stricken oak has a grim beauty of its own, a suggestion of timelessness—a reminder, if you like, that even death takes many years to fell an oak; for even while the process of decay is destroying its vitals it often continues to stand stark and upright, a grand, contrasting background for the new life shooting up all around it."

"Go on," she urged quietly.

"I'm making a fool of myself."

"No, Theo, you are not. I should like you to tell me what else you see in these woods."

Because he knew that Julia was speaking with sincerity he did so. "The twilight mist, which adds softness and mystery to the bare trees; the grey squirrels—even if they are pests; the carpet of leaves; the red berries of holly trees; and mistletoe, too, perched aloft in odd bunches. And then, in the winter, one can discover vistas which are hidden at most other times. Think of Nature's colouring throughout the year. In the spring the general colour scheme, with fresh greens and yellows predominant, has all the crudeness and bold brushwork of youth. Summer is mostly a season of dazzling reds and purples, of every possible shade, from the delicate pink of a Dorothy Perkins rose to the deep, velvet red of a peony; from the sedate lilac to flamboyant clematis. Autumn, on the other hand, is beautiful with soft browns and russets."

"But winter is colourless, Theo. How can you find beauty in—in—colourlessness?" She laughed slightly at the cumbersome word she had coined.

"There is a predominant colour even in winter. A neutral colour, perhaps, but one that can still create startling effects. I mean grey, of course. Chalky greys, pastel greys, black greys. Grey skies, grey mists, grey water, a carpet of grey-black leaves, even the grey squirrels I mentioned just now. I have often seen you dressed in grey, Julie. If grey suits you, which it does, why shouldn't it suit old Mother Nature equally well?"

Terhune's descriptive arguments might have impressed Julia, but he quickly learned that they had failed to convince Murphy.

"Granted that these woods can look beautiful to you at this time of the year, Mr. Terhune, would that fact make you prefer living in a draughty wooden shack, in the middle of nowhere, to a solid brick building within easy distance of the local?"

Terhune felt impelled to admit that his appreciation of the woods was not that enthusiastic.

"Well, then, what made that poor devil live here for ten years?"

"As long as that?"

"So Giffen told me. The truth is, I suppose, that he was a bit soft in the head. Lord! It makes me shiver to think of him trudging through these woods during the really cold winters, like those just before and during the first two years of the war."

"By the way, Sergeant, who was he? Do you know?"

"Not at the moment, but it shouldn't be hard to find out. He must have been issued with identity and ration cards during the war."

"Didn't you find anything in the shack to identify him?"

Murphy started to laugh, but, hearing the woolly echo which the trees flung back at them, he stopped abruptly, and muttered something about a blasted noise. Then he went on: "Yes and no, Mr. Terhune. You see, we've found a couple of things which might help to identify him. But then again, they might not."

"Is one of them the something which you thought might interest me?"

"Yes. In fact, they both might. By the way, do you know anything of the old man?"

"Only about as much as anyone else in Bray. He used to come into Bray every Thursday and Sunday morning. On Thursdays he used to earn an odd shilling by lending a hand to anyone who could make use of him—looking after a horse and cart, or carrying the shopping home, or keeping an eye on a car, or helping the stallholders erect and dismantle their stalls. On Sundays he stood outside the *Almond Tree* and sang for coppers."

"I remember giving him a copper once when I had a drink there with you, Mr. Terhune. He smelled to high heaven on that occasion."

"He always did," Julia said. "Mother used to give him a sixpence because she felt so sorry for the man, but he never touched my heart. Perhaps he might have had more success with me if he had taken the trouble occasionally to wash the stains and bits of food out of his beard. In my opinion he was just a dirty old man who was too lazy to work for a living."

Julia's verdict was harsh, and Terhune would have argued it with her, but before he could do so a bend in the footpath brought them within sight of the hermit's shack, so Terhune remained silent.

Originally the building of the shack had been a work of ingenuity, and a credit to the young boy who had—in a sense—designed it, for Giffen's son had used, as natural corner-posts, four trees which had grown up at each corner of a small area of space approximately square. The lad, it seemed, had begun operations by lopping off the lower branches of all the four trees up to a height of seven feet. He had then adopted the simple stratagem of making three walls of long planks, which he had nailed, one above the other, to the tree trunks. The roof had been made just as simply, by forming a foundation of other planks, which had been nailed to the topmost wail planks, and then covering the roof planks—and all the gaps left by this rough-and-ready method—with some of the galvanized-iron advertisements which disfigure the average railway station—and which, Terhune doubted not, had been 'borrowed' by Master Giffen from sundry stations up and down the line without the express permission of the Southern Railway.

Use had been made of similar advertisements, of various shapes and sizes, to make the walls air-and watertight, and though the weather had wrought some damage to the enamelled surfaces, it was still possible to recognize Colman's Mustard, Huntley and Palmer's Biscuits, Camp Coffee, and other products.

The fourth side of the shack, which contained the doorway, had been built with equal simplicity, for, at the right distance between two of the trees, two uprights had been driven into the ground to serve, firstly as a frame for the door—a respectable prefabricated door—and secondly as posts to which shorter planks could be nailed, and thus complete the building.

For the most part, time had been kind to the crude shack. Perhaps this was due largely to the rock-like stability of the corner-posts; perhaps, also, to the thick umbrella of interlaced boughs which created a second, natural roof, as it were, over the lower plank-and-metal roof.

Still, there was evidence that the building had not entirely escaped the ravages of time. One or two of the metal advertisements had fallen, and exposed draughty gaps in the plank walls. Some of the planks themselves appeared to be crumbling away in decay. Some were green, others black with fungus. Altogether, the decay, the stark surroundings, and the sombre twilight made the shack look dismal and unhealthy.

The local policeman—Gibbons—stood on guard outside the shack. As the other three people approached he saluted Julia, grinned in a friendly way at Terhune, and said to Murphy: "Best not be too long, Mr. Murphy. It'll soon be dark, and this ain't no place to be caught in when it's dark."

"Anybody been near?"

"Not a soul. I wish they had been. Gor! It fair gives me the creeps, this place does. You wouldn't get me to live here a week for a thousand quid. I allus said old Peter was dotty. Now I knows it. You can hear the worms moving about."

Murphy glanced at his companions. "Shall we go in?"

Terhune nodded. Gibbons opened the door—it opened outwards with an eerie squeaking noise—and held it open to admit what light there was left. The other three entered, and looked around. Julia shivered.

The shack was roughly twelve feet by nine. The floor had been stamped and pounded into an uneven but hard and comparatively dry surface. In the centre of the room was a tattered rug, a three-legged stool, and an upturned plywood tea-chest. The greater part of the top of this tea-chest was covered with a thick layer of dirty grease, the drippings of countless candles; the rest of the available space was occupied by a chipped plate, coated with dripping-grease, a knife, fork, and a bent leaden spoon, a chipped enamelled mug, and a piece of stale bread.

A rough fireplace of sorts occupied part of the right-hand side of the shack. This was made of old bricks cemented together to form three sides of a square, a foot high. On top of the bricks was laid a gridiron, on which, in turn, stood a blackened iron kettle. Below the gridiron was a pile of wood ash. On one side of the fireplace was an iron saucepan, half filled with some revolting greasy substance which the visitors had to assume was, at any rate in name, a stew. There was no chimney of any kind above the fireplace—evidently there was sufficient ventilation from the holes and cracks in the plank walls to carry off the smoke from the fire.

Against the wall facing the door somebody had built a sleeping-bunk. In the bunk was a straw palliasse, shockingly stained and dirty, two nondescript blankets, equally filthy, and a crumpled pillow. Underneath the bunk was a flat wooden box about four feet long, three wide, and one foot in height.

Some attempt had been made to decorate the walls of the shack by pasting or nailing up about eight pictures in all. Dampness, and smoke from the fire, had made the illustrations almost indistinguishable, but on striking a match and peering closely at the one nearest to him Terhune saw that it was the cover of a boy's magazine, and depicted a Buffalo-Bill-like cowboy astride a galloping pinto in whose flank was buried the shaft of an Indian arrow.

"How could anyone be content to live in such ghastly poverty?" Julia asked.

"That's my argument, miss," Murphy said quickly. "Only a loony would." He pointed towards the bunk. "He was there when he was found this afternoon. The doctor said that he had been dead about nineteen hours. That puts his death some time about eight p.m. last night. The doctor thinks that he was probably seized with a heart attack, managed to stagger into the bunk, and died with the effort of climbing in and pulling the bedclothes over him."

Julia's eyes clouded. "Poor fellow!" she murmured sympathetically. "What a dreadful death!"

"Who found him?"

"Giffen himself. He was doing a bit of rough shooting, and as he was passing with a well-filled bag he entered this hole to leave a rabbit for the old man's supper tonight—apparently Giffen was in the habit of leaving something here whenever he was out shooting. Anyway, to Giffen's surprise he found old Peter apparently asleep. When he tried to wake the old chap up he was stiff, so Giffen went straight off to bring Doctor Edwards back here. Of course, the old man was already dead, so Edwards reported to Gibbons, and Gibbons telephoned through to Ashford for an ambulance. When the Super was told of the death he suggested my coming out here to see what I could find to help identify the old man."

"Well?"

"You can see for yourself all there was to be seen."

"What's in the box underneath the bunk?"

"The remainder of his belongings—a couple of pairs of stinking socks, a lousy pair of pants and a vest, half a dozen ties and so on. Nothing of any interest, and not a darned thing of use to my investigation. I was on the point of giving up the search when I noticed that old sack on the floor, just behind the door. Would you like to pick it up, sir?"

Terhune did so. The soil beneath was loose and disturbed as though somebody had been digging there.

"Something has been buried here?"

"Yes." Murphy approached the tea-chest, lifted it, and pulled from under it a small wooden box. He replaced the tea-chest on the rug, then opened the box. "This, for instance!" He passed over to Terhune an old newspaper, yellow with age, and splitting.

Terhune carefully unfolded the newspaper. To his astonishment he saw that it was printed in a foreign language, which he could not vaguely identify at first glance. He searched for, and found, a date. The month he could not recognize, but the year was in Arabic numerals: 1923.

In his excitement Murphy moved closer to Terhune, and peered over his shoulder. "Do you know what language that is, sir?" he asked eagerly.

"I haven't the foggiest notion. Does it convey anything to you, Julie?"

Julia joined the two men. She, too, examined the paper for some seconds, then shook her head. For a further thirty seconds or more all three continued to stare with speculative eyes at the yellowed newspaper.

"I could make a rough guess," Terhune said presently.

"Well, sir?" Murphy asked anxiously.

"Mind you, Sergeant, I'm only guessing, but I've an idea this is one of the Balkan languages."

"The Balkans!"

"Yes. And if you want me to narrow the choice down I should say Bulgarian."

"Why?"

"Because some of the advertisements advertise an address in Sofia."

"Sofia! That's the capital of Bulgaria, isn't it?" Murphy asked somewhat diffidently.

"Yes."

"Well, if you're right—and I shouldn't mind betting you are—why do you reckon the old man was treasuring a twenty-four-year-old Bulgarian newspaper?"

"Was Peter the Hermit English, Mr. Murphy?"

"Well, miss, if it weren't for that newspaper in front of us I'd have said yes. But I don't know anything about him, and haven't started making proper enquiries yet, so I can't tell you much."

"Haven't you spoken to Giffen?" Terhune asked.

"Not since I found the newspaper. I've talked to Gibbons, though, and he says that he would take an oath that the old chap was English."

"To find an Englishman able to read Bulgarian is rare enough—assuming Peter could read this paper, and surely he wouldn't treasure it if he couldn't—but to find one who not only can read it, but who remains satisfied to live the life of a dirty, starving old tramp—well, by George, Sergeant, you were right about my being interested!" Terhune's voice confirmed his growing excitement. "What was the other thing you found?"

Murphy returned to the box and produced a second newspaper, more recent than the first, to judge by its colour, and printed in English—a copy of the *Daily Mail*, Terhune saw. Apparently the *Daily Mail* was not in itself the second article, for the sergeant unfolded it and revealed a wide, flat wad of yellowed cottonwool. This he carefully pulled apart.

"Look!" he announced, thrusting his hand forward in the direction of Julia and Terhune.

They stared down with astonishment at what lay exposed on the palm of the detective's hand—a comb; large, handsome, brightly coloured with jewels.

"Well, I'll be damned!" Terhune exclaimed at last.

Chapter Three

"It's very beautiful," Julia said presently.

"That shade of emerald green would look fine on your head, miss, if you don't mind me saying so," Murphy added respectfully. "That is, if women ever wore combs like that in this country. It's foreign, isn't it? I've never seen one like it before."

"I think it must be Spanish, Mr. Murphy."

"Spanish!"

"Yes. I remember seeing combs of that type in the shops at Las Palmas—though none so beautiful as this." The sparkle in her eyes matched the fire of the gems. "I wonder what the value of that comb would be if the stones were real."

"Worth a lot, wouldn't you say, Miss MacMunn? More than a hundred pounds?"

"Quite that."

"The stones *are* real—or my name isn't Murphy!" the sergeant said huskily.

"You're joking, Sergeant."

"I'm not, Mr. Terhune. Honest to God, I'm not! Of course, I'm no expert, but I've had something to do with precious stones on and off, and until an expert tells me they are paste, I'm saying they are real."

"But I thought you said old Peter died of starvation and exposure?"

"That's what Doctor Edwards told me."

"Then why in heaven's name didn't he sell the comb and buy himself a square meal?"

"Yes, why? Because he was loony, I say. Or a miser—and what's the difference, anyway?"

"Perhaps the comb was stolen property, so he was afraid to sell it," Julia suggested.

"I wouldn't say that guess was so far off the mark, either."

"I wonder!" Terhune shook his head. "The old man looked an honest sort of a bloke."

"Theo, my pet, you are an incurable sentimentalist."

Murphy nodded quickly. "One or two of the crookedest men I know have the faces of angels. Beards are particularly deceptive: they usually soften a face, and give it an air of benevolence and innocence."

"If he weren't honest he wouldn't have hesitated to sell the comb, would he?"

The sergeant shrugged. "If he had any sense left he would have known that it might have been too risky to try and sell it."

"Why?"

"If you were a jeweller or a pawnbroker, and an old tramp like Peter came into your shop to try and sell you a lady's comb worth a hundred quid or more, what would you have done?"

"I see what you mean," Terhune agreed slowly. "You think I should have sent for the police?"

"Either that or you would have sent him packing, with a flea in his ear."

"I suppose so—but all the same, if I were starving I think I should have taken a chance on selling it. Unless—"

"You think there is a story attached to that comb?"

"Don't you, Sergeant?"

Murphy chuckled. "Between ourselves, I suppose I do, sir. That's why I thought you might be interested in seeing the comb. I should think you ought to be able to write a pretty good story of an old tramp starving to death rather than sell a jewelled comb which had once belonged to his dead wife—"

"Please, Mr. Murphy!" Julia shivered. "What a horribly morbid idea!"

"I'm sorry, miss," the sergeant apologized quickly, contritely. "We policemen get hardened to tragedies." He looked at the bunk then at the loose soil behind the door, then at the crust of stale bread on the upturned tea-chest. It was easy to follow the trend of his thoughts. "I suppose his death was a morbid affair when you think about it," he mused aloud. His voice became brisker as he dropped the comb into a pocket and collected the newspaper from Terhune. "Well, that's all there is to show you, Mr. Terhune. We ought to be moving before it's too dark."

"I'm ready," Terhune agreed promptly. "What about you, Julie?"

"Yes."

They moved on out of the shack. "All right, Gibbons. Just put everything shipshape first. And close the door when you leave."

Gibbons nodded. "You can leave everything to me, Sergeant. Good night, miss; good night, Mr. Terhune." Gibbons vanished into the interior of the shack.

The other three returned along the muddy footpath. "By the way, Sergeant, very many thanks for letting us come along."

"That's all right, sir. I thought you might be interested."

"I am, exceedingly. As a matter of fact, I'm not going to get the recollection of that comb out of my head very easily."

"I shall look forward to reading about it one of these days, Mr. Terhune. Which reminds me, before I forget—would you care to give me a hand in trying to identify old Peter?"

"Of course. What do you want me to do?"

"If you wouldn't mind asking some of your customers from round about here if they know anything about Peter the Hermit it might make matters easier for me. You know what some people are like the moment anybody in the police force starts to ask questions. They shut up like oysters."

"I'll be glad to do anything I can."

"I'll let you know what progress I make. It may be that something will come to light pretty soon, but on the other hand I've a feeling it won't."

Julia was vaguely surprised by this remark. "Why should you think that, Mr. Murphy?"

The sergeant laughed. "Perhaps it's the Irish blood in me, miss. In any case, it's never easy establishing the identity of old tramps who wander all round the countryside—some forget their own names as they get on in years, and not ten per cent of 'em remember their age, or the date of their birthday. In this case I can't help feeling that the comb—and the newspaper too—may complicate the problem."

"Why?" Julia asked once more.

"It's like this, miss. If old Peter could really read Bulgarian, that must mean that he had had some sort of education—which is more than you can say of the majority of old tramps you see around, most of whom can't even read English. That fact doesn't mean a lot by itself, but it does when you stop to consider the comb.

"Now, I don't think that that comb was stolen. If it wasn't, how did it come into Peter's possession? The obvious answer is—as a gift. A memento, a—a—"

"Keepsake?" Terhune suggested.

"That's the word! Keepsake! Well, people don't give away bits of jewellery worth a hundred pounds unless they can afford to part with money just like that—" Murphy waved an expressive hand in the air. "And people with that much money usually associate only with people of their own class. Please don't think I'm trying to make all rich people out to be snobs,'" he hastened to explain, half turning towards Julia. "But you know what I mean—"

Julia smiled tolerantly. "Of course we do, Mr. Murphy, though I'm afraid that the criticism, even if you didn't mean it as such, is justified."

"Not as much as you pretend, Miss MacMunn," the detective asserted gallantly. "The point I'm trying to make is that old Peter must once have had some money of his own, or have belonged to a family that possibly wasn't too badly off."

"So?" Terhune prompted.

"If we allow that the old chap once had money, or else belonged to a family which had, how was it he practically starved to death?" Murphy raised his hand to prevent the arguments which he knew would quickly be forthcoming. "I know there are probably half a dozen different answers," he went on hastily. "He might have gambled all his money away; he might have become the black sheep of the family, which then refused to have anything more to do with him; every penny of the family fortune might have been lost in a financial crash; he might even have been the only son of an only son, and so have had no blood relations. But if he had any relations at all—and there are few people who haven't—surely somebody would have had enough pity for the old man to give him a few shillings now and again to help keep him alive?

"I don't think I'm making myself very clear," Murphy continued uncertainly. "But I'm getting to my point now, which is this: if he had relatives, but no money from them, then it was possibly because pride, or sentiment of the kind which let him starve to death rather than sell that comb, made him keep the knowledge of his poor circumstances from them and from any friends. In that case, to be absolutely certain of them *not* learning about him, don't you agree that he would have taken care to live in a part of the country where he wouldn't expect any of his relatives or friends to find him? In short, because the old man lived in Kent I'm ready to bet that Kent is the one county where none of his near relatives or friends is living. And that is why he lived here throughout the year instead of wandering from county to county like all the other tramps. Does that theory make sense to you, Mr. Terhune?"

'It's a little far-fetched, don't you think, Sergeant? But go on."

"Alternatively, he had no relations anywhere. In either case, however, whether he had no friends or relatives anywhere, or whether any who exist live in some other part of the country, I shouldn't mind betting that the police have a pretty hard job identifying the old man."

"Wasn't he old enough to be drawing the old-age pension?" Julia asked unexpectedly.

"Undoubtedly."

"Then shouldn't the post-office be able to help?"

"Yes, miss, *if* he drew a pension. But my own opinion is that he didn't. If he had spent even a small proportion of the pension money on food he wouldn't have been as starved as he was."

"If he were entitled to a pension I can't believe that he would have starved to death rather than draw it."

The strange note in Julia's voice made Terhune glance up from his task of looking for the least muddy parts of the footpath. "Old Peter's death seems to have upset you a bit, Julie."

She nodded, without turning her head. "It has," she admitted frankly. "It seems horrible to realize that even in these days it is still possible for an old man to die of starvation and exposure."

"If any man dies of malnutrition in these days he has only himself to blame," Terhune pointed out. "I am beginning to agree with the sergeant, that old Peter must have been a loony."

They came in sight of Julia's car, and saw a group of five or six people clustering round it and gazing in their direction,

Murphy laughed drily. "The news of Peter's death has started travelling. Well, I suppose now is as good as any other time to begin making enquiries. Would you like to stand by, sir, or are you in any hurry?"

"We are not in any hurry—or are you, Julia?"

"No."

"So if our presence won't embarrass you—"

"Embarrass me!" The sergeant chuckled. "You are too well known for me to be embarrassed by your presence, Mr. Terhune. Do you know what happened to me the other day, when I was investigating a burglary at South Willesborough? The old lady whose fur coat had been stolen said to me: 'If you don't get that coat back for me by the end of the week I shall send for Mr. Theodore Terhune, of Bray. I am sure he is clever enough to know who stole my lovely coat.'"

There was no malice in Murphy's voice, only genuine humour, but Terhune reddened.

"I'm sorry, Sergeant—"

"Bless me heart, sir, there's nothing for you to be sorry about. I know too well that you aren't out for publicity—"

"Or detective work!"

"That's right. Nor are you. But here we are." Murphy's voice faded as he got within earshot of the people round about the car.

Of the six people there, Terhune recognized five. Foremost, and standing in a somewhat expectant attitude, was Ted Shore, landlord of the *Dusty Miller*. Shore was a little chap, looking somewhat like an overgrown and overweight jockey, for he was dressed in close-fitting breeches and gaiters, a brightly coloured green jersey, and a cap several sizes too large for him. His face was sharp, but as brown as a berry.

Next to Shore was Giffen, owner of Hilltop Farm, and the woods in which Peter had lived for so many years. Giffen, also, was dressed in breeches and gaiters, but he was as large as Shore was small; his shoulders were massive; his face was rubicund in part, and purple-veined round the base of the nose, but the colouring came from winds blowing from the north and the east, not from too much alcohol.

Just behind the two men were two people holding bicycles—Snaith and his wife. Seeing them, Terhune recollected that they lived at Great Hinton, and concluded that they must have just arrived from Bray. Talking to Mrs. Snaith was the fifth person known to Terhune. She was a thin-lipped, prim-looking woman, with greying hair drawn tightly back from her forehead to make a tight bun at the nape of her neck, upon which rested, somewhat precariously in the chill wind, a hat which had seen its best days during the First World War. Nobody would ever have guessed from her appearance that she was a cook, employed at Strangeways, Mrs. Fawcett's home.

The sixth person was a man with fair curly hair and an adenoidal expression. He looked no more than twenty-five, but his face was tanned with health, and his clothes were those of a farm labourer. Aware how flatteringly deceptive a countryman's complexion can be, Terhune was quite prepared to believe the other man's age to be nearer thirty-five than twenty-five.

"Hullo, Mr. Murphy, have you found anything?" Giffen questioned loudly, in a manner which suggested that his find entitled him to feel that he had become an important member of the community.

"Found anything!" Murphy repeated sharply. "Such as?"

The farmer looked a little taken aback. "I don't know," he mumbled. "I thought you was there to see what you could find."

"Well, there was nothing to be found," the sergeant retorted curtly. "But as you are here I'd like to ask you a few questions. I suppose these other people have heard the news?"

"Yes. Leastwise, we've all been talking about old Peter."

Murphy glanced at each of the five people in turn, then addressed them as a group. "Do any of you know anything about the old man— his rightful name, where he came from, and so on?"

The people shuffled about uneasily. A dribble of saliva trickled from the corners of the adenoidal's hanging lower lip.

Mrs. Newman, the cook, was the first to speak. "I know nothing about him except that he was a dirty old man who ought to have been taken away years ago and put in a home," she said, biting each word off from its predecessor with an air of outraged distaste.

"What sort of a home?"

Before Mrs. Newman could answer there was an interruption from the adenoidal one. He chuckled splutteringly. "Then why did you used to give the old 'un a bite of pie every now and agin, Mrs. Newman?" he asked with a leer.

"You hold your tongue when you ain't spoken to, Jim Cooper," she said with asperity.

"Used you to give him food now and again?" Murphy asked the cook.

"What if I did? Nobody was worse off, except Jim Cooper's pigs. The old man might have starved to death long before this if it hadn't been for them bites of pies. Just because I think he ought to have been put away in a proper home, was that any reason why he should starve to death for want of a helping hand?"

"All right! All right!" Murphy exclaimed soothingly. "Suppose you tell me what you do know about old Peter?"

Mrs. Newman was not to be won over so easily. "And me catch my death of cold in this perishing wind?"

Shore spoke up quickly. "Why shouldn't we all go into the *Dusty Miller?*" he suggested eagerly. "There's the club-room there you could use, Mr. Murphy."

The cook's expression became severe. "I'll not enter a public for anyone. Good day to you." She turned and began to walk away from the group. Murphy glanced quickly at Terhune, who winked and shook his head so the sergeant knew that the identity of the thin-lipped woman was known to his friend though not to himself.

"What about the rest of you?" he asked.

Giffen did not hesitate to nod agreement. Nor Snaith, although Mrs. Snaith gave his sleeve a slight tug as though to draw him away. Jim Cooper gave another spluttering chuckle.

"Does that mean a drink for all o' we?" he asked slyly.

Murphy nodded, and with Shore by his side began to lead the way down the road to the *Dusty Miller.* Terhune joined the others; but

Julia got into the car, started the engine up, and turned on the side and rear lamps, which were, by now, necessary. Upon reaching the inn the Snaiths leaned their bicycles against the wall, while Julia parked her car close by, then all entered the low, squat building, and gathered in the club-room, which was across a narrow, flagged passage from the only public room.

A bright log fire was crackling cheerfully in the bricked-up inglenook. Mrs. Snaith edged her way towards it while Shore put a match to the swinging oil-lamp. In a few moments the small room was alive with the movement of softly wavering shadows, and odorous with the pungent scent of smouldering logs and burning paraffin.

"Mine'll be a mild-and-bitter, Mr. Shore," Jim Cooper said, with the sly air of a man who wasn't going to allow Murphy's promise of free drinks to go unredeemed.

At a nod from the sergeant Shore took the order for drinks, and vanished through the door into the saloon bar opposite. All who remained sat down on one or another of the forms which stood each side of the two trestle tables. Except Murphy. He sat down on the corner of the right-hand table, with his back to the fire.

"You all know that Peter the Hermit has died," he announced. "The doctor says that the old man died as a result of heart failure following years of undernourishment and exposure. There's nothing strange about his death, so don't start imagining there is. But the police want to find out who the old fellow really was, so that he can be buried with his name on the tombstone, and his relatives, if any, can be advised. Now, first of all, do any of you know who he was?"

"Ay," said Jim Cooper. "Peter the Hermit."

"Don't be daft," Giffen snorted. "That's only what us round here called him."

"Do you know who he was, Mr. Giffen?"

"I'll be danged if I do." Giffen rubbed a round, bald patch on his head with a coarse red hand. "I never asked him who he was."

"Suppose you start at the beginning, Mr. Giffen, and tell us how he came to be on your land?"

"I don't know how he came to be there in the first case. He must've just found that old shack, I reckon, and settled in without a word to anyone."

"How and when did you first know he was there?"

"How?" Giffen rubbed his bald patch again; evidently this habit was his source of inspiration. "Well, I was doing a bit of rough shooting in the woods one day when I saw some smoke coming up from a hole in the roof of the shack which my boy built when he were a kid—him what was killed in the war, not Ted, who ran away to sea—"

"Go on."

"'Poachers,' says I to myself, so I cocked my twelve-bore, crept up to the door, and pulled it open. But there weren't no poachers. Just a dirty old tramp cooking a rabbit over a wood fire. One of me own rabbits, I reckon, an' all. Well, I wasn't going to have no tramps making use of my woods, so I told him to—to..." Giffen hesitated, glanced at Mrs. Snaith, and went on: "To dratted well be off and quick. He saw I meant business, for suddenly he—he—" This time the farmer did not continue.

"Go on, man," the sergeant urged irritably. "What happened then?"

Giffen rubbed his mouth and chin with his hand—if his face had not already been so purple and red Terhune would have sworn it was reddening with embarrassment.

"He—he went down on his knees and begged me to let him stay—he offered to pay me a shilling a week rent..." Giffen laughed hoarsely with relief as Shore entered with a tray full of drinks.

Chapter Four

B y the time everyone in the room had a glass in hand—Mrs. Snaith and Julia had chosen sherry, Terhune gin and orange bitters, the rest ale—Giffen had recovered from the embarrassment of having to confess that another man had once kneeled before him. At the first convenient opportunity Murphy resumed the interrupted interrogation.

"Now, Mr. Giffen, what did you do when the old man asked you to let him live in your son's old shack?"

In a deliberate manner the farmer took one more satisfying swallow, placed his tankard down upon the trestle before him, and wiped his mouth with the back of his hand.

"Well, mister, as a general rule I don't encourage tramps, nor gyppos neither, upon my land, but the old man looked so danged harmless and old that I reckoned that it couldn't do nobody no harm to let him sleep at the old shack for a few months—the weather was just beginning to turn warm about then—so I told the old man that he could stay there for the time being. But mind you, mister"— Giffen stared challengingly at the detective, then at the rest of his audience in turn—"I didn't take his bob a week, either then or at any other time."

"I am quite sure of that," Murphy agreed soothingly. "Did the old chap stay on from that day to this?"

"Ay. He did an' all. Even through the winter months."

Jim Cooper glanced sideways at the farmer. "But you didn't mind the old 'un giving you a 'and now and agin, eh, Mister Giffen, when there was a bit of stuking or picking or 'edging to be done. I seen 'im, I 'ave."

"You'll see too much for your own good one of these days. And why shouldn't he have give me a hand, Jim Cooper? Tell me that, if you can. I only asked him to do what a kid of five could've done. 'Sides, wasn't everyone asked to give us farmers a hand during the war? Wasn't we asked that?"

Murphy hastened to put a stop to a controversy which threatened to side-track the main issue. "Of course we were, Mr. Giffen. But getting back to your first meeting with the old man, did you ask him his name?"

"I didn't. It didn't mean a rap to me what his name was as long as he behaved himself."

"How did you find out that his name was Peter?"

The question put the farmer off his stride. He stared blankly at the detective. "Blowed if I know," he replied at last. "One day nobody called the old man nothing, the next day the whole danged village was calling him Peter."

"I know who first called the old 'un Peter," Jim Cooper volunteered.

Murphy gave his attention to the labourer. "Who?"

"Young Charley Binks."

"Charley Binks?"

"Bert Binks's kid—Bert Binks what runs the garage."

"Ah!" Murphy knew the garage, it was on the outskirts of Great Hinton, at the junction of the main Ashford-New Romney road. "Had Charley met Peter before?"

Jim Cooper guffawed. "Naw! Him and his ma was walking to Bray one day when they sees the old 'un coming their way. 'Who's that funny old man, Mum?' asks Charley. Charley's ma says she don't know, she ain't never seen him nor once or twice before. 'He's like the old man what teacher's been learning us at school,' goes on Charley. 'What man is that?' asks his ma. 'Peter the Hermit, what preached to men to join the army to fight them heathens in Asia,' the kid says, and pipes up: 'Peter the Hermit! Old Peter the Hermit! Peter the Hermit!' Before you could say 'Jack Robinson' everybody was calling the old 'un Peter the Hermit."

"Who told you that story?"

"Charley's mum herself."

"That's right enough," Snaith confirmed, speaking for the first time. "Mrs. Binks told me the same story."

"I see!" Murphy was not too happy with Jim Cooper's story, which did nothing towards helping to identify Peter. "Do any of you know where he came from before he settled down here?"

There was no immediate answer to this question; the four people from Great Hinton just looked at one another in anticipation.

"Does that mean that none of you knows anything?"

"I reckon we don't," Giffen replied. "Leastwise, I don't."

"Nor do we," confirmed Snaith. "Do we, my dear?"

"No," his wife confirmed.

"Nor me neither," added the innkeeper.

Jim Cooper alone was silent. Murphy faced him squarely.

"What about you, Jim Cooper?"

"It's no use you asking me. I don't know nothing about where he came from." Although Cooper's slack lips mouthed the words with a somewhat furtive air, Murphy accepted the assurance for the time being, and turned back to Giffen.

"How long had Peter been living in the shack when you first saw him there?"

"Two weeks at least. Longer for all I knows."

"What makes you allow him even two weeks?"

"Because I found out some time later that Tom Thompson, one of the men working for me, had seen him there two weeks before I found him, and hadn't said anything to me."

"Do you know why he kept quiet?"

"He said he felt sorry for the old man, and thought that I should be sure to turn him out if I heard. To hear Tom carry on one would think I was a hard man," the farmer grumbled on. "It's only gyppos I don't like, and some of they rascally tramps who make off with anything they can find lying around loose."

"Had the shack been used at all by other tramps?"

"Not for two or three years, at least. Once I found a couple of old rascals there, but I turned them out quick."

"Then how did Peter come across the shack? It's a goodish way from the road, and well hidden."

When Murphy saw the farmer beginning to rub the bald patch he guessed the answer was going to be unsatisfactory. So it was.

"Blow me! I don't know. But, by crikey, I'd like to! It's funny how he came to find it, now I come to think on it."

"Do any of the footpaths in the wood lead to any place in particular?"

"Only to me own land, and Mrs. Fawcett's. There's one path leads into Woodcock Close, another into Fifteen Acre, and the third into High Paddock. The other two paths stop at Mrs. Fawcett's fields; one at the edge of Craddock's Close, t'other at North Close."

"Do you know why Peter lived for so long at the shack?"

"Because he wanted to, I reckon."

"Would you be content to live the last ten years of your life in a shack like the one in your woods?"

"By crikey, I wouldn't be content to live ten years of my life as a tramp!" the farmer retorted drily.

Jim Cooper guffawed, and Murphy appreciated that his last question had been rather a senseless one.

"Have you spoken to him on any occasion other than the time you first saw him?"

"On and off. On and off," Giffen said boomingly. "Everybody round about here has too, I reckon."

"I stood the old gaffer a beer every Christmas," Ted Shore offered. Snaith nodded. "I've spoken to him now and again."

"Good!" Murphy exclaimed briskly. "Then perhaps you can tell me this. What sort of a man was he? Was he educated? Did he speak with any sort of a dialect, and could you recognize it? Did he ever speak of any other part of the country, or of people living elsewhere?"

A silence followed this string of questions. But just as the detective was losing patience three of his audience began to speak together—the farmer, the innkeeper, and Snaith.

"All right! All right! One at a time. You start, Mr. Giffen."

"Well, mister, as you asks me. I'd say he was a Londoner—"

"That's right!" Shore interpolated, with a quick nod of his smallish, pointed head.

"I'm not saying I'd like to make a bet on it, 'cause he were a bit of a mumbler, if you follows me," the farmer went on. "Nor am I much of a one for telling places where people comes from neither, though I knows a Scotchman from a Welshman, I reckon. But I knows one or two men from London what speaks much like old Peter used to."

"That's right!" Shore confirmed for the second time. "I'll take my davy he lived most of his life in London."

Snaith shook his head. "I don't agree, Sergeant. Old Peter rolled his 'r's too much to be a Londoner."

Murphy turned quickly. "Where do you think he came from? Scotland?"

"I don't think he was a Scot, but he may have come from one of the border counties."

"Northumberland or Cumberland?"

Snaith nodded. "Possibly."

"Have you spoken to him very often?"

"Two or three times a year, maybe."

"Did you form any opinion of his educational standard?"

The other man shrugged. "I never thought of Peter the Hermit as being anything but an old tramp. Do you think he wasn't, then?"

"I don't think anything about him; I haven't anything to go on. Why used you to talk to him?"

"I didn't make a bosom companion of him, if that is what your question means. He's done a couple of odd jobs for me in the years he's lived in the woods, so naturally I talked to him on those occasions. I'd have had him more often if I'd had the money to spare, because I was sorry for the old chap. The other times we talked together were mostly when I was out walking. Old Peter was apt to pop up in the most out-of-the-way places and hail one as a bosom companion."

"In what way?"

"Well, you could be leaning on a five-barred gate, for instance, looking at the corn growing, and suddenly find him next to you, telling you the weather was holding good, or asking whether you thought the harvest would be a good one, or had you heard that Jones's son had nearly been drowned in the canal."

"Then you would say that, to some extent, his manner was familiar?"

"I should," Snaith agreed, with a touch of asperity. Then he added, apparently as an afterthought: "He was like that with everyone who lived in Great Hinton."

Giffen chuckled gleefully. "Ay! He were that an' all, mister. He had only to see Mrs. Fawcett to make a bee-line for her. Many's the time I've seen him jawing to her till she were red with fury."

Terhune grinned at the farmer's obvious relish for this story, for he had heard of the strained relations which existed between the farmer and Mrs. Fawcett, who was the daughter of a Malayan rubber planter and the widow of a schoolmaster.

Murphy, however, seemed unaware of the significance of Giffen's remark, for he went on seriously: "Would you say, then, Mr. Giffen, that Peter's familiarity towards the people round about here was that of a man who had once been something better than just a tramp?"

The farmer's hand worked overtime in rubbing the bald patch—in fact, Terhune began to think that the habit had caused the baldness, rather than the baldness the habit.

"Well, mister, I haven't never given the matter thought, but if you put it like that, perhaps you're right." He nodded vigorously. "Ay, I'd say you've cottoned on to something there, mister," he announced ponderously.

"That's right!" chipped in Shore. "And there's something else I can tell you now, Mr. Murphy, seeing Mr. Giffens reminded me of it. One Christmas, when we were in the bar having a drink on the house, I heard him argyfying with old Mr. Fife, and you wouldn't guess in a month of Sundays what they was argyfying about."

"Well, what?"

"The size of ships what can go through the Suez Canal. Mr. Fife said that ships of thirty-five thousand ton could go through the canal—or did he say twenty-five thousand?" the innkeeper asked doubtfully.

"How should I know?" Murphy asked irritably. "Does it matter? Anyway, what did Peter say?"

"He said no ship larger than seventeen thousand ton had ever gone through the canal."

Murphy exchanged glances with Terhune. Both knew that old Peter's contention was unfounded, but the important fact was that he was intelligent enough and sufficiently knowledgeable to argue such an unusual and uncommon subject.

"That's good enough for me," Murphy declared, with some decision. "I'm satisfied that the old man hadn't always been a tramp."

Snaith smiled derisively. "Because he could discuss the displacement of ships in relation to the Suez Canal?"

"Yes," Murphy stated defensively.

"Shades of W. H. Davies!" Snaith murmured.

The detective glowered. "What's that? What did you say about a man named Davies?"

"W. H. Davies was a poet," Terhune explained quickly. "Among the books he published was one called *The Autobiography of a Super-Tramp*."

"Oh!" Murphy pursed his lips. "Anyway, none of the tramps I've had dealings with could write poetry, or talk about the Suez Canal." He glared at Shore, as though the innkeeper had been responsible for causing his embarrassment. "Is there anything more you can remember about him?"

Shore shook his head. "Nothing at the moment, Sergeant, but if I does remember anything come tomorrow I'll give you a ring on the telephone."

"Thanks." Murphy turned his attention to Jim Cooper. "You've been pretty dumb after getting me in here to give you a drink. What do you know about the old man?"

Cooper leered at the detective. "You should 'ave brought Mrs. Newman in here. She can tell you more than us can."

"How do you know that?"

"He's one of Bill Blakes's men. Bill Blakes what works the land for Mrs. Fawcett," Giffen explained.

"And a mortal fine job he do make of it too, don't 'e think so, Mr. Giffen?" the adenoidal one jeered.

The farmer turned wrathfully upon the sly-looking, fair-haired labourer, but Murphy hastily intervened. "Does that mean that you work at Strangeways?" he asked Cooper.

"On and off."

"Is that how you knew that Mrs. Newman was in the habit of giving food to old Peter?"

"I got eyes in me head, ain't I?"

"What else did those sharp eyes of yours see?"

"It ain't only what me eyes seen. It's what me ears heard, too."

"Well, what?"

For one moment Jim Cooper created an impression upon the others present that he was not going to say much more, but suddenly he gazed round the room and seemed to appreciate, either from the expression in the eyes of his audience, or from the tense quietness, or both, that this was his little moment. His own pale-blue eyes gleamed with malicious satisfaction; his slack lips formed into an idiotic grin.

"One day, when I were taking a rest in the hay, soon after the old 'un had settled in the woods, him and her passed by. Jabbering fifteen to the dozen, they were, and presently I heard him say to she..."

He paused, with the mischievous intent of provoking curiosity, and slowly and deliberately stared in turn at every person in the small club-room. At last, Giffen, with the natural impatience of an employer of several farmhands, shouted out testily:

"G 'wan, man, spit it out! Us haven't all night to waste. What did her say to the old man?"

The sly, watery-blue eyes winked at the floor, as the grin of satisfaction broadened.

"Who's supposed to be finding out about the old 'un? You or him?" He jerked his thumb at Murphy.

A low, growling noise in Giffen's throat gave warning of the scene which might follow if it were left to its own volition. Murphy hastily intervened.

"I am, so suppose you tell me what you overheard?"

"All right, mister. I don't mind telling *you*. The old 'un said to she: 'Thanks for telling me about the hut in the woods, missus. I've settled down all snug and shipshape—'"

An angry roar from the farmer drowned the remainder of the sentence.

"The damned, interfering old busybody—" he bellowed. "Making free with my hut and woods, was she...?"

I I

In time Murphy succeeded in soothing the farmer's ruffled feelings, whereupon he continued his questioning. Nothing more of any consequence came to light, however, and after another fifteen minutes he decided that there was not much object in remaining longer at the *Dusty Miller*. So he and Julia and Terhune left the little club-room.

Outside the inn, Julia asked: "Can I take you back to Ashford, Mr. Murphy?"

"I have a car, thank you, miss. I left it just up the road, outside the vicarage."

"Have you time for a quick one, at the *Almond Tree*?"

Murphy hesitated, then yielded to temptation. "Why not, Mr. Terhune?" he agreed cheerfully. "Ten minutes more or less won't make any difference to my supper. I'll go back for my bus and follow you there."

So it was fixed. Murphy disappeared along the now totally dark road, while Julia and Terhune entered the coupé and started slowly off in the direction of Bray. It was not long before Julia saw a pair of dancing headlights reflected in the driving-mirror, and when the car behind made no attempt to pass they knew that Murphy had caught them up.

It did not take them long to reach Market Square, where they parked the cars and entered the lounge bar of the *Almond Tree*. There they were greeted by the usual crowd—Winstanley, Jeffrey Pemberton, young Arnold Blye, son of Major Blye, Edward Pryce, Isabel, Shelley, and others—who clamoured for the three newcomers to join their noisy party. But Julia waved her hand in negation, and as long experience of Julia's noes had left the young men of the district in no doubt as to their meaning they left her and her companions in peace.

Presently, when they had been served with drinks, Julia said invitingly, "Well, Mr. Murphy?"

He shook his head in doubt. "You would have thought somebody in Great Hinton would have found out by now all there was to be known about the old man."

"Perhaps somebody has—you've only spoken to five or six people, Mr. Murphy."

Terhune saw Murphy's wry expression, and chuckled.

"Why the laughter, my pet?"

"Because Julie old girl, you can be quite sure that if any one person in Great Hinton had known anything about the old man, every man, woman and child would also have known about him long before now."

She spoke to Murphy again. "But you are not going to stop at five or six people, I know."

"Certainly not, miss. But Mr. Terhune has about hit the nail on the head, and I haven't many hopes of finding out much. I hadn't from the first, you'll remember. Mrs. Newman may be worth a special visit. So might the man Fife who argued about the Suez Canal. And I have an idea that Jim Cooper is holding something back. But as for the rest..."Murphy shrugged his shoulders, and turned to his drink for solace.

For another ten minutes or so they discussed the matter, but without much knowledge to sustain them their arguments and suggestions were very half-hearted. When Murphy looked at his watch and stated that he really ought to be moving, the other two made no attempt to detain him. As soon as he had gone, Julia and Terhune joined the party which surrounded Winstanley, and promptly forgot about Peter the Hermit.

III

During the two following days Terhune spoke to scores of people about the old anchorite, especially during Thursday morning, which was Market Day at Bray-in-the-Marsh. Of course, everybody had seen him at some time or another, many had given him a copper or two upon occasions, some had spoken to the old man. But not one of the people whom Terhune questioned was able to offer any information which he thought would be worth while passing on to Murphy.

To begin with, none knew him by any name other than Peter. He was either Peter quite simply, or Peter the Hermit, or old Peter, or that old tramp, or Old Looney—and once, Old Methuselah! Nor did anyone know for certain whence he had come, although there were few who were not ready to make a wild guess. "A Londoner born and bred," stated Doctor Edwards, who came from Wales. "From some-where in the Midlands, I'd say," was Lomax's opinion—Lomax was the lessee of the *Almond Tree*. Mortimer said, "Yorkshire, without a doubt, me boy," but Mortimer was a retired business man, Lancashire born and bred, so perhaps it was prejudice on his part. As no doubt was equally the case with Joshua Higgins, who owned a newspaper-shop overlooking Market Square. Higgins, being a Yorkshireman, was sure a dirty, useless old tramp like Peter must have come from Lancs. Dai Lluellyn—who didn't hail from Scotland—agreed that Peter had a Cockney accent. Brian Howland suggested Cornwall. And so the story continued.

On Thursday afternoon Murphy 'phoned. Could he visit Terhune later on that night? Of course, there was only one answer to that request. So, just after eight o'clock, Murphy called upon Terhune, and quickly settled down in the study before a cosy log fire.

"Any news of Peter?"

"Not a darned thing!" Murphy replied, biting on the end of his pipe. "Didn't I say from the first we were going to have trouble in tracing the identity of that bird! What about you, sir? Have you had any luck?"

"As much as you have, Sergeant."

"That's helpful." The detective chuckled unexpectedly. "But I didn't come here tonight to talk about the old man. I've got something to deliver over to you which was wrongly delivered at my home."

"By post?"

"Yes."

Terhune stared at his guest. "How could anything for me get left at your house?"

"Look for yourself."

Murphy handed over a large foolscap envelope addressed to:

Detective-Sergeant Theodore I. Murphy,
26, Worthing Road,
Ashford.

As soon as he saw, by the expression on his host's face, that Terhune had read the address, Murphy laughed loudly.

"Somebody seems to have got us both well mixed up, sir. Theodore I. Murphy! By old Harry! I hope nobody in the Force gets to hear of this. I should never hear the last of it—to say nothing of the fact that it's ten to one they would nickname me Tim, which is a name I could never abide."

Terhune grinned back. "I wouldn't wish the name of Theodore on my worst enemy, so I sympathize with you, Sergeant." He fingered the envelope, which he now noticed had been wrongly delivered to Ashford, Middlesex, and re-directed: *Try Ashford, Kent.*

"But it's only the Christian names that are wrong, Sergeant. The rest of the address is correct, isn't it?"

"It is that. But the contents are for you, all the same, and if you don't believe me, have a look, sir."

Terhune opened the flap and pulled out a small wad of quarto-sized, typed pages which looked exceedingly like a short manuscript. Unfolding it, he saw that he was not mistaken. The front page read:

TEN TRAILS TO TYBURN

NO. I. FAME

Chapter Five

Terhune flipped over the title page. On the next page began a short story, which continued for seven pages more. The story, apparently, was located in Paris—outside the Café de la Paix, according to the first paragraph. He examined the title page again, but there was no author's name upon it. Nor the author's address. He turned to page eight again, both sides, but on neither side was there any hint of name and address.

He then opened out the envelope and looked inside.

"There was no letter with the story, if that is what you are wanting, sir."

"Funny!" Terhune's forehead creased with perplexity. "Have you a favourite nephew or niece who's been bitten with the ambition to write?"

"That story is intended for you, not for me, Mr. Terhune."

"For me!"

"Yes."

"Why should anyone send me the manuscript of a short story?"

"I can answer that one easily. My idea is that somebody has got the notion that, as you are a writer yourself, you should be a good critic, and has sent you that story so that you may read it and give him—or her!—your opinion of it. Alternatively, the author may want you to give him your advice on what publication he ought to try first and sell it to." Murphy shook his head commiseratingly. "There are so many cranks in the world I shouldn't put it above one of them to try and wangle a little free advice and help from you."

Terhune was not satisfied with the explanation. "Then somebody would be wasting his time—" He grinned. "*His* time, I said, Sergeant. You see, I don't know the first thing about short stories—at least, not other people's. I've sold a few of my own to the *Saturday Evening Post*, of course, but that doesn't make me a critic. Or a tame literary agent." He inspected the envelope again. "Besides, Sergeant, here it is in black and white: your title, Detective-Sergeant, your name, Murphy, and your rightful address. It must be for you." He pushed the envelope forward to the other man.

Murphy shook his head, and made no attempt to take the typed pages. "Don't you believe it, sir. That story is for you right enough. What has happened is that the author has read about you and me taking a hand in one or two criminal cases together, and has got us so mixed up that he's given me half your name, and also your talent for writing books." The detective grimaced wryly. "I wish he was right."

"He's also given you your talent for detective work, Sergeant, so he hasn't left *me* much. But if you are right, and the author intended to send the story for either my criticism or my help, why didn't he send a letter with the script?"

"He probably intended to do so, and forgot to enclose it." Murphy chuckled. "Read the story, sir. I'm anxious to know what you think of it."

"Have you read it?"

"Yes. It's a blinking funny story, to my way of thinking. But there, I'm no judge of stories, like you are. Just give me enough blood and thunder to keep me from falling asleep and I don't mind much if the heroine does start off with brown eyes and finishes with blue. I can't keep all the personal details in my memory when I'm reading a good, exciting novel."

"Yet you do when you are at work. Are you in any hurry, Sergeant?"

"No, sir. The wife's got a friend at home, and it won't worry me overmuch if she's gone by the time I return—the friend, I mean," he added, with a grin of delight at his own unconscious humour.

There were a quart bottle of beer and glasses on a small table close to the detective's elbow. "Help yourself to the beer," Terhune invited.

Murphy did not wait to be asked twice. He filled the two glasses, and passed one of them over to Terhune.

"Your very best, sir."

Terhune nodded. "The same to you," he murmured, as he began the story of *Fame*.

I I

FAME

A group of four men sat at the Café de la Paix on the Boulevard des Capucines.

They had not spoken much, for each was intent on watching the passing throng. Of the passers-by some sauntered leisurely; the day's work was over, it only remained for them to enjoy themselves as they pleased. Some were hurrying, for at home the little ones would be waiting for their good-night kiss, the good Maman listening only for the click of the key to order dinner.

Nevertheless, the ever-moving stream presented an interesting study of a cosmopolitan crowd. There were rich Americans, phlegmatic Englishmen, aristocratic Russians, affluent Brazilians, temperamental Italians and immaculate Parisians; and, not the least important, the amorous Parisienne, the painted 'little *poule*'.

One of the group, Charles Dassier, was on the staff of *Le Grand Journal de Paris*. He it was who spoke most often, for there were many he recognized; some he had interviewed, others he had often described.

"See, *mes amis!*" he exclaimed, his voice excited, "there passes Hiram Chapman, the famous oil-king and philanthropist. They say that his income tax is yearly one half million dollars. *Dieu!*" he added wistfully. "That would mean many millions of francs. More than enough for two, three, even the four of us."

There was silence while each of the four comrades pondered on the many things which a quarter of half a million American dollars would render possible.

Soon their interest was again distracted.

"Ah!" exclaimed Charles significantly. "See—that little man on the kerb just hailing a taxi. Professor Xerxes: his theories are world-famous. Throughout Christendom philosophers hang upon his words."

Suddenly a mischievous smile slowly crept across the face of the journalist. "Professor! Professor!" he murmured reprovingly. He turned to the others, and his voice lowered. "See who is with him! It is the great Adéle!"

Instantly the interest of the other three was centred on the great Adéle, about whom each one of them had heard much, but until this moment had never seen.

"She is beautiful!" In hushed tones Georges Préjoul signified his appreciation.

"So chic, so glorious. What divinity!" Not more backward was Jacques, the young art student. He noted her curving figure, her exquisite shape, and sighed. If he could have but the chance to paint her.

The third man, Pierre, grunted, but said nothing. Perhaps the others were aware that his forehead was creased, his eyes dull; but, if so, they took no notice.

Scarcely had Professor Xerxes and the great Adéle disappeared, their taxi whirling rapidly away into the vortex of raucous traffic, than Charles, his memory as keen as his eyesight, was speaking again.

"Here comes a famous *flâneur*. For many years past he has frankly expounded his views on the Government. See, even now he stops, as he meets a crony. He is for ever against the Government, as indeed all of us are; but his biting scorn, his bitter tongue...

"Behind him, some seven paces, comes Kaviesosky—Kaviesosky the great, the wonderful! See his long white fingers, how beautifully they taper. Do they not unblushingly pronounce themselves as artistes, each one in themselves? How tenderly they pluck the strings of his violin, how gracefully draw the bow!

"His music is the hum of bees, the call of the wild, the plashing of water, the wail of the mystic Orient—they say his fee in London is £1,000 for one performance; in New York even more."

Kaviesosky passed on in the wake of the others; his shadow no longer in the sun, even though he was the famous virtuoso Kaviesosky. Others came and passed even as he; many others who were non-entities, who never would be known or applauded, criticized or immortalized.

And Pierre's brow grew more wrinkled, his lips tightened and drooped.

"Ah, look you, Charles! Even I recognize the car that passes. It is that of Vaudin, the actor. Only last week I saw him at the Comédie-Française'

"Indeed, you speak rightly, Jacques, for it was Vaudin himself who sat in it; by his side the equally famous Italian sculptor Giuseppe."

Suddenly there came an interruption. Pierre brought his fist down upon the iron table with a jar which caused the glasses thereon to jump; his three friends turned amazed faces towards him.

"*Dieu!*" said Charles, "what is wrong?"

"It is you; your chatter, *mon ami*," replied Pierre, his eyes blazing angrily.

"If I annoy you—" Charles shrugged his shoulders.

"But no! 'Tis not yourself, but the people of whom you talk. Bah! Why must you speak of them? Are they not talked of enough? Are they not already famous?"

Georges laughed suddenly. "Surely you have not turned Bolshevik, Pierre?"

"No!" Quickly Pierre snapped out the reply, but his face softened and his shoulders drooped. "Forgive me, friends, this stupid outburst. It is that I am consumed with jealousy, that envy of them all eats into my heart.

"I, too, would be famous—I, who have always prayed that I might be great, that people might point to me and speak in hushed tones, even as Charles has spoken of the American, Chapman, of Xerxes, of Adèle, of Vaudin and Giuseppe.

"As a boy I dreamed of fame and its attendant adulation. I would be a great orator, I would become a Senator, I would rise—Premier— perhaps President. There were no pinnacles too high upon which to build my dream castles.

"Then I would be an explorer. The North Pole, the South Pole, the unreached fastnesses of South America; here and there, throughout the world, there would be no place too inaccessible for me to reach, too dangerous for me to explore.

"Now—what am I? An insurance clerk—one of hundreds." His voice broke slightly, and his listeners were aware that a sob had crept into his throat.

"Not on this earth shall I achieve my ambition, the urging impulse which burns me up. A clerk. What likelihood is there of my ever becoming famous? None—none. You, Charles, you are a journalist, you use your pen. Perhaps one day you may write a book, two books, then more, you may be read from Dieppe to Marseilles: it is possible that the Académie will recognize you; there is the Legion of Honour to reward you.

"Georges, you are a cadet. Come a war and you may earn promotion, you may earn the Baton; why should Joffre, Foch, be more famous than you? Perhaps you may protect France, be its saviour, its hero. It rests with you, Georges.

"What of Jacques? Even now his brush becomes more skilled every day, his colours surer. Why should he not one day hang in the

Salon? Fortunes may be spent to obtain his pictures, perhaps in the days to come critics will argue the merits of Raphael, Gainsborough and friend Jacques.

"Do I exaggerate? Perhaps! Remember all I have said is that at least you, all of you, have the road before you. It may be rough, pit-strewn, littered with unbelievable obstacles, yet at the end is the golden gate, the sparkling entrance to the world of fame.

"Me! What of me? What road lies ahead of me? None; nothing but an insurmountable, unbreakable, immovable wall. Work I ever so hard, till my eyes flicker out, my brain turns soft, my flesh dries up on my bones, I shall die as I live, a clerk in an insurance office. Perhaps in due course be a manager, perhaps even higher; yet still I shall remain unknown, unrecognized.

"Who, but those who know me or my work, could write my epitaph, what unknown bourgeois could relate my life, my work? Yet there is not one of us who could not compose a paragraph, however small, about Xerxes or Vaudin."

His passionate speech faltered, came to an end, and he bowed his head in his hands, whilst his friends gazed at him with sympathy, conscious for the first time of the unsuspected tragedy of this man's life, so unexpectedly laid stark and bare before them.

Georges leaned across the table. "I am sorry," he murmured, and laid his hand upon the other's shoulder. Pierre rose, his eyes blinded by tears, and roughly brushed his arm away. The next moment he was crossing the crowded road, unconscious of his actions, heedless of the speeding traffic, immersed in self-pity.

How narrowly the world escaped the throes of another international financial crisis was revealed by the *Echo de France*.

With a fiery, exotic pen the tale was told, beginning with a description of the little house in Dreux. Here, one day, were gathered together a party of conspirators awaiting the arrival of their leader.

In the meantime, their Chief, a man of letters, unsuspected spawn of the Devil, confidant of Senators—and Senators' wives—waited too: he boasted of his punctuality.

Watch in hand, he waited for the hour. At the stroke of six he stepped into the purring automobile, and with scarcely a sound the chauffeur clutched in, en route for Dreux.

In his pocket the Chief carried, written in full, the complete details of a plot, its ramifications spread throughout the world. A plot which could easily ruin the money markets of the world—and all to line the pockets of half a dozen unscrupulous financiers.

Throughout Europe, America, India, the Orient, the lieutenants waited; waited for the word which their Chief should give—and their Chief was to give the signal at the meeting in Dreux.

The automobile moved along: the chauffeur was dreaming of his Mimi. Only two months now and they would be married—

Too late he applied shrieking brakes. The thudding wheel flung aside the helpless pedestrian. Then a crash, a horrible grinding of metal, the musical tinkling of glass. When the ambulance came there were two corpses—one that of the leading financier.

There was no world-wide financial manipulation. The French police saw to that, when they read the mass of private papers which lay strewn about the two corpses.

One man saved the world, and from north to south, from east to west, the news was flashed by wireless, cable and photograph.

But Pierre could never know that in death Fame was his, for his was the second corpse.

III

Evidently Murphy had been carefully watching for the moment when his companion should finish reading the story, for even as Terhune lowered the script on to his lap the detective asked eagerly: "What do you think of it, sir?"

Terhune stared down at the title page. 'That depends," he began absently. "If this is the work of a beginner, well—I've seen worse."

"It's written in a funny kind of a style, isn't it?"

"It is, certainly, out of the ordinary. But you were wrong in concluding that the script was intended for me."

"For the love of Mike, who was it intended for?"

"For the person to whom it was addressed."

"What, me?"

"Yes."

Murphy looked reproachfully at his companion. "You're pulling my leg, sir. Why should it be meant for me? What do I know about short stories? Or long ones either, for that matter?"

"Possibly not much, Sergeant, but you do know something about Peter the Hermit."

Terhune chose an unfortunate moment for the exploding of his metaphorical bombshell, for Murphy was lifting his glass—and it was still fairly full—to his lips. The consequence of this unfortunate timing was that the detective started, and spilled most of the beer down his jacket. A damp rag soon disposed of the beer, and soon all was peaceful again. With unconscious deliberation Murphy took a long pull at his glass.

"Now, sir, you're not trying to tell me that that short story has any bearing on the death of Peter the Hermit?"

"I know it's a far-fetched theory, but that is just what I do say."

The sergeant looked dubious, but experience had taught him initial respect for Terhune's far-fetched theories. "Go on," he said in a business-like manner.

"Briefly, the plot of the story is that of a man who had lived all his life as a nonentity, but at the moment of his death, when it was too late, achieves notoriety."

Murphy grinned. "It needs a writer's imagination to think out a plot like that. But I still don't see——"

"Listen, Murphy. Peter, too, was a nonentity—to such an extent, in fact, that after two days' work you have failed to find out who he was, or where he came from, or why he chose to settle down in Great Hinton."

"That's true enough."

"Now, you have kept neither your enquiries secret, nor the fact that you believe him to have been a nonentity whose death is so unimportant as not even to cause a ripple of excitement among the local inhabitants. In fact, I'm quite sure that the death of George Barker's Angus bull would have caused a greater stir."

"If you mean that dangerous-looking beast he paid all those thousands for, you're certainly right, Mr. Terhune."

"Suppose, however, that somebody in the district knows, first, that you are on the wrong tack, and secondly, that if the truth of old Peter's going were made known, his death would create a sensation, wouldn't the events of the story parallel, to some extent, those of the hermit's death?" Terhune did not give Murphy a chance of answering. "But there is another clue even more significant," he went on.

The sergeant nodded a query.

"The name of the cashier who was killed," Terhune replied.

"The name——" Murphy frowned in perplexity, unable, it seemed, to remember the name of the cashier.

"Pierre," Terhune explained. "Pierre is the French for Peter."

Murphy's face was expressive, but he took time to consider the proposition. He puffed away at his pipe extravagantly, and filled the small room with blue-grey smoke and the aromatic odour of an Empire mixture.

He spoke presently, in a slow, deliberate manner. "In short, Mr. Terhune, you think that somebody sent the story to me as a warning that old Peter's death is not what it seems to be on the surface, and that if enquiries are pursued instead of being shelved—as I'm expecting will happen at any moment—something sensational will develop?"

"I told you that the theory was a far-fetched one, Sergeant. But, after all, there must be an explanation to account for that short story having been sent to you."

"A straightforward letter would have been simpler to write, and a darned sight more to the point."

"I wonder."

Murphy removed the pipe from the corner of his mouth. "Another theory?"

Terhune did not directly answer the question. "On Tuesday you admitted that most people avoid, if they can, being questioned by the police."

"I still say so."

"Don't you think that the existence of such a general feeling of embarrassment, or whatever it may be, answers your question about why somebody sent you an anonymous short story instead of a letter?"

"I still think that an anonymous letter would have been easier to write than an anonymous short story."

"Easier, undoubtedly, but perhaps—in the mind of the sender— not so efficacious."

"Why not?" Murphy demanded bluntly.

"I can suggest two reasons. One, because many people believe that the police pay no attention to anonymous letters—"

"If they only knew—" Murphy groaned.

"And two, because the sender has somehow got your identity and mine mixed up. Suppose that you were me, as well as yourself, don't you think that you would find yourself more interested in advice conveyed in a short story than in the same advice contained in an anonymous letter?"

The sergeant made a wry face. "I suppose you are right, but you do complicate life, Mr. Terhune, with your theories. But now, if you don't mind, I'm going to start destroying your theory."

"Go ahead, Sergeant."

"Do you mind passing the envelope the story was sent in?"

Terhune did so. Murphy went on: "Did you see that this packet went first of all to Ashford, Middlesex?"

"Yes."

"To my way of thinking that fact disproves your theory. If the person who sent the story to me had been living locally, the sender would have been careful to address the envelope to Ashford, Kent."

Terhune shook his head. "I disagree. I think it merely proves that the sender wasn't aware that there are two Ashfords. By the way, when was the envelope posted?"

The detective examined the postmark, and laughed his triumph. "The story has nothing whatever to do with Peter's death, Mr. Terhune. It was posted in the West One district of London, on Sunday, the sixteenth—more than twenty-four hours before old Peter died."

"Good heavens!"

Murphy glanced at Terhune's expression, and all signs of amusement vanished from his own face. "What's the matter, sir?"

"Are you quite sure the date says the sixteenth—not the eighteenth or nineteenth?"

The sergeant inspected the postmark for the second time, and nodded. 'The six is as plain as a pikestaff."

"Then I don't believe old Peter died a natural death, Sergeant."

"Didn't die—" Out came the pipe from the corner of the detective's mouth. "But I saw the poor old man with my own eyes—as stiff as you like..."

"I believe Peter the Hermit was murdered," Terhune stated quietly.

IV

Taken all in all, the sergeant accepted Terhune's assertion with astonishing equanimity. He just smiled, good-humouredly, and shook his head.

"Now you're pulling my leg, sir," he accused lightly.

"On the contrary, I mean every word of what I said."

Murphy studied Terhune's expression, then frowned. "But that's ridi—I mean—er—impossible. According to the post-mortem examination he died from natural causes. And why not? He was old enough to."

"Listen, Sergeant. If we assume that the short story refers to Peter's death—"

"If!" Murphy interposed pointedly.

Terhune ignored the interruption. "But if it's certain that the story was posted on Sunday, then the sender must have known that Peter was to die in the near future. How could a person know, with such certainty, that a man was soon to die, unless somebody else had planned deliberately to kill that man?"

Murphy shook his head stolidly. "Now you are moving in realms of imagination where I can't follow you."

"Why not?"

"Because I still don't believe that the story was meant for me. But even if it were—*if* mind you!—and even if I could stretch a point by believing that somebody with a queer sense of humour had written and sent the story to me as a hint that old Peter's death is of more importance than I think—which the postmark proves otherwise..."Murphy faltered into silence, and looked miserable. "Now I can't remember what I started off to say."

Terhune's eyes twinkled "I can guess, Sergeant. But before you entirely damn my theory to Hades, don't overlook the title."

"The title! You mean—*Fame!*"

"I mean the title of the series, not the individual story. *Ten Trails to Tyburn*. Tyburn was the name of the hill where the Middlesex gallows once stood. In the circumstances the title is significant, don't you think?"

The argument shook the detective, but he asked gamely: "Are you quite sure you're not an Irishman, Mr. Terhune?"

"Why?"

"You have an Irishman's facility for twisting facts to suit your own side of an argument. But you're not seriously suggesting that the title has any real significance?" Murphy pleaded wistfully.

"What other reason could the writer have for such a strange title? There's no other connection that I can see between a story of the Paris boulevards and Tyburn."

"Ah!" Murphy cheered up. "But if there are Ten Trails to Tyburn, where are the other nine?"

"Perhaps they are to come—later! That is, if you don't soon arrest the murderer of Peter the Hermit!"

"By Saint Patrick! Save me from the other nine!" Murphy exclaimed feelingly.

V

For long after Murphy had gone Terhune sat before the fire and stared at its glowing embers as he tried to analyse to what extent he had been serious in arguing with Murphy that the short story had some connection with the death of Peter the Hermit. The original thought had occurred to him just as he read the last line of the story, for the idea of a man's achieving world notoriety through his death had, at that moment, suggested this question: 'Funny if the death of an old, unknown hermit should bring about a similar result!' But the reflection, instead of passing away into the vast never-never land of rambling reflections, established itself, willy-nilly, as a substantial subject for mature meditation. He found himself thinking: 'I wonder.' Then, from the 'I wonder' stage he moved quickly on to the next, that of analysis and deduction. And so, half earnestly, half tentatively, he had voiced aloud the possibility because imagination whispered, 'It could be' just a little louder than common sense's 'Fantastic and unlikely'.

The ensuing argument certainly had not convinced the prosaic police detective. True, Murphy had said: "How about coming with me to visit Doctor Edwards tomorrow? He will soon tell us whether there are any grounds for thinking that Peter might have been murdered. I have an appointment with Mrs. Newman, too, at eleven o'clock." But a persistent twinkle had lurked in his eyes, which had convinced Terhune that the sergeant hadn't any faith whatever in the idea that the story contained a subtle message.

Of course, it was a fantastic idea, when viewed dispassionately. Despite its strange, and possibly significant, title, despite the fact that the story had been addressed to a police detective, despite the coincidence of its plot being comparable, by a stretch of imagination, with the death of Peter the Hermit, could he himself, Terhune reflected, honestly believe that the story was a clue to some hitherto unsuspected aspect of Peter's death?

The answer—the honest answer—to this question was: yes and no. Yes, because he could think of no other explanation to account for the circumstances surrounding the sending of the story to Murphy; no, because it was equally difficult to imagine what sort of a mentality could be responsible for conveying so abstract a clue in such a circuitous manner.

As Murphy had rightly pointed out—how much easier, how much more straightforward, a simple letter would have been! Something like this: Dear Sir, You are mistaken in thinking that the death of Peter the Hermit is a matter of no importance. If you investigate the

circumstances properly you will cause a sensation. Faithfully yours,
Pro Bono Publico.

Simple enough! But would Murphy, or the police authorities,
have paid genuine attention to such a communication? Up to a point,
yes. Terhune was sure of that, for he had heard, both from Murphy
and from Sampson, of the C.I.D., that the police always investigated
such letters, anonymous or otherwise. *Up to a point!* They were the
operative words, for, lacking any further information, would the police
be in a position to learn any more than they would do in the ordinary
course of events? Scarcely.

What sort of a person was he who had sent such a curious little
short story, instead of a simple letter? Somebody, surely, with a mind
not altogether balanced. Somebody who had the habit of beating about
the bush instead of proceeding directly to the point. Somebody with
low cunning. Somebody, indeed, with a mind not unlike Jim Cooper's,
but vastly more educated.

Educated! Terhune started. So far, he had overlooked that point.
The story revealed evidence of its teller's having received a somewhat
better education than that obtainable, and obtained, by the majority of
the inhabitants of Great Hinton. Great Hinton was a charming little
village—old and untouched; one might almost say sleepy—composed,
for the most part, of farm labourers, smallholders, and three or four
tradesmen. Within a radius of two miles of its centre—the vicarage—
there were only two estates which were not owned by farmers. One
was Mrs. Fawcett's Strangeways. The other was Monksholme, the
property of one Max Bullett. Apart from these two property-owners
there lived in Great Hinton the vicar of St. Agnes's, the Rev. Septimus
Andrews; his daughter; Nicholas Harvey, a retired bank manager,
who lived with his spinster daughter in a cottage; and, lastly, Jeremy
Cardyce, an elderly recluse who had bought a small cottage near the
church in the spring of 1941 after being bombed out of rooms in Gray's
Inn which he had occupied for many years. Terhune had been told that

Cardyce was a barrister-at-law, who had once featured as Counsel for the Defence in a famous divorce case.

While he was considering these five names, and wondering whether any one of their owners could have sent the story to Murphy, another aspect occurred to him, which he thought worth keeping in mind. The atmosphere of the story of the Boulevard des Capucines suggested that its writer had some knowledge of Paris. The knowledge could be second-hand, of course; but, on the other hand, if it were personal, then it might possibly be significant that old Peter had treasured a Bulgarian newspaper, and a comb that could have come from Spain. Bulgaria—Spain—France...

The circumstances surrounding the death of Peter the Hermit were beginning to suggest a distinctly European background.

Chapter Six

Early the following morning Murphy called for Terhune. "I don't know what the Powers-that-Be would say if they knew I was taking you with me," he began, as Terhune stepped into the car beside him. "But what the eye doesn't see the heart can't grieve about."

"Would you rather I didn't come?"

The sergeant laughed boisterously. "There's nobody else I'd rather have with me, Mr. Terhune, and if anything does leak out—well, I wasn't born an Irishman for nothing. I'm not going to start leaping hedges before we come to them." With the obvious intention of changing the subject, he went on: "Did you give any more thought to that theory of yours?"

"I thought about it for the rest of the evening," Terhune admitted. "And the more I considered it the stranger the whole affair became."

"Why?"

Terhune gave a quick resume of the conclusions at which he had arrived, adding: "I have made out two lists of people who might have written that short story. The first is a long list, and has eleven names; the second has only six. The long list consists of those people whose education was of the kind which might have enabled them to write the story—although, mind you, Sergeant, I'm not trying to make out that people who have had only an elementary education aren't capable of writing a story. Some are—and have."

"All the same, your list will do to go on with. Who are they?"

"Mrs. Fawcett, the Vicar, his daughter, Mr. and Mrs. Max Bullett, Nicholas Harvey and his daughter, Jeremy Cardyce, Arthur Snaith, Miss Evelyn Tucker and Henry Rolfe."

"Wasn't Snaith one of the men we met at the *Dusty Miller* on Tuesday?"

"Yes. From the little I know of him I should guess that he had a secondary education, later improved by some adult self-education and contacts with city life."

"What is he?"

"I'm not sure, but I think he's living on a small pension."

"How about the Miss Tucker, and the man Rolls?"

"Rolfe, you mean. Miss Tucker is a retired schoolmistress. Rolfe, I have heard, is a second cousin, twenty times removed, of some titled person from whom, at the age of twenty-three, he inherited a few thousand pounds. He invested the capital, and has lived on the interest ever since."

"Doing nothing else?"

"Nothing."

"He sounds a spineless sort of man."

"I haven't a very high opinion of him," Terhune admitted. "Still, to give the man his due, he volunteered for the Observer Corps at the outbreak of war, and served throughout."

"What about the short list?"

"The second list is made up of people who, to my personal knowledge, have visited Europe at one time or another. The Bulletts, Mary Harvey—the daughter of Nicholas; she was educated in a convent in Belgium—Mrs. Fawcett, Miss Tucker, and Rolfe."

"Haven't any of the others been abroad?"

"Neither the vicar nor his daughter have. I can't say that Cardyce and Snaith haven't travelled in Europe, but I haven't heard that they have, Nicholas Harvey once went on one of the day trips to Boulogne, from Folkestone, but that was his one and only excursion out of the country, so I haven't put his name on the short list. On the other hand, I've included Miss Tucker, not because she has travelled to Europe, but because I happen to know that she has dabbled in literature now and again—a few short articles on folk music, some bits of verse, and so on."

"Ah-ha! A writer, eh! Now we are getting hot!" The sergeant chuckled; it seemed evident that he was not being very serious. "How old is Miss Tucker?"

"What an ungallant question, Sergeant! It forces me to be equally ungallant by guessing that she won't celebrate her fiftieth birthday again. By the way, she lives in the cottage which is immediately opposite the *Dusty Miller*."

"Is she one of your customers, Mr. Terhune?"

"Yes, she cycles regularly into Bray every Monday, Thursday and Saturday morning."

"Then she couldn't have mistaken you for me, or my address for yours?"

"No," Terhune admitted. "Not by accident."

"*Accident!*" Murphy stressed the word. "Does that remark mean that you think she might have done so purposely, as a means of remaining anonymous?"

"Not really. I don't believe Miss Tucker has enough guile in her to think out a plan like that. She's not a bad sort at heart, but she's a bit— well—schoolmistressy, and quite forthright. By the way, Sergeant, have you any news of the Bulgarian newspaper?"

The sergeant nodded. "Yes, a report arrived from New Scotland Yard this morning. It was published in Sofia on the twenty-first of August, nineteen-twenty-three. The translator has made a summary of all the paragraphs which might have interested old Peter. As far as I can judge from the quick look-through which I gave the report before leaving to pick you up, there's only one short paragraph which appears to have any significance."

"And that?"

"One which reports the marriage of a Señorita Bázan, daughter of the Spanish Vice-Consul in Marseilles."

"Marseilles! France!" Terhune became excited. "That's another link between Peter and the short story, Sergeant. And also one between the Spanish comb and the marriage of the Spanish señorita. Don't you think it likely that the owner of the comb was the Señorita Bázan who was married?"

"Perhaps," Murphy agreed cautiously.

"Did the paragraph explain why the marriage of the Spanish Vice-Consul's daughter in Marseilles was reported in a Sofia paper?"

"Because Señor Bázan had been attached to the Spanish Consulate staff in Sofia from nineteen-thirteen to nineteen-twenty-two."

Terhune whistled his satisfaction. "That may explain quite a lot, Sergeant. Don't you think we are justified in assuming that Peter first met the Bázan family in Sofia, fell in love with the señorita, and persuaded her to give him the comb as a keepsake? For some unknown reason Peter didn't marry the girl. In due dourse Bázan was promoted, moved to Marseilles, and there the girl was married. Peter, still in Sofia, reads of her marriage in the Sofia paper, and realizes that he has lost her for good. In an access of sentimentality he keeps the newspaper and the comb, both of which he treasures for the rest of his life. How does that sound?"

Murphy chuckled. "Like a book, sir. Or a sieve, if you don't mind me saying so."

"Is the theory so full of holes?"

"I'm afraid it is. The biggest hole of all is the comb—by the way, it's been officially valued at one hundred and twenty pounds. I don't know a lot about how much money a Consul earns, but I shouldn't imagine his salary would be big enough for his daughter to give away a comb worth more than a hundred pounds. No, sir, I don't think you are right this time."

"Probably not, but the newspaper and the comb have to be accounted for, haven't they?—and I can't imagine what reason other than love caused the old man to keep the comb instead of selling it."

Murphy did not attempt to argue the point just then, for they were approaching Doctor Edwards's house, which was situated approximately half-way between Bray and Great Hinton. The doctor welcomed them in his consulting-room.

"Good morning, Murphy." His eyebrows twitched as he recognized Terhune. "And you, too, Terhune. I didn't expect to see you this morning—"

The sergeant hastened to apologize. "I hope you don't mind, Doctor—"

"Mind! Why should I mind?" Dai Edwards laughed as he gave Terhune's hand a genial shake. "I'm merely surprised because I thought Terhune was only interested in crime—and unusual crime at that. There was nothing unusual about the old man's death—or was there?" he finished abruptly.

"That is what we want to ask you, Doctor."

"Me?"

"Yes, sir. We have a vague suspicion—a very vague suspicion, mind you, Doctor—that old Peter's death was not all it seemed to be on the surface." Murphy hesitated from embarrassment. "You carried out the post-mortem examination, didn't you, Doctor?"

"I did."

"Then—then—you are quite sure that old Peter was not—not murdered?"

"Murdered!" Edwards laughed jovially. "My dear man, the P.M. revealed these: a total absence of subcutaneous fat and the fat round the internal organs."

"What does that mean, sir?"

"Confirmation of what I told you at the time—that the old chap died a natural death from the effects of emaciation practically amounting to starvation."

"Didn't he die of a heart attack?"

"That was the immediate cause of death. His heart was as dicky as a rotten elm. Long undernourishment, and the cold snap, were secondary causes, so when he suffered a heart attack last Monday his life flickered out like a snuffed candle.

"Naturally, we made the usual tests for other possible causes of death—examined the body and scalp for cuts, bruises and limb fractures; and the mouth, stomach and blood for evidence of poisoning, but all reactions were negative." Edwards emphatically shook his head. "No, Sergeant; you can take it from me that, as far as the P.M. is concerned, the verdict of the inquest will be Natural Causes. When is the inquest to be held, by the way?"

"Not until Monday morning, sir. We have asked the coroner to postpone it until then in the hope of obtaining evidence of identification." Murphy rose to his feet; Terhune and the doctor did the same. "Well, thank you, sir. I am sorry to have wasted your time."

"Not at all, Sergeant. Glad to be of help to the police at any time," the doctor murmured politely as the three men moved towards the door. "By the way, if it's not an indiscreet question, what made you think old Peter might have been murdered?"

"Oh, just a vague idea of mine," Murphy replied generously. "One must check up on everything if there's the least doubt."

"Of course! Of course! But there can't be in this case."

They reached the door, passed into the small lounge-hall, and so to the front door.

Edwards held out his hand. "Good-bye, Sergeant. Good-bye, Terhune. No news of that book on Toxicology?"

"Not yet."

"Keep trying, there's a good chap."

"I will, Doctor."

The door closed behind them.

"Well, that's that!" Murphy exclaimed, as the two men returned to the car. "I'm afraid Doctor Edwards's evidence washes out your theory of murder, Mr. Terhune."

"Then I wish I knew how it happened that the author of the story was so certain that old Peter was due to die in the near future."

"Look, Mr. Terhune, I think you are making too much of this short-story business. You believe that it was sent to me as a hint to investigate Peter's death, don't you, and argue that, because it was posted twenty-four hours or so before Peter died, that the author of the story—let's call him Mr. A—knew that somebody else—Mr. X—was proposing to kill the old man in the near future. Now, if Mr. A was aware of Mr. X's intentions, why didn't he advise me *before-hand* of the proposed murder, which would have given me a chance of saving the old man's life? On the other hand, the fact that Mr. A didn't give me a chance of doing that makes him an accessory before the fact, doesn't it?"

"Kind of," Terhune agreed, as they stepped into the car, and the detective started up the engine.

"Very well, if Mr. A was willing to stand on one side and do nothing—nothing worth while, at any rate—to prevent the old man being killed, why should he now be so darned anxious to have me investigate the death? He must know that prevention is better than cure. No, Mr. Terhune, I think your theory is an ingenious one, but frankly I can't swallow it. I still think that either someone has played a practical joke on me—on us, if you like—or, as I suggested in the first case, somebody got the two of us properly mixed up, and really intended to send the story to you for your criticism or advice, or both."

"Then why was no letter enclosed?"

"As I said last night, the man might have written one and forgotten to enclose it. That has been done before now." Murphy chuckled.

"And not excluding present company, meaning myself. I once sent something to my mother-in-law without the letter—she thanked her second daughter. When the wife came to hear of what I had done—" He chuckled again. "Well, one marries for better, for worse. That episode comes under the second alternative." He added tactfully: "But you were saying, sir—"

Terhune wasn't, but he took the opportunity. "I still think there is something significant about the title."

"You mean the reference to Tyburn?"

"Yes."

Murphy shook his head. "I've often read books with queer titles, sir. Do you remember a novel, published a good many years ago, called *Cat Across the Path*? Of all the dam-fool titles—"

"Not really, Sergeant. It was a good, provocative title, and subtle. Did you read the book?"

"No."

"You should have done so, then you would have understood the title. It had reference to the old superstition that bad luck follows anyone across whose path a black cat walks—"

"That is supposed to be good luck."

"In some countries, yes. In others, it is bad. Well, a black cat crossed the heroine's path—I forget whether actually or metaphorically—and the story is of the bad luck which followed her from that moment."

"I see!" the sergeant mused. In the same mood he went on: "If *Ten Trails to Tyburn* was chosen on the same principle, then the title has what you call a subtle reference to the story—"

"Or the reason for the story."

"Or the reason," Murphy repeated. "Yes, I understand what you mean, but if old Peter died a natural death, then he couldn't have been murdered, could he?"

"Hardly."

"In which case," Murphy continued, still in a musing manner, "as you say, how did the author know that old Peter was to die before the story reached me? And then—"

"Wait, a minute, Sergeant," Terhune interrupted. "If the story had been correctly addressed to Ashford, Kent, you would probably have received it by the first post Monday morning?"

"Yes."

"Then the story *was* sent to you as a warning of Peter's death!"

"For the love of Mike! Mr. Terhune. Even if I had received the story in time, how was I expected to interpret it as a warning that old Peter was to die—or be killed, perhaps! I'm just a plain copper, not a mind-reader, or puzzle expert—or even a fiction-writer."

"But then the sender apparently did look upon you as a fiction-writer—as me, Sergeant—"

"Give me a plain, straightforward, dishonest anonymous letter," Murphy lamented, as the car arrived opposite Strangeways.

A minute or so later Terhune and the detective were shown into a small and extravagantly warm servants' sitting-room, and thither came Mrs. Newman some thirty seconds later.

She appeared somewhat flustered. "I don't think Madame would like you to be here in the servants' room, gentlemen, even if it is me you want to see. Madame isn't in, but I'm sure she wouldn't mind me taking you into the morning-room."

Murphy glanced at the fire, towards which he edged discreetly. "If it's all the same to you, ma'am, we'll stay here."

She nodded. "Will you sit, please, gentlemen?" They did so. "I suppose you've come to find out all you can about Peter?"

"We have, ma'am. I think you were in the habit of talking to him more than many of the people in the village."

Her thin lips tightened. "That's that good-for-nothing Jim Cooper who has been saying too much," she said angrily. "I'll ask Mrs. Fawcett to speak to Farmer Blakes and see that Cooper isn't allowed to work on her land any more. Well, what more did he say about me after you had all gone into the *Dusty Miller?*"

Murphy decided that frankness would probably produce better results than prevarication.

"One day he overheard you talking to old Peter—"

She interrupted with a sniff. "Where I come from we called that kind of overhearing by the good old name of eavesdropping."

The sergeant ignored the correction. "According to him, Peter said to you: 'Thanks for telling me about the hut, missus. I've settled down there snug and shipshape.' Did the old man say that, Mrs. Newman?"

With a slight movement of her head she gestured an unspoken defiance. "As I am not in the habit of telling untruths, Mr. Murphy, I must admit that what Jim Cooper said is true. I did tell Peter about the hut in Farmer Giffen's woods."

"Why, Mrs. Newman?"

"Because I was sorry for the poor old man. I think it is a wicked shame that poor old men like him should have to tramp about from workhouse to workhouse, in search of a bed to sleep in. Of course, I didn't think he was going to stay there for ten years—he only spoke of a few weeks, while the weather kept warm enough."

Murphy did not think it worth while to explain the reasons which prompted tramps always to be on the move. "Suppose we begin at the beginning, Mrs. Newman. Can you remember when and how you first came to meet Peter?"

She answered the questions in reverse order. "He came to the tradesmen's door and begged for some food because he was so hungry. Anna—one of the maids—was just about to send him packing when I remembered the slice of stale Melton Mowbray pie which I had put aside for Jim Cooper's pigs. I told Anna to give it to the old man, though I don't know why, for I don't hold with feeding tramps, for once you start doing that you can never get rid of them."

"Quite! Quite! And then—"

"This was one day in May nineteen-thirty-seven—I can't forget the date because it was the week before Coronation. Well, when Anna took the pie out to the old man I overheard him telling Anna to thank the missus of the house, and God's blessing on her and her children—which she's never had, and wasn't likely to have by then, what with her being the age she was, and having no husband—and all the usual things tramps say when you give them something—" Although she seemed set for a long speech, Mrs. Newman paused, and glanced at her visitors as if to ask them whether they were following her.

Murphy nodded understandingly, and the cook continued:

"It wasn't the words which attracted my attention, gentleman, but the voice. He spoke like no other tramp I've ever heard speak. Not quite like a real gentleman, mind you, but—but like—" She paused, mentally grappling for a simile. "Well, like Mr. Terhune or yourself, now, Mr. Murphy."

Terhune felt his lips twitch and was careful to avoid the detective's glance. Murphy, however, appeared to be unconscious of the cook's backhanded compliment, for he went on:

"So you were curious enough to go out and talk to him yourself, Mrs. Newman, to find out what sort of a man this tramp was?"

She nodded. "That's right, Mr. Murphy. I did."

"And what did you find?"

The question defeated the cook. After two false starts, both of which dissatisfied her at the moment of parting her lips to begin, she said: "Didn't you ever see him for yourself?"

"Now and again."

She breathed with relief. "Then you know what he looked like?"

"He looked and smelled dirty."

"He was not a very—very clean man," she admitted.

"He was also too lazy to work."

"He was old," she protested.

"Not so old as old Tom Hobby, who's getting on for eighty. But never mind about his looks," Murphy said testily. "What about his voice and manner? Did he speak as though he had been fairly well educated?"

"Oh, yes!"

"And where would you say he came from?"

"London," she answered promptly. "But he was born in Liverpool."

"Ah!" Murphy's exclamation was sharp and pleased. "What part of London?"

"I don't know. He only said London."

The detective muttered something under his breath. "Did he come to Great Hinton directly from London?"

She shook her head. "Oh, no! He had been tramping about England for several years."

"Do you mean every part of England?" Murphy queried sharply.

"Well, England and Wales. I think he had been everywhere in that time, from Land's End to Berwick, from Carnarvon to Yarmouth."

"Then what made him settle here permanently, after tramping about for all those years?"

"He hadn't intended staying—not at first."

"Well?"

"At least, that is what he told me the day I gave him the remains of the pie. He said he had come from Hothfield and was going on to Hillhurst in a few days' time, then to Hythe."

"A *few* days?"

"That is what he said."

"Why in a few days? Why not the next day?"

"I don't know. But three or four days later he came up to me and asked for some more food. He said he was leaving the very next day. I gave him some bread and cheese, and told him that if he came along in the morning I would make up a parcel for him. He thanked me and promised to come along not later than eight-thirty."

"And did he?"

"No. Not until seven o'clock that night. He said he had changed his mind about leaving for Hastings, and that he was going to settle down in Great Hinton, at least for the rest of the summer. When I asked him why he had changed his mind he said..."

"Well? What did he say?"

"That he had found what he had been searching for for nearly ten years."

In his excitement the detective sucked in his breath with a hissing sound. He leaned forward, tense, vibrant.

"What was that, Mrs. Newman?"

Slowly came the answer. "I don't know," she said regretfully. "He never told me."

Chapter Seven

No amount of questioning on Murphy's part succeeded in shaking Mrs. Newman's conclusive statement that Peter had never mentioned, in her hearing, any other details of the object he had so unexpectedly found.

"It's no use, Mr. Murphy," she said presently, thin-lipped. "I know no more about it than what I told you just now. I didn't ask the old man any questions, and he didn't offer any explanations. All I can tell you is that he stayed in the old shed in Farmer Giffen's woods from that day in May, of nineteen-thirty-seven, to the day he died."

"But you have talked to him many times since then, Mrs. Newman?"

"Quite often, but never for long. I couldn't properly abide the dirty old man."

"Yet you often gave him food."

"I was sorry for him. He always looked half-starved."

"Were you able to form any opinion of his nature? Was he unhappy, discontented, or anything of that sort?"

"He was just a lazy, shiftless old good-for-nothing, in my opinion."

"But was he unhappy?" the sergeant persisted testily.

"Goodness me! I shouldn't say he was anything in particular. I don't believe that that type of man ever have any real feelings. Otherwise they wouldn't remain what they are. If you ask me…" She paused for reflection.

"Well?"

"I should say that if a man like him was capable of any feelings at all they would be sort of contented. Like a well-fed pig or cow that doesn't know any better."

"Peter wasn't well-fed," Murphy pointed out quickly.

"Well, I've always understood that the less you eat the less you want to eat. Just as long as you get enough to keep body and soul alive."

"I think Mrs. Newman is right on that point, Sergeant," Terhune slipped in.

Murphy nodded. "P'raps so! So you don't think, Mrs. Newman, that Peter was any happier for having found something for which he had been searching for many years?"

"Haven't I already said so?" she retorted tartly.

Murphy wisely changed the subject. "How long have you lived in Great Hinton, Mrs. Newman?"

"Ever since my husband was killed in nineteen-seventeen. At that time I was living in Hythe. When I heard about poor Ernie's death I decided to look for a job. I saw an advertisement in the local paper for a Cook Wanted, applied for the job, got it, and have been here ever since."

"You must know almost everybody in Great Hinton?"

"I shouldn't be surprised."

"Then I'll ask you some questions about them, beginning with your mistress—"

"If you think I'm going to gossip about her, or anyone else, Mr. Murphy, you're mistaken. I'm not like that Jim Cooper. So there!" she snapped. "You can ask the people themselves."

Murphy tried to point out that the questions he wanted to ask were simple ones to which there could be no objections from anyone, but she remained obdurate. Soon Murphy tired of the unequal contest, and the two men left.

"Silly woman!" Murphy exclaimed irritably as he reversed the car.

Then, as he straightened out in the direction of Bray: "I don't think we've made much progress this morning, Mr. Terhune."

Once again Terhune noted the use of the plural pronoun, which was a generous gesture on Murphy's part considering his scepticism of Terhune's theory. But then Murphy was like that.

The sergeant went on: "Doctor Edwards's evidence seemed fairly conclusive, don't you think?"

The meaning behind the detective's words was plain enough. Terhune nodded. "It seems as if it is, Sergeant. I suppose the time of the story's arrival was a coincidence. The sender guessed old Peter hadn't long to live, but didn't know he was going to die quite so soon as he did. And yet..." He became silent.

"And yet—what, sir?"

"If Peter wasn't killed—if the only reason for sending the short story was to warn you that an investigation of his identity would lead to a sensational disclosure of some sort—why that silly title: *Ten Trails to Tyburn?*"

"Aren't some of you writers fond of alli—alli—what's the word?"

"Alliteration."

"That's right. Perhaps *Tyburn* was used only for the sake of alliteration."

"Why not Tottenham? Or Tyneside? Or Torquay? Why especially Tyburn?"

Murphy grinned. "Don't ask me, Mr. Terhune! I can't make head nor tail of the story business at all. If you don't mind me saying so, I think the best thing we can do is to ignore it." He added, apparently as an afterthought: "I'll bet it was a practical joke, after all."

Terhune felt inclined to agree on all counts. The practical-joke theory was the only one which was not open to criticism. If somebody like Jeffrey Pemberton, or young Arnold Blye, or Ted Pryce had wanted to pull his leg, no better prank could have been devised than the sending of the short story to 'Detective-Sergeant

Theodore I. Murphy'. There was just the right touch of malice, just sufficient significance to make the joke amusing without being offensive.

"It must have been, Sergeant," he agreed slowly. "Yes, I think you are right."

II

Murphy left Terhune at the shop before continuing to Ashford. As Terhune entered the door Anne Quilter greeted him with: "Miss Armstrong was here twenty minutes ago."

"To change some books?"

"Yes, Mr. Terhune, but she left a message that she wanted to speak to you personally. She is coming back about twelve-thirty."

"Thank you, Anne. Did anything else of importance happen while I was away?"

"Nothing out of the ordinary, sir. Mr. Justice Pemberton's chauffeur collected some books, and left a message asking if you would be sure to get a copy of the latest Eric Linklater—"

"It's already ordered, Anne."

"Also Paul Tabori's latest. And Mrs. Mann sent young Alf along to say that she's in bed with 'flu and won't be able to come along for two or three days."

He grimaced. Not good news that; he would have to be his own cook and housemaid until she returned.

"And Arthur Wood came in and asked for you, Mr. Terhune."

"Arthur Wood! The bus-driver?"

"Yes sir."

"What did he want?"

"He has collected a number of Peter Cheney's books which he wants to sell to help pay for the new baby. He asked whether you would care to buy them. I told him to bring them in so that you could make an offer for them."

"Good!" He glanced at his watch. "We'll check the proofs of the new catalogue, Anne, until Miss Armstrong returns."

With only a few interruptions Terhune and Anne worked upon the proofs of the new catalogue until the arrival of Helena, at twelve-twenty-five.

"Hullo, Tommy." She greeted him with a warm smile, and for no apparent reason he told himself that she had never looked prettier, or more attractive. The cold wind had flushed her cheeks with a rich glow, and ruffled her hair into charming disorder. She was dressed, as nearly always when she visited Bray or the neighbouring villages, in a tweed costume, cut for trim comfort rather than in close-fitting style. The costume was a new one, he noticed; a sort of heather mixture in which shades of rust and olive green were predominant.

"Lady Kylstone says will you dine with us Sunday week?" she went on.

He never refused an invitation to Timberlands, if circumstances permitted. Despite their disparity in ages they understood each other, he and Lady Kylstone, he believed. At any rate, on his part, there was no other person in the world he liked more sincerely. Perhaps the fact of his having no near relatives helped to foster this feeling. He looked upon her scarcely as a mother, because she had children of her own, but certainly as an affectionate 'aunt'. Besides, she stocked a marvellous Manzanilla.

"The answer is in the affirmative," he answered promptly. "Is it a special occasion, by the by?"

Helena nodded. "Yes, Wesley Cruikshank is arriving back in England next Wednesday, bringing with him a distant relation from Minnesota. Mr. Cruikshank cabled that he would be dining with Lady Kylstone the Sunday following his arrival."

Wesley Cruikshank was Lady Kylstone's brother. During a trip to the U.S.A. some time previously Terhune had stayed one week-end with Wesley, at his home in Albany.

"It will be nice meeting Wesley Cruikshank again," he commented. "He gave me a good time in Albany. About the only person he didn't introduce me to was the Governor."

"Then we shall expect you?" Helena's eyes shone.

"You bet!" he exclaimed wholeheartedly.

I I I

During the quieter moments of the week-end Terhune gave some thought to the short story which Murphy had left with him. He also re-read it several times, seeking to find in its two thousand words some other clue to the why and wherefore of its creation and delivery to. Murphy; some subtler reference to the death and identity of Peter the Hermit, perhaps, which had previously eluded him. But without any success. Except for the title, the coincidence of the name Pierre, and the manner of Pierre's posthumous fame, his more careful study of the story yielded nothing except added mystification with its attendant exasperation.

Finally he stopped thinking about Peter and the story. Now that he could no longer doubt but that Peter had died a natural death, the old man's demise ceased to interest him. Only a mild curiosity as to identity remained, and the aggravation of wondering whether or no the news of his death, if the identity could be revealed, would really cause a sensation.

Nevertheless, on the Monday morning he attended the inquest on old Peter. It was a very tame affair, however, and soon over. Dr. Edwards, who had performed the autopsy, stated his opinion that the deceased had died from a heart-attack following years of exposure and undernourishment. Afterwards Murphy gave evidence that the police had failed to identify the deceased. The proceedings closed with a verdict in accordance with the surgeon's evidence. Time taken, nineteen minutes. And that was the end of that—or so Murphy and Terhune and everybody else thought. But two days later Terhune received a large envelope, correctly addressed to himself, at 1, Market Square. Inside was a short story, entitled

TEN TRAILS TO TYBURN
NO. 2. GENEROSITY

IV

Terhune gazed down at the manuscript. Behind the tortoiseshell glasses his eyes shone with unmasked excitement and perplexity. Question upon question occurred to him in quick succession. Why had the second story been sent to him instead of Murphy? Had the sender discovered his mistake? Had the first story been intended for him, after all? Was the second story, and the corrected name and address, all part of an elaborate hoax? What was the postmark? London again? What of the story itself? Was it intended for him as a writer, and not as a poor sort of amateur detective? Would the story reveal the answer to the last question? If it contained another clue of some sort, what was it? Was it a clue to Peter's identity?

He looked at the envelope again, and examined the postmark. It was not London this time, but Hythe, Kent. So the author of *Ten Trails to Tyburn* apparently lived somewhere in the neighbourhood. Perhaps at Hythe, perhaps at Dymchurch, perhaps at Bray, perhaps even at Great Hinton itself.

"I'm going upstairs for ten minutes," he told Anne. "Let me know if I'm wanted."

"Yes, Mr. Terhune."

He went upstairs to his workroom and settled himself in the one comfortable chair—the only other chair was a stiff-backed office chair behind a small table-desk. Then, as soon as he had lighted a cigarette, he began to read.

V

GENEROSITY

There is a little old antique shop just round the corner, monsieur. You have perhaps seen it, yes? You noticed the name. It spreads right across that long dirty black plank, the letters are almost illegible, but you may have solved the puzzle when the dipping sun threw a rosy reflection upon it. Monqueston Mélenaire. Did you think that the first name was Monquest? Ah! yes, Monsieur l'Anglais—or is it Monsieur l'Americain? You need not imagine your eyesight is failing you, the ON was shot away when Danton ruled.

There was a young man lounging at the door when you passed? I am right, you say. No, monsieur, I am no thought-reader. He is always there, never inside. No one buys from him. You see, he is not like Monsieur Mélenaire. Monsieur Mélenaire no longer stands by his shop wearing his ragged old skull-cap, and a big red bandana hanging out of the side pocket of his old velveteen jacket, selling antiques for one third of what he should demand. It is not a long story. Have I time? Monsieur, I smile. I am old now, nearly eighty-four. I have no young limbs to run hither and thither. All my time is free. No, monsieur, I should prefer a *café noir, s'il vous plait. Merci bien, monsieur.*

The original Monqueston Mélenaire was a gentleman, who lived in a fine hotel and attended the Court. That was many years ago, when my great-grandmother's father was lackey to the Duc de Champien.

Monsieur Monqueston did not know the lackey of his oldest friend, yet the time arrived when they lived but a few yards from one another.

One day Monsieur Mélenaire met the daughter of the lackey of his oldest friend, and oh! *Mon Dieu*, monsieur—he married her. He should have made her his mistress, as became a gentleman of the Court, but monsieur he was foolish and honourable.

His friends—the Good God prevent me from ever having such friends. The daughter of a lackey! It was terrible, impossible. Monsieur Mélenaire. One did not know him. One shrugged one's shoulders and looked the other way.

Our Lady smiled upon my grandfather's father, for he was happy with his petite Marie, and in time to come they had a big fat boy. Him they called Monqueston after his father.

Soon the money disappeared, and so the noble gentleman sold antiques, and made just enough money to live and be happy.

The little boy grew up and married, and his father died, so the son took on the business. He lived happily, and soon he had a son.

The years rolled on. There was a blessing on that old antique shop, for all were happy that lived beneath its roof. Then I was born, a younger son for the first time. Before there had been but one son. I caused complications. Still, monsieur, I would not cause unhappiness—far be it from me to spoil my brother's life—so I ran away to sea, and lived just such a life as I would live again had I the chance. Were this a story of my life, monsieur, I would tell you many strange tales of foreign lands, but I tell you of the little old antique shop round the corner, where I do not belong. I am a second son.

Pierre, my brother, was born happy, monsieur, and his father and mother, my father and mother too, you understand, were happy also. Indeed they were all happy till I came along. You see, they worried about me. A second son was unheard of in that little antique shop.

Pierre was five years old when I first suckled at my mother's breast. When my mother was able to return to her housework she found that

Pierre was fond of me, and he was put to take care of me. Generous Pierre! He never objected, though he looked with longing eyes at the other boys playing in the street below. Thus at the age of five did the systematic robbery of his generosity begin. He was robbed of his play-hours.

Generosity was the keynote of his character. Monsieur, when I grew older and had understanding I realized this. We were put to work side by side—washing dishes perhaps. It was I who shirked, I had a thumb which hurt me when put in water, or I remembered a message which Madame Touvon of the Blanchisserie had sent "*à ta brave mère, et tout de suite*". Pierre would smile, and finish his work.

Then when I was fifteen I ran away to sea, and I stole my brother's spare clothes, and the few centimes which he had saved up since Easter, and which he kept in a little tin box. Poor Pierre lost his only boots; robbed by his own brother. Yet, monsieur—and see I wipe a tear from my eye—when he wrote me later, he blessed me.

He was twenty-three when he met Fanchette. Beautiful Fanchette. I saw her once, and straightway fell in love with her myself, but I was honourable. The wide ocean, and whispering west winds had taught me more than seamanship. I am sorry in a way, though please God my conscience is clear. Young André, the saddler's son, stole her from him instead of me. Look, monsieur, there goes their youngest grandchild—she is a fine, strong woman. She might have been my great-niece, someone to comfort me when the tolling bells announce the coming of eventide, someone to love me, to close my eyes when the Good Lord calls me, to burn a candle for me. But there, monsieur, heed not the feeble whining of an old man. Listen, I will continue.

Pierre had a noble heart. This last loss, which would have soiled my soul, or any other man's, only served to make him more gentle than before, more lovable, more sacrificing. *Dieu!* I would have put a knife through the heart of André, and ripped it out, and left it bleeding in the kennel, but Pierre blessed him.

He was happy. Can you doubt it! Yes, monsieur, Pierre was happy, for how could such a gentle soul suffer the torments of misery? He was too good, too noble. He did not fall in love again. No, he died a bachelor, and so the tradition of the eldest son became no more.

Three years after Fanchette deserted Pierre his father died, and then, in quick succession, his mother. Thus he became possessed completely of the business, which paid its way sufficiently to keep him alive.

One day a man came in. He picked up a Venetian glass, worth a hundred francs. He offered thirty, and with a pleading look in his eyes bewailed the fact that he could not afford it. Bah! the bastard son of the Devil! I was there, so I say the truth. I had just finished a trip to Buenos Aires. Gentle Monqueston! He sold that glass for thirty francs; it was worth three times as much.

See, I shake my head in despair. It is because memories of that day flood my brain, what little I have left. I pleaded with him to harden his heart, to remember his business, that a fair profit on turnover was necessary to keep him alive, but he smiled in that slow, gentle manner of his, and shook his head, and said, "Hush, *inori frère, le bon Dieu* takes care of His lambs. Is it not better to give unto others than to receive? though verily in giving one receives—peace and joy. That gentleman was poor, and he wanted that Venetian glass so much; who am I indeed to deprive him of his earthly pleasure for the sake of a few centimes?"

You see, monsieur, it was impossible to argue with him. His heart conquered his brain, in fact cheated him. He did not realize that he was told nothing but lies, lies and yet more lies. He believed what he was told. Now had I that business I would have outlied the 'poor' gentleman who came to buy. Where I wanted twenty francs I would have demanded fifty, and perhaps eventually have accepted thirty. Therefore should I have prospered.

The Devil's spawn who purchased that Venetian glass must have told his friends, and thereafter my brother did big business. Yes, monsieur, very big business. In two weeks he sold nine hundred francs' worth of antiques for six hundred, and my poor brother was robbed of three hundred francs in addition to his due margin of profit.

My father had bequeathed a fine stock of antiques, for he was hardheaded, but as time went on so this stock was gradually depleted, for my brother often had not the wherewithal to purchase, and when he did, of course, he gave twice as much as he should have done. Alas! He gave more and received less.

Notwithstanding this, monsieur, he smiled and laughed, and his heart bubbled over with joy of life. Fortunately he was of moderate taste and inclination, and so he lasted twice, thrice as long as I should have. Me, I am a man fond of women, of wine, and the money goes like the devil when one keeps the companionship of this twain.

The time came, monsieur, as the years passed, when receipts dwindled as my brother's stock was reduced and was not replenished. Gradually the bills began to mount. Then, and then only, did my brother begin to feel unhappy, for a debt to him was a millstone round his neck. He paid off his first crop, but they came again as more weeks rolled on.

They worried him, those bills. They mounted up, and the total became ever larger. Yet he smiled. Yes, monsieur, he smiled still, though the heart wept. That I know, for one day he unburdened his heart to me during one of my brief visits home. I had not the heart to reprove him. All I could do was to slip some francs in the till when he was not present. What was money to me? Bah! Merely a woman and a few drinks less.

After I had gone once again his position was worse, and one day he totalled up his bills. He owed three hundred francs, monsieur.

For three days he was sick at heart—oh! so sick. Three hundred francs, and no prospect of being able to pay. To him this was hell in its worst circle.

Then, monsieur, his Guardian Angel saw fit to come to his rescue at last, for on the evening of the third day the postman brought him a letter. He opened it, and miracle of miracles he was left a fortune. A fortune of three thousand francs and fifty-two centimes. Enough to pay up all his bills, renew his stock, and buy champagne for Mère Anna, across the street, who was expecting travail.

His heart swelled within him in his gratitude to *le bon Dieu*. He sank to his knees in prayer, and prayed and prayed, while his heart still swelled. Then, monsieur, he drooped, and gasped, and muttered my name (this I heard from a neighbour), and the next moment he lay stretched on the floor—dead. For the last time he had been robbed. The grim Reaper had robbed him of his right to pay those bills, to renew his stock, to give champagne to Mère Anna, who subsequently died through lack of strength to undergo the pangs of childbirth.

My poor brother. That is his tale, monsieur. I have nothing more to say. The light is failing. I must hobble to my bed whilst I still can see, for I am blind in the dark. *Bonne nuit, et merci, monsieur! Bonne nuit!*

VI

As soon as he had finished reading the story Terhune turned to page one and read it through for a second time. Then he left the workroom and returned to the shop below. His expression was reflective, and a little distrait. That was obvious even to the young eyes of Anne Quitter, his assistant, so, diplomatically, she left unasked for the time being a question about obtaining a book for which a customer had enquired.

He went to the telephone and dialled the police-station. Presently he was through to Murphy.

"Good morning, Mr. Terhune." The sergeant's voice conveyed an undercurrent of eagerness; evidently he guessed there was a reason for Terhune's call, but he patiently restrained himself from asking a direct question.

"Good morning, Sergeant. There's been a fresh development this morning—I'm referring to old Peter's death, of course. I've just received another short story."

"*You* have?"

"Yes. It was addressed to me correctly at this address."

"That's funny! Have you read the story?"

"I have."

"Does it have any bearing on Peter's death?"

Terhune laughed. "I thought you had no faith in my *Ten Trails to Tyburn* theory?"

"I don't know that I have," Murphy admitted quite frankly. "But I'm curious to read the second story—and to know why it was sent to you. Don't you think it rather confirms my opinion that the first story was meant for you?"

"No, Sergeant, I don't."

"You *don't*! Then the story does bear upon Peter?"

"I should rather you read the story first before we discuss it, Sergeant. Any chance of your meeting me in Ashford this afternoon?"

"I think I can manage between four-thirty and five o'clock."

"Will you have tea with me? Say, the Odeon Cinema?"

"Sure, Mr. Terhune. I'll be with you as soon after four-thirty as I can make it. By the way, was there a letter enclosed with the second story?"

"No."

"I don't understand the business at all, at all. The first omission could have been accidental, or forgetfulness, but not both. What do *you* make of it, Mr. Terhune?"

"I don't know what to say. If the stories are clues, why was the second sent to me? If they have nothing to do with old Peter, why was the first sent to you?"

"Ah! Bad cess to the man who wrote them! I'll be seeing you this afternoon, sir."

The two men met in the restaurant-ballroom of the Odeon Cinema at the time appointed. Terhune handed the second story, still in its original envelope, over to the detective, and ordered tea while Murphy read the first page. Presently he looked up sharply.

"Pierre again!"

Terhune nodded. "Read on, Sergeant."

Murphy read through to the end without further interruption. Then he laid the script upon the table before him and flicked it with his finger-tips in angry gesture.

"Don't tell me you can make anything of this rubbish, sir, for I won't be believing you. Apart from the name Pierre the story has no more connection with Peter's death than with—with— " He struggled to find a simile. "Than with the other story," he finished off with a rush.

"Are you sure?"

Murphy stared at his companion. "Do you make any sense of that nonsense?" Once again he flicked at the manuscript.

"Quite a lot, but you'll probably think it fantastic—"

"I shouldn't be surprised," the sergeant agreed with a grim laugh. "This story' business is fantastic whichever way one looks at it. But go on, sir. Tell me what you make of it."

"In the first case I believe that the story was written many years ago."

"For the love of Heaven! You're not telling me the author is a ruddy fortune-teller, and knew so many years ago that that old tramp was destined to die in this particular year of Our Lord?"

Terhune chuckled. It was not often that he had the opportunity of seeing Murphy lose his usual phlegmatic composure.

"I am beginning to think that when the author first wrote that story, and the one you received, he did so without any definite purpose in mind, except that of writing a short story which he hoped to sell to a magazine or newspaper."

"Then—then—you *don't* think they have any meaning?" Murphy spluttered. "I mean, with regard to Peter's death."

"But I do. I think that the author wanted to convey something to us, and being afraid to do so directly, he looked through some old, possibly unpublished stories which he had by him, and, finding some which he thought would convey what he had in mind, he revised them just enough for his purpose, altered the name of the principal character to Pierre, and then retyped them after adding the general title of *Ten Trails to Tyburn*."

"And you deduce all that from this story here?" Murphy asked in a voice slightly hoarse from astonishment.

"Yes."

"Glory be! Then I take me hat off to you, sir," the other man exploded: in his excitement a slight brogue revealed his nationality, though normally he was more Cockney than Irish. "And how do you make all that out, now?"

"In the first case, Sergeant, because the stories seem vaguely old-fashioned in style. In different circumstances I should have guessed their date to be somewhere about the latter part of last century, not the middle of the twentieth."

Murphy shook his head in self-commiseration. "As if meself could be expected to deduce anything like that from a miserable bit of a story."

"But for something still more significant, Sergeant, look at page five."

The sergeant turned over the pages. "And what might there be on page five to be seen?" he growled.

"Doesn't it say something there about gentle Monqueston selling a glass for thirty francs?"

"It does that, indeed."

"But the name of the character is Pierre, not Monqueston."

Murphy deliberated, nodded. "That's right now, so it is. But I don't see—"

"Wasn't the name of the original Mélenaire Monqueston? And didn't he call his eldest son Monqueston? In those days many fathers gave their own baptismal name to their eldest sons."

"Sure, and I've known that happen. But what about this Monc—Monc—whatever his name is?"

"I think that when the author first wrote the story he called the elder brother by the name Monqueston. But when he retyped the story he changed the name Monqueston to Pierre, except in that one instance, which he overlooked. And why did he take the trouble to change the name to Pierre? As before, to draw our attention to the fact that there is a similarity between the death of 'Pierre' Mélenaire, and the death of Peter the Hermit. A cup of tea, Sergeant?"

Murphy stretched out his hand with undisguised eagerness.

Chapter Eight

For quite a minute Murphy glared balefully at the manuscript before him, and ate the cream bun which he had chosen from the plateful of pastries which the waitress had set before them.

At last he said: "I wish I could pick holes in your new theory, Mr. Terhune, but I can't. Not for the time being, at least. Well, what is the similarity between the death of Pierre and that of Peter?"

"Can't you see it, Sergeant?"

"I've been trying to for the past minute. But I'm just a plain, commonplace bloke at heart. Give me a decent human clue, like a laundry mark, or a particular kind of boot, or a hint that unemployed Bill Bailey is spending more money than usual, then I'm your man. But when it comes to looking for clues in a retyped, nineteenth-century piece of nonsense, then I'm lost and I don't mind admitting it. I don't believe our friend Sampson, of the C.I.D., would be any more successful. It takes a—a writer's brain to understand another writer, damned if it doesn't."

The speech was quite a long one for Murphy, and well before it was finished Terhune's eyes were twinkling, and his lips twitching. Perhaps his mood was infectious, for as he finished speaking Murphy, too, began to grin.

"I know what you're thinking I'm thinking, Mr. Terhune, but I'm not. Not all writers are eccentric, and you're one that isn't, thank the Lord! I was working on the principle of a thief catching a thief."

Terhune's chuckle developed into laughter, but he did not embarrass the detective further by referring to the second unfortunate simile.

Instead, he said: "Pierre of the story died from joy, didn't he, Sergeant? Well, that kind of a death may not happen often in real life, but there are not many years in which the newspapers haven't reported one or two deaths from happiness. Do you remember, during the war, when the first batch of repatriated prisoners returned home? One of them died a few hours after reaching home. His heart was too weak to stand the strain of the happiness which he felt at being home again."

Murphy nodded. "I remember," he said, as he helped himself to a second cream bun.

"I have read of other deaths from a similar cause, from time to time. There was a man who worked for years to complete an important book, and died the day it was published. There was a mother who died from the joy of hearing that her son, whom she had believed dead, was still alive."

The sergeant suddenly stopped worrying his pastry. "Are you suggesting that old Peter died from the shock of hearing he had inherited a small fortune?" he demanded crisply.

"I don't insist that the particular item of good news was necessarily concerned with a bequest of money; the author deals with symbols rather than facts. But suppose, for the sake of example, that the old man had inherited a sum of money. Put yourself in his place. For years you have been an old tramp, living in a draughty shack in the middle of some woods, and starving except for what food you could beg from Mrs. Newman, and a few other kind-hearted people like her. Through many years of exposure and undernourishment your heart is in the last stages of collapse. One day somebody informs you that you are a rich man, that you will henceforward be well enough off to live in a nice brick cottage, buy as much food as you can eat, and hire somebody to wait upon you day and night. Don't you think your heart would start working overtime, just out of happiness?"

"It would do that without my being a bag of bones like old Peter," Murphy agreed drily. "And I shouldn't ask for a fortune, either. Say a sum of five thousand pounds or so." He stared across the empty dance floor, and suddenly stood up. "Like to come with me to the telephone?"

Together they entered a telephone booth. Murphy dialled the operator and asked for Bray 231. Soon a voice at the other end said: "Hullo."

"Doctor Edwards?"

"Speaking." Terhune could hear the words distinctly, although Murphy held the earphone.

"This is Detective-Sergeant Murphy speaking, Doctor. May I ask you a question about Peter?"

"Peter the Hermit?"

"Yes."

"Of course. What do you want to know?"

"Do you think it possible that the old chap could have died as a result of unexpectedly receiving some very good news?"

"Ah!" The exclamation was significant. "If you are asking me, as a medical man, whether—to speak colloquially—a heart can fail as a direct consequence of a man's receiving a mental shock, good or bad, my answer must be that, in my opinion, it cannot."

Murphy was disappointed. "Then——"

But Edwards continued quickly: "Mind you, Sergeant, I am prepared to go farther, and admit that a shock can have *indirect* physical consequences which may fatally affect the heart. For instance, on receiving good news, a man might evince his joy by an impulsive physical act, such as dancing a jig, or jumping on to a chair, or down from a bed. The strain incurred by the sudden exertion could react upon a diseased heart, and so cause it to cease functioning."

"Just let me get this straight, please, Doctor. If old Peter had been told some good news, the news itself would not have caused his heart to fail?"

"That is so."

"But if, as a consequence, he had jumped hurriedly to his feet, or done something energetic, then his heart could have failed as a result of sudden strain?"

"Yes. With some reservations which need not concern us at the moment, I should be prepared to subscribe to that deduction. Particularly so in Peter's case, because, as I testified at the inquest, his heart was particularly unhealthy. Yes, certainly I think it *possible*— mind you, I only say *possible*—for good news to have been indirectly responsible for the old man's death. Anything more you wish to know?"

"Not for the moment. Thank you for your help."

"Not at all, Murphy. Good-bye."

They walked back to the table in silence, but directly he had sat down the detective said abruptly: "If you are right, Mr. Terhune, somebody knows more about the death of Peter than he has cared to admit."

"Not *somebody*, but some people—two at least."

"Two?"

"The one who passed on the good news to Peter, and the one who has sent the two stories."

The mention of the stories again roused the paddy in Murphy. "Why the devil didn't this damned story-teller write a letter saying that Peter died after having heard some good news from Mr. So-and-so? Glory be! What sort of a crazy lunatic is this story-teller, anyway? Tell me that, Mr. Terhune—if you can."

"I can't. But I can make a guess why the man with the good news has kept quiet."

"Why?"

"Do you remember my original theory—that Peter was murdered?"

"Murdered! Oh, come, come, Mr. Terhune! And after what the police surgeon said at the inquest!"

"Don't you agree that it is possible—only just, perhaps, but still possible—that the man who took the good news to Peter anticipated the possible effect which it would have upon the old man, and deliberately divulged it in such a manner as to ensure that it should have that effect?"

Murphy gulped down some tea. "Lord save the man!" he spluttered. "What next will you be thinking of, sir?"

"Don't you agree?" Terhune persisted.

"Indeed, Mr. Terhune, and I don't. I've never heard of one man murdering another just by giving the victim some good news, and I hope I never shall. That theory might make a good film, now, and I'll not be denying that a writer like yourself mightn't make it sound convincing, but those fancy crimes don't happen in real life. For instance, sir, how would a man be knowing that good news *could* kill an old man with a weak heart, and, what is more to the point, that it *would*? It's meself that wasn't knowing the first, anyway. And only somebody knowing the old man well could have guessed the second."

"I think that a man with some knowledge of physiology would know, firstly, that an emotional shock could kill old Peter, and secondly, from a superficial acquaintance with the circumstances of the old man's life, that his heart probably had been weakened by malnutrition and exposure."

Despite Murphy's undoubted scepticism it was apparent to Terhune that the sergeant's shrewd brain was, nevertheless, scrupulously weighing up the possibilities of the theory which his companion was propounding. For no sooner had Terhune finished speaking than the detective came back with: "If Peter was killed in the manner you suggest it would be necessary to search for a man possessing some knowledge of medicine, and probably living in or near Great Hinton?"

"Yes."

"And how would such a man be coming into possession of news of such interest to Peter?"

"He might have read an advertisement in the Personal Column of *The Times* or the *Daily Telegraph*, asking for news of old Peter."

"He might," Murphy agreed, still business-like. "But in such a case he would have to know the identity of the old tramp."

"Of course."

"Then why hasn't he identified Peter? Anyone living locally couldn't fail to know that we were after having news of the dead man?"

"Of course not."

"And lastly," the sergeant continued, in a jubilant voice, "what object would a man be having in mind to kill a poor, starving devil like Peter?"

Terhune pointed to the manuscript. "Who tells the story of *Generosity*, Sergeant?"

"Pierre's younger brother."

"Exactly!"

"Devil take it, sir! You'll not be asking me to believe there's a younger brother of Peter in the neighbourhood?"

"If the story is meant to convey any meaning, Sergeant, then the answer is, Yes. A younger brother who may be next in succession for a fortune left in trust, or who would inherit from Peter under the Intestacy Law of nineteen-something-or-other."

An ominous "Go on."

Terhune obliged cheerfully. "A younger brother who might well be the 'object' for which Peter had searched for ten years, and found in Great Hinton."

"And it is myself that is responsible for having to listen to your reveries, Mr. Terhune!" Murphy exclaimed feelingly. "For wasn't it myself, the spalpeen, that dragged you into the case?"

II

In his misery Murphy consoled himself by asking for a third cup of tea. Terhune squeezed the pot, but the result looked unappetizing.

"I'll order another pot, Sergeant. This isn't tea."

"It mayn't be tea, but it's wet and warm. It'll do." He grabbed the cup and saucer from Terhune's hand, and with one swallow emptied the cup. "That's better," he sighed contentedly as he replaced cup and saucer on the table. "I was needing that after listening to your theories, Mr. Terhune."

"Then you don't agree that there's anything in them?"

"Agree! Haven't I told you that I'm just an ordinary police detective, not one of your Sherlock Holmeses or your Lord Peter Wimseys. But I'll not deny the habit's catching."

The remark aroused Terhune's curiosity. "In what way?" He chuckled. "Don't say you've caught it, Sergeant?"

"But indeed I'm thinking I have, sir. Suppose, now, there is something in this idea of yours, that these stories are meant to be clues, I'm wondering whether you are right in thinking there are two people who know about old Peter being murdered, in a manner of speaking, by his younger brother."

"There must be two."

"Why?"

"Surely it is obvious. Because—" Terhune paused abruptly. "You are not suggesting that the writer and sender of the stories is himself the younger brother?"

"That's just what I am." The detective's grin spread across his round, plain face, from ruddy ear to ruddy ear. "That is, if you're not claiming a monopoly of these here fantasies."

Terhune returned the grin. "Go on, Sergeant. It's your turn, anyway."

The smile slowly vanished from Murphy's face. "I'm going to tell you a story Sampson told me a good many years since—it came back to me a few minutes ago. Away in the nineteen-thirties Sampson and me didn't live far from each other, him being attached, at that time, to the division of the Metropolitan Police which borders the area of the Kent

Constabulary, and me being stationed on this side of the border, quite near the same place. Sometimes, during my time off, I used to have a drink in the *Prince of Wales*. That's where I first met Sampson. We got to talking of a recent crime—I don't remember what it was—and we pretty soon found out that we were both police officers, although he was already in plain clothes by then.

"Well, after that we used to meet there every now and again. Then, when I got married, he used to visit my new home for a yarn over a glass of beer. One day he told me of a queer case in Gigins Court which he had just heard. I don't suppose you've ever heard of Gigins Court, have you, sir? It's a small court just a stone's-throw from Southwark Bridge."

"No."

"It doesn't matter much. I hadn't heard of the place either until Sampson told me of it, and I've never seen it to this day. Anyway, it seems that there were about half a dozen small houses in this Gigins Court, and one day the Assistant Commissioner of the C.I.D. himself went there to visit an old family servant who was on his deathbed—I don't mean the present A.C., Sir Arthur Summers, but his predecessor, Colonel O'Donnell. This O'Donnell, it seems, was a bit psychic, and he came away from the place convinced that something was wrong with Gigins Court."

"What do you mean by 'something wrong', Sergeant?"

"Ah! That's the point, sir. The mystery of Gigins Court was—what was the mystery? Preliminary enquiries failed to answer the question, but the Colonel was so impressed by his hunch that he instructed one of the younger members of the C.I.D., a man named Hugh Arnold, to live in Gigins Court for a week or two in the hope of finding out what was wrong with the place.

"This man Arnold, it seems, was a bit out of the ordinary run of us plain-clothes men. He had been educated at Oxford, but when his old dad crashed financially, and he had to look for a job, he decided to become a police constable. Being a bright spark, he got on well enough to join the C.I.D., and was doing quite well there when this Gigins Court affair popped up. You see, O'Donnell chose Arnold for the job of investigating the mystery because he had been told that Arnold had studied advanced psychology at Oxford, and he thought that Arnold would not laugh so much at the idea of investigating something that wasn't something, if you follow me." Murphy paused, and grinned. "Arnold ought to be in my shoes; I'll bet you and he would get on famously together.

"To get back to Gigins Court; Arnold managed to find a room there, pretending he was a writer—"

"Just a minute, Sergeant," Terhune interrupted unexpectedly. "Was he the author of that series of articles on Southwark which appeared in the *Strand Magazine* nearly twenty years ago?"

"That's the chap. One of the articles dealt with the history of Gigins Court according to what Sampson told me. Well, during the course of the investigation he chummed up with another resident of the Court, an old boy by the name of Prentiss. One day Arnold told Prentiss the real reason for his presence in the Court, and the old boy was so interested that he promised to give Arnold a helping hand, and started by throwing out hints—"

"What kind of hints?"

"I'm darned if I know; Sampson didn't tell me. Anyway, Arnold and Prentiss spent hours together, discussing psychology, the old boy's pet subject, and bit by bit, prompted by Prentiss, Arnold unravelled the mystery of Gigins Court. To cut a long story short, Arnold discovered that one of the houses in Gigins Court had a secret cellar, which some ingenious person had converted into a workshop for making counterfeit money. And who do you think that person was? Old Prentiss himself! He had deliberately handed out clues which led to himself as the guilty party."

"Why?"

"Why? Well, if you were to ask me I'd say because he was a bit soft in the head. But according to Sampson, Prentiss's darned silly motive had something to do with psychology. He was a—a—what's the word, sir—something to do with pain—"

"A sadist?"

Murphy shook his head. "Not that. A sadist likes to make other people suffer. I'm talking about a man who gets pleasure from suffering himself—"

"You mean a masochist?"

"That's the word, Mr. Terhune. Apparently old Prentiss was a masochist, and got a devil of a kick from watching and helping somebody else bring about his own arrest and punishment. Personally, it's not my idea of amusement, but if there really are such people about, mightn't the chap who has been sending us the short stories be one of 'em?"

The theory was a fascinating one, and Terhune welcomed it with enthusiasm, for if it were true to the real facts, then it explained much that hitherto had been inexplicable to him—the indirect allusions in the stories to old Peter, the vague clues, the hint of other stories with other clues to follow, the absence of covering letters. Everything, in fact, pointed to the existence of a brain affected by one or other of the several psychological 'isms'.

As usual, Terhune's frank countenance was a reflection of his thoughts, so Murphy chuckled with satisfaction.

"So you think there might be something in my suggestion, sir?"

"I do, Sergeant, though psychopathic neurosis and Great Hinton make strange bedfellows. Still, it may be a help in finding the assumed killer to look for a man who has some knowledge of medicine, psychology, literature and European countries—which should narrow the search fairly considerably."

Murphy looked suddenly embarrassed. "I am afraid you will have to do the searching on your own, Mr. Terhune," he pointed out regretfully. "As far as the police are concerned the verdict of the inquest has closed official enquiries; it would take substantial information to cause them to be reopened. Of course, if there is anything I can do unofficially you have only to ask me. But I'm sorry about the official end of the affair."

"You don't have to apologize, Sergeant. I'm not surprised. As a matter of fact I was half expecting your news." His eyes twinkled. "And I suppose it wouldn't do any good to pass the stories on to the Chief Constable, and tell him our deductions?"

"It would *not*," Murphy agreed vehemently, with a smile of delight. "Glory be! I can just see his face—" His expression became anxious. "But you'll not be dropping out altogether, will you now?"

"Not on your life!"

"That's good! It's myself that is curious to hear what all this story-telling is leading up to, anyway." He glanced at his watch, and whistled. "I must be going now, sir. May I 'phone you one night?"

Terhune nodded. "I'll try and get along to Great Hinton Friday morning."

"Then I'll 'phone Friday night. Thanks for the tea, Mr. Terhune. And the cream buns. It's a pig I am, to be sure, eating two cream buns at this time of the day. If my kids knew I don't know what they would say, at all, at all." With a warm smile lighting up his homely face Murphy hurried away.

Chapter Nine

Friday morning was cold and crystal-clear. Overnight a north-west wind had clean-swept every vestige of cloud from the sky. The wind still blew; more gently, but with the tormenting caress of ice-chilled fingers. A large sun floated in a background of scintillating blue icicles, and shone with the dazzle of molten gold. The air was champagne, and turned the breath of man and beast into fleeting wisps of gaseous steam. The ground was sparkling white with frost. Dew puddles crackled underfoot.

Terhune pulled a cap well down over his forehead, donned a warm overcoat, pushed his hands into fur-lined leather gloves, and set off, on his bicycle, for Great Hinton. Before he had travelled the length of Market Square the wind which blew into his face pricked his eyes to tears, chilled the tip of his nose into insensibility, and ice-burned his ears. But none of these minor tortures worried him—for the oxygen-charged air exhilarated his mental faculties, and refreshed his coursing blood-stream; he felt happy, and hummed silently the haunting melody of an old-time waltz which he had heard on the radio not an hour previously.

Through tears he glanced quickly round the almost deserted square, and reassured himself for the thousandth time how much he loved the sleepy, rural town. Yesterday, at the same hour, the square had been a scene of cheerful commotion, for yesterday had been market day, and the old cobbled square had been crowded with booths, stalls, motor-vans, carts, dogs, and, above all, people. Ready buyers, bargainers and hagglers from Bray-in-the-Marsh itself, from Willingham and Wickford to the east, from Great Hinton and Little Hinton to the west, from Bracken Hill to the north and Farthing Toll to the south. Sellers, from many of the larger farms in the district, exhibiting local produce: Brussel sprouts, broccoli, leeks, celery, radishes, lettuce, scorzonera, salsify, artichokes, root crops in profusion; Bramley's Seedling, Worcester Pearmain and Laxton's Superb apples; Doyenné du Comice and Conference pears; Dutch medlars, fat geese, early turkeys, plump chickens, rabbits, wild and tame, eggs; butchers from Ashford with prime beef and local lamb, luscious pork; the Women's Institute members, with tempting jars of honey and rich preserves, trugs, local handicrafts; Slick Sims, Dutch-auctioning warm clothing of mentionable and unmentionable varieties; fishmongers from Dover; greengrocers from Ashford, with almonds, walnuts, grapes, lemons, oranges, bananas, and other imported fruits; local seedsmen; a lone representative from the Salvation Army; a venerable ancient selling *Old Moore's Almanac*; people, people, and still more people, treading on toes and heels, buying, selling, arguing; children playing tag in and out of the stalls, children being cussed at, children with open mouths and envious eyes watching the display of live rabbits for sale; dogs barking, yapping, snarling, fighting and courting; voices, loud and boisterous, high and low; laughter; Slick Sims' penetrating cajolery; the stamping of hooves; the scared clucking of hens for sale; a harmonium—noise, cheerful, vivacious, strangely exhilarating.

That was Market Square yesterday. Today the wide expanse of cobbles echoed only two pairs of iron-shod heels—old shepherd Hobby, who had forgotten more about the management of sheep than the majority of farmers were ever likely to learn, and Fred Botts, the local bad lot, who did national service by fathering, on an average, one new citizen per annum, known and legitimate, and an unknown number, alleged and illegitimate. The two cronies were making across the square in a south-easterly direction. St. James's Road, Terhune guessed, where the Parish Church was situated—also the *Three Tuns*. Botts must be out of yet one more job!

Terhune reached the north-west corner of the square, where he turned left, along Windmill Wood Road, part of which formed the west boundary of the square. All the houses fronting Market Square from the west were Georgian. As he passed Doctor Harris's house on the corner, Mrs. Harris waved to him. Farther along he passed Brian Howland's place—Howland was a dental surgeon. Mrs. Collis, the grocer's wife, was just going in—it was about time she had that bad tooth of hers seen to, he reflected; she was always complaining about it, according to Miss Amelia, who lived in rooms above the shop.

The Ashford road, which ran east to Willingham, and west to Ashford, via Great Hinton, formed the southern boundary of Market Square. When he reached the Ashford road Terhune turned right. As he did so Sir George and Olive Brereton flashed past in their Hillman, presumably on their way back to their home at Willingham. One minute later he saw Isabel Shelley coming towards him in a Standard two-seater. She waved her tiny gloved hand and (he believed) smiled, but as the lower part of her face was muffled in a sable wrap it was difficult to be certain. Still, she usually smiled at him. As she never tired of telling him quite frankly, Isabel Shelley had a soft spot in her heart for him, chiefly, she readily admitted, on account of his unassuming youthfulness, which was in such marked but welcome contrast to the artificial and exaggerated poses adopted by so many of her theatrical companions. But then, being quite a good actress, she was an adept at making every man believe that he was the nicest man she knew. She lived just outside Bray, on the road to Bracken Hill, whenever she was free from theatrical engagements.

From time to time other people waved to him, or smiled, or called out a greeting, from a car, a bicycle, or from the pavement. He was known to so many, and well-liked, but he was quite unaware of the regard in which he was held, partly because he was retiring, partly because he was too normal to be introspective, partly because he didn't give a damn anyway. All the same the sight of so many familiar faces made him feel very contented with life.

Many times had he been asked why a young and intelligent man like himself was content to live his life in a sleepy, unknown little market town. Surely there could be no future for an ambitious man tucked away in a neglected corner of Kent, that could only be noted, if it could be noted for anything at all, for its serenity and the richness of its non-friable clay soil? The people who had put this, and similar questions, to him neither knew him nor Bray-in-the-Marsh. In the first place, he had no ambition to speak of; he asked no more of life than that he should remain healthy and happy, and that his book business and his writing should bring him in enough money to live as simply and comfortably as he had lived from the day he had moved into Bray-in-the-Marsh and opened his book shop in Market Square. He loved the serenity of rural life, and hated the thought of enduring the hot-house atmosphere of city Bohemianism, the unfriendly snobbery of suburbia. He loved green pastures white with sheep, rippling cornfields, rose-covered cottages, squat, beamed farmhouses, snug inns; he loved slow, reflective speech, the lore of good husbandry, forthright honesty; he loved the smell of farmyards and hay, the fragrance of wild herbs, the tang of new-ploughed land, and above all the incense of log fires; he loved the clucking of hens, the crowing of cockerels, the bleating of lambs, the lowing of cattle, the grunting of swine, and the rattle and whirr of tractor and plough, the combined harvester and threshing machine; he loved the sight of apple orchards, lichen-covered trees, shadowy woods, haystacks; he loved deserted roads, slow-plodding horses, and the music of rippling water.

As he rode slowly along the Achford road he looked to either side of him, and thought how good it was to be alive, living in a place like Bray. Already the smaller brick houses, and the Dickensian-fronted shops, that clustered round about the vicinity of Market Square, which was the heart of the little town, already these were giving way to blocks of cottages, and prim-looking detached houses, each with its own neat garden, and greenhouse or garage or shed for potting or potterer. Perhaps the younger generations were conspicuous by their absence, for Bray was a centre for retired people, like Mortimer, and Harvey, and others, for people with entailed estates—like the Kylstones, the Breretons, the MacMunns, the Blyes, the Huttons, and many more, and people who were doing well enough in their chosen professions to live away from London, like Mr. Justice Pemberton, Isabel Shelley the actress, and Edward Pryce the artist. But if youth was lacking, so was impatience; if age and wealth were present, so were experience and culture.

The detached houses gave way to occasional cottages, and isolated farmhouses; the prim, orderly gardens to arable fields and pasture land. The pavement stopped; the footpath, the ditch and the green verge began. The last lamp standard slipped behind him, a fine old beech loomed up in the distance. The road itself lost its slide-rule orderliness and began to curve hither and thither without apparent rhyme or reason. The soot-black smoke of coal became the sweet-smelling grey wisps of a smouldering log. The muffled blaring of the radio gave way to the softer music of nature.

He had cycled that stretch of road a thousand times, and a thousand times he had warmed to the checker-board of green and brown squares. Round about the countryside dipped in a succession of little pockets, none of any real depth, but the irregular rises which separated one pocket from another served, at the same time, to shut off the world beyond, and each pocket became, in a sense, a little world of its own with a few fields, a copse or two, a handful of houses and cottages, a farmhouse, some sheep. A little world that was friendly, secluded, intimate.

Presently he passed by Hinton Manor, which lay on his right as he proceeded westward. Hinton Manor was a fine example of the

Georgian era, even if its trim, orderly architecture seemed just a trifle out of place in a neighbourhood that was charmingly wayward, with its complete disregard for any system of planning, its crooked chimneys, its bending, mossy roofs, its crazily shaped timbered walls, its many styles of windows, more picturesque than useful, its sloping but still sound walls. Hinton Manor, in fact, somewhat resembled the prim, ample-bosomed figure of a stern-faced matron—but one with twinkling eyes—who had stepped unexpectedly into the playground, and found herself in the midst of a tribe of happy, romping and woefully untidy schoolchildren. Even the carriage-drive which led from the road to the imposing entrance was aggressively straight, and further formalized by the existence, on either side, of a number of clipped box trees, each one differently shaped. But then, after all, Hinton Manor possibly reflected the personality of its present owner, for Mr. Justice Pemberton lived there with his family. Like so many other houses in the district, Lady Kylstone's Timberlands, for instance, and Mrs. MacMunn's Willingham Manor, Hinton Manor stood on the fringe of a fair-sized acreage of woodland—a perfect green-brown background for the bright red-bricked residence.

A little farther along, on the opposite side of the road, was a building which was in utter and complete contrast to Hinton Manor, for Chalk Lane Cottage was, as its name implied, a small four-roomed cottage, built of stone and rubble. Doors and windows fitted only where they touched—and didn't fit, and had to be permanently wedged shut—because the north-east foundation had sunk an inch or so. Bulging walls had been secured with S bends. Three chimneys emerged from its thatched roof, mouldering-green, but all three were of different shapes and different periods. All the same, the cottage was colourful with chintz curtains, a new coat of paint, a pump—which didn't work—and a strip of garden that was bright with late-autumn flowers, and hadn't a weed showing. Mildred Hetherington lived there on her own, a spinster with an abiding passion to travel all over the world, and an income which just about cared for ordinary needs.

Terhune rode on, mounted a slight rise, left the world of Hinton Manor and Chalk Lane Cottage behind him, and descended into the next world of Maid-of-Honour Farm (no antiquarian had yet supplied a really convincing explanation of how or when the farm had come by that name), Peartree Farm (but not Bram Hocking's farm of the same name, which was at Willingham), and Kenilworth. Kenilworth was Doctor Edwards's house—mid-Victorian, substantial, quite unbeautiful, but redeemed by its situation, and its beautiful rose garden, upon which Dai Edwards devoted both his surplus cash, of which he had plenty, and his surplus time, of which he had little. Peartree Farm, farther on, had no personality of its own, but Maid-of-Honour Farm had, even apart from its name. To begin with, it boasted a water-mill. Also a stream which was so amply stocked with fish that local wits declared that so many carp leaped for every luckless fly that ventured near that it was often possible to see one floating on the surface, unconscious as a result of colliding with one of its competitors. Farmer Wright, the owner of the farm and the riparian rights, refused positively to allow anyone to fish his stretch of water—even Sir George Brereton had failed completely in all attempts to do this—although there wasn't another stretch of water for miles around which Sir George hadn't fished and left as well stocked as ever. In consequence, Farmer Wright was more often known by the rather crude nickname of Farmer Wrong, which some wag had bestowed upon him in a moment of pardonable exasperation.

Another rise and yet one more private world, one shared this time by Mrs. Fawcett's Strangeways, Farmer Giffen's farm, the *Dusty Miller*, and Rose Cottage. The last, together with two acres of land, was owned by Nicholas Harvey. Once it had been called Botts's Cottage, because the Botts family had lived there, but when Harvey bought and renamed it, he had had his favourite hobby in mind. Like Doctor

Edwards, Harvey was a keen rose-grower. Like Doctor Edwards, Harvey devoted both his surplus cash and surplus time to his flowers, but whereas the doctor had much surplus money and little surplus time, Harvey had all the time in the world, and next to no money to spare. As a result Harvey took all the first prizes at local flower shows, while Doctor Edwards had to be content with the seconds.

In the next 'pocket' lay the village itself, but Terhune had arrived at his destination, so he went no farther. By now he could not be sure that he had fingers, ears or a nose left, but he stood his bicycle up against the outside wall of the inn and pushed open the heavy oak door which opened into the narrow, flagged passage just inside. Warm, pine-scented air flowed against his cheeks—a sensuous joy, that. A warm smell of cooking titillated his senses—so he still had a nose, then!— and made him feel hungry. Blending with the smell of cooking—a chicken, or a loin of pork, for certain—was that of burned paraffin, beer, and the musty tang of old timber and sweating flagstones which is inseparable from very old houses.

He turned to his left, into the bar. A bar, so-called, for it was really a low-ceilinged sitting-room, with wooden chairs and forms grouped round a roaring fire. The only evidence of the real business of the cosy-looking room was a short counter, and an old dresser, with shelves for odd bottles, and hooks for tankards used by Regulars.

Ted Shore was the only occupant of the bar. He sat, in a reclining position, in front of the fire, so close to it that it seemed he must be scorching. His feet were stretched out stiffly, either side of the fire, his hands were thrust deep into his pockets, a short pipe dangled from his teeth, and emitted strong-smelling blue puffs from the blackened bowl. However, when he heard the door of the bar close he turned his head. He recognized Terhune immediately.

"Good morning, sir," he said as he pushed his chair away from the fire—regretfully, it seemed to the visitor. "Draw a chair up, if you want to get warm." Then he added, half-apologetically: "'Scuse me sitting afore the fire like this, sir. I weren't expecting nobody quite so soon; the Reg'lars won't be in for another half a nour yet." As Terhune sat down the innkeeper went on: "Can I get you a drink, sir?"

"You can get us both one."

"Much obliged to you." Shore rose with celerity. "What would you like, sir? Gin and something?"

"What about some rum?"

"You couldn't choose better on a sharp day like this. Just the stuff to warm the cockles."

There was an enthusiasm in the innkeeper's voice which informed Terhune that Shore himself was partial to a drop of rum.

"Will you have rum, too, Shore?"

The other man beamed. "That's very generous of you, sir, and I'm real obliged." He winked broadly. "I've got a bottle of the real stuff, sir, not the watered-down muck you buy from the wine-merchants. I've got a chum in the Merchant Navy what visits Jamaica reg'lar-like, who knows my tastes and brings me back a bottle or so each voyage. Between ourselves, as a rule I only sell it to my own chums." Shore juggled with an aspidistra, and some books, produced the promised bottle from a well-concealed hiding-place, filled two sherry-glasses, and quickly concealed the bottle again, the whole with a flurried manner which convinced Terhune that the other man had spoken the truth about selling it, generally speaking, only to his own particular cronies.

"My best respects, sir."

Terhune nodded his thanks, and sipped the rum. It was dark, syrupy, aromatic; its velvet fire warmed his stomach with miraculous quickness.

Shore's eyes anxiously searched Terhune's face. "What do you think of it, sir?"

"I've never tasted anything like it before," Terhune admitted with absolute truth.

"And you won't taste anything like it again, this side of the West Indies," Shore said deeply. "'Cept here, sir, whenever you feel like dropping in, and I still has a tot to spare." For a few moments both men stared into the heart of the fire. Then the innkeeper went on: "So the police haven't found out the identity of old Peter yet?"

"Not yet."

"You would have thought they wouldn't have had no trouble, what with ration cards, and one thing and another."

"Apparently he's never had ration cards."

"What did he live on, when things was at their worst during the war?"

"He lived on what he could beg."

"Then the poor devil must often have gone hungry during the war, unless he lived on stale bread and potatoes."

"I think that is what happened." After a slight pause Terhune continued with: "You know pretty well all there is to be known about the people living round about here, don't you?"

"I daresay I can lay claim to knowing as much as anyone. I've lived in this house all my life. My father was here before I was born, and when he died I took on. But I told Detective-Sergeant Murphy all I knew more'n a week back." A shrewd expression crossed his peaky face. He became immensely eager. "Has something new turned up since then?"

"Nothing of importance. Just a possible hint. But as far as the police are concerned the inquest has closed the case."

Shore winked his eye. "But that don't mean that it's closed as far as Mr. Terhune is concerned, do it—meaning no disrespect, sir."

"Perhaps not."

"Then if there's anything I can tell you, don't you be afraid of asking it of me, sir. We all knows, round these parts, how much of a helping hand you've given the police on more than one occasion."

"Can I speak in confidence, Shore?"

"You can that, sir," the innkeeper replied earnestly. "You ask anyone round here how far Ted Shore is to be trusted—they'll soon tell you."

This fact was already known to Terhune. "Then please don't let anyone know anything about the questions I ask, or the answers you give."

"You can trust me, sir. What is it you want to know?"

"First of all, whether anyone living in the neighbourhood has a knowledge of medicine."

"There's Doctor Edwards—" Shore began.

"Excluding Doctor Edwards."

Shore stared into the fire again. Presently: "There's Mr. Holmes—Percy Holmes. He might know more than most about medicines and what not, him being a veterinary."

Terhune did not remember having previously heard of Percy Holmes. "Where does he live?"

"Not so near," Shore admitted. "Up Bracken Hill way, just this side of Tom Hicks's farm."

Bracken Hill was several miles from Great Hinton, but Terhune recollected the existence of a footpath which proceeded from a point one mile south of Bracken Hill to just north of Great Hinton, and skirted Giffen's land en route—even passing over it at one place. By way of the footpath the distance between the two villages was probably reduced by a half. He thought it worth keeping a mental note of the vet, at any rate for the time being.

"Anyone else?"

"There's Mrs. Wilkinson. She was a midwife, somewhere up Manchester way, before she married Bert Wilkinson and settled down here." Shore saw by Terhune's expression that the name Wilkinson, too, was unknown to the visitor. "Wilkinson's the grocer: he took over the shop when Quirk died three years ago."

A midwife! Midwives, Terhune knew, often pick up a fairly extensive, if rudimentary, knowledge of medicine; enough, probably, to give Mrs. Wilkinson an idea of old Peter's condition, and what effect a shock might have upon him. It might be well, he reflected, to learn something of her character, and of Holmes's character, too, but not until Shore had exhausted the list of possibles.

"Any more names?"

The innkeeper slowly shook his head. "Not that I can think of, sir. No, that's the lot." But then his face gave the lie to his words. He stuttered out a correction. "There's a gentleman live—living in the village who—who—might know a bit about medicine, Mr. Terhune. Leastwise, he ought, to, seeing that both his father and his grandfather were doctors."

He paused provokingly, so Terhune obliged.

"Who?" he questioned, with simulated excitement.

Shore mouthed the tit-bit. "Mr. Max Bullett," he replied, grinning from ear to ear.

Chapter Ten

Terhune was very conscious of Shore's widespread grin; there was a salacious quality about it which convinced the visitor that his companion knew some spicy gossip concerning Max Bullett which he was anxious to divulge. But Terhune hesitated to proffer any encouragement, because gossip was at all times distasteful to him, more particularly when circumstances forced him to be the means of encouraging it. It was this aspect more than any other which prevented his developing too great a liking for the detection of crime. The mental stimulus of deducing material facts from insignificant trifles—that was fine. The excitement of the chase—that, too, had its grim moments of pleasure. But the type of furtive, second-hand interrogation, the prying into the intimacies of other people's lives, that kind of attack, however necessary, was abhorrent, so he usually took good care to have nothing to do with it.

At the same time he experienced a feeling of justifiable interest in the name of Max Bullett—after all, was it not one of those already on his 'short' list? He recollected the man: of medium height, about five-nine or ten, with dark, sleek hair turning white round the ears; he always kept it overlong for the average man, but it curled handsomely—sometimes too handsomely to be altogether natural. He had the black-brown eyes of the Middle East, eyes with impenetrable depths of mystery, though there was nothing else about Bullett to suggest that he was anything but pure British by birth. His face was smooth, slightly sallow, and firm. His lips were over-red for a man, and sensuous. His body was enviously slender considering his age, for he was nearing his fifties.

Terhune tried to think of Bullett as a victim of psychopathic neurosis, and found this to be easy. There was, now he came to con the matter over, something about Max Bullett which was not entirely normal; some elusive quality about the man which it was not easy to define. It could be that he was over-fond of women—Terhune had once surprised Bullett staring at Julia with an expression in his eyes which was anything but brotherly. The bold stare had left Julia unmoved, but on her behalf Terhune had experienced an unpleasant if momentary spasm of repugnance. Or that elusive quality could be the consequence of Bullett's being—well, one of several things: a mystic, maybe, or a hypochondriac, a drug-taker, a pervert—

Shore's patience was not proof against long silence. "It was lucky for young Daisy King that Mr. Bullett knows as much as he does about medicine—leastwise, we're all sure it was Mr. Bullett what helped her. It wasn't Mrs. Wilkinson who Daisy went to first; she wouldn't have nothing to do with it for a hundred pounds."

Though the innkeeper's words were obscure, the inference behind them was clear enough. Terhune understood, and reddened with embarrassment. Daisy King was a nice girl, not twenty yet, he believed. It was damnable to think of people talking about her so openly. He determined to change the conversation as soon as possible.

"Yes, yes, but returning to Percy Holmes—"

Shore was not so easily side-tracked. "Of course, nobody knows for certain that it was Mr. Bullett, but Jim Cooper seen him coming out of George King's home one night, and it was soon after that Daisy was all right again. Not that Mr. Bullett did more for Daisy than he should have," the innkeeper continued gloatingly. "Daisy wouldn't never say who the man was, but her Dad says that Daisy didn't work as Mrs. Bullett's maid without learning a thing or two from the master."

Conscience made Terhune glance uneasily behind him so as to make sure that nobody had entered without his knowing, but save for the innkeeper and himself the room was still empty. He turned back to the fire again and recognized the look of decision on Shore's face. Shore meant to have his say, willy-nilly. In face of this determination Terhune feared he would do more harm than good in trying to prevent the other man's gossip—Shore might turn sullen, and say nothing.

Quite unaware of his visitor's scruples, Shore went on: "Doctor Harris says that Jim Cooper would have lost his life if it hadn't been for Mr. Bullett."

This sounded more interesting, and less intimate. "What happened?"

"Some years ago Jim swallowed some rat poison by mistake. Ma Cooper rushed over here for some brandy. Lucky for her Mr. Bullett was here having a drink quiet-like; he asked her what she wanted it for. When he heard what had happened he told her to 'phone up Doctor Harris quick while he did what he could for Jim. By the time Doctor Harris had arrived Jim were all right again. Mr. Bullett had given him something to make him sick up the poison."

"Where did Mr. Bullett's father practise?"

Shore shook his head. "I don't know as I can rightly say that his father practised in Bedford, but that's where Mr. Max Bullett came from when he moved here sixteen years ago."

"Mr. and Mrs. Bullett travel a good deal, don't they?"

"They used to, before the war, but they haven't gone anywhere far away since then 'cept for a trip to Ireland during the last year of the war."

"Do you know if Mr. Bullett has any relations?"

The question stumped Shore. "I've never heard of any, nor ain't I ever seen any of them. It's Mrs. Bullett what has all the relations. All over the world she has them, and they take it in turns to come to

England and stay with her for a month or two at a time. Especially since the end of the war. You should hear what Mr. Bullett has to say about 'em. Swear! I ain't never heard nobody swear like Mr. Bullett when he gets talking about his wife's relations."

Terhune considered that he had heard enough about the Bulletts to justify his leaving them alone. "Now tell me what sort of a woman Mrs. Wilkinson is."

"Her!" Shore reflected; shrugged. "There's nothing special about her, I reckon, 'cept that she don't hold with her husband coming here to have a drink now and again of a evening." He grinned. "But that doesn't stop old Bert coming."

"Has she ever travelled abroad?"

The grin broadened. "Anybody what doesn't live in England is a heathen. She don't hold with furriners. Thinks they ought to stop in their own country, she says."

"I see! Taken all round, would you say that she's just an ordinary person?"

"Ay, sir, I would an' all."

"Any relatives?"

"Some up Manchester way, I believe."

"And Holmes—do you know anything about him?"

"Practically nothing, 'cept that he has a pretty piece of goods for his missus. And young, too. A blonde. You ought to see the men's eyes whenever she goes by."

Terhune continued questioning the innkeeper until the session was brought to an end by the entry of Snaith and Nicholas Harvey. Conversation quickly became general. Naturally it was not long before the subject of the inquest was raised—by Harvey, who asked Terhune whether the police knew more than they had disclosed at the inquest. Terhune replied that, to the best of his knowledge, the police did not—whereupon, as his glance met Shore's, the innkeeper winked broadly. Other awkward questions followed—both men guessed, apparently, the reason for his visit to the *Dusty Miller*, but he answered them as tactfully as he could and presently left.

Later on, towards eight-thirty p.m., Murphy fulfilled his promise to telephone. Terhune gave as full an account as possible of his conversation with Ted Shore. The sergeant listened through to the end without interrupting, but when he spoke his voice sounded full of interest.

"Max Bullett sounds like our likeliest customer, Mr. Terhune. That business with the King girl was probably only village gossip— personally I wouldn't mind taking a bet that Fred Botts was the man who got her into trouble, *and* out of it. We've had our suspicions of him for a long time, but he's too cunning. But if Bullett was the one, then he sounds the sort of man who is capable of giving a brother a helping hand into the next world for the sake of a small fortune. But isn't he fairly well off already?"

"Fairly well, I'm told. He doesn't work, and he used to travel extensively before the war."

"Well, it's them that has the money who can usually do with more," Murphy said sagely. "And you say that he's a bit peculiar anyway?"

"A bit."

"Then we can't do any harm meanwhile to concentrate on him."

"What do you suggest should be the next move?"

"I think you can leave that to me, Mr. Terhune. I think I could get the Old Man to agree to putting through a routine enquiry to the Bedford police. We might learn something interesting. I'll give you a ring, and drop in as soon as anything new turns up."

"Thanks, Sergeant."

So it was left. Terhune returned to the interrupted task of pricing a library of two hundred choice titles which somebody in Hawkhurst had offered to him.

11

Thanks—or, better, no thanks—to some punctures, Terhune arrived at Timberlands later than he had anticipated. Briggs opened the door to the ring; his wrinkled face smiled with relief as he recognized the visitor.

"I am glad you have arrived, sir. Lady Kylstone was beginning to fear that something had happened to you."

"That's what comes of having a reputation for punctuality, Briggs. The moment one is more than two minutes late everybody begins to imagine calamity. But something did happen to me—two punctures."

"*Two*, sir?" Briggs looked sympathetic as he closed the door behind Terhune. "I think one is bad enough"—for Briggs still rode a bicycle whenever he visited his sister at Farthing Toll. "Would you like to wash your hands before you go into the drawing-room?"

"You've read my thoughts, Briggs." Terhune passed over a small wrapped parcel. "The 'Toff' title you wanted was returned late yesterday afternoon, so I've brought it along for you."

Briggs's eyes shone. "Thank you, sir. I'll be starting on it tonight, the moment I have a minute to spare." Briggs was an enthusiastic reader of 'thrillers', particularly those forming part of a series, written about one central character. Just lately he had discovered 'The Toff', and was eagerly ploughing through the list, one after the other.

Terhune washed his hands and listened to the hum of conversation from the drawing-room. Conspicuous, for once, was Lady Kylstone's own voice; usually it was deep, resonant, very serene, but tonight it trilled with happiness and laughter, and revealed the extent of the affection which she felt for her elder brother.

As soon as Terhune re-entered the hall Briggs announced him. Lady Kylstone greeted her late guest with a severe expression which was treacherously betrayed by the undoubted twinkle in her eyes.

"You are late, Theodore. Nearly fifteen minutes late. We have had the utmost difficulty in preventing Helena from ringing up the police."

He grinned back at her. "I had to make two stops on the way here to mend punctures."

"*Two* stops!" She wagged a reproving forefinger. "Come, come, Theodore; if you really wish us to accept your excuses you should at least make them sound convincing." She turned to her brother. "Do you remember Theodore, Wesley? Since his visit to the States he has become quite a famous person."

"Of course I remember him." Wesley Cruikshank thrust out a huge hand—he was a large man—with which he squeezed Terhune's far slenderer and softer hand. "Glad to see you again, Terhune. And say, it doesn't need Kathleen to tell me of your fame. I've read all about you in the local paper which she sends out to me now and again, so that I can have the news of all my old friends."

Wesley Cruikshank turned to his left, where stood a young man who looked about Terhune's own age. He had curly hair, humorous blue eyes, high cheek-bones, brown complexion, square jaw, a lithe frame. "This is Theodore Terhune I was telling you about on the ship. Terhune, meet a relation of ours from Athens, Alabama; Gary Delaware Jones."

The two men shook hands. Terhune liked the firm handclasp, the unswerving glance.

"Glad to know you," he greeted in a slow drawl. "But you are just about as unlike what I imagined you were as anyone could be, in spite of Aunt Kathy's warning."

Lady Kylstone laughed. "Gary wouldn't believe me when I told him that you both looked and acted like a shy, overgrown schoolboy. Helena, my dear, will you give Theodore a glass of sherry? Theodore, as a punishment for being late you are only going to have one glass of Manzanilla tonight. The meal will spoil unless we sit down at the time Biddy said."

Wesley chuckled. "So that old martinet, Biddy, is still with you, Kathleen?"

"Of course she is. She'll be with me until one of us dies."

Gary Jones inspected the colour of the sherry which Helena served to Terhune. "Say, that's a light-coloured wine, isn't it? What's it like, this Manzanilla stuff?"

"Like nothing that would please your sweet palate, Gary, so you needn't ogle Helena; you've had plenty of drink to go on with, for a young man."

Gary looked somewhat astonished at the outburst. Wesley laughed, and clapped his younger relative on the shoulder. "Take no notice of your Aunt Kathleen, son. She talks like that to everybody, but her bark's worse than her bite."

"I neither bark nor bite, young man, so take no notice of what my brother says of me. I believe in being forthright and saying what I think. And as this is my house I like people who come here to behave as they should, not as they wish."

"Quite right, too, Aunt Kathy," Gary murmured diplomatically.

"And now that we are beginning to know one another, and Theodore has finished his sherry, we will go into the other room." Lady Kylstone rose, and led the way through a connecting door into the adjoining dining-room, Wesley on one side of her and Terhune on the other, with Gary and Helena in the rear. But when they sat down Lady Kylstone placed Gary on her right, with Helena next to him, and Terhune on her left. Wesley she ordered to take the other end of the table.

For a moment the transition from one room to the other caused a brief lull in the conversation, but it was not long-lasting. Lady Kylstone was a born hostess, and charming in spite of her forth rightness—or perhaps because of it. She turned, to her 'nephew' Gary—the actual relationship was rather more vague, Gary being the grandson of Sophie Cruikshank's (mother of Wesley and Kathleen) elder sister, and therefore a first cousin once removed to the two Cruikshanks—and as quickly captivated the young man as she did nearly everyone she met. Soon she and Gary and Helena were sharing a joke together, while Wesley amused Terhune with a succession of anecdotes concerning some of the people in Albany to whom he had introduced the Englishman at the time of his short stay there.

The meal progressed happily. Unexpectedly Terhune's attention was arrested by a question put to Lady Kylstone by her young relation.

"By the way, Aunt Kathy, have you made up your mind yet about the trip to France?"

"I have—on one condition."

"What's that, Kathleen?"

"We go in my car. And Helena goes with us. She needs a change more than I do."

The suggestion was received with enthusiasm by the others, but Terhune, not being concerned, was less enthusiastic about it. Helena and he were in the habit of meeting frequently—they were good chums, very good chums—he would miss her companionship—

Perhaps Lady Kylstone suddenly realized this fact, for she turned to him. "Gary wants to visit the Riviera, and Wesley had promised to take him there for a month or so. Then they had the lovely idea of asking me to go with them, and I could not resist. So much has happened since my last visit to Cannes, in nineteen thirty-eight." She sighed regretfully. "I hope it has not changed too much. There are times when I feel a little apprehensive—"

"Major Blye didn't think it had changed overmuch in spite of damage. He thought the people were so friendly, so grateful, so anxious to please," Terhune said huskily, while thinking: 'Damn it! Two months or more without Helena—

"Arnold is the most cheerful man in the world to know, he invariably sees everybody and everything in its best possible aspect."

"Well, why not, Aunt Kathy?" Gary asked exuberantly.

"Because, my dear Gary, rose-coloured spectacles often distort. What he sees is what his happy-go-lucky nature insists upon his seeing, but it is not always the truth. He boasts that he can sleep anywhere, on bare boards if necessary, with boots for a pillow. He's got the digestion of an ostrich. Therefore, any hotel is de-luxe as far as he is concerned. But in these days my poor old bones demand a real bed. And my digestion, simple but appetizing food."

"Well, folk, when do we start for the sunny south?" Gary demanded.

A discussion followed, one which took them back into the drawing-room, with coffee and liqueurs before them, before it was settled. Tuesday fortnight was eventually chosen. When agreement was reached a happy silence followed. Each of the four would-be travellers stared at the fire in contented reverie, unaware that the other three were doing the same. Terhune, solitary in his thoughts wallowed down his brandy in miserable and indecent haste. For a moment he felt a complete stranger.

Wesley bestirred himself. "Speaking of France, I think you can be of help to young Gary, Terhune."

Terhune smiled feebly. "A guide-book, or Treve's *Riviera of the Corniche Road*—a good book, that, by the by—or *The Lure of Monte Carlo*, by C. N. and A. M. Williamson—"

The American laughed. "Nothing of that nature, but something in the book line all the same. Gary has a first-class knowledge of the French language—reads French literature in the original, and so on. He's just taken the notion that he would like to possess a set of Guy de Maupassant in the original. Do you think there is any chance of your buying a set for him?"

"There are a fair number of translations floating around—"

"No. They must be in French," Gary stated on his own behalf.

"Then you would stand a better chance of buying them in France than over here, especially as you are going there anyway, and can get into personal contact with some of the bookshops."

Gary grinned comically. "I hadn't thought of that." Then he shook his head. "I would rather buy them over here. I want to read them before we go."

"The impatience of youth!" Lady Kylstone murmured.

"It's not only impatience, Aunt Kathy. I want to feel the atmosphere of the country before I go there."

"You won't get it from Guy de Maupassant," his aunt told him. "The France of de Maupassant died in nineteen-fourteen."

Gary was obstinate. "I still want them. Any chance of your buying a set for me during the next few days, Tommy?" The younger of the two Americans had already, with complete ease and as a matter of course, slipped into the habit of calling Terhune by his Christian name—or rather the nickname of schooldays, which Helena had subsequently revived.

"I've just remembered seeing a set advertised in a catalogue about two years ago. There's just a chance they might still be unsold if I can find which catalogue the item was in; I don't think there is much of a demand for Maupassant in the original."

"Will you be a chum and see what you can do?"

Terhune promised he would, whereupon the conversation changed once more. Wesley asked whether Sir George Brereton had produced any more good fishing stories...

Chapter Eleven

The following morning Terhune had reason to bless, by no means for the first time, Julia's insistence upon his engaging Anne Quilter for an assistant. Monday mornings, after Thursday and Saturday mornings, were usually the busiest of the week, for most of the people, having had time over the week-end to read the books which they had borrowed the previous Saturday, hastened along to the bookshop for a fresh supply of literature. The morning after his visit to Timberlands was no exception, but most of the time Anne handled the business of changing some books, selling others, answering enquiries, making a note of wanted titles, and the dozen or so other necessary duties connected with the selling and lending of books. All these things she did with a deft ease, an astonishing speed, and a pleasant, smiling manner which put the people—and Terhune—in good humour.

Because of Anne's presence in the shop Terhune was enabled to concentrate on looking through a large file of catalogues received, in the hope of fulfilling his promise to Gary Delaware Jones. The task required patience as well as time, but he had long since drilled himself into a state of patience, for this business of going through catalogues in search of a title happened often.

This monotonous hunt finished nearly seventy minutes after its start. As he turned to the middle pages of a catalogue sent from John M. McCloud, Bookseller of Antiquarian and Modern Books, Cathedral Bookshop, Canterbury, Kent, his glance was held by the following title:

Maupassant (Guy de). Les *Œuvres Completes, etc., en quinze
volumes*. Published in Paris, 1885. Portrait and plates, 8vo.
Incomplete volumes five and eleven missing..............25/−

This was the set he had remembered, though the catalogue was dated
more than two years ago. Two years! A longish period of time, that, to
retain stock, although some books were apt to remain on a bookseller's
shelves even longer than that. Still…

He considered the telephone. McCloud was on the telephone, so it
need be a matter of minutes only to enquire whether the de Maupassant
books were still for sale. On the other hand, a journey to Canterbury, by
bus from Ashford, was a pleasant trip—or, even better, it was possible
that Julia would gladly run him there in her car. There was an addi-
tional reason for making his enquiry in person rather than by 'phone:
Edward Pryce, the artist, had asked him to try and obtain a copy of
Hassell's *Aqua Pictura*, 1818 edition, and despite his having advertised
the title as 'Wanted', nobody had yet offered it to him. There was in
Canterbury, not far from McCloud's bookshop, but tucked away in a
little, short side-road, another bookseller, who specialized in works of
art dealing with ecclesiastical subjects, also books on art. A funny little
man was he: Tobias Overbury by name old in years, old-fashioned in
outlook, and eccentric. If he liked a prospective buyer a sale could be
concluded; if not, no offer, however high, would tempt him to sell.
Another little peculiarity of his was that in no circumstances would
he enter into correspondence, or buy or sell by post. All business with
Tobias Overbury had to be strictly personal.

Terhune glanced out of the window. The cold had continued, and
hardened. The sun was shining most temptingly. He reached for the
telephone and dialled the MacMunn number.

He was soon speaking to Julia.

"Well, my pet?" There was a warm lilt in her voice.

"Doing anything this afternoon, Julie?"

"Mother's having tea with Diana Pearson. I have been trying to decide whether to go with her, or do some needlework." Julia was clever with her needle and loved making dainty garments, some of which Terhune never saw again, once they were finished. "Why?" she concluded.

"Would you like to run me over to Canterbury?"

"When?"

"Sometime during the afternoon."

"Theo!" The exclamation was one of astonishment, not altogether assumed. But she went on, exaggeratedly: "You are not thinking of leaving your precious books on a Monday afternoon? Whatever will happen to the business?"

He grinned to himself. How many times had Julia snapped at him because he maintained that business must come before pleasure? "I want to go there on business. I've promised to try and get some books for a distant relation of Lady Kylstone's, over from the States." Too late he realized what a blundering fool he was; he should have mentioned Edward Pryce's want instead, for Julia seemed to have an unaccountable antipathy for Lady Kylstone and Helena.

A long pause followed his explanation. His expression became wry. Julia was going to refuse.

But she didn't. "All right," she agreed curtly. "What time shall I call for you?"

"About two-thirty?" he suggested.

"I'll be there."

She was. As nearly always, dead on time. As he stepped into the car he saw that her expression was cheerful. He was relieved. After her abrupt manner earlier on he had half expected her to be cross, and, like the little girl of nursery-rhyme fame, when Julia was bad she was horrid.

Time passed quickly as they travelled to Canterbury, for they had not met for nearly a week, and Julia wanted to know how much progress had been made in the meantime towards solving the vaguely mysterious circumstances surrounding the death of old Peter.

They reached Canterbury in good time, and called in at McCloud's bookshop. A man approached them; he was tall, sparse, had thinning hair, a prominently sharp nose, and was dressed in smart clothes which suggested a floorwalker in a big London stores rather than a small bookseller in a quiet cathedral town.

"Can I help you, sir?"

"Mr. McCloud?"

"Yes, sir."

"My name is Terhune, from Bray-in-the-Marsh."

For a moment McCloud's face was blank; then it lit up with a formal smile. "Ah! Of course. We exchange catalogues—and sometimes cheques, don't we, Mr. Terhune?" The slight humour apparently pleased McCloud; his smile became sincere. "I am glad to have this opportunity of meeting you."

Terhune introduced Julia, and then stated his business. "More than two years ago, Mr. McCloud, you advertised a set of de Maupassant's works in the French language—"

"Less two volumes," the other man corrected precisely.

"Yes, of course. I have just received an enquiry for a set of de Maupassant in the original. Am I lucky enough to find your set unsold?"

Quite a mournful expression settled on McCloud's bony face. "I regret to say that you are not lucky, Mr. Terhune. I sold the books— oh, about five or six months after I had circulated the catalogue." His thinning eyebrows waggled. "To somebody living not far from you, if I remember aright. Hawkhurst, was it? Or Hartley? Let me see, what was the name of the buyer—" He puckered his forehead in deep thought.

"Never mind, Mr. McCloud. Please don't worry. I came here just on chance."

"Perhaps the purchaser would resell. I could probably find the name by turning up my files for that year."

"That's extremely nice of you, Mr. McCloud. Please don't worry—"

"It's no worry at all, Mr. Terhune." His face became shrewd. "Would your client pay up to, say, three pounds for the set?"

Terhune's bookselling instincts rose uppermost. "Two pounds ten—less the usual—"

"Of course, less the usual. Two pounds ten! Well, if I can find you another set would you like me to give you a ring?"

"Please. But it must be within the next ten days."

"Quite. Is there anything else while you are here?" When a shake of the head gave him his answer he held out a bony hand. "Thank you for calling in, Mr. Terhune. I hope we shall have the pleasure of meeting again."

"I hope so."

Terhune and Julia left the shop: As she walked along the street she enquired: "Is he likely to find another set so easily?"

He grinned. "I'll bet the old rascal is going to try and buy the books back from the purchaser, probably at half the price given, so that he can resell it to me for double the original price."

She squeezed the arm she was holding. "So that is how booksellers do business, is it, my pet?"

"We must live, Julie."

"Why?" she countered, not very originally. He did not attempt to answer that question, but crossed the street, away from the parking place where they had left the car.

"Where are we going?"

"Afterwards, to have tea. But first, to Tobias Overbury—"

Unfortunately Tobias did not have a copy of *Aqua Pictura*, but Terhune's journey to Canterbury was not altogether wasted, for what Tobias did have was a copy, in good condition, of Lawrence and Dighton's *French Line Engravings of the Late XVIIIth Century*, for which Terhune had received an enquiry, from a client in Canada, only the previous week.

II

The following night brought Murphy along to 1, Market Square. He looked bewildered, and somewhat tense; Terhune was sure that he had come with some news. So he had, as he made known to his host, without preamble, even before he had lighted his pipe.

"I think you picked on the right man, Mr. Terhune, when you named Max Bullett."

"You've had news from Bedford?" It was a silly question, as Terhune realized the moment he had asked it. But silly prompting questions of that nature are usually born of impatience, and his was no exception.

"Plenty. In the first case, the father was a doctor, sure enough. And a good one too, if money counts for much. He left close on seventy thousand pounds. I suppose Max is living on his share of the inheritance to this day."

"His share?"

Murphy nodded. "One half! The other half went to Max's brother Julian."

There was a certain suggestiveness in the sergeant's manner which obviously lent added significance to his reply. So Max Bullett had a brother; the Pierre, perhaps, of the second story, *Generosity*. Julian Bullett bad inherited half of seventy thousand pounds. So had Pierre. But Julian Bullett, presumably, had inherited at the same time as Max, so the theory of Max's killing Julian for the sake of money collapsed like a house of cards in a draught. Old Peter had died penniless.

Terhune felt puzzled, but he said nothing, for he could see that Murphy had more to say—the sergeant seemed to be bursting with news.

"Now, here's some real news for you, sir. Nobody in Bedford knows the whereabouts of Julian Bullett."

"What's that?"

Murphy laughed mirthlessly. "That bit of information made me sit up too, sir. Yes, Julian went over to Canada sixteen years ago. Some weeks after his arrival there was a bad 'plane crash. Everyone in it was killed, and all the bodies charred beyond recognition. One body, that of a man, was never identified. From that day to this nobody has ever heard of Julian again. People in Bedford have put two and two together and named the corpse—to themselves—Julian Bullett."

"Did his family do the same?"

The sergeant shrugged his shoulders. "There were only two members of the family left by that time. Brother Max, and the mother. Max had left the neighbourhood eight months previously—to settle in Great Hinton."

"And the mother?"

Murphy took his time about replying. "His mother was never told the bad news," he replied at last, ominously.

"Do you mean that she was an invalid, too ill to be told?"

"Only in a manner of speaking, Mr. Terhune. Nearly twenty-two years ago, four years before the death of her husband, Mrs. Bullett was put into a mental home, where she died, in nineteen-thirty-nine, just after the outbreak of war."

Terhune whistled his astonishment, and, prompted by a feeling of nervous excitement, took off his tortoiseshell glasses, which he began to polish.

The sergeant went on: "That information begins to add up to something, doesn't it, sir? If the two sons inherited a streak of insanity from their mother, there lies the explanation for—one—" Murphy held up a finger. "This ruddy silly business of the short stories. You wanted to find somebody suffering from psycho—psycho—whatever it was—"

"Psychopathic neurosis—not that I can guarantee that this is the right description."

"It'll do. Anyway, mightn't Max Bullett be a ready-made example for you? Not mad, mind you, but just touched enough, like the old chap in Gigins Court I told you about, to enjoy seeing us make fools of ourselves by sending in those idiotic stories. And two—" The sergeant held up a second finger. "And if Julian, too, was potty, wouldn't that account for his living the life of a tramp?"

"It might."

Murphy seemed disappointed. "What's wrong with the theory?"

"To begin with, the Sofia newspaper—"

"Ah! I thought you would bring that up. But the dates don't clash. Let's get them properly established. The Sofia newspaper was dated nineteen-twenty-three. Julian went to Canada in 'thirty-one. His father died in 'twenty-nine. His mother was put away in 'twenty-five. She died in 'thirty-nine, at the ripe old age of ninety-something-odd—so she was old enough to have been the mother of old Peter, assuming Peter was getting on for seventy at that time. What do we get? Julian could have been in Sofia in 'twenty-three. He reads about the marriage of a Señorita Bázan—perhaps he loved her himself, as we've already discussed. He returns to England sometime during the next few years, quite possibly after hearing the news that his mother has been put away—quite a natural thing for a son to do, don't you think? Four years later, in 'twenty-nine, his father dies, and Julian inherits a nice packet of Jimmy o' Goblins. In 'thirty-one he goes abroad again, this time to Canada, and there the madness which he has inherited from his mother reveals itself for the first time—well, perhaps not for the first time, but at any rate the attack, if not the first, is worse than the others, and takes the form of disappearing into the blue—" He stopped, seeing Terhune's face wreathed in dry smiles. "What's the matter, sir?"

"Who is making the facts agree with theories, instead of theories agree with facts?"

Murphy was a good sport. He chuckled happily. "You're right, Mr. Terhune. I'm not practising what I preach. The business of deducing and theorizing must be catching. All the same, it's not too fantastic a theory—not if you take those short stories into consideration."

"You don't seem to like those stories, Sergeant."

"I don't, and that's a fact. There's something bizarre about them—and being just an ordinary copper I don't like peculiar cases. But it's time you aired your views, sir."

"Quite frankly, Sergeant, the father's bequest worries me."

Murphy looked puzzled. "Why?"

"You say he left everything in equal shares to his two sons?"

"That's so."

"What about his poor wife? Didn't he make any provision for her?"

"Oh, yes! There was some sort of a trust deed by which each son contributed a sum of two hundred and fifty pounds per annum towards her upkeep and welfare for as long as she lived."

"That trust deed complicates our theories, Sergeant. In all probability it was so worded as to have prevented either son disposing of the capital sum until the responsibility towards the mother ceased."

Murphy looked puzzled. "What difference would that have made?"

"A lot, to your suggestion that Julian might have spent his inheritance either previous to, or subsequent to, his disappearance. Then you must remember, too, that the trustees would have been looking to him to continue paying his two hundred and fifty pounds per annum for his mother's upkeep. I do not know much about law, beyond a smattering of Criminal Law, but I should imagine that, if there had been a genuine possibility of Julian's having died in the aeroplane crash, the trustees would have approached the Courts to presume him dead, in order to legalize the position as between themselves, as trustees for the mother's upkeep, and Julian's heir. Do you follow me?"

"I think so, sir. You mean that whoever came into the money which Julian had inherited from his father would remain responsible for paying out two-fifty per annum until the mother died?"

"That's right. Now, I don't think the Courts would have given their consent to presume the death of Julian unless the evidence was fairly conclusive that he did so die. Obviously, if he really died in nineteen-thirty-one, then he couldn't have been Peter the Hermit."

Murphy leaned forward. "Just a minute, sir. Suppose there had been some doubt as to whether the corpse in the 'plane was Julian's or not, wouldn't the Court have refused to presume death?"

"Undoubtedly. But the trustees could have applied again, seven years later, and if there had been no evidence in the meantime that Julian was alive, then it is almost certain that leave to presume death would have been given. But mark the operative words, Sergeant—'in the meantime'! If Julian had not died in the 'plane wreck, then he would have needed money to live. It would have been impossible for him to have drawn on his own money without the trustees' becoming aware that he was still alive. If this had been the case I am sure that his whereabouts would soon have become known."

"But I still cannot see why his insanity couldn't have caused him to lose his memory, which explanation would account for his still being an old tramp. If he had never recovered his memory he wouldn't have known that he possessed enough money to live comfortably, and wouldn't have tried to draw any. As long as he failed to do that, the trustees might not have heard that he was still alive, and would therefore have applied for leave to presume death."

Terhune shook his head. "I can't agree about the loss of memory."

"Why not?"

"For several reasons. If he had lost his memory he wouldn't have had any recollection of the past represented by the newspaper and the comb, and without some very vivid recollection of what both had once meant to him I very much doubt that he would have clung to them—at least, the comb—and starve in consequence."

A nod of his head signalled Murphy's agreement with this argument.

"Another reason. You remember Mrs. Newman's evidence about old Peter's having found something—or someone, as we now presume—in Great Hinton after a very long search? If Max were that someone, then old Peter knew who he was, and therefore hadn't lost his memory."

"His memory might have returned after the lapse of the seven years."

"Again no, Sergeant. If his memory had returned he would know that he was a comparatively rich man, and that there was no necessity for him to live the life of an old hermit."

"Unless he was mad enough to prefer that sort of life."

There was something in what the detective suggested, Terhune had to admit to himself. Madness, he knew, can take many strange forms.

"Besides, his share of the money might, by then, have been paid to his heir." Murphy laughed. "What would have been the legal position in such a case?"

"Heaven alone knows!"

The sergeant's laugh deepened. "Blow me if you aren't arguing against your own theory, Mr. Terhune, It was you who suggested that old Peter might possibly be a brother Of Max Bullett."

Terhune nodded. "I know. But I am really arguing against only the loss of memory theory. If Julian was insane enough to do what you suggested just now—that is, disappear, and voluntarily remain a starving old hermit—that is another matter, and it could be that Peter the Hermit was Julian Bullett. Would you care to make another enquiry, Sergeant?"

"I'd like to see anyone stop me. I'm in this up to my unofficial neck, and won't be satisfied now till I know what's what. What is the enquiry to be, sir? Whether the trustees of Doctor Bullett's will ever took action about presuming the death of Julian Bullett?"

"Yes."

"I'll do that, Mr. Terhune—just as soon as I can—"

III

Less than twenty-four hours later Murphy 'phoned Terhune up.

"You were right in everything you suggested about the trustees of Doctor Bullett's will. There was such a will roughly on the lines you suggested, there were trustees, and they did ask leave to presume death, six months after the crash."

"What happened?"

"The judges wouldn't hear of it. Seven years later the trustees asked leave for the second time. This time leave was granted. All Julian Bullett's money went to—"

"Max Bullett?" Terhune slipped in quickly.

"Right first time," the sergeant confirmed. "I'll give five to one that Max Bullett is our man sure enough."

As if the unknown author had heard the detective's rash boast, within a few minutes of the call a third story was dropped into an Ashford post-box. It reached Terhune the following morning.

Chapter Twelve

AMATEUR DEDUCTION

I wonder how many writers of detective stories fondly imagine that, given the opportunity, they could successfully play the role of their principal character, the inimitable private detective? Not many of them would admit the fact, of course, but I am sure they believe they could beat the *Sûreté Générale* men at their own game. Once upon a time I had large ideas of my own deductive powers, but I was cured of that, once and for all. It happened not far from my home in Paris. Quite by accident I met an old acquaintance of mine whom I had previously met in New York, a citizen of the United States of America named Andrew Villiers. His real name was André Vila, and he had been born in France, but the lure of the new world had called to him, and at an early age he had emigrated to the U.S.A., where he had, as the saying goes, 'made good'. In due course he had naturalized and changed his name.

Now he was back in our beloved France, strolling along the Rue de Rivoli with a friend of his; we met face to face. Excited greetings followed, introductions, handshakes, questions. His friend, I learned, was Colonel Nadaud. The inevitable duly occurred: we strolled to the nearest café, and placing ourselves at a table just out of the sun, each one of us ordered an *apéritif*.

The conversation turned and veered from one subject to another, as conversations do. I wanted to know what had been happening to

Villiers since I had last seen him: he wanted to know how my latest books were selling. Then, naturally, I had to hear all about Nadaud, who was home on leave from Africa. Time passed by; presently a fourth man joined our party, Jacques Lestrange, whom I knew vaguely as a fairly successful artist, but whom the other two knew well. It was he, in fact, who introduced the topic which led to such a strange result.

"Our poor Colonel has undoubtedly suffered the most of us all," Lestrange said, in answer to a question put by Villiers—I forget now what the question was, but the reply I remember sufficiently well to piece it together here. "While we three have remained in civilized places and have enjoyed the company of charming women, Nadaud, here, has been cast away in the wild deeps of the African forest, losing his fat in the heat, his sight in the sun-glare, and his sense of smell in the vile stench of the rotting vegetation. Still worse, he has not seen the profile of an entrancing beauty, has not been captivated by her inviting smile, her glance of love, nor yet tasted of her lips, no! Poor Nadaud!" Being rather a *poseur*, Lestrange always talked in this flamboyant style.

"You've surely summed it up," Villiers agreed, "but you must know that Jacques has not had all the charming ladies in the world to himself. New York has many attractions for me. To my idea our American women are not unlike the ladies of Paris."

Colonel Nadaud made a grimace and took a deep drink. "You are right, *mes amis*, and now once more in my beautiful Paris I think that Paradise cannot be far away. Yet I assure you that you are wrong in thinking that the sun has destroyed my eyesight. My faculties of observation have considerably improved since my sojourn in Africa. The natives have taught me to take notice of little things which escape the eye of the average person, and to deduce therefrom, to elucidate mysteries of nature."

"Perhaps so, my friend," said Jacques, "but I doubt whether the power of observation of which you speak will be of assistance to you in civilization."

"Test me, my dear chap," replied Nadaud.

"Wait one minute," interrupted Villiers. "I pride myself on being a great reader in my own way, and I am particularly entranced by detective fiction. I believe that I should be able to make some deductions myself, and as for you, de Courtot, as a writer of detective stories you should be particularly adept at observing and deducing. I suggest that we select some nearby object, discuss it, each giving his own particular suggestion as to what it is, or may be, and afterwards we will together make enquiries, and which one of us is farthest from the truth shall purchase four seats at the Casino de Paris tonight."

"Bravo!" ejaculated Jacques. "Only leave me out of it. I am hopeless at anything to do with brainwork."

"I will gladly fall in with your plan," Nadaud agreed. "Moreover, I believe I have discovered our subject. During the last few minutes a pretty girl has just seated herself at that table by the glass partition. If you move your chair slightly, Monsieur de Courtot, you will be able to see her easily. As I 'spotted the target', I claim that Villiers should try his hand first at our amateur detective game of skill. Monsieur de Courtot second, and myself last. What do you say, Andrew?"

Andrew Villiers moved his chair slightly, and under cover of lighting a cigar he gazed at the pretty girl indicated by the Colonel. Presently he spoke.

"Firstly, as to her age, I should imagine that she is between twenty-three and twenty-four. To my mind she is a virgin, for her bust lacks the graceful swell usually apparent in those who have experienced the raptures of love. I suggest that her nature, as a virgin, is mild and docile. She is consequently virtuous. Her parents are probably living, which explains this extraordinary phenomenon! She is habitually neat and tidy, and must have ample means, for I observe her clothes are of good material and the product of a famous firm. She is Parisian born undoubtedly, for she wears her clothes as one used to them from birth.

Being of gentle parentage, she would therefore be well educated, and would speak smoothly. I think that is all."

"Bravo, quite good," approved the Colonel. "And now, my dear Monsieur de Courtot, let us hear to what extent the detectives of your pen have helped you to assume the duties of a police official."

"To tell the truth, Villiers seems to have summed her up very well," I told them. "Though I must disagree with him on several points. To begin with, I see she bears upon her left hand a wedding ring, so that it is rather difficult to make this fact coincide with the statement that she is a virgin. If she is so modest, too, why does she apply cosmetics quite so obviously? Personally, I am inclined to think that she is an actress, who has made a success. Her good clothes suggest money, although it may be that she has a rich husband. I cannot confirm as to her parenthood. I have agreed as to the quality of her clothes, but that red belt is rather too obvious for good breeding, as is her handbag. She sits coarsely. Her drink is scarcely one which I would offer to a young innocent girl. Her age—why, I agree with Villiers. She peruses, you see, the leading article of a political paper. She is interested in politics. Perhaps she is the wife of a member of the Senate. She is quick-tempered, I imagine—she has red hair. She is a deep thinker. See, she frowns over a certain paragraph. She has sufficient brains and intelligence to disagree with the leader-writer. Yes, she makes an ideal wife for a man who loves his spouse, who has made his way in the world, has plenty of money, and was once fond of a gay life. Why the gay life? Because he married—if I am right—an actress. The next, please!"

Villiers clapped his hands. Nadaud (being nearly old enough to be my father) patted me on the back. "You almost convert me to reading 'Monsieur Lecoq' and 'Vidocq'. Nevertheless, I fancy that the natives of Africa can still give a few lessons to the modern writers of detective fiction. When examining her hands you have both passed over the fact that they are red and coarse, and that her nails are not manicured. From that I deduce that she performs a certain amount of manual labour. She cannot be of gentle upbringing, otherwise she would attend to her finger-nails, despite the hard work. Personally I believe her age to be less than you have both suggested. To my mind she is but seventeen or eighteen years old. I do not think she is married —but I do not think she is a virgin, from which I will leave you to conclude just what I imagine the girl to be. Perhaps she has but lately fallen into this life. She is careless as to her attire: there is a small ladder in her silk stocking.

"She does not live far from here. She walked here, therefore did not come by either motor-bus, or taxi, or Metro. She is not shopping, for she has plenty of time on her hands, and just now the shops are the most empty. You, Monsieur de Courtot, imagine her to be country born, and only just in Paris, do you not? I, to the contrary, think she has lived in Paris the best part of her life. She knows her way around. She is highly temperamental. She glances from side to side, with quick jerky movements, even as she reads. She works too hard. That is all I have to say."

Lestrange laughed. "Quite diverse opinions. Now, how are we to know the truth? But, *Mon Dieu*, what is happening?"

A taxi had driven up and stopped before the girl. Out of it jumped four men in uniform, who seized the girl firmly.

She, as she caught sight of them, immediately dropped her paper, and struggled fiercely with the men when they approached her, shrieking at them meantime in vile abusive language, with the harsh dialectal timbre which could only belong to the very roughest Parisienne. Before anyone could intervene, she was inside the taxi, which had driven off, leaving one of the uniformed men behind.

Lestrange called him over. Assuming the role of chairman, he motioned the man to sit down, called for a drink, and put the following question to him.

"Monsieur, forgive our impertinence, but you would earn our

thanks by giving us some information as to the girl who has been so summarily abducted," and he proceeded to tell the man why.

The man laughed. "Abducted, did you say, Messieurs? Say, rather, recaptured. The girl, as you call her—really she is a woman of nearly forty—is an inmate of the lunatic asylum. She escaped from us several days ago, stark naked, so those clothes which she now wears are probably stolen. She must have broken into an apartment and dyed her hair red and made up.

"From what I know of her history she was born in Marseilles, and came at the age of five to Paris with her parents. She was deserted, and while trying to find her way about was knocked down and has been hopelessly insane ever since. She cannot read or write, and is witless. Her vocabulary is confined to words unknown to any dictionary, though where she picks them up I cannot say. She is as unruly as possible, and always gives us keepers a tremendous amount of bother. Well, messieurs, I thank you for your hospitality, and I trust you are satisfied. *Merci, et bonjour, messieurs.*"

I am afraid we all looked at one another with shamefaced expressions, and none of us cheered up until Lestrange ordered another round of drinks. That is why I have not applied for the position of unofficial adviser to the *Sûreté Générale*.

II

Murphy read the story. His face remained expressionless. Without comment he passed the script on to Julia, who—having learned from Terhune, earlier on in the day, that he had received a third short story, and that Murphy was due at Bray in the evening to read it—had insisted upon being present.

She, too, read the few neatly typed pages, but she had one comment to make. "What a peculiar style of writing!"

Terhune nodded absently. "What do you make of it, Sergeant?"

"Look, Mr. Terhune! Will you do me a favour, and tell me your reactions to this story first? I have a reason for asking."

"Of course I will." After a slight pause Terhune continued: "I think the message—or the clue, if you like—contained in this story is more obvious than the previous two. The author is telling us—me in particular—that we are making fools of ourselves—"

"We are doing that by taking any notice of the stories," the sergeant grumbled.

"Are we? I wonder. Anyway, the significance of the chief character's being a writer—that's me in real life—and the subject of our amateur deduction being a lunatic—Max Bullett, in other words—is too marked to be anything else but obvious. The author is telling us, in his usual roundabout way, that our deductions are wrong: that Max Bullett is not what we have made him out to be, and that we shall waste further time and efforts if we continue to treat him as our suspect number one."

"Anything else, sir?"

"Yes. Two things. The first confirms our suspicions that these stories were first written many years ago—"

"I knew you would spot the mention of the *Sûreté Générale*," Murphy interrupted, generously jubilant.

Julia looked at the two men in turn. "What does the mention of the *Sûreté Générale* signify, Theo?"

"You've heard of the *Sûreté Générale*, Julie?"

"Isn't it the equivalent of New Scotland Yard?"

"Roughly, yes, but the point is this: after the Stavisky scandal of nineteen-thirty-odd the name of the police headquarters was changed from *Sûreté Générale* to *Sûreté Nationale*. Therefore this story was probably written before the change of name."

"Is it necessary that the story must have been written previous to the Stavisky scandal, Theo? Or could it be that the writer's knowledge of France is out of date?"

Julia saw the two men exchange glances. "Have I said something stupid?" she asked tartly.

"Oh no, Miss MacMunn!" Murphy hastened to assure her. "But some time back Mr. Terhune said that the first story was written in an old-fashioned, out-of-date style." When he saw that his explanation satisfied Julia he turned to Terhune. "Anything else about the story which strikes you as significant, sir?"

Terhune nodded with decision. "Yes, but it is something to which I cannot give a precise explanation. Let me put it this way—as I read each story for the first time I received an elusive impression that it was vaguely familiar—"

"You mean, as though you had read it before?" the sergeant questioned eagerly.

"Yes and no. That is why I stressed the *first* time of reading. I have re-read both the first two stories more than a dozen times, and consequently I am absolutely convinced that I have *not* read them before. For all that, they still remain familiar. Have you ever visited a strange place for the first time, Julie, and felt, for a moment or two, as though you had been there before?"

"I don't visit enough strange places to have the opportunity of feeling such impressions," she snapped. "But I think I know what you mean, my pet."

"I do," Murphy added eagerly.

"Well, when it happens to me I often close my eyes before I have seen too much, and try to identify definite objects in the visual picture in order to see whether they are there in the real scene. I have never succeeded. The visual objects have always been too nebulous, and have dissolved before my mental eyes could focus and hold them. The Tyburn stories have much the same effect upon me. They are vaguely familiar to me, as I said just now, yet when I concentrate on trying to remember where, or when, or how, I get no results." Terhune paused. "That's about all," he finished off presently. "What about you. Sergeant? How does the latest story strike you?"

Murphy shifted. "As unnecessary," he replied, his manner provoking.

"Unnecessary?"

He nodded. "I have some more news of Julian Bullett," he explained grimly. "A Mr. Dingle 'phoned me up this afternoon, and asked whether I was the Detective-Sergeant Murphy who had caused enquiries to be made concerning the fate of Julian Bullett. When I said that I was he went on to tell me that he was the senior partner of the firm of Trevelyan, Wright and Cameron, solicitors of Bedford and Chancery Lane, London, who had been appointed as executors and trustees in Doctor Bullett's will. Apparently he had been absent in Cornwall at the time of the enquiry, and had only just returned to Chancery Lane. He wanted to know what I had been told, and what I wanted to know.

"I told him. He started to hum and haw, and then came out with this information. What the police had been told was the truth, but not all the truth. Julian *had* disappeared, there *had* been every reason to believe that his was the unknown corpse, the trustees had twice applied for permission to presume death, and Julian's money had gone to his brother Max. But in actual fact Julian is still alive."

"I'll be damned!"

"Yes, Mr. Terhune. Julian is still alive. We weren't wrong in assuming that he had gone potty, and disappeared of his own accord. He went completely off his nut, crossed the frontier into the States, travelled down to Louisiana and demanded an interview with the Governor. When he was asked his name and mission he said he was Napoleon's grandson, and had come to redeem that State from pawn so that it could be returned to the French."

"Poor man!" Julia murmured sympathetically.

Murphy was more hardened to other people's sorrows, and beyond a nod of his head ignored the exclamation. "You can guess what the police did with Napoleon's grandson. They clapped him into an asylum, and made enquiries as to his real identity. They learned nothing. With the cunning of a madman Julian had covered up his tracks. So the State of Louisiana had to accept the lunatic as an unwanted guest for the next twelve years. Then, one day in nineteen-forty-three, Julian had an unexpected lucid period, and told the doctors who he really was.

"Enquiries were made, and his statement proved. Long before that, however, he had lost his reason again. Meanwhile, the American Embassy over here got in touch with Max Bullett, and, through him, with the trustees of Doctor Bullett's estate. I don't want to make a long story of this, Mr. Terhune, but eventually Max made a voluntary arrangement whereby his brother Julian was transferred to a private home, and kept there at Max's expense. He's still at the home, and looks like living as long as his mother. Mr. Dingle then finished by explaining that Max Bullett wasn't anxious for it to be generally known that he had a brother in a mental home, so be persuaded everyone concerned to keep the affair quiet. That is why the C.I.D. man who made the enquiries for me had heard only as much of the truth as it had been agreed the rest of the world should be told. Of course, when Mr. Dingle learned what had happened, he promptly got through to Scotland Yard, who put him on to me."

Terhune grimaced. "And that's that! We've got to start again from the beginning."

"I'm afraid so, sir. But there's one little point about the third story which we mustn't overlook."

"What is that?"

"You referred just now to the significance of one of the amateur detectives in the story being a writer—who is supposed to be you—also the subject of their deductions being a lunatic—in other words, Max Bullett. I go farther than that. To me the fact that the girl was taken back to a lunatic asylum is also intended to be a clue. A clue that a lunatic asylum is somehow mixed up with the story—as we now know is the case."

"But Mr. Max Bullett doesn't live in an asylum," Julia argued.

"I know he doesn't, Miss MacMunn, but you've got to remember that all the hints and clues in these crazy stories are not inferred directly. One has to read between the lines, rather than the lines themselves. No, to me the significance of the mention of madness in the third story is—how did the author know that we had become suspicious of Max Bullett, and how does he know that Julian Bullett is still in a lunatic asylum, considering the pains Max has taken to hide the existence of his brother?"

"Sorry, Sergeant, but I must disagree with you on the last premise. There is no hint of a brother anywhere in this story. The inference of lunacy may refer only to Max—perhaps the author knows enough about Max to be aware of the fact that his mother died in an asylum."

Murphy reflected, and expressed disappointment. "Perhaps you are right, sir, which is a pity indeed."

"Why?"

"Because I hoped that the author's apparent knowledge of Julian's existence would be a clue to the author's identity, because it would have meant that he was on intimate terms with Max. Anyway, there is still the other point I mentioned. How did the sender of this story know that we had suspected Max Bullett?"

An embarrassed silence followed. "I have not spoken to a soul," Julia murmured.

"Of course you haven't, miss. No more has Mr. Terhune, I'll be bound, except to—"

"Ted Shore?" Terhune suggested.

"That's the man I have in mind."

"He promised not to talk."

"Sure, now, and probably he meant not to. But a drink or so soon loosens a man's tongue. I don't doubt he said a word or two too many;

enough for the man who sent us the story to put two and two together and make four."

"Which means that the writer of the story probably lives at or near Great Hinton and drinks at the *Dusty Miller?*"

"Maybe—maybe," Murphy agreed cautiously.

"Moreover, if Shore would frankly admit having gossiped, and will reveal the names of those to whom he passed on the information, we might have a clue to the writer of the stories?"

The sergeant still looked dubious. "Perhaps," he said; "but for every one who heard it from Shore I'll bet another six people heard it in less than that number of hours."

Terhune could not dispute Murphy's statement; he knew only too well how quickly gossip can spread in a small, rural community.

"All the same, I'll pay another visit to Shore tomorrow morning—"

III

Not altogether to Terhune's surprise, his visit to the *Dusty Miller* proved disappointing, but not for the reason he had anticipated. He had half expected the innkeeper to deny having gossiped, and this Shore did, but with a sincerity which impressed the visitor as being absolutely reliable. Shore swore that he had not spoken to a living soul about either Terhune's visit or its purpose.

Terhune was satisfied that Shore spake nothing less than the truth. He prepared to leave, but another reflection occurred to him—some men, he knew, shared all secrets with their wives, regarding them loyally as part of themselves, as one flesh.

"Nor to Mrs. Shore?" he questioned, with diplomatic casualness.

For a moment Shore's sharp eyes actually twinkled. With a quick, precautionary glance towards the door, and in a lowered voice, he replied: "Least of all to the wife, sir. She's a real good 'un, my missus is, and I wouldn't change her for any other woman in the world, but she is a bit free-like with her tongue. Not that I blames her," he added quickly. "Talking comes natural like to most women. But if I wants to keep a secret, you understand, I just don't say nothing to the old woman."

His expression sharpened unexpectedly. "Come to think on it, though, Mr. Terhune, she did ask me what you were doing of over here in Great Hinton."

"What did you tell her?"

"That you'd come for a drink like everybody else what comes here. Then she says: 'Are you sure it weren't nothing to do with old Peter's death? Mr. Terhune don't usually come here but once in a while. Partic'ly on a Friday, when you'd think he had work to do in that there bookshop of his.'"

Terhune had only seen Mrs. Shore from a distance, and never to speak to. He reflected that she must possess a disconcerting shrewdness.

"What did you say in answer to that?"

The innkeeper laughed confidently. "I told her you'd been over-working, and needed a breath of fresh air to buck you up."

Terhune wondered whether Mrs. Shore had accepted that uncon-vincing lie. He doubted it, if she were as shrewd as he believed. But as Shore, presumably, had not satisfied her curiosity further Terhune failed to see how he could hold her responsible for the leakage of information. Anyway, there seemed little more he could do towards solving that particular mystery, but he remained at the inn a little longer, dropping discreet hints that his previous enquiries with regard to Max Bullett were a mistake. By doing this he half hoped that a whispering echo would eventually reach the ears of the writer of the short stories, who would understand that the latest clue had been understood. He also let Shore know that he was now at a complete standstill—though to be sure he had never, in actual words, admitted that he was investi-gating old Peter's death, and trying to identify him. But he was quite certain that Shore was capable of inferring that much. This admission, he further hoped, if it should ever reach the unknown author, might result in another story—and another clue.

In this respect Terhune later came to the conclusion that he had been too optimistic. Day after day went by without any fresh development taking place. Further spasmodic and indirect enquiries, along the lines of his discussion with Murphy, yielded no results. No more manuscripts arrived further to provoke his curiosity, and irritate Murphy. Just nothing happened, and he began to lose interest in the case as the time for Lady Kylstone's and Helena's departure for the Continent drew closer.

On the Saturday night previous to the Tuesday scheduled for the start of the journey, Terhune dined at Timberlands. Although in the nature of a farewell, the meal was *en famille*—just Lady Kylstone, Helena and Terhune.

As usual the evening began with sherry—the serving of which had become almost a ritual with Lady Kylstone, who had no scruples about admitting her liking for one glass of her favourite Solera. As soon as Terhune had poured out three glasses—Manzanilla for himself—and had settled before a toasting fire his hostess asked, with her customary forthrightness: "Well, Theodore, have you received any more of those funny stories?"

He nodded. "A third one reached me last Thursday week."

"Dear me! And was there still no letter, or hint as to the author's identity?"

"No. Not directly. But the circumstances surrounding the receipt of the story make it very certain that the author lives either in Great Hinton or not far away." Without pause Terhune went on to tell his small audience of everything which had taken place since his last visit to Timberlands.

They listened attentively, but Terhune noted, subconsciously, the difference revealed upon the faces of his small audience. Lady

Kylstone's serene expression scarcely changed throughout; it remained in characteristically sweet repose. Her eyes alone betrayed the uncommonness of his story. Vivid and alert, they alone mirrored an increasing, and not unexcited, interest. The whole of Helena's face, on the other hand, unwittingly supplied a silent obbligato of emotion ranging from breathless interest to disappointment.

"Extraordinary!" Lady Kylstone murmured. And again: "Extraordinary! We have met Max Bullett and his wife, haven't we, Helena, my dear? Let me see, didn't they have a stall at the Rector's garden party?"

"Not a stall, Lady Kylstone, but a bran-tub."

"Ah! yes, of course. I recollect having a dip. My prize was a pack of playing cards. I remember his face more than hers. Isn't he dark complexioned, with a changing expression, and vivid eyes? Too vivid to be stable. Have you never seen him, Theodore?"

He shook his head.

"Had you done so you would have been more than ever convinced that he was the writer of those stories. He is quite exotic. But there, if his brother is still living, Peter the Hermit must have been somebody else. What have you just thought of, Theodore?"

"Just now you described Max Bullett as exotic."

"Well?"

"I believe 'exotic' is the word which has eluded me—I have told you that there is some aspect about the stories which I have been unable to define! Exotic exactly describes them. Perhaps he wrote and sent them to me not with the intention of incriminating himself—as we recently assumed—but the real killer of old Peter."

"Why should he write stories to do that, Tommy?" Helena asked.

"It is hardly to be expected that the insanity which his brother inherited from their mother has completely passed him by. But in his case perhaps the disorder is very slight, and its only effect upon him is to make him exotic—which is more or less a form of eccentricity. The stories may be the result of that eccentricity."

Lady Kylstone nodded. "That theory is more reasonable than the one about the writer of the stories incriminating himself. But if the writer of the stories is not the assumed brother of Peter the Hermit, will you be any nearer to solving the mystery of Peter's identity?"

"If I could definitely establish the identity of the writer the police would probably complete the investigation, Lady Kylstone. They could interview Max Bullett—or whoever the writer is—and demand the source of his information."

Lady Kylstone smiled slightly as she shook her graceful head. "I think you are being too optimistic. From what you have told me of all the circumstances of old Peter's death, and the clues of the short stories, I do not believe that the writer of the stories would give straightforward answers to a police interrogation. I think he would deny that any inference was to be drawn from the stories."

"I think you are right," Terhune agreed gloomily.

Helena looked puzzled. "But couldn't the police force him to answer their questions?"

"Not unless he were put in a witness stand and sworn. Even then they couldn't *force* him to answer, Helena. All that the magistrates or the judge could do would be to commit him to prison for contempt of court. But if no crime had been proved there could be no indictment, no trial in open court, threatening him with contempt of court. To complete the vicious circle, without the evidence which the writer alone appears to possess—with the exception, possibly, of the murderer himself—there can be no evidence of crime, no accused, and no trial."

There was a rather long silence. Presently Lady Kylstone spoke again.

"Are there no other clues, apart from those contained in the short stories, which might lead to identifying that poor old man?"

"There's the jewelled comb, but I should imagine that one would have to go abroad to get that identified—possibly Spain, or one of the Spanish possessions, or one of the South American countries."

"The comb does not sound very helpful."

"Then, of course, there was the old newspaper which Murphy found in the box with the comb."

"Tell me more about the newspaper, Theodore."

"I don't think it is of much more help to us than the comb. It was a Bulgarian newspaper, published in Sofia in the August of nineteen-twenty-three. We cannot even be sure why he kept the newspaper for so many years, unless it was on account of a paragraph which reported the marriage of a Señorita Bázan, daughter of the Spanish Vice-Consul in Marseilles. The reason we picked upon that paragraph is the fact that, for many years previously, Señor Bázan had been on the Spanish Consular staff in Sofia. And the Spanish comb. It is possible that old Peter had once been in love with the Señorita Bázan, who gave him the comb."

"You believe, do you not, Theodore, that when Peter returned to England he searched everywhere for his brother, and finding him in or near Great Hinton, settled down to live the rest of his life in the woods?"

"That is not an absolute conviction, Lady Kylstone."

"Just a highly imaginative notion?"

Terhune grinned. "Yes."

"Has it not occurred to you that it might not have been his *brother* for whom the old man searched, but his former *love*, the ex-Señorita Bázan?"

"Señorita Bázan!"

"She might have married an Englishman, Theodore? Other foreign women have been known to marry Englishmen, and settle down in this country." Lady Kylstone smiled teasingly; born a citizen of the U.S.A., she had herself married an Englishman.

Terhune glanced wryly at his hostess. "I haven't had even a glimmering of that notion," he confessed. "The second story, *Generosity*, must have hypnotized me into a brother complex. Well, I'll be darned! What a fool I've been!"

Behind the tortoiseshell glasses his eyes blinked with an expression more comically youthful than usual. Lady Kylstone's laughter pealed out with a deep bell-like resonance. Helena remained wistful, for the expression reminded her of her first meeting with Terhune, when she had thought of him—but how wrongly!—as a diffident, overgrown rabbit.

"For Heaven's sake don't take it to heart, dear boy! Possibly the story-teller intended deliberately to deceive you. Perhaps Peter never had a brother."

"Then why present us with a clue in one paragraph, and deceive us in the next?" He asked the question with no thought of an answer, and continued dismally: "I wish there were some way of finding out the name of the Señorita's husband."

"There is," Lady Kylstone said briskly. "Apply to the office of the Spanish Vice-Consul in Marseilles. Somebody there might be able to supply the information you want, or turn up past records."

"Do you think notice would be taken of a letter—"

"Letter! Letter! I said nothing about writing a letter, Theodore. I do not believe in letters when personal visits are possible," she continued, her manner challenging argument or opposition. "You can drive, can you not, dear boy?"

"Yes, but—"

She waved a firm, weathered hand. "Then you and Wesley and Gary can take it in turns to drive the Daimler; Gibbons can follow by train." She turned to Helena. "Don't you think it would be fun to have Theodore accompany us as far as Marseilles, my child?"

Helena's eyes shone. "It would be fun," she agreed happily. "But can Tommy manage to come?"

"Manage it! Of course he can," Lady Kylstone exclaimed masterfully. "That young man seems to have a strange aptitude for managing affairs when they have to do with a case of crime. Of course he will come. Or am I wrong for once, Theodore?" she concluded, challengingly.

His beaming face was answer enough.

Chapter Thirteen

With Helena and Gary by his side, Terhune watched the coast of France slowly materialize as the Southern Railway Channel packet thrust forward at a steady speed through a slight swell which did no more than give the passengers the not unpleasant sensation of being aboard a vessel that was joyfully alive, and not merely an inanimate hull.

It was not easy to see clearly, for the sharp east wind which chilled his cheeks and nose also blew behind his tortoiseshell glasses, and misted his eyes with tears that were doubly salted. All the same he leaned his elbows on the rail and stared with excited eyes at the undulating coast, silent and wondering. How would he find France—which he felt he knew so well, not from personal contact, for this was his first visit, but from the countless books he had read and the many conversations he had had with Francophiles? How would he find her and her people after their cruel oppression, their occupation by a hated enemy, their martyrdom? Would he find many of their towns and cities ruined beyond hope? Would he find the inhabitants bitter and resentful towards the people of Albion whose lot during the war had been, despite all trials and tribulations, so incomparably easier? Or would he find the country less devastated than he believed? And find, too, that much of the spirit of the Entente Cordiale still remained?

He had listened to other travellers recounting their experiences and airing their views, but had learned nothing reliable. For the many statements and opinions had cancelled one another out. The Little

Englanders, as usual, found little good to say of a people they could not understand, while the Francophiles were amazed by the warmth of French gratitude towards allies who had helped them to rediscover their own soul.

Soon, he reflected, they would be able to sort facts out for themselves. In a matter of minutes now the packet would be nosing its way into what was left of Calais harbour—or would it enter stern first, perhaps? Anyway, before the striking of another hour they would land on French soil. He was neither prejudiced for nor against the French. He knew they had faults; he had been told about them often enough. At the same time he was not unaware of the faults of his own people. He had listened to bitter words about the British from an American in New York, who had had the misfortune to be cheated out of money, health and happiness by an English girl who had bigamously married him when he was a Doughboy stationed in the Midlands. In consequence the American was sincerely convinced that all English women were diseased and vicious, which Terhune knew to be as false to reality as any other similarly prejudiced generalization applied to a foreign people.

The coastline loomed up, bolder and clearer. He brushed the tears from his eyes. Objects became visible. A skyline. A car streaking along a road inland. A belt of trees. Stretches of brown earth. And nearest of all, grey houses and buildings. The harbour mole and signal-mast.

He did not feel in a mood for conversation. He wondered if Helena and Gary were similarly affected. Gary, he knew, was not on his first visit. Not many years previously he had been fighting on French soil. Helena, too, was not a newcomer to the country. She had frequently travelled in France before the outbreak of war. But she stood between the two men, her gloved hands resting in the crook of their arms, and stared at the harbour with a rapt look in her eyes. Gary's expression was much the same. Yes, he told himself, both his companions were experiencing emotions comparable to his own.

So nearer and nearer, until Helena broke the long silence. "Look!" she exclaimed in an unsteady voice. "Look at the end of the mole. A man fishing! There always has been a man fishing there. I can almost believe he must be the same man." She laughed tremulously. "Do you think it is an omen that France hasn't changed overmuch?"

"I sure hope so, Helena," Gary said at last. "My old Dad used to love visiting France. He used to say that it was the one country in the world where you could be yourself, and do what you darned well wanted without a lot of busybodies interfering."

By now the landing pier was visible. To Terhune's unknowledgeable gaze the scene did not look as though it could have changed very much. There was a long Customs shed to be seen, station buildings, a long, unwieldy French train with a trail of black smoke blowing out to sea from its massive engine—surely the war had passed over this part of Calais? But then he saw something which he had missed at first sight. There was a certain newness, in comparison with others, about parts of the buildings, also parts of the quay, which suggested that some rebuilding and repairs had already had time to assume a slightly weathered appearance.

His gaze travelled to the right, to the town. Much of this, he saw, was still standing, its age plain for all to guess. But there were many gaps, gaps which he felt sure were unnatural, gaps which created the impression of having been building sites. Other buildings were obviously new; their brickwork and paint was garish against the dull blue-grey and sand-brown surroundings of pre-war houses; the style of their architecture was modernistic, in startling contrast to the rest of the town. There was also much building work in progress; he could see three houses in the course of erection, also a warehouse; two others, towards the edge of the harbour area, were undergoing considerable repairs. Through one extensive gap he could see a distant road being relaid.

He looked once more at the quay. A line of blue-smocked porters clustered near a wheeled gangway; two gaitered gendarmes stared incuriously at the travellers above; a light-blue-trousered local *sergent-de-ville* talked with another uniformed man: a railway official, Terhune guessed—the harbour-master maybe, or the stationmaster. A handful of civilians stood by, handkerchiefs or hats waving, according to sex: friends of the travellers, these, without a doubt. There were two or three other civilians, in more formal clothes, with black brief-cases under their arms. More officials, no doubt. A dark-moustached man in the uniform of the A.A. walked in leisurely fashion towards the gang-plank. A fat-bosomed, fat-bellied woman stood just inside the doorway of the men's *urinoirs* and gossiped with a Customs officer. Other Customs officers stood by the entrance to the Customs shed.

Wesley Cruikshank joined the other three. "Nothing's changed, by heck! I last saw Calais nearly ten years ago, but it seems like only yesterday. Same old gendarmes, same old porters, same old Customs men. It doesn't look like war has treated the old place too badly."

"It looks like somebody's done a thundering fine job of work," Gary commented. "It wasn't looking so good when I passed through it, a few months after the German defeat. Though they had made a start even then." He pointed to a building on the far side of the harbour. "That place had a hell of a great hole through it. It looks sound enough now."

Whistles blew; the ship's telegraph rang; the vessel shuddered as the propellers began to churn the black water into yellow spume. By some mystery incomprehensible to the landlubber the packet began slowly to edge broadside on towards the quay. Winches chattered, an electric crane hummed; the porters began to shout. The propellers stopped thrashing; the winches quietened; a slight thud shook the vessel. A pregnant silence followed during which, seemingly without reason, everybody and everything remained motionless and quiet. The next moment, a mild commotion. "*En avant!*" Two gangways appeared to lift themselves into the air and bridge the downward gap between the saloon deck and the quay; twin lines of shouting porters scrambled up them.

"*Porteur! Porteur! Porteur! Porteur, messieurs? Porteur, madame?*"

A babel of voices, noise, commotion, movement—Terhune felt deliriously excited. He could still recollect his arrival in New York. That moment had been an exciting one, too. But this landing was different, somehow. Mysteriously it possessed added delight, not by way of comparison, but in its hint of adventure and romance. It was nice to land in a strange place, like New York, where one could speak one's own tongue knowing that it would be understood and replied to, where one felt comfortably at home. That very sense of 'at-homeness', however, was just enough to rob a visit of that indefinable something which contributes an intoxicating zest to the exploration of the unknown.

Helena squeezed his arm. "Thrilled, Tommy?"

"Immensely."

"So am I," she said ecstatically. "It's wonderful to be able to travel again."

She turned to her other side, and while she talked to Gary, Terhune studied the faces of the French porters and wondered what they were thinking of as they hurried about with large loads of luggage suspended from their shoulders. He could detect nothing from their dark eyes and impersonal expressions. Perhaps they were not consciously thinking. They had a job of work to do, and were doing it. But he suspected that some, at least, were not quite so impersonal as their dark olive faces made out. Were they generous enough to forget that their allies from across the strip of Channel had *not* suffered an enemy occupation for years? Had *not* sweated blood to maintain the imposed costs of the army of occupation? Had *not* near-starved to death while their foreign overlords waxed fat on such good things as France could still produce even in war-time? Could they forget the countless years their million countrymen had rotted in German prison camps, while their British allies had waited, and waited, and waited before launching the final devastating blow? Could they resist the temptation of comparing the rape of their country with the comparative immunity of Britain? Were they even possibly resentful, with outraged pride, that the British Commonwealth had continued the fight, at one time entirely on her own, against incredible odds? Did they resent, too, this influx of travellers which seemingly indicated that the British could still afford to live indolently, to travel luxuriously, to take their ease? In their eyes was every fresh shipload of travellers added evidence that they had fought and suffered and bled in vain because the brave new world was just the same bad old world?

On the other hand, were they as logical as of old, these French porters? Did these strong, sloe-eyed, small-statured men realize that the money which was needed to rebuild France had to come from somewhere, and that it could only come from those few fortunate countries who had some balance left after social service had claimed its lion's share? Did they reflect that the passengers whose luggage was weighing down their shoulders were bringing foreign currency into France, currency which would oil the wheels of French industry? Did they remember that their soldiers had marched and died side by side with Tommies from old Albion, and Doughboys from the States? Did they frankly acknowledge that their own liberation could never have been effected without the help of allies? And were they, when all was said and done, grateful for that help?

Terhune could not make a guess at the truth. The porters were polite, willing, even occasionally cheerful. But their faces were masks which revealed nothing. They had a job of work to do, and they meant to finish it off as soon as possible.

Presently Terhune realized the foolishness of his thoughts. There was no reason to imagine that the porters were thinking along such lines, either pro or con. Many tides had washed in and out of Calais harbour since the bells had rung out the end of war. Many shiploads of passengers had landed at Calais, and gone their separate ways to every part of France and Europe. At first the novelty of resuming the old jobs might have made them ruminate on the immediate past. Besides, take himself and Gary. Had he experienced any feeling of gratitude towards the Americans for having helped to save Europe from German domination? He had not. Had he thought: 'These damned Americans; they still seem to have enough money to globe-trot whenever they feel inclined!' He had not. He had merely reflected—Gary seems a nice chap. Not much of a family resemblance, though, to Lady Kylstone, or Wesley Cruikshank. I wish my shoulders were as broad as his. Some tie and shirt he's wearing. He never bought those in this country.

The passengers aboard thinned out as the luckier ones—who would seize the corner seats in the train—streamed down the gangways, along the quay and into the Customs shed. Lady Kylstone and her companions waited for everyone else to go ashore before themselves following suit. For them there was no immediate hurry; the Daimler had to be unshipped and formalities complied with before they would be free to set out.

The A.A. man stared at them rather anxiously as they descended the gangway; probably he was wondering whether the owners of the car had missed the packet. When he saw Lady Kylstone advancing very obviously in his direction he swept off his hat, and smiled so expansively that his fearsome upturned mustachio threatened to reach his eyes.

"Messieurs, mesdames—it is your automobile which is to be landed, no?"

"It is. Will it take long to complete the business?"

"But certainly not, madame," he replied with decision. "Yours is the only automobile to arrive today, so the Customs officers will hurry it through. *Zut!* It is not like it was ten years ago, when the special packet-boats brought so many there was not enough room on the quay for them all."

"Were you doing this before the war?"

"But yes, madame," he said eagerly. "But I was younger then. *Alors!* now I am an old man."

He wasn't, of course—in the early fifties, probably—so Lady Kylstone accepted the obvious cue. She smiled charmingly. "Nonsense, monsieur. You are many years younger than I, and I do not call myself an old woman."

"I may not be old in years, madame, but in spirit—*Dieu*. The war lasted half a lifetime, and a man has not nine lives, like a cat. I lost my early manhood in one war and became old in another." He became briskly formal. "If madame will give me her papers—"

The man took the documents away. Lady Kylstone turned to her brother and spoke. Gary caught hold of Helena's arm. "Say, Helena, come with me. I want to ask that old chap over there—" The rest of his words were snatched away in the wind. Terhune watched the departing pair, and saw Helena take Gary's arm.

Terhune felt unpleasantly alone.

II

The formalities entailed by the temporary import into France of a foreign-made car were quickly completed. Less than a quarter of an hour after the train for Paris had left the A.A. man informed Lady Kylstone that she was free to depart.

She thanked him for his attention and trouble. This he pocketed with one hand while gracefully declining with the other the necessity of proving it.

"But it was my pleasure, madame, and I wish you a pleasant and easy journey."

"May I hope for just that, monsieur?"

The forthright question shook the Frenchman a little, and he hesitated.

"I want the truth," she added firmly.

He shrugged his shoulders. "How do I know the truth, madame? I have not moved out of the Pas de Calais district since my return from a German prison camp. But I hear talk. We French are not perfect, madame. Some of us find it hard to realize that what has hurt us personally was done for the sake of France."

"By which you mean...?"

"Before the war Jacques Pégaud owned a small garage on the outskirts of Calais. One day it was smashed to ruins by a British bomb. The Government has promised that it shall be rebuilt, but poor Jacques wants to know when. Meanwhile, to keep his family from starvation he drives a *camion* and transports bricks which are being used for more important buildings. But what would you, madame? Then there is Etienne Riondel. While he was a prisoner of war in Germany his wife and child were killed by a British bomb which was aimed at a German ship. There is also Monsieur de Rignon. He owned a small villa near the road to Boulogne. All his money was in the Renault firm, but since the R.A.F. destroyed the Renault works Monsieur de Rignon has received no dividends, and has to live in a small *appartement* near the Pont Saint Pierre."

The man hurried on, anxious to have his say before he could be interrupted. "But there are other Frenchmen, who have suffered equally, madame, but who are grateful to the British and the Americans for having helped to free them from the Boche. An American bomb killed the daughter of Henri Foissac, but Henri will not hear a word against the Allies. Georges Baroché lost a son in one of the Fighting French warships which was helping to defend a British convoy to Russia. But Georges takes off his hat to every Briton he sees in the streets in Calais. And Madame Huygen, who keeps a café in the Boulevard Léon Gambetta, she lost her husband in Hamburg when that town was bombed by the British. *Mais oui*, madame, France is still divided politically into opposing camps. Perhaps one day——" He shook his head dismally, then cheered up. "But me, madame, I like the British. I would like the devil himself if it had been he who had pulled down the barbed wire from that *sacré* German camp, where I was imprisoned for four accursed years. And my son-in-law, he, too, likes the British, because he was in London with General de Gaulle, and he does not forget what the British did for him and his friends."

With the A.A. man standing stiffly to attention, his hand at the salute, the Daimler drove off, with Wesley at the wheel, there on Lady Kylstone's instructions because he was used to right-hand driving. As they bumped over the cobbles, the railway lines, the floating bridges, and entered the town they saw further evidence, both of the tremendous damage which had been inflicted upon the unfortunate town during successive waves of war, and of the equally tremendous efforts which its inhabitants were making to restore what was restorable, and to rebuild at least a small proportion of the buildings which had been smashed to rubble.

They passed across what had once been the Place d'Armes, into the Place Richelieu, and so into the Boulevard Jacquard. The scene was a sad one, and brought mistiness to Lady Kylstone's eyes, although she was normally an unemotional person.

"Even after all these years," she murmured. "And all the hard work—" She stopped abruptly, for no apparent reason.

Terhune looked out for the new, and consequently was less affected by the old. His eyes missed—at any rate consciously—the empty places of which the others were so acutely aware, concentrating instead on the people and, especially, the shops. The wine shops, their windows displaying a greater variety of bottles than he had ever seen before at any one time: bottles of every shape, design, colour and size. Liqueurs, beers, ciders, gaseous lemonades, wines from the Burgundy and Bordeaux districts, from the Côtes du Rhône, Alsace-Lorraine, Anjou.

Many of them he suspected were dummy bottles, there to make the display fuller rather than a truthful advertisement of what was to be purchased within, but nevertheless, the sight was one to make eyes brighten, in the hope that it would not take too many years to fill the dummy bottles with the genuine article.

The *pâtisseries*, too, made his mouth water, though in this instance he was less affected than Helena, who had always adored the light rich creations of the French pastry chef. For all that, his enjoyment was the greater, for it missed the bitter which modified the sweet: he looked at the luscious-looking pastries and saw them as they were at that moment, but Helena could remember what they had once been, and the comparison, like most comparisons, was, if not odious, at least unsatisfactory.

There were the cafés, too, to inspect with interested eyes. One or two had tables outside, but it was a gesture of defiance rather than hope, for none but an Eskimo could have stomached sitting outside while the east wind blew so coldly. Behind the huge, uncurtained windows, however, there were crowded tables and chairs, some occupied by men who drank black coffee from glasses, smoked, talked, played dominoes or cards, read newspapers, or else just *watched*— that most fascinating of all *boulevard* pastimes.

The *épiceries*—the ubiquitous groceries of France—they, too, were a source of delight to him. There were cheeses in variety to be seen —at least, not the actual cheeses, but advertisements and price lists, and what not to titillate the palate. Gruyère—Pont-l'Évêque—Port-Salut—Brie—Camembert… Perhaps they were in very short supply—but they had returned to the world to which they belonged, those cheeses of France, and that knowledge was a joy in itself. Wine vinegars, too, which he scarcely knew existed. Strange cereals of which he had never heard. Salads which he could not recognize.

Yes, indeed! There were sights to warm the cockles of the heart even in ravished Calais. And something else, too. The sight of a man who stared curiously, even enviously, at the big Daimler, then glanced at the registration number plate, and lastly, recognizing its nationality, suddenly saluted. And a rather obvious-looking Frenchman, dressed in the blue smock of the French workman, with blue eyes, unshaven cheeks, carrying a long loaf under one arm and a basket of shopping with the other—this obvious Frenchman calling out familiarly to Wesley, in a voice just as obviously from the New Cut: "Whatcher, mate?"

So to the right along the Boulevard Léon Gambetta, into the Rue de Boulogne, and the outskirts of the town. And here another man looked with envy at the shining automobile, and recognized its nationality. He glanced nervously in all directions and spat. Not such a pleasant sight, this, but he had taken the precaution of ensuring that nobody but the occupants should see him spit at the car. This unconscious little gesture told its own story, and caused more cockles to warm.

So into and through Boulogne, en route for ruined Abbeville and more fortunate Beauvais.

Chapter Fourteen

Lady Kylstone and her companions proceeded southward at a steady but unhurried pace. There was every reason for not speeding. First, to have attempted to keep up a consistently high average would have injured the car, for the road had deteriorated badly during the past decade, and though patches of it had been relaid, and were being relaid where it was most needed, the greater part of the surface was in a bad state and, at speed, would have placed a great strain on the springs. There was, however, a second reason for travelling at a moderate speed: Lady Kylstone's wish to that effect. Apart from a personal dislike for unnecessary speeding, she desired, so she said, to enjoy every minute of a pleasure long deferred.

With the possible exception of Gary, who sometimes chafed at his 'aunt's' speed restriction, the rest of the party were in sympathy with the comparatively slow progress. Superficially the party was an unbalanced one; a mixture of age and youth, of nationalities and customs. In actual fact no other five such dissimilar people could have combined together more happily. Lady Kylstone and Wesley seemed never to tire of each other's company—it was a surprise to Terhune to realize that brother and sister were on such affectionate terms. Besides, they had so much to talk about, having been parted for several years.

Helena and Gary, too, seemed to have much in common. Two young people only half their ages could scarcely have chattered more, or have been more light-hearted. Indeed, Lady Kylstone had frequently to scold them good-naturedly whenever she wanted a little peace and quietness for a change—which was usually between two and four o'clock in the afternoon!

This unconscious, and certainly unintentional, pairing left Terhune, to some extent, odd-man-out. He did not mind—he was probably no more aware of what was happening than the others—because his was, to some extent, a solitary nature. He was always content with his own company. At Bray he lived by himself. When he rambled through the surrounding country during his free hours, more often than not he went unaccompanied. Indoors he could always occupy himself with books, sometimes reading them, sometimes writing them, sometimes just handling them in the course of his business. Out of doors his chief preoccupation was observation and reflection. He loved Nature in all her moods, and loved, equally, her living subjects. Trees, birds, insects, all were an open book to him, a book which he read and reread with ever increasing pleasure. As for reflection, his being a quiet, studious nature, he was never at a loss for a subject on which to ruminate. Except himself! He was too healthy in mind and body to indulge in dangerous introspection.

So he was in no way troubled to find himself somewhat apart from the domestic intimacy of brother and sister, and the joyous inconsequence of Helena and Gary. These intervals of mental isolation gave him the opportunity of leaning back and enjoying the sight and sound and smell of the country through which they were passing. After two days of this pleasure he began to appreciate, for the first time, something of Julia's passionate longing to travel. He had always maintained, quite truthfully, that he had no desire to travel; that he was happy to live at Bray—rusticating in a forgotten corner of the world, as Julia had scornfully described his manner of living—and would be quite content never to move far away from there. It was this state of mind which had made him look upon Julia's restlessness merely as an outlet for a discontented nature.

Now he began to see how wrong he had been. How narrow-minded and prejudiced. Although he remained convinced that Bray was still the one place for a permanent residence, yet there was certainly a fascination to be obtained from actual travel which no books on the subject could possibly supply.

Another curious result of this odd-man-out situation—besides his better understanding of Julia's extraordinary mentality—was the greater amount of driving he did than the other two men of the party. This was entirely his own fault, and, be it said, his own desire, for he had found that, by occupying himself at the driving-wheel, it was both easier to observe the country and to ruminate. At first Wesley and Gary had protested, believing that Terhune merely wanted to do more than his share of work because he was embarrassed by not being one of the family, as it were. But Lady Kylstone, having watched him with understanding eyes, insisted upon Terhune's being allowed to do as he wished. Perhaps she was curious to watch his reactions to the growing friendship between Helena and Gary.

Thanks to their leisurely rate of progress, Terhune had good opportunities of studying France and her people. During the two days of their journey they were made very conscious of the effects of war, this despite the valiant efforts of the people to repair the damage. Abbeville, where Lady Kylstone had slept on several occasions, was little better than a ghost town. Nearly all the rubble of ruined and destroyed buildings had long since been carted away, but the gaps thus left were mute reminders of the holocaust which had overtaken the sleepy, inoffensive town. Those of the pre-war era which remained stood out in stark and pathetic loneliness, often among new buildings which flaunted their newness with the scorn and arrogance of young brides in wedding finery at finding themselves set down among a company of toothless, senile nonagenarians.

Some towns had suffered less, and many of the scars were hidden from the casual passer-through. But there was other grim evidence to be seen far away from towns and villages: the bombed aeroplane hangars and buildings of temporary airfields. The fields themselves were no longer visible, for the land had been returned to the farmers and quickly ploughed up, but the ruined structures remained until such time as more important work eased off. Then there were the few houses here and there which had been only partially destroyed, and which had since been repaired, but now, half old and half new, resembled grim-looking jesters.

There were ruined bridges cheek by jowl with temporary structures of steel, or pontoon bridges. Some roadside fields still sheltered the smashed or burned-out hulk of a tank, or an armoured vehicle, or a transport lorry. Other fields held ruined hutments; others, rusty, battered cannon; still others, temporary cemeteries with their neat rows of short, wooden crosses. In one field there was evidence of clearance; a mounted crane was bodily hoisting a smashed field-gun into a six-wheeled lorry. Some twenty kilometres farther on a vast area had been converted into a huge dump for damaged machines of war. Here a number of men were at work separating into component parts cannon, vehicles, equipment of all kinds and of many origins.

As they progressed southwards, the signs of war grew less until they became the exception instead of the rule, and all save Terhune felt that they were back again in the France of old. Only the people were changed. Where once their weathered faces had expressed the serene indifference of ageless peasantry, now they were grim with determination and anxiety; determination to restore their country to its former status and stability, but anxiety about the future—an anxiety which, Terhune felt, would take a generation to disperse.

So, after several happy days, to Marseilles, and a parting of the ways; Terhune to the Hôtel de l'Oasis, the rest to Cannes.

II

Terhune's French was of *la-plume-de-ma-tante* variety, but it sufficed to carry him into the office of the Spanish Vice-Consul, and to start him talking with the official concerned. He then quickly discovered that the Vice-Consul knew some English.

Terhune began in French. "*Bonjour, monsieur.*"

The Spaniard scrutinized his visitor with the frankness of the Continent. "*Bonjour, monsieur. Vous êles Anglais, non?*"

Terhune nodded.

"*Bueno! Bueno!* I speak the English, too, señor. What can I do you for?"

Terhune had to hold himself in rigid control. Fancy that old joke making a genuine reappearance! Or was it genuine unconscious humour, and not just a wisecrack? He stared back at the Vice-Consul, but there was no sign of mischief in the dark eyes.

"I have come to Marseilles on a rather curious errand, monsieur—er—señor." He paused. "Can you read English?"

The answer came pat, in a flurry of French, Spanish and English. "*Mais oui, certainement. Leo los periódicos ingleses todos los Domingos. Si! Si!* All the Sundays I read the English newspapers. I like to read about your Everton footer team; *mi hermano*—my brother, he play the footer for Everton team first eleven. *Zut! Quel homme celui-là!* What a man! He does everything, as you say, under the sun, *si!*"

Terhune passed a slip of paper over to the Spaniard. "Can you read this, señor?"

Señor Prieto took from the desk before him a pair of rimless spectacles, which he carefully adjusted on the bridge of his nose, and to a muttered commentary in three languages began to read.

"*Si! Si!* I read it *fácilmente*. It is from a newspaper *publié*—published in Sofia, on the 21st of August, nineteen-twenty-three. Our correspondent in Marseilles reports the marriage of Señorita Francisca, daughter of Pedro Bázan, Spanish Vice-Consul in Marseilles—*ah comprendo! Comprendo!* Señor Bázan? Señor Bázan. I have heard the name. *Mais certainement.* I know it. *Mais oui, certainement!* The many friends in Sofia of el Señor Bázan and his beautiful daughter will remember that he was a member of the Spanish Consulate Staff in Sofia from nineteen-thirteen to nineteen-twenty-two. It is rumoured here in Marseilles that Señor Bázan is to be promoted again, and may soon be leaving for Sout' America. *C'est trés, trés intéressant!*"

The Vice-Consul looked up from the paper. "Well, señor?"

"I am particularly anxious to trace the whereabouts of Señor Bázan's daughter."

"The—the—what said you—ware—wareaboots? *No comprendo, señor.* I do not you understand."

"The present address of the señorita."

"Ah! *Perdóneme. Si! Si!* The address!" He shrugged. "But I do not know it, señor. Señor Bázan has not lived in Marseilles *depuis vingt-quatre ans*—for more than four-and-twenty years."

Terhune was disappointed. "I thought you recognized the name."

"But yes, indeed, señor. I recognize the name because of it I have heard now and again, no! But I have never met him. He did never return to Europe from Sout' America. He went as Consul to Montevideo, in Uruguay, and in some years coming, to Mexico, where he die, eight, ten years ago."

"I suppose you have no records which you could turn up, señor?" Terhune suggested.

"Records!" Señor Prieto laughed boisterously. "Not of marriages, señor, and I should not know where to look for them. But I have an idea." He gesticulated flamboyantly. "She is *buena*, my idea."

"And that—"

"Perhaps *le bureau du journal du pays*—*Le Petit Marseillais*—you know it, señor?"

Terhune didn't, but he nodded. That was probably the simpler course, he thought, and why in Heaven's name hadn't the idea of consulting the files of a local newspaper occurred to him long before this moment?

Then suddenly the Vice-Consul bent his head. "*Peste! Je suis fou!* I am fool! I am idiot! I am nincompoop! The concierge! He might know. He has been concierge of this building these forty years. Ah, señor! If anyone can tell you it is he. Albert, *le méchant*, knows all secrets. You must ask him about the beautiful Señorita Bázan, and only if of her he can nothing tell you, then must you go to the newspaper bureau and enquire."

Albert sounded worth trying, so having thanked Señor Prieto for his trouble Terhune returned to the ground floor and tapped on the concierge's door. Albert was within, and if Terhune had been told that the old man had been there twice forty years the fact would not have astonished him. Albert was round-shouldered, thin-haired, wrinkled, and tight-gummed. But he was still belligerent.

"Yes, monsieur?" he demanded, as if resentful of being disturbed in mid-morning.

Albert was a little deaf. That is what *he* said. In actual fact he was a whole lot deaf. Between that affliction and Terhune's uncertain French (Albert could not speak English) a situation was produced which needed exquisite patience at best, and was fraught with potential disaster at worst. Fortunately Terhune had patience, even if the old porter hadn't, and at last understanding dawned.

"Mademoiselle Francisca Bázan? Ho! But yes, monsieur, I remember her. Little Franci, we called her. She was so *petite*, you understand. And merry! She used to call me Uncle Albert." He shook his head, mumbling words to himself which Terhune was unable to interpret. Then: "It's a long time ago, monsieur, and I am an old man. Too old, some say, to be still working. But what else is there for me to do but work? My wife is dead. My children are dead. My friends are dead. Soon I shall be dead, but meanwhile…" And once again he lapsed into unintelligible mumbling.

"Do you remember her marriage?"

The skull-like head nodded several times. "Yes, monsieur. I have not forgotten poor little Franci's marriage. She did not want to marry the man who took her away from her father. She was in love with another man. She used to talk to me about him. He was so handsome, she told me. So brave and dashing and attractive."

"Who was the man she was in love with? Did she ever tell you that?" Terhune asked eagerly.

"Who was the man?" Having repeated these four words, Albert was so long silent that Terhune began to fear that the concierge had fallen asleep. He held on to his patience as long as he could, but at last he opened his mouth to prompt Albert. At that moment Albert came to life again.

"He was an Englishman, monsieur, like yourself, but I cannot remember his name. I never was good at remembering names. My poor wife—the good God rest her soul!—said to me once: 'One of these days, Albert, you will forget your own name. Then you will forget to come home and I shall have to find another husband!'" His bowed shoulders shook; his breath whistled through his shrunken lips. "She was always one for a laugh, poor Marie."

"This Englishman mademoiselle was in love with, why did she not marry him?"

"Ah, ha, monsieur! That's a long story, but I will tell it to you. This sweetheart of hers had been left behind in another country—"

"In Sofia?"

"Sofia! I have never heard of that country, monsieur."

"It's a city; the capital city of Bulgaria."

Albert shrugged his shoulders. He was not in the least interested. "Who can say, monsieur? I am not good at remembering names. Once my poor wife—the good God rest her soul!—said to me—but I have already told you what she said." His expression became vacant. "What was I saying, monsieur? I have forgotten."

"The man whom Mademoiselle Francisca loved—he came from another country—"

"Yes. She had promised to marry him. He told her that he would make a fortune soon, and follow her to Marseilles." He cackled with laughter. "He came—five—no, six years too late. But not too late for the message which I had to give him."

"From Mademoiselle Francisca?"

Again the old man cackled. "No, monsieur. From the husband. He gave me a hundred francs and said to me: 'If ever Franci's sweetheart comes to Marseilles, old man, tell him that his precious Franci has married—'" Albert paused, and Terhune's spirits drooped, fearing that the concierge's memory had failed again. But he was wrong; this time Albert had paused for the sake of dramatic effect.

"For once I remember the name, monsieur. It is the only name I have ever remembered in my life. My dear wife, God bless her, used to be afraid I should one day forget my own name. But I remembered the name of the man Franci married. It is strange, is it not, what a hundred francs can do to one's memory?"

It occurred to Terhune that Albert's last remark was highly significant. A hundred-franc note changed hands.

"A thousand thanks, monsieur, a thousand thanks. (Terhune was amused to notice that the concierge hadn't limited his thanks to a hundred!) The name of the man Franci married was—Alec."

"Alec—"

"But yes, monsieur, Alec."

"Alec what?"

"I do not understand, monsieur. Just Alec."

"Alec is a Christian name. Like Albert, or Jules, or Henri."

The familiar shrug greeted this explanation. "What would you, monsieur! Perhaps Franci's sweetheart only knew the Christian name of Franci's husband."

A significant remark, that. "Then the sweetheart knew the husband?"

"But certainly, monsieur. From being very sad he turned angry. *Zut!* I have never seen a man more angry. Then he went away."

"And next?"

"That is all. I have never seen him, or Franci, or Franci's husband, or Monsieur Bázan, again."

"Do you know why Franci married the man named Alec instead of waiting for her sweetheart to reach Marseilles?"

The old head nodded. "Yes, monsieur. Franci told me. When Monsieur Alec arrived in Marseilles he told Monsieur Bázan that Franci's sweetheart was not good enough to marry Franci. Monsieur Bázan believed him, and agreed to his daughter marrying Monsieur Alec instead of her sweetheart."

Terhune continued to question the old concierge, but without gaining any further information of any value. So he left Albert and proceeded to the offices of *Le Petit Marseillais*. There, after a patience-trying interview, and a long search through yellowing files, he came across the information he wanted.

On the 1st of August, 1923, Francisca Bázan had married Alexander Crawshay, of 33, Falkirk Road, Hampstead Heath, London.

I I I

Within an hour of Terhune's return to Bray, Murphy arrived, thin-lipped and angry.

"Look!" he exclaimed loudly, after a most perfunctory enquiry about Terhune's well-being. "Sent to *me* this time!"

He drew a long, familiar-looking envelope from his pocket and flung it down on Terhune's desk. "If ever I lay my hands upon that crazy devil—"

Terhune withdrew the script from the envelope. It was shorter than the others, only four and a half quarto pages, and was titled:

THE BEST LAID SCHEMES...

He left the irate detective to help himself to cigarettes and a whisky-and-soda, and settled down to read the fourth 'Trail to Tyburn'.

Chapter Fifteen

B oth men had pleasant open countenances, yes one was a notorious jewel thief, known to his associates as 'Diamanté', the other was Pierre Sichel, absconding clerk.

They had no secrets from each other, had these two men, for they had shared the love of the same woman. Now both were in the famous Orient Express: Diamanté was en route to Belgrade to receive a packet of jewels which he hoped to smuggle into the United States; Pierre Sichel was on his way to Athens, there to live the remainder of his life in ease and luxury.

He did not mind boasting of his future. "Think of it, *mon ami*; I am free for the rest of my life: no more work, no more drudgery, the sun, wine, laughter and love—that's my future."

"You are young to be so lucky—not yet thirty, I believe?"

"Twenty-seven."

"Twenty-seven! And the rest of your life before you! Come, come! You must tell your old friend your secret, your touchstone."

Sichel was nothing loth. "It really all started soon after I had completed my military service, when it became necessary for me to look for work. After nearly starving to death because my family would not assist me, I joined the staff of Bossuet et Cie, bankers, merchants, and insurance brokers. Do I need to tell you that that first year was hell; for do not you, better than anyone, know the free life I had been leading before I was conscripted?"

Diamanté grinned. "I do indeed, *mon vieux*!"

"Well, anyhow, I hated my employers, I hated the staff, I hated the work, I hated rising so early in the morning, I hated the vile journey in the Metro each day, for the office was near the Rue de Rivoli, and I was living in the Buttes-Chaumont district. Most of all I hated the sight of the *sacré* office, where I worked from eight to six, with figures and more figures all day long, until I was sick of the everlasting sight of them."

Diamanté smiled salaciously. "You always did prefer the other kind of figures."

Pierre's eyes sparkled with memories, but he went on: "I remained at the *sacré* office because, from the first, I had a plan in my mind: I went to an office because it was all part of that plan. I remained patient, and later my patience was rewarded. Five years after I had joined the staff I was promoted. I became cashier, and instead of juggling with figures I handled money instead: hundreds of thousands of francs weekly."

"*Mordieu!* If my hands had handled so much money I should have made sure that some of it stuck to my fingers," Diamanté ejaculated.

"*Mais oui!* That is just what you would have done, my stupid one! You were always a short-sighted ass. You would have taken a few thousands of francs and bolted. Then you would have been arrested and sent to the *bague* for five years or more. But I used my brains."

"Go on, then, tell me what happened."

"For the next two years I lay low: you see, Diamanté, I knew that if I did the thing properly I could get away with as much as a quarter of a million francs."

Diamanté whistled. "*Merde!* You had big ideas, my friend. If you got away with that much I give you best in the matter of brains."

"Wait until I have finished. I have more to tell you. I worked out an absolutely infallible plan! I waited until the annual audit was over, and then I began to put my plan into action. Week by week I abstracted money, which I sent straight away to a branch of the Peloponnesian National Bank in Athens, in the name of Robert Léguyer."

"How did you do that without being found out?"

"Never mind how. The means do not matter. Only the result. By the end of the financial year I had managed to transfer more than half a million francs to the Peloponnesian National Bank."

Diamanté gazed in amazement at his friend. "You have all the luck! Do you mean to tell me that, as soon as you get to Athens, you will have all that money to yourself?" Sichel nodded. "But supposing you are traced?"

"No fear of that, *mon vieux*! I have taken all my precautions. While I was on my summer vacation last year I shaved off my moustache and had a passport photograph taken, but by the time I was back in the office my thick moustache had grown again, so I forged references and secured a passport in the name of Robert Léguyer."

"You were undoubtedly cunning."

"Naturally. Later I made a collection of U.S.A. immigration propaganda, which I hurriedly and partly burned at the last moment. I also half burned one or two credit slips from an American bank to give the impression that I might have transferred money to New York. Which I did indeed do—but not too much. Next I booked a third-class passage by an English ship, under a third name and with a second passport."

"*Tonnerre de Dieu!*" Diamanté muttered admiringly.

"A few days ago everything was ready. That night I caught the boat train to Le Havre, and with my luggage I actually boarded the ship, was shown to my cabin, spoke to as many people as I could, and then, shaving off my moustache, and changing my clothes, I left the ship as a visitor, two minutes before the boat sailed."

"Pretty smart work," Diamanté complimented. "As you say, infallible. You guessed that the *Sûreté. Générale* would be on your track, realized that they would track you to the ship, and after that presumably all trace of you would be lost. You hoped that your disappearance might be put down to accident or suicide?"

"Exactly. Anyway, having got back to Paris, I took a taxi to the Gare de l'Est—and here I am, on my way to Greece."

*

Later, 'Robert Léguyer' arrived in Athens. Everything was strange to him, but he scarcely noticed. For the rest of his life he was free—ample time to get used to a new country.

He sought out an interpreter, and engaged him for the rest of the day. The first thing he did was to make the man call a taxi, which he directed to the Peloponnesian National Bank. Soon they arrived at the handsome building: it was surrounded by an excited, gesticulating crowd.

"What's the matter?" Sichel asked the interpreter.

"I do not know, but I will find out." The interpreter grinned. "Perhaps it is the beginning of another revolution." He left the taxi and mingled with the crowd. Presently he returned.

"Not so bad as I thought," he offered casually. "Something to do with the manager of the bank. Apparently he absconded with the bank's money, so that it has had to close up for good—but what is wrong, sir?" he asked, suddenly alarmed.

Sichel did not reply: he had quietly fainted.

I I

"When did you receive this script, Sergeant?"

"Three days ago."

"There was still no letter with it, of course?"

The detective grinned his reply to this question. At least, if an expression which closely resembled a canine snarl could rightly be termed a grin. Anyway, Terhune understood its inference well enough. His eyes twinkled.

"Of course not!" he slipped in hastily, before Murphy could speak. "But the fact of its being sent to you is proof of one certainty, at least— that the sender is taking care to keep abreast with events."

"Sure, he is that." The sergeant leaned forward; a sly look of suppressed triumph glowed in his eyes. "It wasn't only on account of you having gone abroad which caused the author to send me this particular story."

"Indeed?"

"No, sir, it wasn't. The spalpeen had another good reason for sending it to me."

Terhune played up to the obviously jubilant detective. "What was the other reason?"

Murphy leaned back, contentedly. "May I smoke my old pipe, Mr. Terhune?"

"Go ahead."

The pipe was soon erupting puffs of fragrant smoke. "Before I answer your question, Mr. Terhune, would you like to tell me what you make of the story?"

"Of course, but frankly. I am a little worried."

"Why?"

"The clue in this story seems too obvious to be true."

A wry expression on the sergeant's face warned Terhune that he had said something in the nature of a *faux pas*, but as it was too late to retract he did not aggravate the mistake by trying to explain it.

"What do you reckon the clue is?"

"The reason for Pierre's—or old Peter's, if you like—being in Europe. He fled to Europe to escape being sent to prison for embezzlement."

"That's what I took the meaning of the story to be. And that answer does more than give a reason why Peter went to Europe: it darned well explains why the old man kept his identity a secret, and why he didn't apply for an old-age pension, and so on. He didn't want to be asked awkward questions because he knew there was a warrant out for his arrest, and that if the police got to hear of his real identity he would be sent to jail as sure as God made little apples."

Terhune began to appreciate the meaning behind the sergeant's earlier remarks. "So the writer sent the story to you instead of to me because he reckoned you were in a better position to put a real name to the man Pierre Sichel?"

"Sure! Sure! And bedad he was ruddy well right!"

Terhune started. "Does that mean you have discovered Peter's identity?"

The sergeant smiled all over his homely, unhandsome face. He was very pleased with himself. "It does that, sir, though, glory be to God, why he didn't send this story first instead of last, it's not me that can be knowing. It would have saved me a few headaches, and you a few whiskies, to say nothing of a journey all the way down to the South of France."

"In that case I'm glad he didn't send it first."

"That means you've enjoyed the trip, if I'm knowing anything?"

"Immensely."

Murphy was too full of his own news to be genuinely interested in Terhune's. "To get back to the story, Mr. Terhune," he hurried on. "The first time I read it I didn't see much more in it than you did, so I read it through again. Then suddenly something clicked in me memory. I suppose you don't remember the Chetwynd Private Bank—you weren't born then."

"I've read about it, Sergeant."

"I don't doubt you have. Well, I'll take my davy that old Peter was indirectly responsible for that crash."

Terhune whistled. "Have you established that he was employed at the bank?"

"Not absolutely, sir. But it is my own belief that Old Peter was a cashier at the Liverpool office of Brandreth, Foster and Co., East India merchants. I don't know whether you know anything about the old-time East India merchant companies, but they used to have fingers in half a dozen pies, and carry on umpteen different types of business—shippers and ship-owners, cotton-mill-and mine-owners in India and Burma, financiers—they even owned vineyards in Spain and Portugal from which they imported sherry and port. I'll bet you've drunk Brandreth's Sherry in your time?"

Terhune nodded.

"Well, old Peter became an employee in the firm, just like the Pierre of the story, and after a few years was promoted to a cashier's job. He determined to embezzle some of the money which passed through his hands, and made his plans. The cashier, whom I believe was Old Peter, got away with the money, right enough—more than thirty thousand pounds, and promptly vanished into thin air."

"Thirty thousand! Phew!"

"A tidy sum, especially in those days, when the Government only asked for a few coppers in the pound, and money would really buy things. Anyway, a story of the embezzlement appeared in the Press. Not that much was printed at that time, because there was something else to occupy the headlines. One of those damned international incidents; Agadir, or Fashoda, or something of the sort. Still, there was enough in the papers to make one of the shareholders of Brandreth, Foster and Co. wonder what kind of book-keeping system the firm employed, which enabled a cashier to embezzle thirty thousand pounds.

"At the next general meeting of the company this shareholder—his name was John Meredith—raised Cain, and demanded that another firm of auditors should be appointed to reorganize the book-keeping system. The directors did their damnedest to defeat the resolution, but for once in a lifetime the shareholders got their own way, and new auditors were appointed.

"That was the beginning of the end. Before long the new auditors began to smell a rat. Their investigations became really searching. Then the truth came out. Brandreth, Foster and Co. were as rotten as a maggoty apple, with liabilities equal to half the National Debt, and assets not sufficient to buy a meal for an abstemious beggar. Apparently they had been carrying on like that for years, becoming more and more involved as time passed."

"How did they manage to carry on so long?"

"Ah! That is where the Chetwynd Private Bank comes into the picture, Mr. Terhune. It came out that both firms were controlled by Hiram Brandt, who was a naturalized Englishman with a German father and an American mother. He was one of those financial geniuses who can juggle with accounts until hell freezes. I don't know the exact details of the transactions, or precisely how they were manipulated, but the main point is that the bank had been 'carrying' Brandreths for some time past—by discounting ninety days drafts, advancing cash against bills of lading, and so on.

"You can guess what happened next. An investigation of the bank's affairs followed, and it was found to be as rotten as Brandreth's. A large part of their clients' money had gone to bolstering up Brandreth's. Naturally, as soon as certain facts leaked out there was a run on the bank. In next to no time it closed its doors for good.

"Both firms were unlimited. As a consequence hundreds of shareholders were ruined. Four or five of them committed suicide. But the after-effects didn't stop at that. Several other firms crashed through being involved in the affairs of Brandreth's or the bank. More people were ruined. Three more committed suicide. Altogether it took nearly three years for the ripples caused by the crash to die away. And all this, mind you, came about as a direct consequence of old Peter stealing thirty thousand pounds. The newspapers made the most of that fact, as you can well guess. For weeks on end not a day went by but what his name wasn't to be found in most of the morning and evening newspapers. You know the kind of nonsense I mean: 'The Man Who Brought About the Bank Crash', 'One Man Ruins Thousands', and so on. His crime and disappearance were a sensation. I'll bet my last shirt that his death would have caused a second sensation if it had been known that old Peter was really Wilfred Crawshay Foulis, the embezzler."

"Was—*who*?"

"Wilfred Crawshay Foulis! Do you remember the name?"

Terhune answered indirectly. "The name of Crawshay is familiar. Alexander Crawshay was the name of the man who married Francisca Bázan," he told Murphy.

III

The sergeant was more pleased than surprised. "That's right! Alexander Crawshay was Wilfred's youngest brother. There was a third brother, Sydney Crawshay—Crawshay was the mother's maiden name. Sydney emigrated to Australia forty years ago, soon after the bank crash."

"You've made enquiries about the family?"

"I've made a few telephone calls, and everything tallies up to old Peter being Wilfred. This is what I have learned. All three boys were born in Liverpool, the sons of a grocer who had worked up a very nice business there. The eldest son, Wilfred, was born in eighteen-seventy-seven. The next, Sydney, was born five years later, in 'eighty-two; and Alexander, the youngest, in 'ninety-four.

"The two elder sons grew up as two quite ordinary young men, except that both had a wild streak in them which revealed itself every now and again by their getting into scrapes from which their poor old Dad had to rescue them. Wilfred, in particular, had extravagant tastes, and was a spendthrift. As soon as he had finished school his father put him to work in the shop, but a few years of having to keep the boy in check was enough for Father. He approached one of his best customers, whose brother had an important position in the Chetwynd Private Bank, to find young Wilfred a job. The customer promised to do what he could, and later was able to tell Father that Brandreth's had a vacancy. So Father put young Wilf into the job at Brandreth's, with what result you know, while Sydney took his place in the shop, where he worked, for the most part, satisfactorily, except for an occasional 'drunk', and making love to girls, one of whom he got into trouble, but didn't marry because he was only seventeen and she was twenty.

"During the next few years Alec's parents had the satisfaction of seeing their youngest child growing up to be entirely different from his elder brothers. He was quiet and studious, and from quite an early age showed a determination to pursue a career in—" Murphy paused, his eyes twinkled with interrogation. "Can you guess?"

"Medicine?"

Murphy nodded. "Medicine it was, so your guess was right. Well, by this time Father Foulis was doing quite nicely, thank you, so he promised to do his share in helping young Alec to achieve his ambition. He paid for Alec to have special tutoring so that he could pass the entrance examination into a good-class public school. Alec passed the exam with flying colours, was accepted as a pupil, and began there in the autumn of nineteen hundred and seven.

"That was the situation when Wilfred vanished with thirty thousand jimmy-o'-goblins. I've told you how the ripples caused by that splash travelled far and wide. One of the ripples—and it wasn't the smallest by any means—washed into the neighbourhood where the father Foulis had his shop. To begin with, it so happened that Foulis had always banked with a local branch of the Chetwynd Private Bank, so he lost every penny of his reserve capital. Unfortunately, that wasn't the worst of his troubles. Many of his customers also lost all their money in the crash, including the rich customer whose brother had got Wilfred the job in Brandreth's. He lost the brother, too, for he committed suicide.

"I don't wish to make the story too long, Mr. Terhune, but the upshot of all this to-do was that the once-rich customer unjustly held the elder Foulis to be the indirect cause of his ruin, and determined to see that Foulis should suffer for having fathered such a son. As some of the other customers who had also lost money as a result of the crash felt much the same, and as there were others who wouldn't be seen going into a shop owned by the father of a now notorious thief, it wasn't long before Foulis realized that he would have to face ruination if he tried to carry on business at the same old shop.

"He hadn't the courage to start a new life. He raised what capital he could, paid Sydney's fare out to Australia, paid two years' schooling for Alec in advance, and then left the gas on when he and his wife went to bed.

"That left Alec on his own. According to what I was told over the telephone by a Chief Inspector who, when he was a lad, lived in the neighbourhood where the Foulises had their shop, and was friends with Sydney, Alec determined to work hard during the two years the school fees had been paid for in the hope of winning a scholarship." Murphy shook his head commiseratingly. "Poor little devil! He didn't have a dog's chance! It didn't take the young savages in the same school long to find out that Alec's brother was the notorious Wilfred Foulis, and that his father had committed murder and suicide—which was the verdict of the coroner's inquest. Add to this the fact that the Headmaster had lost money in consequence of the bank crash, and that several of the boys' fathers had likewise suffered, and you can guess what sort of a life young Alec was forced to lead.

"He didn't stick it out. One day he was missing from school. From that day to this he has never been heard of again. One woman in Blackpool was sure she had seen a boy resembling him walking along the front just before dusk, but she was the only one. When no other trace of him was ever reported the Lancashire police came to the conclusion that he had followed his father's example, and committed suicide by swimming out to sea and drowning. But now..." Murphy tapped some charred tobacco out of his pipe. "Well, everything points to Alec Foulis being alive, and living not a hundred miles from Great Hinton."

Terhune nodded reflectively. "The theory sounds feasible," he agreed. "I wonder how far it agrees with the facts of the case as we know them. Let's take Wilfred first. After he had robbed Brandreth's of thirty thousand pounds or so he vanished, and was never subsequently picked up by the police. The chances are that he left the country for some safer part of the world. Perhaps even Greece, as suggested in the latest story."

Murphy broke in excitedly. "I was going to bring that point up, Mr. Terhune. By a bit of a coincidence, one of the banks in Athens crashed about the time Wilfred Foulis disappeared. The chances are, I should say, that that part of the story is approximately true to the real thing." He chuckled grimly. "I wonder what his feelings were when he discovered that he was just as poor as he had ever been. Fancy having spent years planning to rob a firm of thirty thousand pounds so that you could live the rest of your life without working, and then having the money disappear overnight! Bedad! If ever a man was paid out in his own coin Wilfred Foulis was—if that story is true."

"Suppose we assume that it is true. What happened to Wilfred when he found his money gone? He couldn't return to England unless he was willing to serve a sentence for his crime. There was only one obvious course for him to take: start life afresh, as both his brothers were apparently doing. In normal circumstances I presume he would have made his way to one of the English-speaking countries, but this he daren't do, so he probably decided to stay where he was, and scratch a living as best he could.

"Probably we shall never know what happened to him during the next ten years or so, but it seems safe to assume that he eventually arrived in Sofia, where he met Francisca Bázan. They apparently fell in love with each other, and as a token of their love Francisca gave him the Spanish comb—" Terhune paused. "I wonder!" he exclaimed presently.

"What, sir?"

"It's just an idea, Sergeant, which may or may not be true. In the light of what we know now, that Wilfred hadn't any moral scruples,

I wonder whether he stole the comb with the intention of giving it to his Franci. Or, for that matter, he might have saved up enough money to buy it as a present for her. Whatever the facts of the comb may be, however, it seems that the romance was interrupted by Bázan's promotion, and orders to proceed to Marseilles.

"The family moved to Marseilles, presumably leaving Wilfred in Sofia. And then—" Terhune paused in doubt. "It's not much use our making a guess what happened next, because we have nothing upon which to base any supposition. In what circumstances did Alec meet Francisca? How did he know that the man Francisca was in love with was his brother Wilfred? You see, Sergeant, if the latest story is to be believed, Wilfred was living under another name. In any case, that was the most likely thing for him to have done. Alec, too, was living under the assumed name of Crawshay. So, one way and another, there are a number of gaps in the story which need filling in."

"What made Alec marry the Spanish girl—and how did he persuade her to marry him instead of Wilfred?"

"Exactly! I can make a guess at those questions, Sergeant. I think it quite possible that Alec married Franci to spite his brother. Isn't it likely that Alec hated Wilfred for the harm he had done to Alec? I am prepared to go further, and say that that hate persisted until the day of Wilfred's death. Alec hated his brother Wilfred for having ruined his possible career as a doctor. That is why he did nothing to stop his brother living the life of a starving tramp for ten years. And why he had no conscience about murdering that brother."

"That's a reasonable-enough assumption, sir. But what made the wench give up one brother to marry the other?"

"Perhaps Alec went to Señor Bázan and told him the truth about Wilfred's embezzlement. That would have been enough to make any self-respecting father refuse his consent."

"Would the father have been any keener on his daughter marrying the criminal's brother?"

"No," Terhune agreed. "I am sure he would not. But don't forget that Alec was masquerading under the name of Crawshay—possibly he kept his relationship to Wilfred a secret."

Murphy nodded agreement with this theory. "But why should the girl have been willing to marry Alec, seeing that she loved Wilfred?"

"Perhaps Alec did some blackmailing, Sergeant."

"Ah!" The sergeant's exclamation was significant. "You mean that he probably threatened to expose her sweetheart to the English police unless she married him—Alec?" Then he shook his head, wonderingly. "I thought that sort of blackguardism only succeeded in old Victorian melodramas!"

Terhune grinned. "There's still no accounting for the sacrifice some people will make for love, even in the middle of the twentieth century! And when a Latin loves, Sergeant, she loves with passion."

"Lucky devil, that Alec!" Murphy murmured regretfully. He became business-like again. "The message Alec left for Wilfred becomes a bit clearer. 'Tell him that'—what was it?—'Tell him that his precious Franci has married Alec!'"

Terhune nodded.

"That message must have startled Wilfred, even if it was five years or so too late. Come to that, *why* was he so late turning up? Did he expect the girl to wait that long for him?"

Terhune shrugged. "I could offer you half a dozen explanations, none of which might be right. For instance, he might have been so keen to follow her to Marseilles that he tried stealing the necessary."

"But that time he wasn't smart enough, and was jugged by the Bulgarian police?"

"Something of that sort. Anyway, he reached Marseilles at last, only to hear that his brother had stolen his girl. Then follows another gap which we can't fill, and maybe never will, now that Wilfred is dead. But at long last he takes the risk of being arrested by the police, returns to England, becomes an old tramp, and begins a long, long search for the woman he still loved, despite all the passing years. He reaches Great Hinton, stays for a few days, is about to move on to Hastings, and then—*eureka!* He finds her. So he settles down in Farmer Giffen's wood, to spend the rest of his life as near as he can get to his old sweetheart."

"Time for soft lights and sweet music!" Murphy muttered. "You've worked out a moderately sound chain of events, sir, but, of course, it has its weaknesses."

"Naturally."

"Here's one of them. If old Peter hoped to find Mr. and Mrs. Alec Foulis—under some other name at that—before the present century had expired, what made him spend two or three days at a tiny little village like Great Hinton?"

"You remember Mrs. Newman telling us he had come from Hothfield, and was planning to go on to Hillhurst and Hythe?"

"Yes."

"All those names begin with an H. So do the Hintons, Great and Little. I don't think coincidence is responsible for so many H's."

"You think Wilfred heard, by some means or other, that his brother was living in a town or village with a name beginning with an H, and was visiting each in turn in the hope of catching up with Alec?"

"Something of that sort."

"You may be right, sir, and I wouldn't be for contradicting you without more knowledge." Murphy rubbed his chin. "And now, all that remains to be done is to find out where the Crawshays are now living?"

"That's all," Terhune agreed drily. "But there are no Crawshays living at Great Hinton as far as I know, which probably means that he must have changed his name once more. And *that* means—"

"That we are practically back where we started?"

"Exactly," Terhune agreed.

Chapter Sixteen

Of course, Murphy's statement, and Terhune's agreement, that they were back where they started was merely another example of the Briton's traditional under-statement. In actual fact they had gone some considerable way towards achieving their original aim, namely establishing the identity of Peter the Hermit. Indeed, everything pointed to their having done more than that. They had, to their own satisfaction, learned the cause of Peter's death, also the probability of the name—the real name—of his murderer, and the approximate whereabouts of the murderer.

Unfortunately, there was the usual fly in the usual ointment. All their assumptions were based on hypotheses which were practically unsupported by evidence of a more material nature. The old newspaper and jewelled comb! What did their positive evidence amount to? Just this: that a certain Señorita Bázan had, in 1923, married an Englishman. There was no positive proof that old Peter was Wilfred Foulis, or that Alexander Crawshay was Alec Foulis. There was no proof that Alec 'Crawshay' had brought his bride to England, or that Francisca's former sweetheart had followed them there. There was no proof that old Peter had been ingeniously murdered. There was no proof, even, that he had been left a fortune, as suggested by one of the short stories.

Even worse than the fact that all their deductions to date were no more than reasoned guesswork was the unlikelihood of ever being able to check their deductions. As Murphy pointed out, however certain they might be that old Peter and Wilfred Foulis were one and the same, how were the police to prove the identity? Wilfred Foulis had left England as a young man in his late twenties—his corpse was that of an old man of seventy years of age. In the absence of any marks of identification, or finger-prints, was it conceivable that any living person could look upon the disinterred corpse of an emaciated septuagenarian and swear: "That is the body of the young man I last saw in Liverpool, forty years ago"?

And next, how were they to learn of Alec Foulis's present alias, if, as Terhune believed, there was nobody by the name of Crawshay living at or near Great Hinton?

"Have you still got those two lists of possible suspects, Mr. Terhune?"

Terhune had, and produced them, together with a word of warning. "They were only suspects as far as the authorship of the stories is concerned."

"I know, sir, and in the light of what has happened since I suppose you haven't much faith left in the maso—maso—"

"Masochistic theory?"

"I never can remember that word. But I'd like to go through the list again to see if we can possibly spot Alec Foulis's new alias."

The sergeant read out the first name. "Mrs. Fawcett, the Vicar and his daughter—those three are out. Mr. and Mrs. Max Bullett—they are out, too, I suppose, in view of their history which the Bedford police gave me. By the way, I haven't told you—while you were away in France I spent a little time in both the Hintons, and had another long talk with Ted Shore. I saw Mrs. Bullett close to—she's quite foreign-looking, in my opinion. I think I must try to get a description of Max Bullett from Bedford."

"In case he isn't Max Bullett at all, really, but Alec Foulis?"

"One can't be too careful."

"But the Bulletts live pretty well. Isn't that part proof that he is the real Bullett, living on the money he inherited from his father?"

"It goes a long way, but on the other hand we don't know anything about Alec Foulis's financial circumstances. He might have made money before retiring to Great Hinton. Anyway, it can't do any harm having a further check-up on the Bulletts." He referred to the list again. "Nicholas Harvey and daughter! They're out—"

"Why?"

"He's a widower—" Murphy stopped, then looked a little crestfallen. "I'm a fool. Of course, there's no reason for assuming that Francisca is still alive. She might have died. Let me see, what age would you give his daughter? Twenty-two—twenty-three?"

"About that."

"Then she could have been Franci's daughter, which would explain why she was educated on the Continent. I'll make a cross against Harvey's name. Next, Jeremy Cardyce. Better check up on him, too, though I'm pretty sure he is who he says he is. I was talking to him about some court cases, and what he doesn't know about the law isn't worth knowing. Arthur Snaith—humph! What's your opinion of Snaith?"

"My opinion of him, Sergeant, is not flattering, but I suppose you mean the possibility of his being Foulis." Terhune reflected, then nodded. "He could be. His wife is dark enough to be a Latin."

The sergeant put a cross against Snaith's name, and carried on: "Miss Tucker—out! Henry Rolfe! It's ruddy strange, but Shore wasn't able to tell me much about Rolfe. From what you told me I believe you know more about him than Shore does."

"It's precious little I know about him, Sergeant, except that he doesn't strike me as having enough guts to murder anyone. I remember talking with him once when he said something to make me think he has been married, but what has happened to his wife, if any, I've never heard. Perhaps there was a separation or a divorce. I think I should put a cross against him, too."

Murphy did as Terhune suggested. "That finishes your list, Mr. Terhune. Now here's one of my own, which I made the night I last talked with Ted Shore." He pulled a piece of paper from his pocket. "Do you know the Trevors, at Two Ponds Farm?"

"Not personally. I've seen him from a distance, but never to talk to. I have never seen Mrs. Trevor—at any rate, not to my knowledge."

"She's no chicken," the sergeant admitted. "But her complexion is dark, her eyes are brown; she is short and plump like the Italian women you see at the pictures, and she talks in a funny way. Shore says she has an impediment in her speech, but I'd like medical evidence before I swear that she doesn't speak like she does because she was born a foreigner. Trevor doesn't seem a bad sort, but he could be Alec Foulis.

"Then there's Ayres—Ayres, who's a lodger with Farmer Giffen's sister. Ayres has only lived in the district for fourteen or fifteen years. He's supposed to have come here from Hayward's Heath. He's a shopwalker at Forrests'." Forrest and Sons was the name of a fair-sized stores in Ashford—Evan Forrest lived in a large house near Bray.

"Then there are Mr. and Mrs. Bacon. Mrs. Bacon is as English as you make 'em—a blonde, one of the blowsy kind, with a Cockney accent you could cut with a knife—but Shore says he's heard she's a second wife. I've put their name on the list because they've only lived in Hinton just over ten years, and came from somewhere in Lincolnshire, or so they say. They live in Cooper's Cottage, and just about scratch a living by selling honey, eggs, vegetables, fruit, and so on, which they get out of the twelve acres which go with the cottage."

He put the paper down on Terhune's desk. "That's the lot, sir. If you would care to find out what you can about them it might be useful. Meanwhile, I'll have a check made on that address which Crawshay gave when he married Francisca Bázan—it might lead us somewhere." Murphy leaned back in his chair and refilled his pipe with an air of being rather glad to relax for a few moments from the mental exercise of discussing the circumstances arising from the demise of old Peter.

II

The day after Terhune's return from France the local carrier delivered a number of parcels. Every one consisted of books, among them the Guy de Maupassant novels which he had purchased in France and brought back with him as far as Ashford.

These he unpacked himself; the rest he passed on to Anne, to be dealt with as usual. His self-allotted task took some time, for each volume was separately wrapped in newspaper and tied with string, but as the work of unwrapping books was one from which he never failed to derive maximum enjoyment, he was more sorry than otherwise when there were no more knots to be patiently unravelled, no more handsome leather bindings to examine and gloat over.

He surveyed the line of volumes before him with intent but jubilant eyes. He was quite confident that Gary would not be dissatisfied with the buy. With every good reason, for the set was a bargain, and Terhune had been lucky to find it. The purchase had come about by accident. After he had achieved the main purpose of his trip to Marseilles he had visited all the principal bookshops in that city in his search for a complete set of de Maupassant. Towards the end he had been warned by a pessimistic bookseller that his search was likely to be futile: the bookseller seemed to harbour doubts about the existence of such a set in matching bindings. If monsieur were not insistent upon companion bindings, there was a nice copy of *Yvette*, also of *Les Dimanches d'un Bourgeois*— Or perhaps a modern novel, one of a series on the Châteaux of the Loire; *Chaunont, Retraite d'Amour*. Monsieur would appreciate the sub-title: *Love in Retreat*...

But monsieur wanted neither the odd volumes of de Maupassant, nor *Love in Retreat*, nor any of the half a dozen books, 'not quite proper', which the anxious bookseller offered him, so he continued his unsuccessful search. By the end of the day he realized that he would have to break his homeward journey at Paris, to search the bookshops of that city for his requirements—to say nothing-of the famous portable bookstalls which border the banks of the Seine. And then, within a few minutes of reaching this decision, chance—in the shape of an attempted short cut—had led him along a lesser street where Monsieur Heuleu, *Antiquaire*, displayed behind a dust-streaked and fly-soiled window a not-so-choice collection of bric-à-brac and historic but useless pieces of furniture. Terhune had pressed against the window-pane and peered with difficulty at the mass of near-rubbish. At first lazy curiosity had been his only impulse, but the sight of a piece of cheap jewellery gave him the idea of buying a present for Julia. Monsieur Heuleu's window scarcely seemed likely to produce anything worth while, but while he was still looking Terhune had noticed, well away to the side, a number of half-leather volumes, with gold-leaf lettering, badly rubbed. A true bibliophile, his interest had been immediately awakened; he rubbed the window-pane in the hope of seeing more clearly. The effort was not entirely successful, for most of the dirt was inside, and not out where the glass was sometimes washed clean by the rain. Because of the film of dust he blamed his imagination for making out the author's name on the nearest see-able volume to be something like G— de —upassan—. It couldn't be that he had found that for which he had been searching all day?

The more he stared the more clearly it had seemed to him that the half-obliterated name was Guy de Maupassant, especially when he was ready to swear that the title of another volume was *Contes de*—*Contes de la Bécasse*! Another of de Maupassant's works!

He had entered Monsieur Heuleu's shop, and found, to his too-revealing joy (for Monsieur Heuleu's eyes were no less sharp than his business acumen), that his search was ended. Every published work of Guy de Maupassant was within, all in matching half-leather bindings—the one-time property of a nobleman whose hobby it had been to bind by hand all the books he intended adding to his library.

Now the books were at Bray, en route for the U.S.A. Terhune picked up one of the volumes, *Notre Cœur*, and handled it with loving hands. How often had he longed to have his own books bound according to his own special wishes? How often, indeed, had he considered having lessons in bookbinding so that he might do just what Monsieur le Baron de—what was the name?—Bracieux, or some such name—what the Baron had done?

The book was in moderately good condition, and had suffered nothing from the journey. He picked up a second, a third, a fourth. Then a fifth: *Mademoiselle Fifi*. All short stories in this volume. He opened it casually and tried to read one of the stories. Progress was slow, but better than he had expected; to his surprise the few days in France had quite appreciably brushed up his French. Soon the story itself was holding his attention. It concerned a Monsieur Lantin, a widower still suffering from the bereavement of his wife. Madame Lantin had been a good housekeeper. While she lived existence, despite his meagre salary as a clerk, had been satisfying; the dining-table had rarely lacked good food, even luxuries, and wines of repute. A perfect jewel of a wife with but one fault—a passion for trashy trinkets. Now Madame Lantin was dead, and Monsieur Lantin was in debt, and almost starving. There was only one thing he could do to tide over his present difficulties; he must sell his dear wife's jewellery for the few francs it was worth.

Terhune read on, unable to translate word for word, but getting the sense of every sentence as a whole.

III

Monsieur Lantin decided to sell the heavy necklace which she seemed to prefer (Terhune mentally translated), and which, he thought, ought to be worth about six or seven francs; for although paste it was, nevertheless, of exquisite workmanship.

He put it in his pocket and started out in search of a jeweller's shop. He entered the first one he saw, feeling a little ashamed to expose his misery, and also to offer such a worthless article for sale.

"Monsieur," said he to the merchant, "I would like to know what this is worth."

The man took the necklace, examined it, called his clerk and made some remarks in an undertone; then he put the ornament back on the counter and looked at it from a distance to judge of the effect.

Monsieur Lantin was annoyed by all this detail, and was on the point of saying, "Oh! I know well enough it is not worth anything," when the jeweller said: "Monsieur, that necklace is worth from twelve to fifteen thousand francs; but I could not buy it unless you tell me now whence it comes."

The widower opened his eyes wide and remained gaping, not comprehending the merchant's meaning. Finally he stammered: "You say—are you sure?"

The other replied drily: "You can search elsewhere and see if anyone will offer you more. I consider it worth fifteen thousand at the most. Come back here if you cannot do better."

Monsieur Lantin, beside himself with astonishment, took up the necklace and left the shop. He wanted time for reflection.

Once outside, he felt inclined to laugh, and said to himself: "The fool! Had I only taken him at his word! That jeweller cannot distinguish real diamonds from paste."

A few minutes after, he entered another shop in the Rue de la Paix. As soon as the proprietor glanced at the necklace he cried out:

"Ah, *parbleu*! I know it well; it was bought here."

Monsieur Lantin was disturbed, and asked:

"How much is it worth?"

"Well, I sold it for twenty thousand francs. I am willing to take it back for eighteen thousand when you inform me, according to our legal formality, how it comes to be in your possession."

This time Monsieur Lantin was dumbfounded. He replied:

"But—but—examine it well. Until this moment I was under the impression that it was paste."

Said the jeweller:

"What is your name, monsieur?"

"Lantin—I am in the employ of the Minister of the Interior. I live at No. 16 Rue des Martyrs."

The merchant looked through his books, found the entry, and said: "That necklace was sent to Madame Lantin's address, 16 Rue des Martyrs, July 20, 1876."

The two men looked into each other's eyes—the widower speechless with astonishment, the jeweller scenting a thief. The latter broke the silence by saying:

"Will you leave this necklace here for twenty-four hours? I will give you a receipt."

"Certainly," answered Monsieur Lantin hastily. Then, putting the ticket in his pocket, he left the shop.

He wandered aimlessly through the streets, his mind in a state of dreadful confusion. He tried to reason, to understand. His wife could not afford to purchase such a costly ornament. Certainly not. But then, it must have been a present!—a present!—a present from whom? Why was it given her?

He stopped and remained standing in the middle of the street. A horrible doubt entered his mind. Then all the other gems must have been presents, also! The earth seemed to tremble beneath him—the tree before him was falling; throwing up his arms, he fell to the ground, unconscious. He recovered his senses in a pharmacy into which the passers-by had taken him, and was then taken to his home. When he arrived he shut himself up in his room and wept until nightfall. Finally, overcome with fatigue, he threw himself on the bed, where he passed an uneasy, restless night.

The following morning he rose and prepared to go to the office. It was hard to work after such a shock. He sent a letter to his employer requesting to be excused. Then he remembered that he had to return to the jeweller's. He did not like the idea; but he could not leave the necklace with that man. So he dressed and went out.

It was a lovely day; a clear blue sky smiled on the busy city below, and men of leisure were strolling about with their hands in their pockets.

Observing them, Monsieur Lantin said to himself: "The rich, indeed, are happy. With money it is possible to forget even the deepest sorrow. One can go where one pleases, and in travel find that distraction which is the surest cure for grief. Oh! if only I were rich!"

He began to feel hungry, but his pocket was empty. He again remembered the necklace. Eighteen thousand francs! Eighteen thousand francs! What an amount!

He soon arrived in the Rue de la Paix, opposite the jeweller's. Eighteen thousand francs! Twenty times he resolved to go in, but shame kept him back. He was hungry, however—very hungry—and had not a sou in his pocket. He decided quickly, ran across the street in order not to have time for reflection, and entered the shop.

The proprietor immediately came forward, and politely offered him a chair; the assistants glanced at him knowingly.

"I have made enquiries, Monsieur Lantin," said the jeweller, "and if you are still resolved to dispose of the gems, I am ready to pay you the price I offered."

"Certainly, monsieur" stammered Monsieur Lantin.

Whereupon the proprietor took from the drawer eighteen large notes, counted and handed them to Monsieur Lantin, who signed a receipt and with a trembling hand put the money into his pocket.

As he was about to leave the shop, he turned towards the merchant, who still wore the same knowing smile, and, lowering his eyes, said:

"I have—I have other gems which I have received from the same source. Will you buy them also?"

The merchant bowed. "Certainly, monsieur."

Monsieur Lantin said gravely: "I will bring them to you." An hour later he returned with the gems.

The large diamond ear-rings were worth twenty thousand francs; the bracelets thirty-five thousand; the rings, sixteen thousand; a gold chain with solitaire pendant, forty thousand—making the sum of one hundred and forty-three thousand francs.

The jeweller remarked, jokingly:

"There was a person who invested all her earnings in precious stones."

Monsieur Lantin replied, seriously:

"It is only another way of investing one's money."

That day he lunched at Voisin's and drank wine worth twenty francs a bottle. Then he hired a carriage and made a tour of the Bois, and as he scanned the various turn-outs with a contemptuous air he could hardly refrain from crying out to the occupants:

"I, too, am rich!—I am worth two hundred thousand francs!"

Suddenly he thought of his employer. He drove up to the office, and entered gaily, saying:

"Monsieur, I have come to resign my position. I have just inherited three hundred thousand francs."

He shook hands with his former colleagues and confided to them some of his projects for the future; then he went off to dine at the Café Anglais.

He seated himself beside a gentleman of aristocratic bearing, and during the meal informed the latter confidentially that he had just inherited a fortune of four hundred thousand francs.

For the first time in his life he was not bored at the theatre, and spent the remainder of the night in a gay frolic.

Six months afterwards he married again. His second wife was a very virtuous woman, with a violent temper. She caused him much sorrow.

IV

Terhune chuckled. A typical de Maupassant story, that. Vaguely familiar, too. In past years he had read a number of de Maupassant's works. In English, of course. Probably the story of the false gems had been one which he had read. He turned the pages, slowly, reflectively. Queer effect reading the de Maupassant tale was having upon him. His memory was excellent where anything to do with books was concerned. Although there was something vaguely familiar about the story, yet nothing of its plot jogged his memory; whatever his subconscious might remember of the story, his conscious self could not recollect one tittle of it.

The ingenuous blue eyes behind the horn-rimmed glasses became unseeing as his mind wrestled with the irritating problem of how, on the one hand, he was ready to swear that he had never previously read that story, and yet, on the other, there was something about it which was vaguely familiar. Had he dreamed a somewhat similar situation? That might well be the answer, for his memory was of something recent, whereas he had not read one of de Maupassant's stories for at least three years.

Or was the answer to the problem one of style? Was it, perhaps, the stilted, outmoded style which was familiar, and not the plot? Or its Continental locale—

Continental locale! The two words were the key which opened the doors of memory. Old-fashioned style, a background of Paris boulevards, an exotic morality, unconventional endings—all these were part and parcel of the four stories which a person unknown had sent either to him or to Murphy.

It was not strange that a haunting familiarity with the stories had plagued him. They had reminded him, subconsciously, of Guy de Maupassant. Perhaps they were, in fact, by de Maupassant, but had been adapted and bowdlerized to make them convey a clue to the circumstances of Peter the Hermit's death.

With unusual haste he began thumbing through the pages of the book he still held, in the hope of recognizing or associating some of the shorter stories with those received from the unknown. Time passed, for he found the task a slow and laborious one, especially when his brain began to fag from the unusual exercise of reading a foreign language. The first three volumes yielded nothing, but neither his time nor his work was wasted, for his quick skimming of the stories convinced him that he was on the right tack; that the stories had either been lifted from de Maupassant or, alternatively, the writer had so based his own style upon de Maupassant's that the origin was unmistakable.

He picked up a fourth volume, *Pierre et Jean*. This tale was a short novel rather than a short story, but he lingered long over its pages because of several significant coincidences. The title, containing as it did the name of Pierre. The fact that Pierre and Jean were brothers. Pierre's ultimate choice of medicine as his avocation. Jean's inheritance of a small fortune. The rivalry between the brothers for the love of one woman. There, however, resemblance ceased, for, in de Maupassant's story, although Jean wins the bride, Pierre, not Jean, leaves his native country—to become a respectable and respected physician aboard an Atlantic liner.

Terhune carried on patiently, but none of the remaining volumes produced any stories from which the four upstairs in his study could have been taken. It seemed that his second theory was the more correct—that the writer of those four had copied his self-appointed master's style so slavishly that he had lost whatever personality of his own he possessed, and had, in consequence, produced stories that were merely imitations of a writer he could never hope to equal.

His reflections expanded and spread like waters seeking an outlet. Who, in Great Hinton, or somewhere near by, so admired Guy de Maupassant's stories that he had modelled his own literary efforts upon them? And the answer presented itself automatically—maybe the person who had purchased the set of de Maupassant's works in the original from the Canterbury bookseller, John McCloud. If McCloud could supply the name and address of the buyer, perhaps the mystery of the writer's identity could be solved.

This time Terhune decided that a personal visit to Canterbury was not necessary. He rose from the corner where he had been unpacking the books—a convenient corner, tucked away out of sight behind some bookshelves—and crossed over to the telephone, which was near the door leading into a small passage, and the private staircase to the rooms overhead.

The connection was made in less than three minutes. He heard McCloud call out an impatient: "Hullo?"

"Mr. John McCloud?"

"Yes."

"Theodore Terhune of Bray here."

"Ah! Good morning to you, Mr. Terhune—" McCloud's voice became genial. "What can I do for you?"

"Have you any news of those de Maupassant books about which I spoke to you a week or so ago?"

"That's strangely funny, now, Mr. Terhune, your 'phoning me up this morning of all mornings!"

"Why?"

"Well, let me tell you that I searched everywhere for a record of who had bought those de Maupassant books, or to what address I had sent them. But I failed. Unfortunately, I accidentally set fire to one of my files two years ago, and the record of the de Maupassant transaction must have been destroyed at that time. That is why I have not telephoned you before this."

Terhune was terribly disappointed. "Does that mean you have no news for me?"

McCloud chuckled drily. "I am coming to that. On the contrary, I have news which I should have been telephoning you this afternoon, during a slack period about tea-time. Yesterday a man and woman came into the shop enquiring whether I had a copy, in the French language, of *Yvette*, by Guy de Maupassant. *Yvette* was one of the two titles missing from the complete works which you were enquiring for, Mr. Terhune."

"Yes, yes," Terhune prompted impatiently.

"When I looked at the faces of the two people I seemed to recognize them as the ones who had bought that set from me. I said to the man: 'Are you from the neighbourhood of Great Hinton?' He said he was, so I said to him: 'Then you are the gentleman who bought a complete set, less two volumes, of de Maupassant in the French language some time ago?' McCloud's words were interrupted by a click. "Hullo! Are you there, Mr. Terhune?"

"Yes, yes. What happened then? What did he say?"

"He nodded his head, and said: 'I am. I have bought one of the two missing titles, but I still need *Yvette* to complete the set. I suppose you haven't come across one yet?' I told him that I had not. Then I asked him whether he was willing to sell the rest of the de Maupassant books if a good offer was made for them. He said he wasn't, and nothing I could say would make him change his mind. When I saw that he intended to be obstinate about the matter I changed the subject. Then, just when he was going out of the shop, I said to him: 'By the way, if you should wish to change your mind about selling those de Maupassant books you should let Mr. Terhune of Bray know; he's the man who has been enquiring for them.' So if somebody makes an offer to sell them, you will know how he came to hear of your requirements."

Terhune mumbled a few words of thanks, then continued anxiously: "Will you do me a very great favour, Mr. McCloud?"

"If I can. What is it?"

"What I am about to do is unethical, as between one bookseller and another, but will you, on this one occasion, give me the name and address of the buyer? I need it most urgently."

"Bless my heart, Mr. Terhune, I'm not a cut-throat rival. I believe in friendly relations, even with my competitors. I should gladly pass on the required information—if it was mine to pass on."

"What does that mean?"

"He refused to give it to me when I asked for it. He said he would call in at the shop any time he wanted to buy more books, but he wasn't going to be bothered with a lot of catalogues. I tried to argue with him, but he said he would soon be leaving his present address, anyway."

"And haven't you any idea of who he is, or where he lives?" Terhune appealed.

"Not the faintest, except that he lives somewhere neat Great Hinton," the Canterbury bookseller answered cheerfully—much too cheerfully, Terhune thought disconsolately.

Chapter Seventeen

It was not coincidence which brought both Julia and Murphy to Terhune's rooms that night: it was part and parcel of Terhune's cowardly design for shielding himself from the first impact of Julia's displeasure and envy of his journey to France in the company of Lady Kylstone and Helena, a displeasure of which he was quite sure he would be the target at their first meeting. In arranging the appointment *à trois*, as it were, he had reckoned that Murphy's presence would postpone, and so blunt, what he anticipated would be an unpleasant thirty minutes or more. So long as Murphy was present, Terhune argued, Julia would restrain her caustic tongue, giving him the opportunity of mollifying her on the one hand, and, on the other, of so interesting her in his new theory that her resentment would vanish. For this fell purpose he had carefully arranged for Murphy to arrive about eight o'clock, but Julia not until fifteen minutes later, to allow for possible accidents.

His simple scheme was no match for Julia. Just as the clock of St. James's Church chimed a half-hour, a firm ring, suspiciously like Julia's, summoned Terhune downstairs to the private door. His caller was Julia.

"Hul-lo, Ju-Julie," he stammered. "You're early. I—I didn't expect you before eight-fifteen."

"I know," she said coolly, as she stepped inside, and led the way upstairs. "But Mother is out, having dinner with the Breretons. As I was feeling bored with my own company I didn't think you would have any objection to my coming earlier than you suggested." She stopped, and turned to face him. "Or have you?" she demanded icily.

"Don't be silly, Julie. You know I'm always glad to see you."

"Then why did you suggest eight-fifteen instead of our usual time?"

"I—I—well, Murphy is coming about then. I have some news for him about old Peter's death which I thought might interest you."

She laughed shortly, and continued upstairs. He reddened, for he realized that she had fathomed the motive for his unusual behaviour. What a fool he was, to think that he could outwit her!

Half-way along the upstairs passage she stopped again. "Which room, Theo?"

"The workroom—if you don't mind that room—"

"I prefer it," she interrupted. "The workroom has personality. It is you; not in flesh and bones, but in bricks and mortar." She pushed open the door and entered the study. "The front room could belong to anybody. But not this room. I don't believe there is another person in the world who could keep it quite so untidy."

She sank into the one comfortable chair. "Well?" she exclaimed challengingly as she relaxed.

He sat on his typing chair and played for time. "Well what?"

"Did you enjoy your mysterious trip to the South of France?"

"There was no mystery about it—"

"Then why did you make a mystery of it, my pet?"

"But I did not."

"You said nothing about it to me beforehand; you did not even take the trouble to ring me up to say you were going. The first I knew of your plans was when I received your note, posted in Calais, to say that you would be away for a week or two as you were going to the South of France with Lady Kylstone and Helena."

"I did not mention Helena's name, Julie."

"She accompanied Lady Kylstone, did she not?"

"Of course, but—"

"Not that there was any reason why you should have told me, Theo, but we had tentatively arranged for you to take me dancing—"

"I know; it was rotten of me to have broken that date without a word of warning, Julie," he broke in hurriedly. "But, honest to goodness, everything was done in such a rush that I had no time to do half the things I intended to do."

"A 'phone call would have taken no more than four or five minutes."

He had not the audacity to contradict her, for the charge was justified. Indeed, on three separate occasions he had half-decided to ring her up to tell her of his plans, but each time he had hesitated, and had ultimately decided not to do so because of her attitude towards Helena. Julia disliked many people—in fact she disliked most people. Aware of her intolerance for slow thinkers, bores of all kinds, the sporting type, and many other varieties of people, he could mostly understand—though, usually, without approving of—her unconcealed dislikes. This understanding did not extend to her antipathy for Helena. He could not conceive it possible for anyone to dislike Helena, who wasn't capable of a mean, a catty, or an unfeeling impulse. Helena was as nice a girl, as jolly a companion, as anyone could ever hope to meet. Yet Julia, though outwardly amiable to Helena—a rare concession on Julia's part—nursed for the other woman a cold-blooded dislike which mystified Terhune whenever he tried to account for it.

"I really was busy," he said weakly. "I had less than two days to make all arrangements not only for going abroad but also for leaving Anne to handle the business on her own. It was a heck of a rush; honestly it was, Julie."

He looked so shamefaced, so incredibly ingenuous, that she almost forgave him. Then she thought of the intimate companionship which must have existed in the car, so she became angry and bitter again.

"I suppose you are still in a rush, as a result of your holiday?"

He fell into her trap. "Not more than usual, Julie," he replied quickly, happy to take advantage of a slight change in the conversation.

"Anne managed very well; she has kept the work practically up to date—"

"Then why have you asked both Murphy *and* me to come tonight? Is it because you haven't enough spare time to have the two of us separately?"

"You know that isn't true," he protested. "Besides, you haven't any objection to Murphy, have you?"

"None at all. He is a pleasant, capable man."

"That is what I thought was your opinion of him, and as I've already told you, I also thought you would like to be present when I tell him of the new clue I believe I've discovered."

She stared coldly at him. "You are a liar, Theodore Terhune. The only reason you asked Murphy and me to come here on the same night is because you didn't want to be alone with me."

Exasperated by her attitude, his own hardened. "All right, Julie, if you insist upon having the truth, then, yes. And I am damned if you're not proving that I had every reason for taking that precaution—or perhaps I should say trying to take it—"

"There is no need to swear, Theodore. And if you are trying to be rude—"

"I am not. I am merely pointing out that you are making a devil of a fuss just because I didn't have a chance of telling you beforehand that I was off to the South of France on a business trip—"

"A business trip, Theo! With Lady Kylstone and Helena?"

"A business trip," he repeated firmly. "And there is fifty per cent of the business." He waved his hand at the pile of books he had brought back with him from France.

"What are they?"

"A set of Guy de Maupassant's works in French which Lady Kylstone's nephew had commissioned me to buy for him. As it is, if things turn out as I rather suspect, perhaps I shall be giving, instead of selling, them to him. As a wedding gift," he added disconsolately.

Her keen eyes did not miss the shadow which flashed across his face. "Whom is he marrying?" she asked quickly, in a voice sharp with nascent jubilation.

"I only said perhaps," he replied moodily. "But—"

He stopped abruptly, and stared at the fire, apparently unaware of having left his thought unsaid.

"Do you mean Helena?" Her eyes, usually so coolly confident, were unsteady.

He nodded.

Julia's self-control vanished; her eyes sparkled with a savage pleasure which would have startled Terhune had he glanced up just then. But he did not turn his head, and the dancing flames from the wood-fire threw his profile into relief.

If the voyage to the French Riviera had engendered romance between Helena and Lady Kylstone's relative, then Julia no longer hated it in retrospect. Light-heartedly she changed the conversation while praying that Mediterranean days and moonlit nights would transform the sprouting seed into a full-grown plant before the spring weather tempted Lady Kylstone to move northward again.

"What was the other fifty per cent of your business in France, my pet?"

"The other fifty per cent?" he began vaguely. He groped for the meaning of her question, and presently grasped it. His mood changed to a livelier tempo. "To call on the Spanish Vice-Consul."

The last vestige of Julia's ill-humour departed. "What happened, Theo dear?"

Cunning, cunning Julia! Never had there been quite such warmth in her manner. He was not directly conscious of it, but the contrast between Julia's subtle tenderness and the memory of Helena's unwittingly cooler behaviour created the desired effect. Cheerfully he told her the story of his visit to the Vice-Consul, and of its results. Then they discussed his theories, and presently Terhune realized that he had jumped the worst hurdle. Julia had forgiven him for the secrecy with which he had left England. Having done so, she would never refer to it again. Harbouring resentment was not part of Julia's brusque forthrightness.

Then came Murphy, ten minutes before he was due. He smiled broadly as he apologized for his early arrival. "You've got me nearly as excited as you sounded yourself, Mr. Terhune," he explained. "What's happened this time?"

So Terhune told him of the de Maupassant stories, of the possible similarity between them and the four original stories under the general title of *Ten Trails to Tyburn*, and finally of his own deductions that the writer of the *Ten Trails* was the man to whom the Cathedral Bookshop had sold the de Maupassant books.

Murphy's face expressed many shades of emotion during the telling, but comical despair was paramount at the end.

"It's a lucky thing that I wasn't left to read those darned stories on my own. I don't know that I've ever heard the name of that French writer Guy de—Guy de—Mope-something-or-other—"

"Maupassant."

"Don't ask me to repeat it, sir; my tongue won't twist itself round most of them foreign words at all, at all. Anyhow, as I was saying, I'd never even heard of him, nor read his stories, so I couldn't have been expected to guess that the fellow who wrote those *Ten Trail* stories is probably somebody who has read the Frenchman's stories, and modelled his own style upon the other man's. Bedad!" he went on plaintively, "as if us 'tecs don't have to know enough as it is without being expected to know whether the style of a silly bit of a story was that of the Guy fellow, or Dumas, or Zola, or any other French writer." His voice became crisper. "Meanwhile, you say that that bookshop fellow couldn't give you any hint as to the identity of the man who bought the set of books some years ago?"

"Beyond the fact that the other man lives in or near Great Hinton, McCloud wasn't able to tell me anything."

"He was able to give you a description?"

Terhune shrugged. "Of a kind, but it would fit any one of a dozen men I know. Doctor Edwards, for one, Giffen for another, Rolfe, Nicholas Harvey, and so on."

"Max Bullett?"

"No," Terhune confessed. "No, the description wouldn't fit Bullett. He's on the short side, and dark, and mostly dresses in tweeds. But the man who purchased the de Maupassant stories was—according to McCloud, who wasn't too precise by the way—about five-ten in height, a little round-shouldered, aged about the middle fifties, wore a formal, well-worn lounge suit, and a hat which hid most of his hair except round his ears, where it was mousey-grey."

"That's not very helpful," Murphy grumbled. "As you say, that's Doctor Edwards to a T. He was clean-shaven, I suppose?"

"Oh yes! And complexion healthy—but who living round about here hasn't a healthy complexion?"

There was a short silence, broken eventually by the sergeant. "There's still something I can't account for."

"What is that, Sergeant?"

"If the man who bought the French books is Alec Foulis, then we've got to get back to our old idea that Alec is sending us the stories in order to enjoy the maso—masochistic—got it!—the masochistic pleasure of seeing us gradually closing in upon him for the supposed murder of his brother Wilfred?" There was a question-mark in his voice.

"Yes."

"Well, sir, I can understand Alec's killing Wilfred for the sake of money—if that second story is to be trusted. I could even understand his doing the crime just out of revenge for having his early life ruined by his elder brother—though I'm damned—begging your pardon, miss—if I can think why he should wait fen years if he killed only for the sake of revenge. But I cannot see the same man deliberately committing suicide—kind of, at any rate—just for the sake of some crazy kind of pleasure. If he was so blooming keen to make himself suffer why didn't he let Wilfred inherit the money? It should have been enough to know that his brother was well off, while he himself was poor, to make the average man feel pretty sore. It would me, at least," Murphy finished up candidly.

"There is no proof that Alec is poor."

"I agree with Mr. Murphy, Theo," Julia said quietly. "All those isms which psychologists reel off so glibly look very learned in books and articles, but I haven't much faith in them myself. I think that most people act according to normal human emotions, and it is neither normal nor human for a man deliberately to help the police hang a noose round his own neck."

"Hear! Hear!" Murphy echoed warmly. "My feelings entirely, Miss MacMunn."

Terhune shook his head. "Nine hundred and ninety-nine people are normal and human, to use your own words, Julie, but the thousandth isn't. Would you call an assault upon a young girl normal or human, Sergeant?"

"Scarcely," Murphy admitted warily.

"But such assaults do happen, don't they?"

"I'm afraid they do."

"Well, you know as well as I do, Sergeant, that a criminal assault upon a young girl is more a mental than a physical crime."

The detective nodded.

"It is possible for Alec Foulis to be one of our thousandth men." Terhune chuckled. "After all, Sergeant, you first raised this psychological business, not me. Personally I'm agin it, which brings us back to the old question—if Alec Foulis isn't betraying himself to us, who is betraying Alec Foulis? And why? And if Alec Foulis is being betrayed, then the man who bought the de Maupassant stories isn't Alec Foulis."

Murphy made no immediate answer to these questions, and the silence which followed was broken this time not by one of the three people in the small study, but by a sharp knock upon the private street door downstairs.

"Who the devil—" Terhune exclaimed; unexpected visitors so late of an evening were unusual.

He hurried out of the room and downstairs. When he was half-way down the short flight he saw a large-sized envelope on the doormat. There was something ominously familiar about it, so that he did not wait to pick it up and examine it. Instead he made a dash for the door, opened it, and ran the few yards along the side-road, on which the private door faced, to the corner where the side-road entered Market Square. In the light of a new moon, and half a dozen street lamps, he saw the Square was empty of pedestrians, but in the far corner was the indistinct figure of a cyclist turning out of the Square into the Ashford road—the road which went through Great Hinton! Was it he who had pushed the envelops through Terhune's letter-box? Terhune was certain of it, for no walker could have vanished so quickly.

He returned indoors, and picked up the letter. Although the envelope was similar to the others which he or Murphy had received from the writer of the *Ten Trails*, yet the alignment and set-out of the typed address seemed vaguely different. Nevertheless, the thickness of the contents assured him that another manuscript had arrived.

He frowned slightly as he wondered why the script had been delivered by hand instead of through the post, as in the past. This unusual form of delivery suggested urgency, a desire on the part of the sender that he, Terhune, should read the story as soon as possible. Tomorrow was not soon enough; it was hoped that he would read it tonight.

He carried it upstairs and into the study, unopened. Murphy took one glance at the envelope and exploded.

"If that's another of thim stories, may all the Saints in Heaven stop me from murthering that haythen if ever I lays me hands upon him." Never had Murphy's brogue been quite so obvious. He was evidently rattled.

"I believe it is. I haven't opened it yet." Terhune began to slit open the envelope with a paper-cutter.

"Then can you tell me what the crazy creature is doing, pushing it through the letter-box at this time of night? Bedad! It's a hurry he seems to be in, to be sure, for us to be reading his latest literary efforts." Murphy choked. "It's myself that will soon be crazy, too, if I have to read many more of them tales."

Meanwhile Terhune had taken the script out of the envelope. As usual, there was nothing to indicate the name and address of the sender: no letter, no author's name. Just the usual front page.

TEN TRAILS TO TYBURN
NO. 5. THE FIRST BRIEF

Terhune hesitated for a few moments. He was exceedingly eager to read the latest clue to old Peter's death, but politeness dictated that Julia should be the first to read the story, then Murphy, and lastly himself. As the fifth story was rather longer than the previous four he foresaw having to wait several minutes before his turn arrived.

As he passed the script to Julia an idea occurred to him. He slipped off the paper-fastener.

"As you finish reading each sheet, Julie, would you pass it on to Murphy? Then he can pass it on to me. In that way we shall all be reading at the same time."

Julia nodded, and began to read. Presently she passed the first sheet on to the impatient sergeant. Murphy read, and passed it on to Terhune. Terhune began reading.

II

THE FIRST BRIEF

The other day I met my old mess-mate Franklin. Before Franklin had been called to the Bar he and I had joined forces in many a rowdy mess at one of the Inns of Court, so, naturally, I was interested in his career.

"How's life?" I asked him.

Of course I realized later that to put such a question to a barrister of six months' standing was asking for trouble. However, in this world one has to pay for experience—often on an instalment system.

"How am I doing?" Franklin's face became rapturous. Had he been an American he might have continued, "Boy, oh, boy!" and I should have signified my complete comprehension with an expressive grunt. Being an Englishman, he said the same thing in a hundred words or more.

A hundred words, did I say? I am underestimating. It took him all of an hour—a perfectly good luncheon hour—to tell me of the glorious success he was making of his chosen career. In short, that morning he had received his first brief.

I did not hear the sequel until three months later. But some sequels, like good wine, improve with age. Here it is.

Having studied the brief for several days, having read every text-book dealing with the subject, having swotted up every authoritative case dealing with a similar charge—his client was to be tried upon a 'complaint lodged against him by the R.S.P.C.A. for monstrously torturing a dog to death—he decided the best course to pursue was to interview his client.

The necessary arrangements were made, and in due course—oh, heavenly moment!—Mr. Smith sat opposite my friend Franklin.

"Er—good morning, Mr.—er—Smith, good morning. Messrs. Gass, Gass and Moregass have sent you along, I believe. Let me see, you are to interview me in connection with—ah, yes! Here is the brief. I have to have it before me, Mr. Smith, to refresh my memory. So many cases, you know," he added absently.

"Now, Mr. Smith, in connection with this affair, this most unfortunate affair, I will be frank with you. It is not an easy case to defend. Not easy at all. You may rest assured that I will do everything possible for you. To assist me in your defence I have invited you here to ask you a few questions. I presume Messrs. Gass, Gass and Moregass made that clear to you?"

Mr. Smith was a vague, insignificant sort of a man, with a vacant stare and a wispy smile. Just the type of man—no doubt mentally deranged—who would torture a dog to death, thought Franklin.

Mr. Smith nodded his head. "Yes, sir."

"First of all you must tell me frankly—have you been in similar trouble before?"

The man hesitated. Franklin could see that he was endeavouring to make up his mind whether to tell the truth or not.

"Come, Mr. Smith," he insisted firmly. "I must know the truth. It will all come out during the proceedings, and I must be prepared to deal with such evidence in the best possible way. You have done it before?"

"Yes, sir," Mr. Smith muttered uneasily.

"Did you—er—dispose of the bitch in the same way?"

"If you put it that way, sir, yes." Franklin's client grinned familiarly.

"Were proceedings taken against you?"

"Yes, sir."

"Was the verdict against you?"

"Yes, sir."

Franklin shook his head dismally, "Pity! Pity! It will make things rather worse for you."

Mr. Smith looked startled. "I didn't realize that, sir. What might happen to me?"

Franklin rubbed his chin reflectively. "If you are found guilty I am afraid it may mean several months."

"Gawd!" Mr. Smith whimpered. "I didn't know that. I wouldn't have taken the risk. I would have had it out on me old woman instead."

It was Franklin's turn to look startled. "Come, come! That would never have done. You never attempt to treat your wife as you did the bitch, I am sure."

"I dunno." There was a smile of sly amusement in his eyes. "I used to before I married her. Gawd! I used to give her a time, I did."

"Humph!" Franklin told himself that being a barrister he should not be shocked by anything his client might say. "Rather unusual method of wooing, is it not, Mr. Smith?"

The man leered confidingly. "There's more of it goes on than what you thinks for. Us men aren't to blame all the time, though. If it wasn't for the way the bitches treated us we wouldn't get them into trouble, which is just what they wants."

Franklin began to feel rather out of his depth. The ways of the people were beyond comprehension! "Well, well! What happens at other times does not concern you at the moment. We had better confine ourselves to your case. What caused you to treat the bitch in the way you did? You did treat her so, I presume?"

"Yes, sir. I just couldn't help myself. I'm made that way."

"Humph! You will have to control yourself more. If this should happen again—"

"It won't do that, you bet yer sweet life. I'm off them for good after this. They've got me into a mess for the last time. 'Sides, they cost too much."

"Oh!" Franklin was interested. For some time he had been considering whether or not to keep a dog. "Do they eat much?"

"Eat?" Mr. Smith threw up his hand. "They'll eat until your pockets is empty, and if you don't give 'em all they want they kick up such a row that you gets afraid of the old woman knowing all about it."

"Did your wife not know you were keeping a bitch?"

"You bet yer sweet life she didn't! She would have given me whot-ho if she had found out."

"But she did find out in due course?"

"Naturally. That's how all this affair started."

"Oh! Did your wife—er—inform the—er—authorities?"

"Yes. She went to the magistrate, and asked him what she ought to do about it, and so the blighter told her." Mr. Smith waxed angry at the thought.

Franklin endeavoured to calm him by reverting to his previous line of questions.

"Have you kept many in the past?"

"Two or three at different times."

"The fact of your having kept some in the past should prove, should it not, your fondness for them?"

"I *am* fond of them. That is the cause of the trouble. I'm too fond of 'em."

"Then why did you do what you did? Was your wife the reason?"

"You've hit it, sir. If it hadn't been for the old woman, nag, nag, nagging every blooming night, I shouldn't have become so fond of the other."

"Perhaps I can understand your reason, Mr. Smith, for want of—er—companionship," Franklin murmured judicially, "but why did you go to the—er—extent that you did go?"

"I've told you, sir, it's me nature. I can't help myself."

"I am afraid we shall have to put forward a better defence than that, Mr. Smith. Let me see: did she ever bite you, for instance?"

"I must say as how she did, on occasions "

"What was her temper like, as a general rule? Bad, for instance?"

"Not too good at times."

"Was she snappy? Did she growl at you?"

"Yes, but then I didn't use to take no notice. I used to take her out to the Park, and that always put her in a good mood. She always was fond of parks. That's where I picked her up in the first case."

"Was she a stray?"

"Yes. A man what lives Walthamstow way had given her the go-by. She looked at me so pitiful I couldn't resist giving her a good cuddle."

Franklin consulted his papers. "You took her home, I see."

"When I knew me old woman wasn't home."

"Considering the circumstances, do you not think that was a very stupid thing to do?"

"Of course it was, but that's me all over. I always was one for taking risks, I was. If I'd been in the Eighth Army I would have won a V.C., if I knows anything about myself."

"Quite, quite. Now tell me, Mr. Smith, the events that happened on the day when you did the—er—fatal deed."

Mr. Smith pulled his lower lip. "It was like this here, mister. Me old woman was in one of her extra specials: you only had to put your head round the door to get a saucepan or kettle chucked at it. So I says to myself, I says: 'Mate, this is where you goes off to enjoy the company of Minnie—'"

"Minnie being the name of the bitch?" Franklin queried.

"Yes, sir."

Franklin noted the fact. "Go on," he murmured, as he finished writing.

"By that time I don't mind telling you, sir, me poor nerves was all shot to pieces. I don't know if you are married, sir—"

"I am not," Franklin replied abruptly.

"Lucky you, sir, is what I says. As I was saying, I was feeling so fed-up that off I goes to Minnie."

"She was glad to see you?" the barrister prompted, when his client paused.

"She was, and she wasn't, so to speak. She jumped up and kissed me all over the face, but all the time I thought to myself, 'There's something on your mind, old gal, you're worrying about something.'"

"You learned she was in pup?"

The sweat gathered on Mr. Smith's forehead. Taking a grubby handkerchief from his pocket, he wiped his face and head. "Yes, sir," he agreed hoarsely.

"I understand that that fact gave you rather a shock."

"It did and all. I was so mad I just didn't know what to do."

"So you seized hold of poor Minnie—"

Smith's eyes gleamed wildly. "I did. I caught hold of her and gave her such a clip across the ear that she went bang on the ground."

"Wasn't that a rather cruel thing to do, especially considering the circumstances? I could understand it more easily if you had whipped her for—for—well, you know what I mean. But because you found that something was to happen in the future—well—"

"All right, mister," Smith growled. "I can't help what you think. I lost me temper. That's what happened."

"Quite, quite!" Franklin hastened to conciliate his client. He felt that the interview was not proceeding as it should do. The man was right: it was not his place to criticize his client's actions, but to defend them.

"Speaking of the deed itself, at the time did Minnie attack you? Perhaps, if it could be shown that she attacked you, and you had reason to be afraid for what might happen to you, we might get you off."

Mr. Smith scratched his head. "I am afraid not, mister. You don't do these things in front of witnesses as a rule."

"No doubt—no doubt."

"But there you are; just as it happened, blow me if there wasn't a witness after all, the dirty spy. Me old woman had become suspicious of me and had hired one of them private detectives what you read about to find out all about poor Minnie."

"A private detective!" Franklin was surprised. The particulars passed on to him said nothing of a private detective. "Did he see you kill the bitch?"

"But I didn't kill her!" Mr. Smith gazed vacantly at the barrister. "All I did was—"

There was a discreet knock upon the door. In answer to Franklin's summons, his clerk entered.

"A letter from Messrs. Gass, Gass and Moregass," he said. "It is marked 'urgent', sir."

Franklin hastily opened the letter.

My dear Franklin [wrote Mr. Fuller Gass],

Through culpable carelessness on the part of one of our clerks, the wrong client has been sent to you. The man you have interviewed this morning (as by now you will have discovered) is involved both in divorce and bastardy proceedings. Your Mr. Smith of the dog torture summons will come along to you later—

Chapter Eighteen

Terhune was still reading page nine of the script when the quietness of the little room, previously broken only by the rustling of paper, was disturbed by loud and gusty laughter from the sergeant. He laughed, and spluttered, and laughed again.

"Ho! Ho! Ho!" he bellowed. "If that isn't the funniest bit of tale I've ever read, then me name isn't Murphy. Bedad! He would have had it out on his old woman instead of the bitch—"

Laughter choked his words, but he could not resist trying to finish what he wanted to say. "He's made that way! And his wife didn't know he was keeping a bitch! It was his nature. He couldn't help himself. Then he learned that she was in pup—" The sergeant rocked, and literally held his ribs. "My ribs are that sore," he spluttered. "I haven't laughed so much for years— He learned she was in pup! Ho! Ho! Ho! Ha! Ha! Ha!"

His laughter was infectious. Terhune hastily skimmed the last page, then echoed Murphy's laughter. The noise was shattering, and must surely have penetrated the party-wall into the neighbouring building.

Presently Murphy wiped the tears from his inflamed cheeks and glanced with guilty eyes at Julia.

"Begging your pardon, miss, for this scene. But a story like that is just up my street. Perhaps you don't know how solemn some of them counsel look when they're interviewing clients. I can just see that there Mr. Smith grinning all over his nasty little face because he thought he was discussing the young woman he had got into trouble—" More laughter threatened, but he choked it back, and turned to Terhune. "I don't mind telling you that those French stories were a bit above my head, but this last one—well, it strikes me as funny. Messrs. Gass, Gass and Moregass—" He gurgled again, irrepressibly.

Terhune glanced quickly at Julia. She was smiling tolerantly, but there was a light in her eyes which informed him that she had personally found the story vulgar. He felt rather happy about that; although a modern young man, he possessed the old-fashioned distaste for women who were essentially bawdy-minded.

As soon as Murphy had recovered Terhune asked him: "Well, Sergeant, what do you make of the fifth story?"

The detective's face became alert and business-like. "My guess is that we are on the wrong tack again. All the cross-questions and crooked answers in the story arise from the fact that the young barrister is working on the wrong brief. Substitute the word 'detective' for 'barrister', and 'clue' for 'brief', and there is your clue. Do you agree?"

"Before I answer your question, Sergeant, let me be sure that I quite understand it. Which wrong clue do you suggest we are working on?"

"The latest; the clue referring to the French books. In other words, we are being told that while everything seems to point towards the buyer of the French books as the man who has been sending us these stories, actually the two men are not one and the same, and we shall not get very far by assuming that they are." Murphy paused. "I can see by your face that you do not agree with me."

"Not entirely, Sergeant. The first point which occurs to me is this: why was the sender so anxious for me to have this story tonight? If he had put it in the post the delay would have been a few hours at the most."

"Perhaps he did not want to have the envelope bear the local postmark on it, for that would have confirmed for certain—almost for certain, at any rate—that he was living in this neighbourhood. That being the case, and as he possibly hasn't planned going farther afield for several days, he decided to deliver the letter personally."

Terhune was not able to point out the fallacy in the sergeant's argument, for Murphy did so himself, with the next breath.

"Bedad! I'm making mincemeat of my own theories. If he had wanted to prevent us knowing for certain that he lives somewhere near he wouldn't have delivered the script by hand. He would have waited until he was going farther afield."

"Exactly."

"Then he *was* in a hurry for you to have the story fairly soon, and if he merely waited for night in order to avoid the possibility of being seen and recognized, then any other would have been as convenient as tonight."

"Do you think the sender knew Mr. Murphy was coming tonight, and wanted to make certain of his reading the story while he was here?" Julia suggested.

"There's something in what you say, Miss MacMunn," Murphy agreed quickly. "But how did he know I was to be here?"

"Did you telephone Mr. Murphy about the time you 'phoned me, Theo?"

"About five minutes earlier."

"Was there anyone in the shop at the time?"

"Not when I started to 'phone, but three or four people came in before I had finished."

"Any one of whom could possibly have put two and two together—I mean, of course, if that one had been either the writer of the stories, or Alec Foulis?"

"Well, yes, I suppose so."

"Who were the people?"

Terhune shrugged. "Heaven alone knows! As soon as I noticed that Anne was coping with them I got through to you."

"Can't you place any of them, Theo?"

Terhune tried to recall the bookshop as he had seen it in between the two telephone calls, but his memory of it was hazy; his thoughts had been elsewhere, so he had not consciously assimilated the details.

"Major Blye is the only person I can remember. He waved his gloves at me."

Julia looked disappointed, but having nothing further to say, she remained silent.

Terhune went on: "What else do you make of the latest story, Sergeant, apart from its clue that we are apparently on the wrong track?"

"Nothing else, except that I liked the last story better than the others, even if they are imitations of that French bloke."

"But that may be an important fact in itself, Sergeant."

"What may be—me liking the last better than the others?"

"Yes."

Murphy's glance became shrewd. "Go on, sir; what's in your mind?"

"To begin with, there isn't a Pierre, or a Peter, in the latest story."

Murphy started. "Nor is there," he exclaimed slowly. "Go on, sir," he repeated. "This is becoming interesting."

"But there is no doubt in your mind what the clue of the last story is?"

Murphy was honest. "There *wasn't*. But I gather that you have, and you're cleverer at judging the meaning of the stories than I am."

"You're wrong about my having doubts about the clue of the last story, Sergeant. I agree with you that it points most definitely to our being on the wrong track."

The sergeant looked confused. "Well, sir?"

"The story of the wrong brief is set in England—presumably in London. All the other four stories are about Paris. But the latest story reads quite naturally to you, doesn't it, whereas the others are old-fashioned and artificial?"

Murphy nodded, and stared thoughtfully at Terhune. "Yes," he agreed, "but isn't the probable reason for me liking the story the fact that it's about London, and the kind of people I've met and know? On the other hand, I don't know anything about Paris, and Parisians, and boulevards, and what not."

"Precisely, Sergeant! And yet our original conception of the first four stories was that they had been written by somebody who must have lived in Europe, and knew France very well. That is why we started looking around for our suspect from among people who had travelled to France, and knew French people intimately."

Comprehension dawned upon the other man. "Bedad! Now I understand what you are driving at. If the stories about Paris and French life were written by somebody who must have known about them, then this last story proves that the writer must know just as much about London, English people, and legal proceedings?"

"That's what I mean—up to a point, Sergeant. But I read more than that in the comparison between the French and English stories. The four French stories were modelled upon Guy de Maupassant, but nobody in their sane senses could say the same thing about *The First Brief*. The French stories are old-fashioned in style. The English story is modern. The French stories have a Continental subtlety about them. The English story is blatantly Cockney."

Murphy smacked the corner of Terhune's desk with his fist. "By God! Then the fifth story was written by another man!"

Terhune was more cautious. "A good sound journalist could write in two distinct and even contrasting styles, so we should not be too hasty in jumping to conclusions which have no supporting evidence."

"Nevertheless, you believe that the last story was written by a different person?" Julia insisted.

"Yes."

Julia knew her Terhune. "You have some theories, too, haven't you, Theo?"

He nodded. "As I said earlier on, I think that the theory of ours which held the murderer of Peter the Hermit to be the writer of the stories was definitely a wrong one. On the assumption that old Peter was Wilfred Foulis, and that his brother Alec helped very materially in bringing about his death, I believe now that Alec Foulis was *not* betraying himself by sending us those stories, but that he was being betrayed by somebody who was obviously aware of *all* the circumstances connected with the identity of both men, and intended seeing that Alec should suffer the consequences of his crime."

"That somebody had a darned funny way of setting about doing that," Murphy grumbled. "But I think I've said that before."

Terhune grinned. "You have, Sergeant. Anyway, this somebody sends us one story after another, and with each one supplies a clue as to the whys, the wherefores, and the hows of the crime. And then, one day, Alec Foulis wanders into a bookshop in Canterbury, and in the course of conversation hears that I am desperately anxious to team who purchased a certain set of Guy de Maupassant books. He is aware that you and I, Sergeant, are collaborating in trying to identify old Peter—who couldn't be aware of that fact, if he is living anywhere near Great Hinton? He realizes suddenly that we are on his track, and that if we should ever get to hear that he is the purchaser of the de Maupassant books he might find himself in a very awkward situation. Do you agree—so far?"

"For the sake of hearing you continue, yes."

"Now, Alec is an intelligent man. Or cunning might be a better word. He realizes that he must do something, if he can, to prevent our continuing enquiries as to the identity of the man who bought the de Maupassant books. He invents a neat solution to the problem. He writes the story of the wrong brief and sends it to us in the hope that it will make us believe that we are on the wrong trail—"

"Which it would have done, too, if you hadn't spotted the differences in style, Mr. Terhune."

Terhune smiled diffidently, and continued: "Whether he hoped that his red herring would have a permanent effect, I don't know, but maybe he is planning to send us more stories designed to lead us further astray, and if his stratagem gives him enough time he will leave the neighbourhood, and vanish, as he vanished once before—"

"How can you possibly know that, Theo?" Julia asked reprovingly.

"I don't *know* that he will do that, Julie, but there is good reason for suspecting that he has that idea in mind. Don't you remember what I told you he said to McCloud—that he would soon be leaving the neighbourhood? In the circumstances it is quite possible that he meant what he said at that moment."

"Of course."

Murphy frowned, and broke in: "Not so fast, Mr. Terhune. As I see it, you are arguing that Alec Foulis wrote *The First Brief* in order to lead us away from his own trail?"

"Yes."

"You also think that the man who wrote *The First Brief* didn't write the four French stories?"

"That is so."

"On the other hand you have also deduced that the man who wrote the French stories is probably the one who purchased the set of the French author's books from the Canterbury bookshop?"

"No."

"What!" The sergeant looked confused. "But I thought you said that McCloud identified the man who called in at his shop a short time back with the man who bought the original set of French books?"

"That is right."

"Then—what the devil—" Murphy came to a halt.

"I agree that it was possibly Alec Foulis who bought the set of de Maupassant's books. But I don't think it was he who wrote the four French stories."

"I know. So you have said earlier. But if it was somebody other than Alec who wrote the stories, then he didn't base his yarns on Mopewhat's-his-name." Then Murphy added reflectively, "Unless he borrowed them from Alec, of course. Yes, that could be the explanation."

"Perhaps."

"But in that case——" The sergeant shook his head in bewilderment. "How in Heaven's name did Alec Foulis get to know that somebody else had been sending clues to you in the shape of stories?"

"Exactly! How?"

Murphy did not have the opportunity of answering the question. Julia spoke first. Excitedly:

"Because that somebody was Alec's wife?"

"His wife," Terhune agreed quietly. "Alec's wife—Francisca."

I I

The sergeant was the first to break the ensuing silence. "The pieces are beginning to fit," he agreed sombrely. "Alec learns that his brother Wilfred has inherited some money. He passes the news on to Wilfred. Wilfred dies. Franci is convinced that Alec murdered his brother. She decides to avenge her old lover. For some reason she is afraid of doing so openly, and writes, or re-writes, one of those blasted stories in the hope that your connection with literature will enable you to put two and two together, and make four, or, in other words, spot the clue. Having got you and me completely muddled up, she addresses the envelope to Detective-Sergeant Theodore I. Murphy, at my address.

"As soon as she becomes aware that we are investigating old Peter's death she sends along a second story, but by that time she has got you and me sorted out. Later she sends a third, and then a fourth, story. Then her husband gets to hear that you are mighty anxious to find out who bought a certain set of French books. He doesn't know what the connection is between the French books and the death of his brother, but having a guilty conscience he determines to act cautiously. He refuses to sell the books back to McCloud, also to give his name and address.

"He returns home, but then what happens? We would do as well not to guess, but just consider what resulted. By some means he succeeds in learning what his wife has been up to. Being a cunning devil, he sees how he can turn this fact to his advantage. He writes a fifth story, and drops it in your letter-box tonight in the hope that you and I will think it has come from the sender of the other four stories, and believe that we are on the wrong trail, and go sniffing around for another. While we are doing that he plans to make his get-away, probably to Europe. Isn't that roughly the idea, sir?"

"Roughly, I think."

"But all that doesn't put us any nearer to knowing under what alias Alec Foulis is living," Murphy continued grumblingly.

"I think the latest story may help us to get that information."

The sergeant's scalp twitched. "How?"

"I'll ask you a question, Sergeant. How does the latest story read, in your opinion?"

The scalp descended again in a slight frown. "Do you mean, do I like it? I've told you that already."

"I do not mean that. Did the story read easily, and smoothly, or did it strike you as being scrappy, or stilted; amateurish, in fact?"

"Seeing you are asking me—though mind you, sir, I don't pretend to be any sort of a judge in such matters—I don't mind telling you that I thought the last story read more smoothly than the others."

"The answer I expected, Sergeant. Now, do you think you could have written a story like that at the mere asking?"

Murphy laughed loudly. "I'm damned sure I couldn't, Mr. Terhune, even if I was to be paid a pretty big sum. But then, I'm no writer, and never was."

"Just so! Why, then, should you think Alec Foulis would have found it any easier than you?"

"He might have a knack for writing. A lot of people can write a bit of a story or an article now and again even if they can't write books like you can."

"Agreed, but it is a strange coincidence if both husband *and* wife possessed an aptitude for writing—for those four French stories weren't too bad. Sergeant. With a little more polish they might, have been worth publishing in one of the pocket magazines. But here's another point. You know something about briefs, and interviews with counsel, and so on. Just now you said that the author must also know something about such matters, because he had sketched a scene which was realistic enough, as far as it goes, for it actually to have happened."

"Uh-huh!" or some such exclamation, from the detective.

"Then who of those in Great Hinton already known to us has such legal knowledge?"

A moment's thought, and then a sharp snap of the sergeant's fingers. "Jeremy Cardyce!"

"That's the man."

"But Jeremy is not married. He's an old bachelor."

Terhune nodded. "I know. I am not suggesting that Cardyce himself wrote the story. But if somebody has been picking his brains and knowledge just lately, and if he is able to tell us the other man's name—"

"Ten to one it would be Alec Foulis!" Murphy interrupted quickly.

"It's worth a chance, isn't it, Sergeant?"

"Of course it is. Without a doubt." Murphy grinned at Terhune. "Tomorrow?"

"As ever was," Terhune eagerly agreed.

Chapter Nineteen

Jeremy Cardyce took little finding. "He lives at Two Oaks Cottage," Ted Shore informed Murphy and Terhune the next morning.

"Whereabouts is that?"

"You know Mr. Harvey's place?"

"Yes."

"Two Oaks Cottage is next to it, on the far side from here."

They left the car outside the *Dusty Miller* and walked as far as Cardyce's cottage. As they approached they saw the retired bank manager at work in his garden. The garden was Harvey's hobby, his passion in life; whenever weather permitted he was to be seen in the garden doing one or another of the hundred odd jobs which a gardener has to do: digging, potting, planting, digging, weeding, mowing, pruning, digging, making compost, carting manure, spraying, picking fruit, cutting the vegetables, lifting the potatoes and digging. Today he was just digging, but as his back was towards the road he did not see them.

"Not my idea of fun," Murphy remarked, pointing his thumb at Harvey. "Though I must say he keeps the place a treat. Regular picture it is in the summer, especially since he's built that rockery." They walked on. By now the two oak trees which gave the cottage its name were to be seen. Fine specimens they were, too, green with age, rugged and tremendous. Their branches interlocked, and made a tunnel of the path leading from the road to the front door of the cottage; their farthermost branches even overhung the cottage, and dimmed much of its light. Apart from the two trees, however, there was nothing individual, or particularly striking, about the cottage. It was neither old nor modern, but just a sound, squat, square-looking building with tarred-stone walls, small windows, tall chimneys, and a red-tiled roof. It stood in about an acre of land, which was part flower and part kitchen garden, with a sprinkling of fruit trees, and soft-fruit bushes. Though the garden obviously received attention of a kind, it suffered badly by comparison with Harvey's scrupulously attended land.

They pushed open a rather decrepit gate, which squealed a loud protest at being disturbed, and walked along a brick patterned path. As they approached the door Terhune began sniffing.

"What are you smelling, sir?"

"I don't know, Sergeant, but the smell reminds me of books."

Murphy laughed. Mr. Terhune and his books...

A knock, a few moments' silence, the dull echo of short, unhurried footsteps. The door opened, and a spare little man with a mane of white hair stared at them through horn-rimmed spectacles.

"Mr. Jeremy Cardyce?"

"That is my name," Cardyce answered, in a quiet, polished voice—Terhune reflected that he had not heard a more pleasant voice for many moons; it was warm, cultured, redolent of wit and humour.

"I am Detective-Sergeant Murphy, of the Kent County Constabulary, Mr. Cardyce."

"Ah!" the little man exclaimed significantly.

"And this is Mr. Theodore Terhune," Murphy continued.

Cardyce nodded his head in acknowledgment of the introduction; enquiry was mirrored in his eyes.

"We should appreciate an opportunity of putting a few questions to you in connection with the death of old Peter the Hermit, if you could spare us a few minutes, Mr. Cardyce."

"Peter the Hermit!" For a moment Jeremy Cardyce looked surprised, but a smile of comprehension quickly supervened. "Of course!

I recollect, now, that the police have been making enquiries as to his identity. Will you please enter, gentlemen; it is more cosy, and certainly warmer, in my room."

He stood aside to let his visitors enter. They did so, whereupon, with a word of apology, he led the way into a room at the back of the house. As they entered Murphy laughed impulsively, for the room was walled with books from ceiling to floor, from north to south, from east to west. There were other books piled up on the floor, and books piled up on the desk.

The sergeant realized that Cardyce was looking at him with surprise. "I must apologize for laughing, Mr. Cardyce, but just now Mr. Terhune said he smelled books, and, by all the Saints, it's right he is! He's a book-lover is Mr. Terhune. Like yourself, I guess."

Cardyce turned eagerly to Terhune. "So you, also, are a bibliophile," he burbled. "This is a pleasure! A very great pleasure! Books make my chief happiness in life. Though, as you will notice, the majority of my books have a legal flavour. Are you interested in the law, Mr. Terhune? Many members of the police are—"

"Mr. Terhune isn't a member of the force, Mr. Cardyce," Murphy interrupted. "He owns the bookshop and library in Bray."

"Indeed! Indeed! Indeed!" Cardyce nodded his head rapidly. "Your visit becomes more pleasing still. I have often thought about calling upon you—I was sure from some of the books I saw in your window that you must share my passion. But I never saw any legal books which I do not already possess."

"He keeps them all for himself," the sergeant explained.

Cardyce's eyes shone eagerly. "Are you interested in the legal profession?"

Murphy seemed determined not to let Terhune speak for himself. "Mr. Terhune is a writer," he answered, proud of shining in Terhune's reflected glory. "Haven't you read about Mr. Terhune in the newspapers? It was he who gave evidence in Rex *v.* Cockburn at Maidstone—"

"*That* Mr. Terhune!" Cardyce's voice warmed with enthusiasm. "I read every word of that amazing case. Every word, Mr. Terhune! The case of Rex *v.* Cockburn was unprecedented in legal history. What did the newspapers call the trial—"

"A Case for Solomon."

"Yes, yes! That is right!" The mane of white hair nodded rapidly again. "A Case for Solomon, indeed—in which one man is tried for murdering another a *second* time." He became suddenly apologetic. "But please sit down, gentlemen. If you will take that chair, Mr. Terhune, and you this one, Mr.—Mr.—"

"Murphy."

"Of course. Mr. Murphy— I shall sit on these books. Now tell me how I can be of assistance to you in your enquiries? I must first warn you that I have only twice spoken to that unfortunate old man."

The sergeant pulled the script of *The First Brief* from his pocket, and passed it over to the old barrister-at-law.

"Would you mind reading through this script, sir, and letting us know afterwards whether the story is familiar to you?"

Cardyce glanced at the typewritten pages. He read the first three pages at a deliberate speed, then looked at the sergeant with surprised eyes.

"Read on, sir," Murphy encouraged.

Cardyce did so, but less attentively. He reached the last page, laid the script face down upon his knees, and looked at his visitors with an expression of astonishment.

"Certainly the story is familiar to me, gentlemen. It is a true story, and happened to a young friend of mine who ate his dinners and was called to the Bar at the Inn of Court of which I have the honour of being a member. But his real name is not Franklin."

"Who else knows the story besides yourself, Mr. Cardyce?"

A mischievous smile lighted up the old man's face. "Franklin himself, of course."

"Naturally!" Murphy was too tense to share Cardyce's humour. "Is Franklin living anywhere near here?"

"No. Franklin—I shall continue to call him by that name unless you insist otherwise—is a puisne judge in India."

"Is there anyone living locally, besides yourself, who might be able to tell the story of Franklin's first brief?"

"I cannot say that there is not, Mr. Murphy, but I should think it most unlikely that there is. The episode happened many years ago."

"Are you a writer, sir?" Murphy asked suddenly.

"I contribute articles to certain publications specializing in legal matters."

"Did you write this story?"

Cardyce looked shocked. "Certainly not, sir."

"Have you told it to anyone lately?"

The old man looked embarrassed. "Yes, gentlemen, I have. Less than a week ago."

Murphy snapped: "Who to?"

"To nobody in particular."

"What?"

"Let me explain the circumstances, Mr. Murphy. Last Sunday morning I went for a walk with Mr. Harvey. Mr. Nicholas Harvey, who lives in the next cottage."

Murphy nodded.

"Just as we were returning to the village the rain started. At first it was gentle, but then it became squally. As we were passing the *Dusty Miller* at the time Mr. Harvey suggested our entering and having a glass of sherry while we waited for the squall to pass on. I agreed. I am not a drinker, gentlemen, but I enjoy a glass of sherry now and again.

"We entered the saloon. There were some people already there, whom I knew. We all joined in a party, and talked. Presently the conversation turned upon some legal point. I was asked to express an opinion. I did so. Then I was asked other questions of a general nature—the difference between the Constitution of Great Britain and that of the United States of America. Before long I found myself the centre of attention, if I may be allowed to express the situation thus. Someone asked about briefs. Soon, I found myself telling the story of Franklin's first brief. It was, perhaps, neither a proper nor a fit story to tell—I was shocked when I read it in type just now, though I did not tell it as a bawdy story—but doubtless I was led astray by the warm, cheerful atmosphere of the saloon."

"Who was present in the saloon when you told the story?" Murphy demanded urgently.

"Mr. Shore, of course, Mr. Nicholas Harvey, Mr. Rolfe—I do not remember his Christian name. Then there was somebody from Willingham, a Mr. Hocking—"

"Mr. Bram Hocking?"

"Possibly. Also Mr. Giffen, Mr. Hicks from Bracken Hill—" Cardyce paused.

Murphy glanced despairingly at Terhune. "All that lot!" he muttered. Then, to their host: "Mr. Max Bullett? Was he there?"

The barrister shook his head. "No, Mr. Murphy, Mr. Bullett was not present."

"Anyone else, sir?"

"Let me try to remember. There was somebody sitting next to the fire— Ah yes! Mr. Arthur Snaith. And next to him, Doctor Edwards—"

Terhune clicked his fingers loudly. The other two men looked at him, surprised.

"Are you on the telephone, Mr. Cardyce?" Terhune asked anxiously.

"I am. The instrument is behind you, Mr. Terhune."

"Might I use it, please, for an urgent call?"

"Of course." Cardyce rose from his pile of books. "I shall retire—" he began courteously.

"Please stay, Mr. Cardyce. The call is not private."

As Cardyce sat down Terhune turned and picked up the telephone, which stood on one of the shelves between two piles of books. To the girl at the exchange he gave a Canterbury number. In a very short time the connection was made. He recognized McCloud's voice.

"Hullo, Mr. McCloud, this is Terhune again. I am very sorry to keep worrying you about a very trivial matter, but concerning the de Maupassant books—"

"Again!" McCloud laughed good-humouredly. "I shall soon begin to think that you want to trace the buyer of the books not as a bookseller but as a detective."

Terhune decided that frankness might pay a good dividend. "As a matter of fact, I do."

The Canterbury man choked in his hurry to speak. "Then the books are connected with a crime, Mr. Terhune? Good Heavens! You have made me feel most excited. Most excited indeed."

"It is by no means certain there is any question of crime, Mr. McCloud—"

"Oh!" The exclamation was one of disappointment.

"I cannot give you much information over the telephone, but I'll call upon you one day next week and tell you why it is necessary to trace the books."

"That is most kind of you. I must confess that you have aroused my curiosity. In the meantime, what is it you want to know this time?"

"The set you sold were less two titles, were they not?"

"That is so."

"Can you remember the titles, Mr. McCloud? It is most important that I should know."

"Let me see—" A long pause followed; one that was extremely irksome to Terhune. Then: "Ah! I have remembered one—*Yvette*—"

"Isn't that the title this same buyer asked for a few days ago?"

"Yes, yes. It is. You have a good memory—"

"It is the other title I want to know about. He didn't ask you for that also?"

"No! No, no! I gathered from his manner that he had found the other missing title elsewhere. The other title! Let me see—the other title…" Another agonizing pause. Longer, this time. Then, at last, in a jubilant voice: "I have it, Mr. Terhune. It has come back to me. The second title that was missing from the French set was the one which, you will remember, converted Tolstoi into a fervent admirer of Guy de Maupassant."

"*Une Vie?*" Terhune broke in.

"*Une Vie*, Mr. Terhune," McCloud confirmed. "That was the other title. Yes, indeed—*Une Vie*."

II

One glance at Terhune's expressive features satisfied the sergeant that something of importance had developed from the telephone call to Canterbury. He turned to Cardyce.

"May I ask you to treat this conversation as confidential, Mr. Cardyce?"

"Of course," Cardyce answered immediately.

Murphy turned back eagerly to Terhune. "Well, Mr. Terhune?"

"You remember that our man was missing two titles from that set of de Maupassant in the original?"

"Yes. He tried McCloud the other day for the other two, didn't he?"

"No, only for one. *Yvette*. McCloud had the impression that he had bought the other title elsewhere."

"Well?"

"The other title was *Une Vie*. Some months ago I sold a copy of *Une Vie* in the original."

The sergeant had no need for the significance of this remark to be pointed out to him. "Who to?" he exploded.

"Arthur Snaith."

"Snaith! My God! And Snaith was present in the saloon when Mr. Cardyce was telling his story of Franklin's first brief?"

Cardyce looked very confused, but he nodded. "Yes, indeed. Mr. Snaith was there. He sat by the fire."

Murphy's excitement increased; he appeared to have lost most of his customary phlegm. "That wife of his, she's foreign-looking—coal-dark hair, olive complexion, ear-rings—unless I'm imagining—"

"You are not," Terhune reassured him. "Listen to this. *Une Vie* is not the only book in a foreign language Snaith has bought from me in the past year. He had a copy of *La Rana Viajera*, by Camba."

Murphy looked blank.

Cardyce also. He murmured: "*La Rana Viajera!* That is not a French title."

"It's not, Mr. Cardyce. It's Spanish."

"Spanish!" Murphy bellowed the word. "That almost clinches the case?"

"Almost," Terhune agreed.

III

After a brief explanation to Cardyce, which was, in the circumstances, due to him, the two visitors left Two Oaks Cottage and walked slowly along the road towards the *Dusty Miller*. They had passed by Harvey's place—Harvey was carrying his garden tools away to a shed—before either spoke. Then Terhune said, somewhat bitterly:

"I'm a blithering idiot not to have thought of Snaith before now."

"Nonsense, Mr. Terhune. Why should you have done so?"

"I can number the people who buy books in a foreign language on one hand—Snaith, Godfrey Hutton, Guy Heather—"

"The schoolmaster-fellow at Bracken Hill?"

"Yes. In the last few months he's been worrying me for children's stories in French—he reads them out in school. Then Judge Pemberton once bought two books in Italian, and lastly, Sir George Brereton —he once asked me to buy for him a book in German—on angling, of course—but I think that was mostly swank." Terhune shook his head in self-reproach. "No, Sergeant, I ought to have thought of Snaith, more particularly seeing that his wife is foreign-looking."

"She's no raving beauty," Murphy remarked in a doubtful voice. "Not the type to cause most men to spend all their lives believing her to be the only woman in the world."

Terhune disagreed. "Her profile is striking. So is her colouring. Even now. I should say that she was stunning in her early twenties, but that twenty-odd years of married partnership to Snaith hasn't helped to preserve her good looks." He finished up reflectively: "I never did care much for the man."

"Talk of the devil!" Murphy exclaimed.

"Snaith?"

"Yes. Isn't that he, walking towards the *Dusty Miller?*"

Terhune peered through the gathering dusk at the man ahead. The back undoubtedly belonged to Arthur Snaith.

"Can you walk quietly?" Murphy continued. "Enough not to let him hear us overtaking him?"

"I think so."

"Then we'll challenge his identity, and see what happens."

The two men quickened their pace, and began to approach Snaith from the rear. Unfortunately Snaith had almost reached the *Dusty Miller.*

"Damn!" Murphy muttered, quickening his pace still more.

Still nearer to the inn, until less than a dozen paces separated Snaith from the door. The two men were still some distance behind.

Murphy funnelled his hand. "Alec!" he bellowed. "Alec Foulis!"

Snaith swirled round.

"You've hit another bull's-eye, Mr. Terhune," Murphy congratulated generously.

Chapter Twenty

Snaith recovered very quickly from his involuntary act of betrayal. He pretended to look about him, then, with subtle cunning, waited for the two other men to approach near enough for him to say, in a casual manner: "I thought you were calling me for a moment, Mr. Murphy." He nodded genially. "Good afternoon, Mr. Terhune."

"We were calling you," the sergeant said grimly.

"Me! But the name you called out was Fowkes or Foley or something like that."

"Foulis was the name. Alec Foulis;"

"Well…" Snaith shrugged. "You know *my* name."

"We do." The sergeant laughed shortly. "Alec Foulis."

The other man simulated anger. "If this is a joke, Sergeant—"

"Perhaps you prefer Crawshay. Alec Crawshay, husband of Francisca Bázan."

The accusation shook Snaith. A nerve in his forehead began to pound. His glance became shifty. Then he squared his shoulders.

"All right," he said boldly. "I was born Alec Foulis. What of the fact? There's no crime, is there, in preferring to be known by some other name?"

"No, there's no crime in changing one's name unless it is for an unlawful purpose. But there are some questions we want to put to you, Mr. Foulis—"

Snaith stared insultingly at Terhune. "We!" he exclaimed softly.

"I was not aware that Mr. Terhune was a plain-clothes member of the Kent Constabulary."

"If you have any objections to Mr. Terhune's presence—"

"Oh! Please, Sergeant Murphy, do not misunderstand me. I have no *objections* to Mr. Terhune's presence. Only to the inference contained in the word 'we'. But have you any right to question me, even if my name is Foulis?"

"I have not, but if you prefer to be interviewed by somebody of higher authority—"

"Tut! Tut! You are *so* hasty! I asked a simple question, which you answered. But that does not mean that I have any more objection to your questioning me than I have to Mr. Terhune's presence. Why should I object? I have done nothing to fear a police interrogation."

"In that case—"

Snaith waved a hand in the direction of the inn. "Shall we go in?"

"In the *Dusty Miller?*"

Snaith laughed, presumably at the surprise in Murphy's voice. "Why not? It is warm and cheerful."

"And private? Unless, of course, you do not mind your friends and neighbours knowing that you allowed your brother to starve for ten years!"

A longish pause. 'Mrs. Shore would probably lend us her kitchen." Snaith sounded less sure of himself.

"Isn't your own home equally warm?"

"Mrs. Snaith isn't there—she is visiting some friends in Bracken Hill—"

"So much the better," Murphy broke in. "We shall not be disturbed."

Another long pause.

"Well, Mr. Snaith?" Murphy said impatiently.

"All right. If you insist," Snaith muttered sullenly. He led the way along the deserted road. By now twilight was deepening into night, and the increasing wind had a sleety chill in it.

As the three men trudged along, pushing against the wind, their feet alone disturbed the restless silence. Their tongues remained still. Perhaps they were too chilled to welcome conversation. That, at least, was Terhune's reason. He turned up his coat collar, and pulled the brim of his hat down over his eyes to protect his glasses from damping. Murphy walked with a lighter step than usual; there was an alertness in the poise of his body which suggested that he was prepared for any move which Snaith might make. But Snaith, although somewhat less defiant than at first, showed no sign of alarm or panic.

They reached Snaith's cottage. He took a key from his pocket and opened the front door with it. Both his companions were surprised; it was not usual for the country people thereabouts to lock their houses and cottages unless they were leaving the village.

They entered the cottage. Snaith fumbled in his pocket for a box of matches, and presently lit the small oil-lamp which hung from the low ceiling. As soon as the wick was burning brightly he opened a door on the left. His companions saw a cheerful glow in the fireplace, and felt a draught of warm air caress their cheeks.

"Will you enter?" Snaith invited light-heartedly, in a voice which indicated that he had recovered his composure. They did so; he followed, and lit the lamp, which stood on a small round table pushed against the wall farthest from the fire.

There were three chairs in the room; a well-padded but well-worn armchair, a rocking-chair, and an ordinary wooden chair. With a rather foreign gesture Snaith indicated the chairs.

"The rocking-chair is my wife's," he explained easily. "Do either of you prefer the rocker?" As neither Murphy nor Terhune answered at once, he continued quickly: "No? Then you have the armchair, Sergeant, and you, Mr. Terhune, the other. I'll take the rocker, but I rely upon you to tell me at once if I begin rocking. It is an odious, but unconscious, habit. I have never succeeded in curing my wife's habit of rocking."

The three men sat down. Both Terhune and the sergeant felt ill-at-ease, but Snaith appeared quite unconcerned. In a queer fashion he dominated the situation, and made his visitors feel as if they, rather than he, were on the defensive.

"Do you smoke?" he continued easily. He held out a packet of Players to Murphy.

"Not for me," Murphy refused sharply. "I only smoke my pet brand, if you've no objection." Without waiting for an answer he took a cigarette-case from his own pocket and quickly lit a cigarette. Terhune's eyes twinkled. He knew that Murphy usually smoked Players.

"Of course not," Snaith agreed genially. He offered the cigarettes to Terhune. "And you, Mr. Terhune?"

Terhune patted his pocket. "I prefer a pipe—if I may."

Snaith nodded, and smiled. The other two had the uncomfortable feeling that he had realized the true reason behind their reluctance to smoke his cigarettes. However, he said nothing, but lit a cigarette for himself. Soon all three men were leaning back in their chairs, smoking.

Snaith was the first to speak. "Well, Sergeant Murphy, what do you want to talk to me about?"

"You and your brother," Murphy said bluntly.

"Which brother?"

"Wilfred. We are not interested in Sydney."

Snaith began to rock; very gently. "You seem to know so much about my family, Sergeant Murphy, that I cannot think of any reason for being interrogated." He glanced at Terhune. "Isn't that the technical term generally used by novelists?"

Terhune nodded vaguely. Snaith turned back to the sergeant.

"I suppose you realize that I resent this interview? I can think of no circumstances to justify it. Certainly not the fact that I once had two brothers, one named Wilfred and the other Sydney."

"Suppose we begin at the beginning—"

"An excellent idea," Snaith broke in, mockingly.

Murphy was not ruffled. "The day old Peter died dates the beginning."

"Well?"

"You knew that the police were anxious to trace old Peter's identity?"

"Yes."

"Then why didn't you give information to that effect?"

Snaith leaned well back, stared up at the ceiling and blew cigarette smoke through his nostrils in wispy trails.

"Are you charging me with having knowledge of that old tramp's identity?"

"I am," Murphy confirmed bluntly.

"Indeed! How interesting! And what makes you think that I have that knowledge?"

"Do you deny that your real name is Alexander Crawshay Foulis?"

"You make my name sound very impressive!" A nod. "Those are my baptismal names."

"And that you had an elder brother by the name of Wilfred?"

"I had."

"And that old Peter was that brother?"

"Ah!" The rocking ceased. "Now we are leaving the realms of fact to sail up into a less substantial stratosphere of imagination."

"Are those fancy words meant to imply a denial?"

"On the contrary, they imply an affirmation."

"Good!" Murphy said briskly. "As you admit that old Peter was your brother, we can continue."

"But I made no such admission," Snaith pointed out with a suave gesture.

Murphy frowned. "I'm not deaf. You said that your words implied an affirmative."

"That is true. An affirmative answer to your question."

"Are you trying to be funny?"

"Not at all, Sergeant Murphy. You asked me if I denied that old Peter was my brother Wilfred. If I give an affirmative answer to that question the result is, yes, I do deny the identity."

Murphy thrust out a lower lip. "It won't help you to juggle with words."

Snaith laughed softly. "I am not aware that I need to be helped. Is it a crime just to be Alec Foulis?"

A quick, seering smile flashed across the sergeant's plain face. "It may well be."

Murphy scored the point. Snaith's lower lip twitched: he threw the butt end of his cigarette into the fire with an uncertain gesture.

"I have seen neither Wilfred nor Sydney since I was a schoolboy."

"Not Sydney. He disappeared. He emigrated to Australia, didn't he? You all disappeared. Wilfred disappeared. He fled to Greece. Then you disappeared."

"You police are so clever in poking your noses into other people's business, aren't you? All right. I did disappear, and I suppose you know why?"

"We do. Your brother fled from England because he had embezzled a small fortune from the firm which employed him. The disgrace ruined your father. He sent your other brother to Australia, paid your school-fees for a couple of years, then killed your mother and himself. Your school-mates taunted you with the crimes of your family. You hadn't the guts to stick it out—"

"Guts! Guts!" Snaith's laugh was shrill, bitter. "God! You don't know what you're talking about. Guts! There isn't a boy alive who could have stuck out those blasted little heathens. 'Wilfred is a theief! Wil-fred is a the-ief! Wilfred is a the-ief! Your father killed your mother! Your father killed your mother!' Damn and blast their mean little souls! They may have forgotten me, but I haven't forgotten them. By God, I haven't! I can still remember them and their names. Every mother's son of them. Jack Boyle, Jimmy Donovan, Bill Stukeley, Joe Dobbs, Joe Crane, John Sankey, Ted O'Connor— Damn you and your guts!"

"All right! All right! I shouldn't have said what I did. You went to another part of the country. Let's leave it at that. Besides, we are talking of Wilfred, and not you—for the moment. Wilfred's theft ruined your life, didn't it? It stopped any chance of your putting M.D. after your name, didn't it? And you hated him for what he did to you, didn't you?"

Snaith's face reflected the degree of his raging emotions, and later, the extent of the rigid control over those emotions which he presently exerted. He laughed, and stared with mocking challenge at the detective. The chair began to rock. Slowly, gently, like the slow, sinuous movements of a snake gradually uncurling.

"I am not a man to hate my brother," he said. "Did my brother ruin my life? Yes, I suppose it is true to say that he did. But I did not hate him for that when I learned that fate had punished him in her own, pretty way—"

Murphy nodded. "We know all about the failure of the foreign bank."

For a passing moment Snaith's eyes filled with the fire of the savage hate which he so suavely disclaimed, but his companions could not decide whether this sudden spasm was caused by the thought of what his brother had suffered or the extent of the detective's knowledge.

"What we don't know is what happened to the brother when he found out that all the money he had sent abroad had gone."

"How should I know what happened to him? At the best of times we were neither of us good correspondents," Snaith sneered. "Besides, neither of us knew the address of the other."

"But you knew he was living in Sofia in nineteen-twenty-three. That is why you took pains to see that the news of Señorita Bázan's marriage should be printed in a Sofia newspaper, and why you left a message for him in Marseilles."

The rocking came to a sudden stop. Once again, it seemed, Snaith was startled by the extent of the detective's knowledge.

"You know so much I don't know why you are troubling to ask me *questions*."

"How did you come to know that Wilfred was living in Sofia?" Murphy persisted.

A long pause. The rocking began again.

"Are you going to reply, or would you prefer me to put the question to Mrs. Snaith when I see her?"

Rock! Rock! Rock! The length of the rock increased. Every time the chair went backward the tips of the rockers pressed on a loose floorboard which squeaked slightly, rather like a cat in pain. Ro-ck—squeak! Ro-ck—squeak! Ro-ck—squeak! Snaith's face remained unrevealing; his self-control still maintaining a check upon his facial expression. But, unconsciously, he sought relief in rocking. To and fro! Ro-ck—a long-drawn-out ro-ck—and then—squeak—a miaowing protest. To-and-fro! Ro-ck—squeak!

"For the last time—"

"Frances—Francisca she was then—told me. Early in nineteen-twenty-three I had to go to Marseilles on business. I met Frances and her father at a party. When we first met she looked at me as if something about me worried her. I questioned her. She said that my face reminded her of her fiancé, whom she had left behind in Sofia. I teased her until at last she showed me his photograph. Then I recognized Wilfred."

"So you determined to revenge yourself upon Wilfred by marrying Señorita Bázan yourself?"

Snaith laughed sneeringly. "Why not? He had ruined my life. Instead of being a G.P., and my own master, I was a clerk in an insurance firm, in the Employers' Liability Department, where I acted as liaison officer between the company and the company's appointed physician."

"Go on."

"What more do you want to know?"

"How did you persuade Señorita Bázan to give up Wilfred and marry you?"

"Her father was a sensible man, and had his daughter's future at heart."

"I suppose you told him that his daughter's fiancé was a thief?"

Snaith shrugged. "I thought Frances was too nice a girl to be sacrificed to the kind of life she would have led with Wilfred as a husband. He was still a fugitive from justice."

This gave Murphy an opportunity of returning irony for irony. "Having saved Señorita Bázan from such a terrible fate. I suppose you then fell in love with her yourself?"

"I married her," Snaith answered crisply. "A man mostly marries for love."

"Was it love for your wife which prompted you to leave the message for your brother?"

"It was certainly not love for him."

Terhune grinned. A rather ingenious answer, that, he thought.

Murphy went on: "When did you next hear of Wilfred? When he made an unexpected appearance in Great Hinton, ten years ago?"

Snaith lit another cigarette. "This is where we must metaphorically part company, Sergeant Murphy. I cannot believe that you are serious in asserting that Wilfred and old Peter the Hermit were one and the same man. After all, if I had had any idea that old Peter was my brother I would have helped him a little with food and shelter, although I am myself comparatively poor—I am living on a small pension from the insurance company for which I worked."

"You are a comparatively young man to be living on a pension."

"Is fifty-three young? A matter of opinion. In point of fact, as the result of an accident I was pensioned off early."

"Old Peter was your brother Wilfred," Murphy repeated dourly.

"Well, if *you* say so—" Snaith gesticulated—it was more a foreign than a British gesture. "I am told that the police never make statements unless they have the requisite proof to back them up." His smile mocked the sergeant.

"As a matter of fact, we have," Murphy agreed casually.

The rocking became slower. The smile vanished. "You have *proof?*"

"Part of which consists of a copy of the Sofia newspaper containing the notice of Señorita Bázan's marriage. It was buried under one corner of the shack which old Peter lived in."

The rocker became still. Terhune mentally timed the seconds. One—two—three—and so to twenty. Then it moved again. To and fro. Evenly, gently, and without an annoying squeak.

"Interesting!" Snaith murmured. "Quite interesting! And suppose that, for the sake of continuing this interesting interview, I agree that that clue points to the possibility of old Peter having been my brother, what then? What other questions would such a hypothetical assumption produce?"

"How much would your brother have inherited had he lived instead of dying?"

Once again Snaith's subconscious self registered a note of alarm. The rocking ceased abruptly. But outwardly his smile was confident, sneering.

"Do I hear you asking that question, Sergeant Murphy, or our novelist here, Mr. Terhune? Really! Really! I am sure only Mr. Terhune could have invented such a fantastic theory. From whom would, or could, my brother have inherited money?"

"That is another question I was going to put to you in a moment. It will save the police a little trouble, but not much. We have a system for searching old newspaper files for solicitors' advertisements."

Snaith's eyes shadowed. Evidently he had overlooked that point.

"All right, I did see an advertisement in *The Times* some weeks ago," he admitted abruptly, and a little less confidently. "It was for

Wilfred and Alexander Crawshay Foulis, brothers, or any other surviving relatives of the late Sydney Crawshay Foulis, who left England for Australia in nineteen hundred and seven."

"And the amount?"

"Seventy-two thousand pounds."

Murphy whistled. "What did you do?"

"Wrote to the solicitors informing them that I was still alive, living under the name of Arthur Snaith, at this address, but that nothing had been seen or heard of Wilfred since Sydney had left for Australia."

"What happened? They sent for you?"

"Of course." Snaith's manner was now somewhat sullen, as if regretting the necessity even of admitting facts which the police could easily check up for themselves.

"Were you informed of the terms of your brother's will?"

"Yes. Wilfred was made chief beneficiary, with remainder to me upon his death, with remainder equally to the heirs of us both."

"So Sydney bore no hatred for his elder brother?"

Snaith shrugged. "According to the solicitors, Sydney was grateful to Wilfred."

"Grateful?"

"If Wilfred hadn't robbed his employers, Sydney wouldn't have been sent to Australia, and wouldn't therefore have made a small fortune from gold-mining."

Terhune chuckled. One man's poison was certainly another man's meat—

"What are the solicitors proposing to do about fulfilling the terms of the will?"

The answer was long in coming. "They are applying to Court for leave to presume death," he said at last.

"And if leave is given you will inherit the whole of your brother's fortune?"

"Yes."

"On the other hand, if your brother had not died you might have had to wait another ten, twenty—who knows?—perhaps twenty-five or thirty years—before being able to lay your hands upon his money?"

"*If* my brother had *not* died!" Snaith laughed jeeringly. "It would suit me admirably to hear that Wilfred was dead—it would mean the money coming to me all the sooner, and without the complications of applying to the Courts for leave to presume death. But where is the person who can do me the favour of proving that my brother is dead?"

Murphy was seeking for the best way of countering Snaith's subtle argument, that he had more to lose by denying than admitting old Peter's identity, when the temporary silence was disturbed by the dull echo of a drumming noise. The slow rocking of Snaith's chair came to a sudden stop.

"What's that noise?" Murphy asked.

"The kitchen window—it must have come unlatched, and is banging in the wind." Snaith spoke loudly.

The sergeant was only partly satisfied. "It sounds like something inside the house. Perhaps Mrs. Snaith—"

"I've told you—she is visiting neighbours."

"She might have come home."

The drumming seemed to grow more insistent.

"She's not due back until nine o'clock. I tell you it's the kitchen window banging in this damned wind. I'll close it." Snaith quickly rose from his chair.

So did Terhune. "I'll close it, Mr. Snaith."

"What the devil—"

Murphy glanced at Terhune's face. "Sit down, Mr. Snaith," he interrupted sharply.

"May I remind you that this *is* my house, and that I am *not* under arrest? I'm going out to shut that window."

"Then we will both go," Terhune announced cheerfully.

Snaith hesitated.

"Well?" Murphy prompted impatiently.

Snaith sat down. "All right! As far as I am concerned the damned window can carry on banging. I'm used to it. It always does bang in a high wind."

Terhune and the sergeant exchanged quick glances. Murphy jerked his head towards the door. Before Snaith could anticipate him Terhune moved towards the door and opened it. Snaith leaped to his feet, but Murphy acted as quickly, closed the door behind Terhune, and stood before it, blocking Snaith's exit.

Terhune moved along the short hall to the back of the cottage. Two doors faced him. The noise came from behind the left-hand door. He opened it. The noise of the drumming ceased. The light reflected from the tiny oil-lamp in the hall was not enough to reveal the interior of the room. He pulled a torch from his coat pocket, pressed the button. The bright, round beam of light sliced the grey darkness, and illuminated a small double-bedded bedroom. But no banging window, no moving object of any kind. He hesitated, stood still. Then the drumming began again. A dullish, hollow sound from low down which seemed to emanate from the far, hidden side of the bed. He moved round the bed in that direction.

Stretched out on the floor, her arms and legs bound, her mouth gagged, was Frances Snaith. Her heels drummed on a woollen rug.

Chapter Twenty-One

Terhune quickly looked about for a light, and saw a candlestick close at hand, on a chest of drawers. He lit the candle, and as its flame brightened after the initial hesitation he bent down to release Mrs. Snaith from her bonds.

Almost before he had finished releasing the gag from her mouth she was speaking to him. "You are Mr. Terhune, aren't you? The light is not very clear—"

"Yes." He began untying the scarf which bound her knees together.

"I could hear voices from the front room. Who was there? My husband?" Her voice was scared but full of loathing.

"Your husband, Detective-Sergeant Murphy, and I."

"Ah!" The exclamation was a sigh of relief, inspired, he was sure by the mention of Murphy's presence.

The knots were very tight. He had to struggle with them. "Who bound you like this?"

"*He* did!" The hate was more perceptible. "*He* did! My husband. When he went out tonight. He has tied me up every time he has left the cottage since Monday." She spoke with a slight accent which now—after the event, as it were—he recognized as foreign, and not the result of an impediment. "He went to Canterbury that day. Later, while I was out, he searched the cottage and found an envelope addressed to you with a new story inside—"

"The fifth story?"

"Yes, yes. I intended to post it on Tuesday when we went in to Ashford for market day. He twisted my arm until I told him about sending you the other stories—"

"The swine!"

"He is a beast! I hate him! I have always hated him. He has always been cruel to me."

"Ah!" The knot gave way; he freed her knees of the scarf. "Please turn over, Mrs. Snaith,"

She did so, and while he struggled with the scarves which secured her arms, one at the wrists, another at the elbows, she spoke into the wool rug. "You have guessed, have you not, that Peter the Hermit was my husband's brother? His name was not Peter, it was Wilfred—"

"We know. Wilfred Foulis, your first sweetheart."

"Holy Mother! How do you know that? None of my stories said anything of Peter's love for me, or my love for him."

He freed her wrists. "We found an old Bulgarian newspaper under the hut in the wood. One paragraph announced the marriage of the daughter of the Spanish Vice-Consul at Marseilles, Señorita Francisca Bázan. With the help of your stories, and after making some enquiries, we put two and two together."

"You are *so* clever! I am glad to have helped you. My husband killed his brother. Do you know that? Did you learn that from my stories?"

"We did." The last scarf fell away from her elbows. "Can you stand?"

"Yes, yes. I am not so stiff as usual. He had not left the cottage more than a few minutes. Take me to the policeman detective. I want to tell him everything I know."

"Come along, Mrs. Snaith." He placed one hand under her elbow, because she seemed less steady physically than she was mentally.

So into the front room, where Mrs. Snaith was glared at by one pair of eyes which were filled with a hatred equal to her own, and by the other pair with a curiosity that had nothing of surprise in it; Murphy had already half-guessed the truth.

Terhune helped Mrs. Snaith into the chair which Murphy had hurriedly vacated upon her entry. The sergeant spoke, relieving the tension: "So you've returned earlier than you expected, Mrs. Snaith?"

"Mrs. Snaith wasn't out. I found her in the bedroom, bound and gagged."

"Bound and gagged, begod!" Murphy swung round to face Snaith. "I don't think we've come here any too soon."

Snaith said nothing. He did not even trouble to look at the detective, but stared at his wife. His glance was vicious.

Terhune explained quickly: "His visit to Canterbury put Snaith on his guard. When he arrived home he searched the place, and found another story all ready to be posted to me. He tortured Mrs. Snaith until she confessed what she had done."

The sergeant's mouth became an unpleasant sight; there was an ominous gleam in his eyes as he looked at Snaith.

"Well, Snaith?" he said harshly.

"Well, Sergeant Murphy?" Snaith mimicked.

"You heard what your wife said, didn't you?"

"I did. What of it?"

"What of it, begod! Do you think you can get away with torturing your wife, and binding and gagging her?"

"Tonight wasn't the first time," Frances Snaith broke in. "Ever since Monday night he has stared at me with those terrible eyes of his. Look at him now. He's still staring. Stop him! Please!"

"Keep calm, Mrs. Snaith," Murphy soothed. "You've nothing to worry about as long as Mr. Terhune and me are here."

"He makes me afraid when he looks at me like that. Ever since Monday I have not been able to move, even from one room to another, without him coming with me and staring at me. And every time he went out he tied my arms and legs together so that I could not escape, and put something into my mouth so that I could not call for help. You must take him away to prison. Please, Policeman, put him in prison."

Snaith laughed scornfully; his composure seemed not to have suffered greatly in consequence of his wife's unexpected appearance.

"I should not be too hopeful about seeing the sergeant take me away to prison, my dear. In this country people are not thrown into jail just because somebody else wants to send them there."

Murphy ignored the man. "You could charge him, ma'am."

"Charge him—I do not understand."

"Make a complaint to the police that he has beaten you, or whatever he's done."

She nodded her head quickly. "Now I know what you mean. Yes, yes, I will charge him—"

"You will need witnesses, my dear Frances," Snaith interrupted jeeringly. "I shall deny everything you say. With only your word against mine the police can't do much to harm me."

"I can testify to having found Mrs. Snaith on the floor of your bedroom, bound and gagged," Terhune pointed out.

"No doubt! No doubt!" Snaith agreed, with mock geniality. "But that is not proof that it was *I* who did the binding and gagging."

"That's what you hope," Murphy said with grim satisfaction. "But I wouldn't bet too heavily on your chances of getting away with that argument."

"Please, please, gentlemen, do not trouble about what he did do to me. That is not important. You must punish him for what he did to his brother—"

"Peter the Hermit?"

"Yes, yes. Old Peter was Alexander's elder brother, Wilfred. His name is not Arthur Snaith. It is Alec Foulis. Alexander Crawshay Foulis." The words left her mouth explosively, and were only just intelligible.

"All right, Mrs. Snaith, all right. There is no need to become excited. There's plenty of time. Suppose we begin at the beginning."

"Why not?" Snaith mocked. "Once upon a time there lived a beautiful fairy—"

"You shut up," the sergeant snapped.

Snaith smiled; his teeth shone whitely in the soft light from the oil-lamp. His eyes shone, too, with a jeering expression. But he remained silent.

"Now, Mrs. Snaith?"

She stared at her husband. The flame of hatred which passed between the two people had the intangible, searing quality of artificial lightning.

"What is the beginning?" she asked huskily.

"When did you first meet your husband?"

"In Marseilles, in nineteen-twenty-three. He was there on business. We met at a party. At that time he called himself Alexander Crawshay. A friend introduced me to him because, having been educated in England, I used to like meeting Englishmen. We danced together and talked. He told me he was a big business man in London—something to do with insurance—he told my father the same lies—"

"What I told your father was perfectly true, my love. I was in the insurance business."

"You let him think that you were of importance in the firm, that you were rich and influential—you did not say that you were only a poorly paid clerk, and that you were in Marseilles only as an assistant to one of your bosses—"

"You and your father's greedy imagination made up that story, my dear."

"You lie! I disliked you the very first time I met you. I only listened to your lies because I was trying to be polite."

"Then why did you marry me?"

"My father forced me to. He thought he was making a good match for me—"

Murphy interrupted. "Take no notice of your husband's taunts, Mrs. Snaith. Just answer my questions."

"I am sorry, sir. What do you want to know?"

"What happened at your first meeting?"

"He tried to flirt with me, so to protect myself from his advances I told him of my fiancé, Wilfred Evans—"

"Evans, eh? Go on."

"He seemed interested. He encouraged me to talk of Wilfred. He asked me if I had a photograph or snapshot of my lover. I had. I showed it to him. It seemed to hypnotize him. He asked me many more questions about Wilfred. I was glad to answer, because I was very much in love with my sweetheart. The next day I learned the reason for Alec's interest. In the morning he visited my father at his office, and told him that Wilfred was a criminal. My father was very upset, and made me swear by my dear mother's memory that I would never see or write to Wilfred again."

"But you didn't want much pressing to do that, my dearest, sainted wife, when you heard that your darling Wilfred was a penniless fugitive from justice."

"Saints in heaven! That is not true. Do not believe him. Not for two days would I make the oath my father wanted me to make."

"Why did you in the end, Mrs. Snaith?"

She made a forlorn gesture of helplessness. "I had always obeyed my father. All my life I had learned obedience. First from my dear mother, and when she died, from the nuns at the convent school to which I was sent. Lastly, from my father. We Spanish women are not like your English women. Or the Americans. We are not allowed to be independent."

Murphy nodded. "I think I understand, Mrs. Snaith. What happened after you had made the oath not to see or write to Wilfred again?"

"I have told you. *He*—" the hatred in her voice betrayed the identity of the *He*—"*he* went to my father, and asked for my hand in marriage. He pretended that he was rich, and would be able to give me everything in life I could wish for. And dear father, because be knew that I was heartbroken because of Wilfred, and because he thought that Alec would make me happy again, gave his consent to the marriage."

"You were married in Marseilles?"

"Yes. We spent the first night of our honeymoon in the night train to England."

"And when you got back to England?"

"I found him out in all his lies. I learned that he was only earning a few pounds a week. We had to live in a tiny house in one of the London suburbs—"

Snaith laughed loudly. "Which didn't please her ladyship at all. Her idea of life was to live in a palace surrounded by servants—"

Murphy lost his temper. "Will you shut up, or must I make you?"

"By God I If you think I'm going to stand being threatened by a ruddy policeman—"

"*I* am not a policeman," Terhune interrupted. "And I have no objection to substituting myself for Sergeant Murphy."

"*You!*" Snaith inspected Terhune's slim, medium figure, and laughed insultingly. Nevertheless, he fell into sullen silence.

"Go on, Mrs. Snaith," Murphy urged.

"There's little more to tell," she replied sadly. "I soon realized that my dislike for my husband was turning to loathing and abomination, but I was his wife. I had been taught obedience for so long I had not the courage to leave him. Besides, I am a Roman Catholic, you understand."

Murphy nodded sympathetically. "It's a pity there ain't a few more women with the same views—there might not be so many divorces." Then he realized that his remark scarcely fitted the occasion, so he hastened to amend it. "Not that there aren't some exceptions, of course, ma'am, and yours sounds like one of them." He hurried on,

"How did you both come to be living in Great Hinton, and calling yourselves Snaith?"

"Twelve years ago he had an accident at work. He was ill for many months. Afterwards the firm gave him a pension. I do not know why he wanted to be known as Snaith. I think it was something he read in the newspaper one day. He wouldn't tell me what it was, but soon afterwards he told me we were moving to a little village in Kent, and that we were going to be known as Mr. and Mrs. Snaith."

"So you came to live in this cottage?"

"Yes."

"By the way, when did you first learn that your husband's real name was Foulis, and that the Wilfred he had denounced to your father was his own brother?"

"About a year after my marriage. I was cleaning out one of the rooms, and came across a bundle of newspaper—what do you say—clippings, no—"

Murphy nodded.

"They were all to do with the robbery of money from a firm in Liverpool, and the failure of a bank—I cannot remember its name—"

"The Chetwynd Private Bank?"

She nodded quickly. "That is the bank. One of the clippings had a photograph of Wilfred Crawshay Foulis. I recognized the photograph as my Wilfred, also the name of Crawshay. Then I knew everything. When my husband returned home that night I showed him the clippings. He told me everything, and admitted that he had married me only to revenge himself on his brother Wilfred."

Murphy's hands clenched suggestively, but he succeeded in maintaining self-control. "Now, Mrs. Snaith, how did Wilfred Foulis come into your life again?"

"One day, about two years after we had been living here, I was walking home from Bray when I saw an old tramp coming towards me. I didn't take any notice of him, but as he was passing by he suddenly called out, 'Franci.' I didn't recognize him, but soon he convinced me that he was Wilfred."

"And then?"

She shook her head. "Nothing. I exchanged a few words with him, and passed on. I never thought to see him again."

Murphy frowned. "You mean—you—you were no longer—interested—"

"No, sir. Neither Wilfred nor any other man could ever have meant anything more to me. My husband had turned my heart to stone."

Snaith jeered. "Don't believe *that*, Sergeant Murphy. Even the Marines wouldn't believe that. She nearly wept when I first told her that her old lover was in Great Hinton."

For the first time Mrs. Snaith smiled. "I made you believe I was upset because I knew that every tear I shed for your brother Wilfred would rile and torture you because it was for him and not for you. But all the time I was laughing at you, Alec Foulis. That is the only pleasure I have had for twenty-four years."

"You dirty bitch!" he snarled—and the two visitors rejoiced that for once Frances Snaith had scored.

"Of course I was sorry for old Peter," she went on of her own accord. "But no sorrier than I should have been for any other poor old tramp."

There was no doubting her sincerity, but her words puzzled Murphy and Terhune both. Hitherto—or rather since their fuller knowledge of the facts—they had assumed that she had sought to betray her husband in revenge for his having encompassed the death of the man she still presumably loved. But if she no longer loved Wilfred, or old Peter, if she had not even a tender feeling left for him, then why her determination to inculpate her husband? Not a sense of justice. Her nature seemed too hard, too emotionless, to possess such impersonal ideals. Then was it vengeance upon her husband for his persistent cruelty to her? Possibly, but why had she waited so long before attempting to avenge her wrongs? She had had that opportunity one year after marriage, when she had first learned that he was a Foulis, a brother of the man who had ruined the lives of so many.

Terhune had a strange feeling that a new element had been insinuated into the affair, but he could not identify it, so he kept quiet and let Murphy continue the interrogation unprompted.

Murphy carried on, somewhat uncertainly: "What happened during the next ten years?"

"My husband encouraged Wilfred to remain in this neighbourhood because he believed it would torture us both to live so near to each other, and yet be so far apart."

"Forgive me, Mrs. Snaith. I do not want to be too personal, but wasn't Wilfred still in love with you?"

"I believe he was," she agreed indifferently.

"But you had no love for him?"

"None."

"I see." Murphy nodded his head in doubt. "And now, what was the next important event which is of any consequence to us?"

"An advertisement in a newspaper asking for information of the surviving relatives of the late Sydney Crawshay Foulis."

"We know about that, ma'am. Mr. Snaith informed the solicitors that his brother Wilfred had not been heard of since nineteen hundred and seven."

"That is because he wanted the inheritance for himself. The morning he read the advertisement he said to me that he was going to kill two birds with one stone."

"What did he mean by that?"

Before Frances Snaith could reply, Snaith broke in: "Would you like to hear the truth first-hand, Sergeant Murphy?"

"Does that mean you are willing to talk?"

Snaith nodded. "Do you want the truth, the whole truth, and nothing but the truth about my brother's death?"

"Yes."

"All right. Then this is it. I killed Wilfred, wilfully and with malice aforethought, to get the money on the one hand, and on the other, to revenge myself on Wilfred. And now—" He laughed loudly, cheerfully, jeeringly.

"Well—now?"

"What are you going to do about it?" he jeered. "What in hell's name are you going to do about it?"

Chapter Twenty-Two

"You hear what he says," Mrs. Snaith called out joyfully. "He has confessed. You must arrest him—"

Murphy waved his hand. "Take it easy, Mrs. Snaith. There is plenty of time."

"Plenty," Snaith echoed cheerfully. "Plenty of time, my dear."

Murphy looked sternly at the self-confessed murderer. "Before you tell me anything more, Mr. Snaith, I must warn you that anything that you say may be used in evidence against you."

"I know all that rigmarole, Sergeant Murphy. I have read too many detective novels not to know the words almost as well as you do. Ask Mr. Terhune here; he has sold me enough thrillers in his time."

"Then we may as well proceed. You admit deliberately killing your brother?"

"I do."

"How did you kill him?"

"In a very subtle way, my dear Sergeant Murphy. I suppose you know his age when he died?"

"About seventy-five?"

"Not quite. He was seventy this year. I suppose the life he has led made him appear older than he was."

"Probably."

"I don't need to tell you anything about his physical condition; you know that from the evidence of the P.M.—you see, I am well acquainted with all the jargon."

"Go on."

"Didn't you mention just now that it was once my ambition to become a doctor, an ambition which dear Wilfred so effectively quashed with his blasted embezzlement?"

"We did."

"I thought so. But what you didn't learn was that my love for medicine remained even though the chance of practising it vanished. I taught myself medicine and the rudiments of surgery from books. Then, when I became an employee of an insurance company, I wormed my way into the E.L. and W.C.A. Department— Employers' Liability and Workmen's Compensation—and, in particular, the job of taking injured employees to the firm's doctor for examination.

"I let the doctor know that I was fond of medicine, so he became interested in me. We often discussed the cases I took along to him, and one way and another I learned a good deal from the old boy. I'm not boasting when I say that I know almost as much about medicine as the average G.P. does.

"At any rate I knew enough to realize that, after the life he had led—did you know, by the bye, that Wilfred has been in the prisons of four different countries, Bulgaria, Turkey, France and Spain?—and especially after the many years of near-starvation and exposure, his heart wasn't exactly as strong as a horse—or should I say horse's? There was something more, too, that I knew about Wilfred, something that not many other people in the world knew—that Wilfred had a passion for money. Not for the sake of hoarding it, mind you. Not Wilfred. He liked spending it, and liked enjoying all the good things in life which money can buy."

He recognized the disbelieving expression on the sergeant's face, and explained: "I can see what you are thinking, Sergeant Murphy: that old Peter's character wasn't very much like that of a man who worships money. It wasn't, but, you see, Wilfred's spirit had been broken by bad luck, and failure. By the time he was fifty he had only one thought left: to find Frances and me. Frances, so that the crazy fool could be near her for the rest of his life—can you imagine anyone remaining all his life in love with that bitch of a woman? There's no accounting for taste, is there, Sergeant Murphy? And me he wanted to find so that he could sponge on me for a few odd bobs each week. What a hope! As if I would have given him a penny of my money after what he had done to me!

"Anyway, he found us here, and lived in Farmer Giffen's wood for ten years. Then I saw the advertisement in *The Times* asking for news of Wilfred and me. I've told you what happened during the first interview with the solicitors. When they told me that Sydney had left seventy-odd thousand pounds I knew that Fate had given me a good chance of killing Wilfred without having to suffer the consequences. That is what my dear wife meant when she spoke of me killing two birds with one stone. By getting rid of Wilfred I should not only get my revenge on him, but, at the same time, make certain of inheriting all Sydney's money.

"I told Frances what I proposed doing—I thought it would give her real joy to know beforehand that her old lover was soon to die…" Hate contorted his face, and his audience appreciated the furious anger which he was experiencing at the reflection that his barbed shaft had not found its billet. But he went on:

"Then I paid a second visit to London so that I could interview the solicitor again. That time I took my loving spouse with me to stop her queering my pitch by giving Wilfred a hint of the pleasant news I had in store for him. It must have been on that occasion when my dearly beloved wife must have sent you the first of those stupid *Trails to Tyburn*. While I was at the solicitors' I persuaded them to give me a letter containing all the information necessary to make Wilfred realize that he had come into a bigger fortune than he had ever hoped to make even in his wildest dreams.

"As soon as I had that letter we came back here. Then, late that afternoon, I called upon Wilfred to pass on the good news." He paused, his eyes dancing. "Can you guess why?"

"You believed that the shock would cause your brother's heart to fail?"

"Believe! Believe!" Snaith laughed. "I *knew* it would, my dear man. Your more cautious doctors can say what they like about having no faith in the theory that a shock can kill. But I was pretty sure that if any heart could fail as a result of a shock to the emotions, Wilfred's heart was in just about the right condition to do just that. Besides, I knew what to do if my scheme failed."

"You intended to kill him by more direct methods?"

"Good Heavens, no! I value my own neck far too much to take any risk of being hanged for murder. Oh no! All I intended to do, if the shock in itself failed to stop his heart beating, was to suggest some exercise which would do the trick quite as effectively. You know— running through the woods towards the village so as to telephone the solicitors before it was too late—"

"You devil!" Frances spat out.

Snaith shrugged his indifference, but otherwise ignored the interruption. "You can take it from me, I laid my plans pretty well. Yes, pretty well!" he repeated. "But it so happened that I did not have to worry about alternative schemes. I showed the solicitor's letter to Wilfred, and impressed the fact upon him that he could spend the rest of his life in ease and luxury. He got to his feet and began to dance a jig of joy, the silly old fool. Well, you know what happened. He just snuffed out, without further to-do." He laughed softly. "It was all so very simple. And so very satisfactory. A neat way of killing a man, don't you think? Though, of course, it might never happen again. The circumstances were peculiar, and possibly unrepeatable. Still, I still say it was a neat little murder. And one which the police would never even have begun to suspect if that bitch of a wife hadn't interfered with her blasted stories—and God only knows why she did so, for she would have benefited from the money almost as much as I." He shrugged. "I think that's about all."

Frances could not contain her jubilation. "You see. He has confessed all. Now you can arrest and hang him." She turned towards her husband. "On the day you hang I shall go to church and thank the Holy Saints in heaven for my freedom."

Snaith laughed. "A touching thought, my dear! But Sergeant Murphy seems in no hurry to arrest me."

She turned again. "Arrest him," she ordered. "You must arrest him. Now. At once."

Murphy sat still and shook his head. "It's not quite so easy as that, Mrs. Snaith."

Snaith's light-blue eyes sparkled with malicious humour. "Tell her why it's not so easy, Sergeant Murphy. My wife takes a lot of convincing."

The sergeant ignored Snaith, but answered the anguished plea in Mrs. Snaith's dark eyes.

"You see, Mrs. Snaith, medical men have already testified, at the coroner's inquest, that old Peter died a natural death. I am not sure that we could find anyone to testify otherwise."

"I do not understand."

"Well, it's this way, Mrs. Snaith. Old Peter did die a natural death, as it were, and if he died a natural death, you couldn't very well say as how he was murdered."

"But you have heard what my husband said—that he told Wilfred the news of his good fortune in such a way as to cause the shock which killed Wilfred."

"I know." Murphy nodded disconsolately. "You know, Mr. Terhune here knows, and I know that Mr. Snaith deliberately plotted to kill his brother, but could we persuade a jury to believe that he did?—that is the point."

"Of course they would believe. Why should they not, if you can?"

"Mr. Snaith might not be so ready to tell that story in court before a judge and jury as he is here, in this room."

"How right you are!" Snaith added. "My opinion of you, Sergeant Murphy, is going up by leaps and bounds."

"But *you* can tell the jury what *he* has told you."

"I could, but he might step into the witness stand and swear that he was only joking."

"Joking?"

"Certainly! Joking! Or he could say that his story was a pack of lies, from first to last. There is no law against telling lies except when you are on oath to tell the truth. Of course, we might afterwards charge him with causing a public mischief, but that wouldn't avenge Wilfred's murder."

"He told Wilfred the story of Sydney's fortune in order to kill Wilfred."

"I know. But there's no offence in telling a person good news. He couldn't have known for certain that the news would kill Wilfred, could he? He took a chance, and it came off. We have no *proof* apart from his story, that he told the story with malice—that is, guilty intention. And if he *didn't* tell the story with the *intention* of killing his brother, the fact that the telling *did* in fact kill Wilfred does not thereby make his act one of homicide. For that matter, we have no *proof* that he told the story at all, either with or without malice. We have no *proof* that he visited old Peter on the night the old man died. We have no *proof* that old Peter was Wilfred Foulis."

"Proof! Proof! Proof! *Madre de Dios!*" Mrs. Snaith appealed to the ceiling with an expressive gesture. "If it is proof you want, Mr. Murphy, *I* can supply it. I can give evidence of what you call guilty intention—did he not inform me beforehand of his intention of killing his brother by giving him unexpected good news? I can testify that

I watched him go into the woods in the direction of Wilfred's hut. I can testify that old Peter *was* Wilfred Foulis—"

Murphy shook his head ruefully. "I would not like to claim that all the evidence you are willing to give would help to convict your husband, Mrs. Snaith, but even if it could, you could not give it."

"Why not? Dear God! Why not?"

"Because you are his wife, and in the eyes of the law man and wife are one entity. Except in certain circumstances a husband or wife cannot be compelled to give evidence against his or her lawful spouse."

"But he or she may give evidence for the defence," Snaith added mockingly. "Isn't that so, Sergeant Murphy?"

"It is," Murphy agreed shortly.

Frances Snaith stared at the detective with growing incredulity. "Are you going to do nothing to punish my husband for the crime he has committed?" she asked harshly.

The sergeant shifted uncomfortably. "Not on my own responsibility, ma'am. Of course, the case will be reported to the Director of Public Prosecutions, but it's my opinion no arrest will be made unless the police obtain other evidence to substantiate Mr. Snaith's confession."

"Then—then—he will go—unpunished?"

"Other evidence may come to light—"

A shrill cry from Frances Snaith interrupted the sergeant's words. She rose lightly to her feet—her left arm moved swiftly in the direction of the oil-lamp. Before Murphy could make a move the room was plunged into a darkness that was relieved only by the glow of the fire. There was a flash of red lightning—a moaning shriek of pain—confusion—the dull thud of a door banging—

II

It was easy to account for Frances Snaith's escape from the immediate vicinity of Great Hinton, for the night was pitch-black, the wind violent. It was possible neither to see far nor to hear much. The police patrols, ordered to watch for and arrest the fugitive, never had any real chance of searching for her. However, nobody doubted but that the coming of daylight would witness the early arrest of Snaith's murderer.

But it did not! One day succeeded another without the expected news being announced. By the time four weeks had passed by everyone had taken it for certain that Mrs. Snaith had avoided arrest by escaping to the Continent.

"I still don't know why she sent those stories instead of a plain, straightforward letter," Murphy said one night to Julia and Terhune.

Terhune grinned. Poor old Murphy! He was still peeved about the *Ten Trails to Tyburn*.

"Do you, Miss MacMunn?" the sergeant continued.

"I think I do," Julia said. "I think it was just a matter of courage."

"Courage?"

"She was afraid of her husband, wasn't she, Mr. Murphy? Desperately?"

"She gave me that impression."

"She was too afraid to risk writing a letter, signed or anonymous, in case he should ever come to hear what she had done, and avenge himself upon her. On the other hand, by some strange reasoning, I think she had convinced herself that the stories could not betray her, because she could deny the authorship of them, and also point out that there was nothing in them which bore any relationship to the death of old Peter."

"Humph! They were obscure right enough, Miss MacMunn. So obscure that, if it hadn't been for Mr. Terhune's brainwave, Arthur Snaith might be alive today, enjoying his brother's inheritance."

"We do not know what clues she intended to convey in the remaining five stories," Julia warned.

"That's true. Each story might have been a little more obvious, according to whether or not she believed we were getting on with the job of incriminating her husband." He shook iris head doubtfully.

"What's still puzzling you?" Terhune asked.

"What did you think of the woman, Mr. Terhune? Did she strike you as being of the kind to want to see justice done for justice's sake?"

"Not particularly."

"Same here. From the little I saw of her I should have said that she would have been more likely to keep quiet and enjoy the money that was coming to her old man, and damn the memory of her one-time lover, for whom she no longer cared a fig. But no! Her one and only desire seemed to be to see Snaith hang. I could understand that attitude if she had been married only for a couple of years or so. But after more than twenty-four years of hell—well, a few years more or less couldn't make much difference, and would have been worth putting up with for the sake of dibs. No, I'm darned if I understand her attitude."

Julia—surprisingly—supported Murphy. Terhune did not. Presently Julia said:

"I am sure Mr. Murphy is right, my sweet. There was an ulterior motive in everything Frances Snaith did—but what it was I cannot imagine."

Murphy laughed grimly. "If there is one thing we can be sure of, it is that we shall never know now what it was."

The sergeant was mistaken. Some months later Terhune received a small packet from Russia. He opened it wonderingly. And...

III

TEN TRAILS TO TYBURN
NO. 10. THE REASON WHY

"Friends," began Musàloff, as he rose to his feet and beamed up and down the table. "I have tonight the extreme pleasure, the honour, I might say, of introducing to you the great advocate, Sasha Uskoff. Introducing, have I said? Nay, friends, that is wrong. He needs no introduction, does Sasha Uskoff, to his old friends and playmates, to ids townsfolk.

"Yet, when I look around I see young faces. Surely, though the name of Uskoff will be engraven upon the pages of history of our little village, some of you here have not yet cast your eyes upon him. Look, then, all of you, upon our great advocate who sits here upon my right hand, and upon his beautiful wife, and his handsome son, who sit upon my left.

"Verily, friends, the history of Sasha, my true friend and comrade of my childhood days, now, alas, long past, is a romance, a tale of energy, hard labour, an inborn genius and subsequent success.

"Listen, all of you, and you shall hear the saga of Sasha, the man whose name rings throughout Russia.

"Many years ago there was born unto Boris Uskoff, our coffin-maker, and Zhenya his wife a son—Sasha. What a joy, what a rejoicing there was in the household of Boris that night! Even I, but five or six years old at that time, can remember it.

"'Thank God for His kind mercy,' said Boris, with the tears running down his cheeks, so my mother has oft told me. 'Thank the good God that my prayers have availed, and it is a son born unto me. Now indeed shall I, in but a few years' time, have an assistant to help me, and more, a son to carry on the business, and support his father in his old age.'

"Yes, friends, there was none so glad that night as Boris. Yet Boris little knew that the small child whom he saw suckling at its mother's breast was to be a great man.

"He soon learned that his son was not born to be a coffin-maker, for there came one day to the house of Boris, almost two years later, good Father Yegor, carrying with him books and papers, which he set down beside him.

"He talked awhile, and then, when he turned round, what do you think he saw? Little Sasha, papers spread before him, gurgling with delight as his chubby little fingers traced the pattern of the letters of the alphabet.

"Good Father Yegor, he realized at once that here was one who needed education, and from that time took the child under his wing.

"A few years passed, and Sasha gradually absorbed the learning of Father Yegor—ay, and more. He read much, became wise, and before long had commenced to ask and answer questions which even puzzled the good father.

"That was Sasha's wisdom—asking and answering questions. Soon there was no question to which he could not give a reply, and before he was eleven years of age he was the wise man of the village.

"To him came one and all. 'Ho, Sasha,' they would say, 'canst tell us why the cost of bread has increased in price by a kopek or more?' And the child would tell them of the shortage of wheat, of foreign orders and competition, and more of which I myself know nothing.

"Then to him would come two quarrelsome wives. 'Sasha, dear,' they would ask, 'tell us who is right,' and to him they would propound a riddle which even Solomon might have found perplexing. Then thought Sasha awhile, and he answered. Always he answered.

"Time passed by, and as he learned and grew older, so his fame gradually spread abroad, and one day there came to him an advocate of St. Petersburg—and, friends, I make no apologies for calling that city by its old name.

"This advocate, he, too, put questions to this boy prodigy, and Sasha answered them well and fully, and his questioners wondered greatly, and that night talked to Boris Uskoff.

"The next day when the advocate returned to St. Petersburg he took Sasha—our Sasha—with him, and so, until this night, we saw no more of him.

"Friends, gaze upon him, Sasha Uskoff, born of Boris, the coffin-maker, and so recognize a wise and famous man."

The speaker sat down, and there was a movement, a stirring. Everyone at the table gazed searchingly at the guest of honour, their bovine glances taking in the famous man and his wife alternately.

To many the fatuous inanity of their expressions would have been embarrassing; the hero-worship which they bestowed would have been almost worthy of contempt, for they were but peasant folk: Sasha Uskoff was a hero because Musaloff said so. In the words of the famous poet, "Theirs not to reason why." Like sheep, Musàloff was their shepherd; he said gaze upon this man who had come into their midst, and they did so.

Sasha gazed round, his face gradually broadening into a beatific smile. Ponderously he rose to his feet, and began to speak, meanwhile he stroked his long heavy moustache, and patted his thick bushy beard.

"Friends, townspeople," he began, theatrically waving his hand, on which gleamed several large rings, "Comrade Musàloff has spoken well tonight, for he has told you nothing less than the truth." His large voice boomed and echoed round the hall, dropping and rising with measured effect.

"Throughout my life, as I quickly fought my way up to fame and fortune, I have never forgotten this little town, wherein I spent my childhood days. Some of you remember me, but I wonder how many who do so knew that the lad, 'Boris Uskoff's boy' you used to call me, was predestined to become the foremost advocate in

Russia, a leader of the people? None of you knew or suspected; it was only I myself who visioned the great future which was in store for me.

"How have I reached such a pre-eminent position in life? Well might you ask, you who can never hope to reach those dizzy heights, yet I freely confess that it is partly due to the brains with which I was endowed by the good God, but mostly because it was I who had the brains. Another might have failed where I have succeeded. Dost thou not agree, wife?" he asked.

He turned to Varka for corroboration. Different from him was his wife, small, petite, still retaining traces of past beauty; her face was drawn and timid.

"Yes, husband, that is so," she meekly replied.

"Ah!" Sasha beamed at his spouse, then turning towards his audience he continued his diatribe. "My wife and I, we are turtledoves. With my usual sagacity I looked for a woman who could most nearly approach my intelligence, and I consider myself fortunate to have found my charming Varka." He smiled down at his wife, and all his listeners murmured, "How charming!" "How he loves her!" But Varka only saw the steely glint in his eyes, and the hardness of his chin, so with an effort she smiled sweetly at the company which surrounded her, the company which disgusted her.

"What goes to make greatness, you ask." Sasha shrugged his shoulders. "Ah, friends, not many of us achieve greatness, yet a great man must be thought kind and generous, wise and sedulous. Of all these attributes I pride myself I possess my full mean.

"Only a week ago my wife received news that her father was dying. He called for her, but in her love for me she did not wish to leave me until she had made adequate arrangements for my well-being; but me, it made me sad to think of Varka's father dying, and so I sent my wife away, merely insisting that she return in time to attend me here at this dinner tonight."

He paused dramatically, and, led by Musàloff, the diners clapped.

"How generous! How noble!" announced Musaloff.

"How generous! How noble!" echoed the others.

In response to the acclamations, Sasha bowed gracefully. "Thank you, my dear friends, thank you. I am indeed deeply touched by your kindly thoughts. Perhaps I should not have mentioned this sacrifice of mine, but it was meant merely to illustrate an act of generosity, a part of my greatness.

"Of course, I am generally known for my ability in replying to questions put to me. It is said in learned circles that I am like unto One Who passed before me, He Who was found in the Temple, answering questions, but, friends…" He waved his hand deprecatingly. Evidently his modesty forbade his associating himself with this suggestion.

"To answer questions, any and every question put to me, has been my aim throughout my life, and I am proud to say that never once has anyone younger than myself been able to pose a question to which I have been unable to reply satisfactorily. Only the sages and the philosophers have propounded perplexing problems which have caused me hesitation. Friends, you may be unable to credit such a statement. Therefore test me. Here I stand before you, prepared to answer any question which you put to me."

He gazed round, but the simple peasant folk merely eyed one another stupidly.

For a moment no one spoke, but then his little son, Abógin, spoke up in a small, piping voice, which echoed weirdly around the room after the booming crescendo of his father.

"Papa, papa," he said, "what was the name of the pretty lady who slept with you last Wednesday?"

I V

"Begod!" Murphy exploded when he read the story some hours later. "What in the name of all the Saints do you make of this, the tenth, and presumably the last, of the ten stories?"

"She must have guessed that we couldn't appreciate her motive for killing her husband.' I think the operative words are contained in the last sentence."

"Another woman, eh? Just downright jealousy? Well, begod!"

"Snaith should have remembered that he had married a Latin. I'm beginning to think that for all her hatred of him his wife would have stuck to him through thick and thin—she was a good Catholic, Sergeant. But the poor fool did the one thing which no Latin woman forgives—religion or no religion. He slept with another woman. It was for that she determined to see him hang. Not for killing his brother."

"Begod!" Murphy repeated monotonously.

THE END